WHEN ALL THE CLOUDS COLLIDE

AN ODEZZA AND THE MIGHTY5 ADVENTURE

KEN GRANT

VINCIT VALOR
PUBLISHING

WHEN ALL THE CLOUDS COLLIDE

Published by Vincit Valor Publishing

Print ISBN: 979-8-9910459-0-2
Electronic ISBN: 979-8-9910459-1-9

AuthorKenGrant.com

This book is a work of fiction. Names, characters, places and incidents are
products of the authors imagination or are used fictitiously. Any resemblance
to actual events or locales or person, living or dead is entirely coincidental.

Cover design by @nabinkarna
Printed in USA
First Edition: July, 2024

To Kristin, Annalisa, Zoë,
Don, Kim, Ryan, David, Bethany,
Hailey, Mat & Gracie.
Thank you for guiding, believing, pushing and trusting

FOREWORD

This fanciful story is set in the not-to-distant future of 2088, where the climate is bleak, but the tech is cool. And the people talk slightly differently and British English is the language of choice.

Here's to all the strong, inquisitive, and bold people out there. You know who you are: never look back, always look forward!

So, kick back and have fun with my first book. I hope you enjoy it as much as I did researching, plotting, planning and writing it.

CHAPTER ONE

Dad's voice echoes off the walls as he yells from his lab come office, but I block it out. All I can think about is the water, its cool embrace calling out to me.

"Not now," I shout back, my patience snapping like a rubber band stretched too far. My heart races with adrenaline and urgency. I've decided. I need to go for a plunge. There is nothing that can stand in my way. But then my dad's words cut through the air again, pleading, desperate. The guilt claws at my chest, but I push it aside. This is *my* time, *my* escape. And nothing will impede that. "I want to go for a swim before it's dark!" I yell out.

"Honey." You can always tell when my dad is getting serious when he calls me, 'honey'. "Please!" he adds.

"But—" I say with a deep sense of guilt mixed with annoyance.

He's a good guy, pretty old-fashioned if you ask me, but still a wonderful dad.

It's just him and me, and it has been that way for the past 16 years.

"Just dash down to the store and grab me some milk and ice cream!" Dad says, again, yelling from his office!

"You're killing me," I say under my breath - get it delivered like every other human in the Western world!

Daylight is fading fast, even this far up in the sky. Not that I can complain. Being on the 299th floor has its perks - better sunsets than most and less street noise. You can take in so many other SkyRisers and sky bridges from up here, creating a web of elevated walkways and vertical gardens. All that vibrant flora still thrives amidst the steel, glass, and lack of water.

My dad absolutely adores this place because it offers panoramic views of London plus his favourite, a breathtaking view towards the South, stretching across the Thames and over to Greenwich.

You know the spot - where the East and West converge and time begins and ends! It's his absolute favourite! My Dad is a visionary, an inventor, a scientist, and a futurologist, yet an old soul with a deep appreciation of history. When he gazes upon the beautiful, lush green lawns of Greenwich, with its rich history and secret mystique, it brings him a sense of tranquillity.

And to think, Greenwich hasn't changed, but everything around it has - I never bore off looking at the Floating Parks on the Thames. They are man-made islands covered in greenery. They're like their own little serene oases providing respite from the bustling, high-tech city surrounding us.

"Honey, could you please get me some milk and ice cream? I think I deserve it after being here for hours!"

What is he working on? I never seem to know - he isn't the greatest communicator in the world, which is ironic given the fact he was on the team that invented the Bio-Tech Network (BTN), the world's greatest comms tech.

The sun is low in the sky, so I'm torn. Hit the floor 300 rooftop pool or hit the store.

"Okay," I say. I cave, and the latter wins out. "Tell me exactly what you want and I'll go right now."

TiM, the family RoboDog, cocks his head at me, like I should have gone swimming. He just wants to join me on the roof. Or maybe he wants to go to the store. I can't totally tell.

Dad continues, "1/2% SynthMilk and CocoICE, please. Hey, and don't get distracted and waste your time at Time Travellers — I'm hungry!"

He's talking about one of my favourite places near our SkyRise, called The Time Traveller's Tea House. It's a quaint little place, not only for tea but 'time-travelling' too. You can sit and sip their Old English tea while gazing through antique-looking windows that reveal glimpses of different eras. Dad explained the tech to me once. The windows, if you can really call them that, are Ultra-Immersive Experience (UIEs). It's a fully immersive 3D experience that uses holographic tech, allowing us to see lifelike images floating in their living space. It's cool. I've seen ancient Turkey, life in Egypt, swinging '60s London, Paris and beyond. Dad is right to know I might get distracted and wander off.

"Hurry, please," he calls out.

He cracks me up - the fact that it is synthetic milk (and has been for years), means it doesn't come in 1/2%. SynthMilk is SynthMilk for gawd's sake! But he's old school, and the fact I have to 'run' down to the store is crazy to me too, when every-one, and I mean everyone, has pretty much everything deliv-ered to the Express Dumb Waiter (EDW). Not sure how that got its name, because the tech that goes into ordering some-thing and getting it delivered within half an hour is kind of crazy-cool.

So, no pool time. Just yet.

A few steps away is our flat's lift. The descent in the glass bullet lift down the outside of Cloud Haven, our SkyRise, never loses its excitement - it's a thrilling ride attached to the exterior of our building. Six identical elevators, perfectly spaced from each other, like a display of impeccable symmetry. Our building has been called a modern marvel of architecture. With three interlocking sections, it looks a tad like a twisted corkscrew. It's almost a thousand metres high. It's not the tallest SkyRise in the city, but it is certainly one of the more unique.

From every floor, the views of London stretch out in all directions, and I make it a point to always choose a different lift each time I ride down. And what a ride it is. 5.5 seconds of pure speed leaves me figuratively breathless. And despite the velocity, there's no sensation of falling or being shot out of a cannon. It's as if we're gliding effortlessly through the air. It's an experience unlike any other.

As the double glass doors open melodically, I step into our sprawling lobby. It's filled with great tech; transparent monitors floating over the greeting spaces, displaying 3D holograms with Cloud Haven sales information. The decor is minimalist yet luxurious, with reflective floors and hidden LED accents. The waiting area furniture has built-in VR capabilities for visitors. But to me, the cool thing surrounding this tech-marvel is the verdant indoor gardens. The variations of plants and colours are intense. And right in the middle of it all is a waterfall, the likes I have never seen before. The rich mixture of real plants and real cascading water almost make me not want to go outside.

Just around the corner from Cloud Haven is the London-Mart. One of the very few, and I mean very few, 'old school' grocery shops in the Greater London area. I have the feeling not only did Dad and I guess my mum back before I recall, picked this building because of its view over history, but its adjacency to this stupid old LondonMart, the LM. LM for lame.

The streets seem busy for the late afternoon.

As I clear the threshold of the LM, I instantly want to spin around and go back home. Talk about a lack of action! Two other people, one looks to be around 110 and the other so much younger, in her 90s. Old school! The place is always clean, not that I have many places to compare it to. I have looked up some other stores like this on my BTN, but have no way of appreciating what they smell or even truly feel like. So I have a sample size of exactly one!

The usual wide aisles are filled with canned goods and soft foods, not modern food here. As I head across the store, I'm aiming for the walk-in cooler. Dad's favourite part of this ancient relic. This is where I'll find this stinking 1/2% and CocoICE, chocolate ice cream. Dang, I'll never get used to how cold that cooler really is! Sub-zero!

As I exit the arctic blast of the cold zone, I spot a display of HandyDandyCandy. Stupid-ass name, but so good! Brazilian chocolate over a biscuit.

This store always smells interesting to me - different! An interesting blend of spices, cardboard, plastic, overly conditioned air, old people, and somehow bread. Which is odd, as bread hasn't had an aroma in twenty years; but somehow they have synthesised the bouquet to make every loaf smell like a French patisserie - or at least what I imagine a French patisserie to smell like.

Grocery bag packed, I head back. I walk past Neo-Modern-Victorian architecture with ornate ironwork, stained glass, and turrets; old-world charm with innovative design.

The streets are busy with RedEls: the red double-decker buses hovering above the streets, powered by solar. They never get old to me.

Back at our building, I ride the lift back up to Floor 299. As the double lift doors open, I can see straight through to my dad's office, doubling as a lab, study and workshop; and TiM sitting outside, trying to spy inside.

Dad quickly leans his back foot out and closes the three-inch thick, reinforced titanium, one-of-a-kind, custom-made door in my face. Not knowing what he is working on is both suspicious, yet intriguing.

"Your 'dairy' products are here!" I shout, as I cross the enormity of our flat. "I'll put them in the kitchen when you're ready," I continue, never really sure if he can hear me through all that re-enforced secrecy.

As I enter my room, I slip out of my black tee, pants, kicks and underwear, and into a one-piece racing suit; like a swim-suit that the pros wear. This is a full-length Olympic pool, heated to 23C, and as this is my sport of choice, the chances of me going fast are a certainty.

I climb the spiral glass staircase to the roof deck above. I checked the Thermal MagIc, its readout showing a pleasant 28C.

It's close to sunset and the views across the pool are intense. 300 floors up with no walls to restrict one's view is never boring. It never ceases to amaze me I'm often the only one up here. Maybe 50 metres is too long for others to swim. Who knows? All I know is, it's all mine for the next 40 laps. 10 breast, 10 free, 10 fly and 10 back.

My arms scream in agony as I push through the final four backstrokes. My breath is coming out in gasps. But as I finish, I roll over on my front and cling to the edge of the pool. I look up, stretching. The sky above catches my attention. The clouds are like none I have seen before - dark lines streak across the sky like looking at the pages of a book on its side, tinted with a foreboding shade of deep orange and purple that makes my stomach churn with unease. Despite my exhaustion, I can't help but feel a sense of dread creeping over me at the sight. What are those clouds and where did they come from?

CHAPTER TWO

As I hop out of the pool, I look around. Still not a person in sight. I love the silence. Complete nothingness. The only sound I hear is the sound of my pounding heart. Those were some tough last laps. I pad off the deck of the pool towards my robe and The Crystal.

The Crystal is Cloud Haven's new outdoor shower. London, and I guess everywhere, are facing major water restrictions, so they installed this to be good Earth stewards. It's crazy that in 2088, with water cutbacks the way they are, we still have a pool like this; but hey, I'll take it.

The Crystal is interesting. Instead of a regular water shower, I'm surrounded by shimmering crystals that fizz gently when activated. These fizzing crystals cleanse your body. Very invigorating.

I'm a nerd, so I did some research on this thing when they installed it a month ago. The shower chamber contains crystal dispensers filled with various types of effervescent crystals. When I step inside, sensors detect my exhausted presence and activate the crystal dispensers. As the crystals dissolve, they undergo chemical reactions. Some release oxygen bubbles, while others emit pleasant scents. And the kicker is, as Dad would say, I can ask for different fragrances like lavender for relaxation, citrus for energy, or mint for invigoration. Mint is my favourite.

I could stay here forever, but life awaits me!

As I step out of The Crystal, I look up to see that the berserk clouds have gone. Evaporated from sight. What the heck?! Nothing.

I turn my eyes back down to the view that fans out all around me. Night time up here is staggering. The energy in this city is palpable with the sounds of people streaming up from the streets far below and the sights of AeroCars and eVTOLs buzzing around the city.

The colours, the images, the wild advertising emitting from the nearby buildings are breathtaking, unnerving, yet oddly calming! The ads are like chaotic fireflies, buzzing and hissing and vomiting oversized images against the building. Although 'against' is probably not the correct term, these images are incorporated into glass.

The commercials advertise everything under the sun, from Nissan's new rockets to lunar bases, to the latest NorLand fashion. There's even a teaser for the new and expanded Terra-Tube routes. They boast that the TT, TT3 and TT2 all promise faster and safer service to even more places around the world. "No thanks," I say out loud. Not my cup of tea.

The air is still warm, it's always warm. That could be me after knocking out those 40 or it might just be the air rising upward from the busy streets below.

I looked up again, hoping to figure out what I had seen when I finished my swim. Still nothing! Just an open night sky, sprinkled with millions of fine dots speckled across the cosmos! Maybe I was full of rubbish and had seen nothing. No. I certainly saw something, something I won't soon forget. It was so different. Intriguing. Scary.

I swiftly head back down the outer spiral staircase. Those were installed just for our penthouse. They're not for the fainthearted, particularly if you don't like heights. But it never seemed to phase me. Not sure why, but I know my dad hates them.

As I head back inside the perfectly air-conditioned flat, I don't see my dad, the SynthMilk or CocoICE. Odd? I wander around, calling out for him. It's a big place, taking up the entire top floor. Yet unless he lost his hearing in the past hour, he should be able to hear me.

It's not like he went downstairs to the street and headed out for a quick walk - he hates going outside. Something about being around 'other people'.

Finally I spot him, out on the west deck overlooking the river, looking west toward the lights of downtown London. That's not like him. He hates heights. It is ironic, given the floor we live on. But he always wanted this view. He is in his custom rocker. Made of a transparent aluminium, so you can see right through it. It never blocks the view from the inside.

"What are you doing, ya crazy old man?" I ask sarcastically.

Dad cuts right to it. "Did you see the sky at sunset? That was the strangest thing I've seen."

"How did you even see the sky?" I ask. His office is located right in the middle of our flat. With no windows, just that crazy ass 'don't-come-near-me door'.

"When I came out for my treats - thanks, by the way - I looked out to the West and saw the trailing edge - it was mesmerising, but a little scary. Did you see it, Odezza?" he adds.

"Yes," I reply, "as I was wrapping up my laps. What do you think it was? It seemed strange to me! Out of place. Something was off about it, right? And then it just vanished."

"I know I'm not a meteorologist," he says, "but you're right, there was something strange about it. Strange indeed."

CHAPTER THREE

The next morning begins like any other, with a comforting breakfast shared by my father and I. OZ, as his team affectionately calls him, or Ozwold as my grandparents named him, makes it a point for us to have this time together every day. It is our own personal ritual, a commitment to connect before the chaos of a frenzied day.

The breakfast spread includes artificial eggs, faux milk, and synthesised oatmeal. All of it was created in a lab mimicking actual food, rich in vitamins and minerals, but lacking any natural ingredients or anything connected to 'real food'. The days of farm-fresh breakfasts seem like a distant memory in this post-BoldWar world.

Sitting down to our unremarkable meal, I couldn't help but acknowledge the monotony of it all. The familiar spread of fake food laid out before us, just as it is. Every. Damn. Morning.

As I glance out the enormous windows and take in the morning grandeur. I couldn't help but notice a similar predictability in the weather. The thermometer reads a mundane 27C, and there isn't a cloud in sight. The bright rays of sunshine beat down on the modern landscape, creating a picturesque scene that seemed almost too perfect. It's as if Mother Nature herself has set the stage for another ordinary day, unaware of the extraordinary thoughts swirling in my head.

Apparently, and I've only read about this, Old-London (my name for it) used to be quite different - cold and rainy for most of the year. As a sixteen-year-old, I find it hard to comprehend such brutal weather. Cold and rainy? The very thought sends shivers down my spine. Yet here we are, basking in the warmth and dryness of our home, enjoying yet another ordinary day in paradise.

One of the great things about our breakfast together is the chance not only to chat about nothing but also to find a topic to focus on - like an icebreaker, not that OZ and I are ever really lost for words!

"That cloud last night. I looked it up," OZ says with a mouth full of faux food! "Nothing on the GlobalNet or even the local blogs. It's like no one bothered to look skyward at sunset and notice anything different from the norm."

"Nothing at all?" I ask.

"In my 56 years, I've never seen colours so intense," he exclaims, his eyes wide with awe as he points out the west window and up towards the sky. "Those shades of deep orange and red smeared across the horizon, painting the landscape in a fiery glow. Wild. There was something unnerving about them - the shape was peculiar." I notice a slight tremble in his voice.

"Didn't you find it breathtaking and yet unsettling?" he continues his ponderance. "The shape looked like the pages of a book."

"I don't get it," shaking my head. "There's no news, no reports about this anywhere? You don't have a gadget that can help us figure out what that was, do you?"

My Dad may be a lot of things and invented many important life-changing tools, but meteorology is not in his wheelhouse, nor mine.

OZ just nods, furrowing his brow. "That's what makes it so off-putting." He seems to muse aloud, unable to wrap his mind around the unexplained phenomenon. "It's like we're the only two that saw it and I don't have a gadget, as you call it, or way of figuring it out. At least not with the instruments I have."

As a little kid, I thought my dad could invent anything, just by spending a little time in his office. Or is it a laboratory? It's always been difficult to tell. I'm not permitted to go inside. I think sometimes he should just post a sign on that damn door that says 'mad scientist at work!'

Over the years, I have caught a peek inside if he has dashed off to the loo or into the kitchen for a late-night nibble. It is insane there, in a cool way.

From the glances I have captured, his office is a dark and mysterious space, with walls that seem to absorb the light rather than reflect it. From my few skating encounters, I've seen recessed lighting that casts a soft white glow around the ceiling. I can't see them, but there must also be hidden speakers, because sometimes, and I mean super infrequently, I can hear him blasting his old-school tunes from Daft Punk and singing! Yep, singing!

I've seen the dark walls are lined with shelves and cabinets, filled with mysterious objects and artefacts from his lifetime of experiences. I've even seen handwritten journals. And a levitating pencil box. His workbench seems cluttered. The whole thing seems futuristic with a subtle touch of old-school. The massive transparent screens take up one entire wall, displaying a wide range of data and information. None of which makes any sense in the seconds I've 'spied'.

I remember the air in his office smelt slightly musty, with a hint of metal, oil, and electronics. My guess is that it's a familiar scent to those who have spent countless hours in space tinkering and experimenting with their various gadgets, because Dad's clothes often smell like his office.

My dad's lair is the core of his existence, where he has shaped the world and left his mark on it for the good of humanity. I've been tempted to go inside and explore, but I know that would disrespect him and his space. Still, curiosity has always gnawed at me. But my respect for OZ keeps me from doing so.

"Damn it, I have to get my ass to school," I tell him sharply, cutting off his ruminations about last night's cloud formation. "Thanks for the mediocre breakfast, Dad." As I sprint down the hall to my room, I yell, "Love you." My heart pounds with anxiety as I frantically throw on my GLS (glasses) and flic my BTN.

Damn! I seem to always be late to class, and if I am again, my friends will ridicule me!

CHAPTER FOUR

I wedge myself into my plush, white study chair, in the corner away from the 5-metre wall-to-wall windows.

I flic on my BTN, which lights up the GLS. My Hello-Helo springs to life - that's not what it's actually called, but every time our holograms shudder to life, we're greeted with the word 'Hello' in whatever your spoken language is.

The Bio-Tech Network is a small tech button we are all injected with at birth and is infused under the skin of our right wrist.

Just then, our SR or Study Room materialises around us.

"Hello, my people," I quip, stepping into the space where virtual meets reality.

"Hi guys," Benny grins, his image popping up beside me, pixels merging seamlessly. He is sitting on his faux-leather settee.

"Oi, you think they'll ever update your decor?" Soren chimes in, their hologram flickering into view, a playful glint in their eyes.

"Only if retro becomes cool again," Juice retorts, materialising with his arms crossed, his eyebrows arching high above his intelligent gaze.

"Ha, like that'll happen," adds Banksia, completing our circle. She leans back against the wall in her SR.

"So, alright, spill then—RC#?" Soren asks, steering the conversation towards our daily routine check-in.

"No, wait," I exclaim. "I have an entirely different topic to start this morning's discussion," I say with all the eagerness of a cat going after a mouse.

Every weekday morning, no matter where we are in the world, the five of us, the Mighty5, connect, just to get our mornings going. It's like the breakfast ritual with OZ, but without the faux food.

I can see everyone's disappointment in me for derailing the standard conversation.

"Okay, but sorry," I say, cutting straight to the chase. "Did any of you catch the crazy sky show last night?" I'm eager, maybe too eager, scanning their faces for a flicker of recognition.

"Dezzy," that's what my Uni friends call me, "you mean the sky looked less like a perpetual sunlit array of nothingness as it streaked toward the perpetual horizon or did you actually see colour?" quips Banksia, with a smirk on her face that is equal parts mirth and mischief. I can't help but grin back at her, despite the fact she has apparently no idea what I'm talking about.

"More than just the colour," I clarify, the memory burning bright behind my eyes. "It looked like a book laying on its side, a book on fire. None of you saw it?" I plead.

"Even if the planet is all messed up and overheating, it is still a big place," Juice remarks in his general dull drone. "We aren't where you are, so maybe it was only in London, Odezza."

Their faces remain blank canvases, untouched by the

phenomenon I'm describing. A part of me wilts with disappointment. The sight was meant to be seen; it can't have been a figment of my damn imagination.

"Why do you care so much?" Juice continues, apparently annoyed by my overzealousness.

I continue in an eager tone. "It was so strange, so different, so off-putting! I wanted someone else, apart from OZ and I, to see it."

"Wait, your dad saw it too?" Banksia adds.

"Yes, we saw it, but from separate parts of the flat, and it freaked us both out."

"Wait?" Banksia continues, "OZ doesn't get freaked. That's not an emotion we've heard you talk about."

"That's my point - that's why I wish one of you had seen it too, just to confirm how strangely out of whack it was!" I replied.

I give up!

"Guess it was just me and the ghosts then," I mutter, trying to keep the conversation light, but there's a weight to my words that betrays the sadness curling around my resolve.

"Hey, if anyone could share a celestial dance with spectres, it'd be you, Dezzy," Soren says, their voice a warm embrace that doesn't quite reach their concerned eyes.

"Next time, livestream it, yeah?" suggests Benny, pointing to his BTN with a wink. "Give us all a shot at witnessing these 'magical colourful clouds'." He's giggling at me. "Because right now, we're not going along with it."

"Will do," I promise sarcastically, tucking away the mix of camaraderie, solitude and pissed-off-ness that nestles within the Mighty5. We're a constellation of purpose and pain, drawn together under the dimming stars of this dystopian sprawl and HC, HoloClass. But I still wanted them to see what OZ, and I did! It seems important to me.

"Alright, forget about you guys," I quip, segueing with a

frown, "so, what were you saying about your RC#, Soren?" An RC# is how many days since it rained somewhere - Rain Check Number.

"Two hundred and seventy-nine here," Benny chimes in, his voice tinged with concern. "Plants at The Circle are struggling."

"One hundred and eighty-four," Banksia reports, her frown mirroring the gravity of the situation. "The water collectors are barely full."

"Sixty-two," Soren interjects, "but only because I was in Paris and a rare storm came down from the North Sea."

"Cheeky bugger," I smirk. "We're hitting ninety-three. Dad hates how dry it's been. But I have my pool and my Crystal Shower, which seems to help."

"Planets gone bonkers," Benny mutters, his usual humour subdued. "The post-BoldWar really fucked with nature." It's a little disconcerting to hear Benny swear like that.

"More like Russian roulette," I counter.

"Hope's our currency," Banksia nods, her determination infectious.

"Speaking of hope," Juice spurts out, a mischievous twinkle returning to his eye, "anyone else excited for today's lesson on subversive tech?"

"Speak for yourself, big man. I have a robolecture on the CG, Central Government, that is as dry as a, well, robot!"

Here's the lowdown on my friends. First, why The Mighty5? It's simple! We can't be The Fighting5, because as far as I can tell, none of us, well, maybe Juice, has ever laid a finger on anyone. We couldn't be The Cool5. That makes me snort through my nose. I guess we could be The Global5, but that doesn't have the same catchy ring.

I'm not even sure how the name came about, now that I think about it - but here we are, the Mighty5, all of us slung around the world connected through a special friendship.

We all met at Tokë University (TU). Gone are my dad's days when people 'went' to uni. TU boasts of being a GOI, a global online institution, as they call themselves. It's based in Albania, so I guess that's something. All I hear is that Albania still has rain, so I'm guessing a low RC#. There aren't a lot of universities to choose from; this is the one for all of us brainiacs.

We five all like the fact that TU has BCI+ (Brain-Computer Interfaces) like Brain-to-Brain learning. The + means they also use bots for teaching; EduBots. Tokë uses BCIs to directly interface our learning content. That includes everything ever published throughout the history of person-kind. Imagine downloading knowledge directly into your brain, bypassing traditional study methods. Like I said, it's the school for smarties, so they use smarty tech tools to teach.

That's why we like this program. We haven't used fully functional robots since the BoldWar, so the bots are the next best thing and still legal; they're like holographic tutors.

Then, there are my uni mates.

Banksia is a cool cat, with a unique style and presence. She hails from New Taiwan and exudes an air of intelligence. She is certainly quirky. Her dark bobbed hair always frames her face to perfection, which often has a funny grin, alluding to her playful nature. But beyond her outward appearance, Banksia seems to have a deep sense of caring for everything and everyone around her.

Banksia's not only nerdy, but also highly tech-savvy. She speaks multiple languages fluently (but has never said what they are). Her field of study is Bio-Composing, which I know little about. It sounds like a blend of art and science. As she explains it, student artists collaborate with biologists and mathematicians to create living artworks.

Banksia has also told us about genetic sequences, protein folding, and cellular automata merging with visual and auditory aesthetics. That involves another class project where they're developing a garden where flowers bloom in perfect Fibonacci spirals, harmonising with fractal melodies. This project's sheer complexity and beauty always leaves our group speechless - what a brilliant mind this girl has!

Then there's Juice! He is a military veteran from Baku, Azerbaijan, yet he has Scandinavian access. Juice seems tall and always maintains a mysterious aura about his background. He's no-nonsense, which we constantly poke fun at him for. I sometimes question how he is in the Mighty5, but he's cool, smart, and not bad to look at! He has a chiselled face, wide eyes, that are deeper than brown, almost black. He also sports a buzz cut.

Juice speaks 17 languages and studies Meta War Game Theory. There's a shock given his background. Apparently, that's where they delve into the strategic analysis of games themselves, specifically war games. If I have this correct, Meta War Game Theory explores how players reason about games, considering not just individual moves but the entire landscape of strategies. It's lost on me, but he says it's like playing 3D chess while also contemplating your opponent's chess strategy. Instead of focusing solely on Nash equilibria (optimal strategies within a single game), meta-game equilibrium considers optimal strategies across different games. When he explains it, all I hear is he gets to play games all damn day!

Soren is an interesting duck. They are well-travelled with diplomatic parents and carry themselves with an air of mystery and sophistication. Soren never speaks of their past. Ever. And their speech bears no trace of a distinguishable accent, leaving their true origin enigmatic. Still, we're pretty sure Soren's from Cyprus or Lebanon or somewhere in the eastern Mediterranean. Soren is stunning. Muscular physique with jet black hair and deep blue eyes. One thing is for certain - they are incredibly intelligent. I can tell by the way Soren's eyes are always darting around, observing, analysing, and processing everything in their surroundings. It's as if they are constantly connected to a network of information and ideas.

In fact, Soren is studying Synthetic Biology - a cutting-edge field that involves engineering microbes to produce essential nutrients in food. As I listen to them talk about it, I am in awe of this tech's potential for creating healthier and specifically designed food ingredients.

But that's not all - Soren also studies Transcendental Gastronomy. They tried to explain it once, but our minds couldn't quite grasp the concept. Something about going beyond molecular gastronomy and exploring food as a multi-sensory experience. In their class, they learn how to create dishes that elicit emotions, memories, and even altered states of consciousness through taste and presentation.

I often wonder if Soren has anything to do with the breakfast OZ and I 'enjoy' every morning. Perhaps they are already experimenting with their own transcendental gastronomic creations or delving into some other intellectual pursuit. Either way, Soren's intelligence and resourcefulness never cease to amaze me.

Then there's Benny, a skinny boy with sandy blonde hair, bright blue eyes and perfect teeth. He hails from NorLand - that's from the merger of Norway and Finland during the war. Despite his impressive academic focus on Planetary Ethics and Extraterrestrial Diplomacy, he is often the butt of jokes among our group, as he has a noticeable crush on me that I seem to be completely oblivious to.

His advanced studies centre around future Mars colonies and lunar outposts - concepts that seem otherworldly and far beyond the three space stations that are currently whirling around our planet every ninety minutes. In his classes, Benny and his classmates are delving into interplanetary ethics, studying how to respect Martian ecosystems and navigating diplomatic protocols for potential communication with extraterrestrial civilisations. He's mentioned pretend exchanges with Martian students and debates on cosmic rights as part of their coursework. It's hard to believe, but these are the realities of life in the Mighty5 - where anything is possible and the boundaries of knowledge are constantly being pushed.

I am a Sustainable Futures Futurist - a class title that often elicits curious glances and puzzled expressions. But allow me to elaborate. In SFF, we delve into the realm of Climate-Altered Futures, analysing the impacts of the climate crisis on societies, economies, and education.

It's a subject that only emerged after the BoldWar, when it became impossible to ignore the consequences of human and robotic actions. We utilise innovative tech, such as quantum computing, AI, and biotechnology, to reshape entire industries, redefine ethical standards, and enhance the human experience. Blah, Blah, Blah! They just changed the curriculum, but rumour has it that in our final year at Tokë, we will start studying topics like colonising Mars, travelling through interstellar space, and negotiating with cosmic entities. It's both thrilling and daunting to contemplate the endless possibilities of our field - I just hope it pays off!

"Okay, guys, we need to split and get to class - let's hope it rains where you are and keep an eye out for those crazy clouds. I'm not kidding - there was something super off-putting about them!"

"OUT!"

CHAPTER FIVE

A few days of exams later and still no more signs of crazy clouds, I shuffle into the kitchen to join my dad for breakfast. My stomach grumbles in protest, longing for something that doesn't taste like cardboard laced with artificial flavours.

I'm about to call for OZ to join me, when a sliver of light catches my eye. It slices through the morning's dimness, a thin beacon beckoning from Dad's office door. It's ajar. That's odd. Dad is as meticulous with security as he is with his research — a door left open with him in there is indeed a rare sight.

"Must've forgotten to seal it," I whisper, my curiosity piqued despite the gnawing hunger. TiM looks up at me like I'm talking to him. OZ's workspace is a treasure trove of unfinished ideas and enigmatic contraptions, a cathedral of innovation.

"Focus, Dezzy! Food first, snoop later," I chide myself, but even as the words leave my mouth, my feet betray me, inching towards the sliver of mystery. Dad's entire world is just beyond that crack, and like the forbidden fruit, it tempts me with the promise of knowledge.

"Two minutes. In and out," I convince myself. It's not breaking in if it's already open, right? Besides, what's a glimpse going to hurt? It's like a siren call I can't ignore.

"Here we go," I say, taking a deep breath as my hand reaches for the door, ready to push it open and find the secrets held within.

"Careful, Odezza," I mutter to myself, sidling along the perimeter.

I peek inside, just enough to see a half-built contraption that resembles the lovechild of a kaleidoscope and a telescope.

"Monday evening's clouds were off the charts," I hear him say, to someone either in the room or on his HelloHelo, his tone laced with both awe and apprehension. "Did anyone else see them?" he asked his guests.

"Never seen patterns like it," someone agrees, the person's voice tinged with the excitement of the unexplained.

Wait, someone else saw it too?

"Ozwald." They still call him that, it's kinda cute. "What do you make of it?"

"Unnatural," OZ replies, pacing before his peers. "Not just irregular... almost as if they're being — directed."

"Directed?" My mind races, snatching at the implications. Directed clouds? Directed by whom? Better still... why?

"Speculation is pointless without data," Dad continues, forever the scientist. "We need evidence, hard facts. The worry is, I think those were Noctilucent Clouds.

I wonder about Noctilucent Clouds and flic my BTN to life and find out. My HelloHolo quickly fills me in: they are thin, icy clouds in the upper atmosphere above the Earth, also known as polar mesosphere clouds (PMCs). They are visible during astronomical twilight and most often seen during the summer months. I read on: recent studies suggest they may be influenced by increased methane emissions. These clouds are the highest in Earth's atmosphere, located around 76 to

85 km in the mesosphere. "But it's not summer here," I whisper.

"Right," says the first speaker, nodularity snapping into resolve. "Facts first, hysteria later," I hear the man say.

"Keep me posted, team. I'm going to dig deeper," OZ says with a sense of authority that I'm not used to hearing.

"Be careful, Ozwald," the woman says, a hint of worry threading through her words. "You're not the only one watching the skies."

"Since when has caution been my strong suit?" Dad chuckles.

"Since never," I whisper, the smile that tugs at my lips is coy. That's my dad, relentless, fearless and wicked smart.

"Alright," he says, as I watch his hologram wink out. Dad is alone in his office.

"Damn clouds," Dad's voice suddenly fills the room.

Several seconds later, I hear, "That can't be right? That shit's illegal."

Minutes go by. I can hear him on his BTN, working. Then I hear him call back his friends on his HelloHolo.

"Sorry to recall you so soon, but I think I just found something that might answer the trouble with the clouds," I hear him address his colleagues.

"Look at this?" I hear him ask, but I can't see anything - I don't dare let myself get any closer to the open door for the sake of being caught.

"Can this be right?" I hear the woman ask inquisitively.

"Are you sure, OZ?" I hear the man ask, tension in his voice.

What the heck are they looking at? It's killing me!

"That's certainly cloud seeding," OZ announces.

"But..." the man's voice trails off.

"I know," OZ picks up the gentleman's thoughts, "cloud seeding was condemned after the war."

What's going on here?

"But that doesn't look like normal cloud seeding from what I recall," the female adds.

"Agreed. I noticed that too," OZ continues. You can almost hear the cogs turning in his head.

"Anomalies in the atmosphere," the man adds, the words thick with confusion. "But what kind?"

"Something's going on up there, something new, something different. Certainly seems rogue. Illegal," says Dad, scepticism lacing his tone. "I think I know. I just need to do more research. If what I'm thinking is true, we need to figure out who's behind this immediately and stop it if we can."

"Ozwald?" the female voice asks firmly. "What on earth are you saying? What's going on?"

"Well," Dad answers sheepishly, "from the little I've seen already, I'm thinking this might not be rogue cloud seeding, but being done deliberately."

Dead silence fills the office. The only thing I hear is my heart beating over time.

WHAT THE HELL IS CLOUD SEEDING?

CHAPTER SIX

"I'll do some 'tapping'," OZ declares, the word 'tapping' a euphemism that has my pulse quickening. That's his cue for code-breaks and data raids. He's about to splice through the UK Canton's digital defences, seeking whispers and shadows about cloud seeding. How have I never heard about cloud seeding before?

"Keep your eye on the sky," he suggests, a last command before the line goes dead.

"Right?" I murmur to myself, slipping further away from the door. "Because the skies aren't full of enough eyes as it is."

The thought sends a shiver down my spine as I make my way back to the kitchen; damn I'm hungry! That, plus my mind is racing faster than my heart. There's a storm brewing, and it could be from cloud seeding? My stomach twists—not with hunger, but with anxiousness. Dad's about to stir up a hornet's nest, and I'm right here, ready and willing to help.

I'd barely taken two steps away from the lab door when I heard it—a harsh utterance that snapped through the silence like a live wire. "That just can't be right? That shit really is illegal," OZ says, echoing his earlier statement! What's going on? I ask myself repeatedly.

I freeze, every muscle coiling tight. Dad's voice pitches in disbelief and carries a kind of horror that could chill your blood. This is more than a simple 'a-ha' moment; this discovery sends ripples across the stagnant ponds of our dismal existence.

My breath catches, hitching in the back of my throat. Illegalities in the world's canton are as common as clouds in the old world sky, but for dad to sound so mortified. It's as if he has stumbled upon a forbidden secret, so outside the realm of our constricted laws, that it seems to shake him. The brilliant inventor who scoffed at boundaries, rattled by an illegality? Now that's saying something.

A brief debate wages war in my mind—do I burst in, and demand answers? No. OZ wouldn't welcome that. He's the fortress, and I'm the shadow skirting its walls.

So I do what any self-respecting daughter of a renegade scientist does—I make breakfast. I truly am famished, even with Dad's level of angst.

I've decidedly lost my appetite. Just the echo of that line, bouncing around the chasms of my skull. "That just can't be right? That shit really is illegal."

"Damn it," I whisper under my breath, impatience nipping at my resolve. What has he found? What spectre from the skies above has reared its ugly head?

I pushed off the kitchen wall, heart drumming a fierce rhythm against my ribs. I need time, space—to think, to strategize. To plan our next move in this 3D chess game of shadows and secrets. Yes, time for a swim.

No sooner do I think 'swim' when OZ calls out from his lab, "Honey", he announces, instantly pulling me out of my deep concerns. When he leaves his office, he yells, "I'm famished! Let's go get some breakfast."

Wait, what? My dad just asked to go out, leaving our tall glass-encrusted shrine and going somewhere other than our beautiful sun-drenched kitchen for breakfast. Did an alien suddenly abduct OZ without my knowing?

"Sure," I squeak out, sounding more like TiM than myself.

As he approaches me, he looks visibly worried, not a look I'm used to.

"Why the sudden need to go out and grab breakfast?" I ask him, trying to find my normal voice.

"I know; shock and horror, your dear old dad wants to go outside, nay, venture out into the great unknown where I rarely dare to venture!" he says with a scoff.

I need to say yes, as this truly is a rare occurrence. "Yes, great, what an idea, let's get going," I add. Before you change your mind, my inner voice squeaks out.

Maybe this is my chance to ask him about cloud seeding.

We grab our stuff, pat TiM on his shiny metal head, and move toward the lift.

In those mere seconds, hurtling down to the ground, you have little time to appreciate the staggering beauty across London.

As we pile onto Ferry Street, we have two choices, head to Island Gardens ModTube stop, the hyper-loop system of subterranean tunnels, or grab the next RedEl we see.

"Your idea to go out, so it's your choice of transportation," I suggest to OZ.

"I'm feeling doubly risky today. Let's take the RedEl," he says, like a renegade runaway.

The RedEl is a modern marvel that graces our venerable streets in London. They're an elongated double-decker red bus that seems to defy gravity; elevated, gliding above the roadscape. It runs on powerful electromagnetic fields generated by the bus' interaction with the Earth's magnetic field, lifting the

RedEl into the air. As a passenger, it feels like you're floating on air.

"Okay, great," I add, "and where to, Jeeves?" I ask in my mock-aristocratic accent.

As if I haven't endured enough surprises already today, he blurts out, "To The Time-Traveller's Tea House, tout de suite."

It's one of my favourite spots, but this means Dad must be stressing out. The Time-Traveller's Tea House is his go-to place when he is feeling strain and pressure. From what I've read, OZ has claimed, "I never felt pressure or anxiety when I invented the Oxolet." This cloud seeding business must really be pushing him to the limit.

The Time-Traveller's Tea House is kind of fun. It's nestled in a hidden corner of Covent Garden. People can sip on steaming cups of Old English tea while discussing quantum physics with fellow time travellers. The menu always features delicacies from various historical eras—Victorian scones, Roaring Twenties cocktails, and molecular gastronomy from today. It's a place you get dressed up for, but in our haste to leave the penthouse, we didn't change our SLAX!

As the RedEl whisks over the streets, you can feel the pulse of neon life. Holographic billboards come to life, and AI-guided rickshaws whisk commuters past vertical gardens and bustling markets. I like this city!

"I need to tell you something important," OZ blurts out as we step off the RedEl, just metres from the glamorous entrance of the Tea House.

Having thought ahead, I used my BTN to make a reservation, thus avoiding the line like all the lemmings.

As we cross the street and approach the grand entrance, I tug on my dad's sleeve and ask, "Can it wait until we sit down? As we walked through the intricate double doors adorned with gold trim, we descended the ornate spiral staircase. "Yes, fine," Dad finally replied with a frown.

I forget how insane this place is. The staircase spills into a magnificent gathering area that models a grand ballroom. As they mill about, the greeters, clad in white dusters, scan our BTN.

Beyond each inner entrance are four enormous rooms, all themed to different historical periods. Like ancient temples, each room is filled with treasures from past dynasties and long-forgotten adventures, each space whispering its own tale.

It looks like we are heading to The Renaissance Room. The Renaissance Room is filled with ornately carved wooden chairs and tables, with intricate designs and patterns adorning every surface. The furniture looks weathered and worn, but also grand and wise, as if it has years of history. The mismatched teacups on the tables add a touch of whimsy to the room, each one unique and beautiful in its own way.

As we wander through the narrow aisles, the intoxicating scent sparkles my senses. When we listen carefully, we can hear music. With a quick flic of my BTN, I discover we are listening to Monteverdi. The haunting melodies of classical music transport me to another time and place.

Amelia, the enigmatic proprietor and Sorceress of Teas, as she is called, heads our way, like she's known us for years. With her silver and turquoise hair framing her face, her clear green eyes appear to hold various long, distant secrets. As she says hello, all I can think about is the fact it's rumoured she brews ancient potions in the hidden basement.

With her salutation done, Amelia excuses herself to make tea, leaving me alone with my father. Leaning forward eagerly, he asked, "Have you heard of cloud seeding?" I hear a blend of excitement and trepidation in his tone.

Without skipping a beat and not allowing me to answer what evidently was a rhetorical question, "I can't be totally certain, but I believe someone is seeding the cloud - that's what's so odd about the clouds we saw - they weren't natural."

WHAT?

Continuing eagerly, he asserts, "in fact, after conducting some preliminary research and collaborating with my old team this morning, I genuinely believe that something terrible is happening above us, and we have only just witnessed the beginning."

Wanting to ask a multitude of questions, I refrain from doing so to avoid revealing that I overheard their conversation, instead holding tight until he shares more.

"Proving beyond a doubt that this is really happening, and where it's happening, is the real challenge." I interrupt, "and I guess, who's doing it."

Just then, our tea service arrives table-side. We are greeted with two large pots of steaming hot Old English tea, faux finger sandwiches, no crust, Petit fours, scones, and Devonshire cream. Yum!

"Yes!" he continues, almost jumping out of his old leather seat, "who is doing this is a key question. Cloud seeding is illegal and has been since the BoldWar. I think this isn't merely rogue cloud seeding. I believe someone is intentionally doing this. I just need to prove who."

After making that startling declaration, we transfer our goodies onto our delicate china plates.

CHAPTER SEVEN

After finishing breakfast, I'm eager to hurry back to the penthouse. I have to share with the Mighty5 what I just heard while we were having tea and faux scones with cream.

OZ covered the history, process, legality, illegality, cessation, reasons, and global taboo of cloud seeding.

He also needed to get back as fast as possible, because he wanted to continue his Tapping. He was the ultimate researcher, so the more he knew, the more we'd all know.

One RedEl ride back, through the lobby and up the exterior glass encased lift, and we were back.

I run off to my room, while my dad heads back to his multipurpose office.

Moments later, my HelloHolo springs to life and my uni mates materialise gradually.

The bright sunlight streaming through my high bedroom windows paints a pleasant background in juxtaposition to my high level of angst. As I wait for the Mighty5 all to join our virtual meeting, my mind races with all the information OZ just shared over tea. It's hard to believe that something as innocent as cloud seeding could be illegal and have such a dark history. But if someone's using it and doing it wrong, as OZ speculates, then we might be in for a total earth-shock! And we have had enough of those this century.

As Benny finally joins the call, I quickly summarise what OZ had explained to me earlier.

"So, here's what OZ told me over breakfast at the Time-Traveller's Tea House."

"Wait, what," Benny jumps over me, "your dad left your flat?! He never to leaves the protection and security of your penthouse!"

"Yes. No. Yes," I bark. "Listen, that's not important right now!"

"Cloud seeding? Heard of it?" I look around the virtual room, "it's a technique that changes the weather, it creates rain from the tiniest clouds in desert regions of the world. Some Yank chemist and meteorologist developed it 150-years ago. OZ told me it involves dispersing substances such as silver iodide or dry ice into clouds to alter precipitation processes."

"There's something about playing with dry ice I find really enjoyable."

"Benny!" Everyone snaps.

"The goal is to either increase rainfall or snowfall. People used aircraft, rockets, cannons, and even ground generators to get this gunk up into the sky. People frequently used it during droughts in Australia, India, the Middle East and other countries."

"Well," Juice finally speaks, "wouldn't that be most of the world right now - completely dry with crazy RC#s?"

"Okay," Soren butts in. "Did you just say it's illegal? Since when?"

"Since the BoldWar! Something happened that OZ wouldn't share, but I think I have a plan to find out."

I go on, finishing what Dad had told me over tea.

As OZ's words swirl in my mind, I am struck by the weight

of a warning he mentioned about the potential consequences of improperly executed cloud seeding. The thought of unpredictable weather changes like torrential downpours or destructive hailstorms sends shivers down my spine, knowing its devastating impact on nature and man-made structures. And the mention of harmful substances like silver iodide accumulating in the very soil, water, and vegetation that sustain us is a chilling reminder of our responsibility to protect our delicate ecosystems.

"But just when I think I can't handle any more knowledge," I continue my story. "Dad dropped another bombshell over breakfast. Supposedly, inefficient cloud seeding not only wastes valuable resources but can also lead to legal and ethical dilemmas if not properly allowed or consented by a community."

I'm seeing a lot of nodding and shaking of heads. I can't tell if it's all coming out the right way, but they cling to every word as I emphasise the crucial importance of precise execution, rigorous monitoring, and strict adherence to guidelines to ensure effective and safe cloud seeding. My mind races with the weight of this information and the understanding of how much is at stake.

"That's great and all," I continue, "but he never told me what the connection was between cloud seeding being banned and becoming illegal and how that pertains to the BoldWar. I guess we'll have to find out on our own!"

The others are just as shocked and intrigued by this new intelligence as I am. We all agree that we need to do some research on our own end and sort out this cloud seeding nonsense.

Banksia is the first to pick up what must sound like EduBot. "So cloud seeding seems like a good thing–"

"If it's done right," Juice charges in.

"Right?" Benny adds flatly. "Bringing rain back to a seriously parched earth sounds like something we could be and could use right about now–"

"But the problem is, it backfired!" I say grimly.

Stunned faces look back at me with concern.

"What?" Soren elicits.

"I forgot one critical detail in my EduBot lectures." Benny cracks a half smile. "The part that has OZ in a panic is the fact that whatever happened with this rogue seeding outfit, they are seeding the wrong clouds. They're seeding Noctilucent clouds."

Blank stares all around!

"I know, I had to look it up," I set off again like some juvenile teacher.

"They're seeding Noctilucent clouds," I repeat, "the really high ones; the super wavy, silvery clouds, way up high," I conclude this part of the lecture.

"I'm not getting it," Benny chimes in, seeming a little dense, but maybe that's okay right now. This is some heavy subject matter.

I go on, "OZ relayed the fact that Noctilucent clouds are a super rare form of clouds. He told me they're made of ice crystals and dust from meteor smoke."

"Sounds like an exotic drink," Benny cracks.

I push on, "that occurs at really high altitudes, such as 80km. They're so far up there that they could create total devastation, as these are the clouds you never mess with. That's why OZ thinks this might all be an error on some companies' side, or worse still, it's being deliberately done."

Too heavy right now! I must change the subject.

"So," I can't stop, "are you guys seeing anything different in the weather where you are?"

"Well," Banksia starts off, acknowledging the change of subject, "since you're asking and because you told us to keep a lookout for any strange clouds, I have seen some changes for sure. And they're pretty wild."

"I have too," Benny jumps in, eager like a primary school kid.

"Just this morning," Banksia continues, giving Benny the stink eye, "there was stuff happening I'd never seen before."

"Where are you, by the way?" I ask quickly.

"Oh, I've been at The Line, Saudi Arabia, for the past fortnight. My parents had to be here for work, so I tagged along. This place is utterly crazy. It's so flippin' long and skinny and everything shiny. It has its own elevated monorail system that goes up one side and down the other. And there's something like a million people living here. It's how I imagine it will be at Living Luna. I'm in Neom Sector 18L, so away from the water on the lower level, we're out here in the desert."

"Everything is a damn desert there, B!" Juice spills."

"Anyway, this morning, it not only snowed. And it has become completely overcast - two unheard of weather events."

We all look at her with the same collective thought, "Seriously!?"

"Wait. It snowed in Saudi Arabia?" Benny challenges. "That can't be good."

"That's what my parents said. The crazy, or maybe I should say, scary part is it was 42C yesterday."

"Nothing like that here," Soren kicks in, "here being the NAC (New Administrative Capital, near Cairo), where every day seems to be clear and hot, hot and clear! Seems like I'm missing out. But I will say," they continue, "this place is to die for. Thousands of palm trees, millions of well-dressed, well-to-do people, and architecture that looks like it's out of the future. It's nuts here and I'm loving it. But no change in the weather."

Juice, eager to share, exclaims, "I'm in The Circle, Dubai, and haven't seen a thing!" But I have heard there is the mother of dust storms coming our way. They're calling it a 'dust tsunami', but no rain!" He turns to Banksia, "We have an elevated monorail style system here too. There are 25 trains that just go round and round in a circle all day. Picking up. Dropping off. And no one leaves here as this is the most climatic-perfect city in the world."

Juice sounds like a spokesperson for a second, putting a smile on my face.

"That's interesting," I chime in. "The three of you are so close, but such distinct weather patterns."

"Benny, where are you and what's going on?"

"I'm down here in the city, the Maldives Floating City that is, and let me tell you, for a place that thinks it's so cool, I am getting worried."

"Why?" We all ask in unison.

"Because since you told us to look up for changes, everyone's been looking down. The water level here has risen almost four centimetres! That's a lot of damn water. And before you throw the jokes my way that it's a floating city," he continues, not sounding like a tourism spokesperson anymore, "save your breath. It might float, but that is a crazy amount of sea rise, and no one can tell where all that water is coming from. But now that I think about it, it has been stormy, but I have seen little rain, not enough to bring about four centimetres."

Silence.

"Listen," I finally stutter, just to break up the chilling hush. "We need to do something, anything to see if we can understand what's going on; seeding clouds, who, where, what, when, and all that kind of nonsense!"

"Let's disperse for now," I continue, "and start digging around for any information we can find, even gossip about meteorological oddities that aren't the norm."

Banksia mentions, "I can start browsing through articles and forums on my BTN and report back."

"Me too," Benny chirps like a canary in a gilded cage.

"Mighty5," I don't always blurt that out, "we need to figure out why people were afraid of, what they couldn't control or understand, and why they banned cloud seeding. And, if we can, what about cloud seeding sparked such intense fear?

Soren chimes in, their voice quivering with pure annoyance, "This is just what this planet needs - another man made disaster!!!!! This shit is pissing me off!"

"OZ is doing Tapping as we speak, so let's get to it."

Juice says, "Well, if he is, we can too."

We? I don't believe I have what it takes to Tap. And I don't think these are skills the Mighty5 have either. But what am I saying? Who knows what secret talents the Mighty5 offers?. We're just uni students; geeky, smart kids that all seem to get along and not totally annoy each other.

Juice explains the skill he has that none of us knew about - stuff he learned while in the mandatory Azerbaijan military. Tough canton. With this underlying tone of pure espionage, we're understanding why he's called Juice.

"Give me some time and I'll report back on my findings!" he says.

With that, we all flic off our BNTs and fade back into reality and get to work!

CHAPTER EIGHT

The Mighty5, we are a constellation of hope in a fast-darkening world. It has been two days since the '5' have been linked. I stand by the massive windows in the study, an obelisk of glass that frames the suffocating darkness above. The sky is a canvas of chaos, painted by mankind's hubris. My eyes search for a twinkle from the past, but find none. "Looks like the night forgot the day ever existed," I muttered to myself and TiM, sitting by my side, obedient as ever.

With the flic of my BTN, we're all back together.

"You guys, you need to hear this," Juice calls out, his voice cutting through the thick air of our cramped holo hideout. His fingers dance across the makeshift keyboard. The screen flickers, throwing ominous shadows across his intent features.

"Spill it," I say, turning away from the wall of windows. Whatever he has found, we are clearly in deeper trouble than we thought.

"I found some internal rumours swirling around the CG (the Central Government) that state that someone's messing with weather patterns," he continues without preamble, his eyes never leaving the screen.

"Someone?" Benny asks. No one responds.

"Yeah, someone's desperate for rain, right?" I reply, trying to keep my tone light despite the sinking feeling in my chest.

"More like desperate times calling for disastrous measures," Juice's hands pause for a moment. "They were cloud seeding, alright, but from the speculation, they screwed up big time."

"Define 'big time'?" I prompt, knowing I might regret asking.

"OZ's speculation was correct. They hit the Noctilucent clouds, Odezza. Eighty-two kilometres over Tunisia. They are claiming it happened unintentionally. And what's unfolding..." He trails off, the implications hanging between us heavier than the darkness outside.

"Wait. Could it be cataclysmic?" Banksia responds with the question on the tip of all our tongues.

"Isn't it obvious?" Juice snorts. "Panic is bad for business, so they're not saying. And speaking of business," he continues, his gaze flicking to a document on the screen, "it seems all roads potentially lead to Roman Polotov."

"Polotov?" I felt a chill that had nothing to do with the temperature. "The tycoon, Polotov?"

"None other," he confirms dryly. "I discovered he owns a cloud seeding company. A large one. Based in Malta. It's all here—" Juice jabs at the screen, "—in black and white. They knew the risks, cut corners, and now..." His voice is speculative, fading as he reads further.

"Let me guess," Soren says. You can see their minds racing. "It's irreversible."

"Looks like it," he muttered. "There's something bigger at play here, and Polotov is potentially smack in the middle of it. If the government is working overtime to bury this, then..."

"Then we dig it up," I state firmly, a spark igniting within me. "We owe it to everyone out there, living under this cursed sky."

Juice nods, his usual sly smile replaced by steely resolve. "We'll need every scrap of information we can get. Every rumour, every secret memo. We expose them all."

"Agreed." I clench my fists, feeling the familiar thrill of the challenge stir inside me. "We've got storms to stave off and scandals and secrets to share."

"Count me in," Juice said, already typing furiously. "After all, what's a little global catastrophe between friends?"

"Nothing we can't handle," I declare, though a part of me wonders if that's just bravado talking. But as I look back at the impenetrable sky, I realise that bravery isn't just about facing down fear—it's about charging headlong into the unknown, armed with nothing but wit, will, the faintest glimmer of hope and friends on a hologram.

"Let's get to work," I say, squaring my shoulders. "Time to bring some light to this darkness."

The HoloMeet disbands, each of us retreating into our own thoughts, our own fears, our own corners of the world. Yet beneath it all, a flicker of hope persists. We're the Mighty5, after all. If anyone can pierce the darkness with light, it's us. Or is blind arrogance speaking?

Darkness continues to cling to the edges of the sky like a malignant shroud, swallowing the once-familiar silhouette of London's jagged horizon. As I press my face against the cold glass of my study window, the unnerving blackness seems to press back, carrying with it a silence that roars louder than any storm.

LATER THAT NIGHT, we reconnect.

"Juice?" I start, "You find anything?"

"Banksia?" Soren interrupts, cutting through the background noise. "Where the hell are you?"

"My parents left The Line, and now are at Rise Tower." Banksia seems more tense than her usual chipper self.

"What's all that noise?" I ask, not trying to seem overly anxious.

"The building feels like it's groaning," she says.

As we look on behind her, the wind looks like an ancient beast lashing against the sides of The Rise, creating a howling symphony of nature's fury. What's going on in Riyadh?

"At this movement," she sounds so scared, "I'm in my bedroom on the 366th floor, and the world outside is a blur of sand and rage. It's a madhouse here, with everyone scrambling for cover. I'm not sure why my parents headed here! I think we're in the middle of the dust tsunami you spoke of, Juice. What's not cool," she adds, "is the fact that this building is two-kilometres high, so we are swaying — a lot..." Banksia's voice trails off in terror, and we can see she is holding an old stuffed teddy bear for protection.

"Well, hang in there," Benny blurts, not sure he realises his own pun. "It truly looks terrifying out there!"

I'm still dying to now, "Juice, did you do any more tapping?" I ask, trying to keep my tone at a normal pitch, fighting the backdrop of terror.

"Plenty!" he shouts back over the sound of battered SkyRiser, his fingers a blur across his holo-screen. His eyes are alight with the fire that only comes from digging through secrets meant to stay buried. "I confirmed it is indeed cloud seeding! I only perused what the GC referred to as 'speculative', but now it's tangible. I discovered an old memo stating that cloud seeding interferes with weather patterns, causing worse droughts, and floods ... end-of-days stuff, so it was banned. Your Dad was correct, Dezza. This rubbish is truly unlawful and has been for two decades.

The BoldWar led to its banishment? I question myself, not putting forth the question to the group. It's odd. How can it create worse droughts and potential flooding?

"Great!" I mutter, the weight of this adding clarity, settling like lead in my stomach. "So they played God with the sky and lost control."

"Seems so," Juice confirmed, tapping into another encrypted file. "And get this—the ban came after rogue states tried weaponizing the tech. Caused more damage than a couple of nukes."

"Fan-bloody-tastic," Soren says, their sarcasm thick enough to cut with a knife.

"And now we're staring down the barrel of today's mess." I motion towards the window, where the storm raged uncontrollably like a possessed entity.

"Still, it's not all bad news," Juice adds with that frustratingly optimistic lilt he always musters. "We've almost confirmed Roman did it, but we still can't figure out why he wanted to start cloud seeding again. We need more data."

"Remember the BoldWar?" I finally ask, trying to connect the dots in my mind, my voice almost lost in the wind's howl in the background at Rise Tower. Everyone nods, and I see the flicker of intrigue in their eyes. "Twenty-two days. That single action was enough to rip the world asunder. It appeared every doomsday scenario from old cinema had combined into one, including nuclear strikes and rogue bots.

"The Internet went poof, too," Soren recalls. "Imagine that, a life without memes, stupid dad jokes and viral videos of puppies scurrying around on frozen lakes."

"Tragic," I quip, but the reality surpasses the mere absence of dad jokes. The BoldWar left scars, not just on the land, but on the very air we breathe. Oxygen levels experienced a drastic drop during those dark days, creating a sensation suggesting the world had decided that humans had overstayed their welcome. Much of the oceans couldn't keep up with oxygen supplied by algae, animals, including domesticated and livestock, died off as did most of the great and ancient forests around the globe. The things we had taken for granted over the past millennia, like the oxygen producers, were actually starving from a lack of life supporting gases - what a crazy circle to be caught in. Yet many of us survived. Well, OZs era.

"Which brings us to the Oxolet." I tap the small device clipped to my left wrist, feeling its familiar hum against my skin. "Dad's brainchild. His way of thumbing his nose at a suffocating planet and saving as much of the world as possible. At least humans," I add with sadness.

"Genius," Banksia exclaims in genuine admiration. "Pulling O2 straight from one's own blood supply. Pretty brilliant of OZ to figure that out."

"Like a tree in your pocket," I finish.

It was classic OZ—practical, lifesaving, and with a disdain for anything that wasn't his brand of innovation. Yet, he had never asked for acclaim after his invention; although it made him rich beyond belief and gave us a delightful view.

"After the war, there were rumours," Juice moves the conversation forward, "whispers about RogueBots sparking the conflict. Humanoid robots so advanced they blurred the lines between synthetic and organic."

"RogueBots," I murmur. The term brings back terrible memories. Dad had always been wary of tech that mimicked life too closely.

"Right. And in the panic, they banned them all, even those that were harmless. Threw the baby out with the bathwater, as they used to say."

"Typical knee-jerk reaction," I muse. "And here we are, twenty years later, still dealing with the fallout."

"Literally," Banksia says, glancing over her shoulder anxiously at the window as another gust rocks the pane.

"I can see why OZ is troubled by this," I say, my voice barely above a whisper. "The cloud seeding, the potential cover-ups... He wants technology to serve, not dominate or destroy."

"Then let's ask him what he has also found and, together, start fixing this mess," Juice states resolutely. "Starting with Polotov and his sky-high ambitions."

"Sky-high—good one," Banksia smirks. Despite the gravity of the situation, I can't help but smile. We need Dad's help, because this might be beyond the Mighty5.

With a hint of trepidation, I turn to look out at the panoramic penthouse view overlooking the fading beauty of Greenwich Park. The once lush lawns are currently being pelted with hail, their vibrancy drained by the harshness of this oppressive weather. The old naval buildings, usually bathed in bright sunlight, seem weary under the unwelcome grey tones washing their stoic walls. A sense of sadness and bitterness permeates the surrounding air, a tone that I have never felt before. It weighs heavily on my heart as I take in the scene before me.

I'm distracted.

"Hey! I'm going to jump you guys. Out!"

I AM HAUNTED by the remarks Juice stated about the BoldWar. It makes me feel uneasy to think it was only a few years before I was born. I have always strayed away from learning about the war. And it's not a subject OZ and I use as one of our breakfast icebreakers. Yet, there is more information to garner.

I flic my BTN and promptly search for the basics. I am acutely not prepared for this, especially given everything happening around us, but to recognise the future is to appreciate our past, or at least that's what our HistoryBots told us when we were kids. Too late now, I must read what's on my holo:

BoldWar: 2066, a catastrophic nuclear war lasting 22 days, brought about by RogueBots; consequences were dire, affecting human lives, massive impact on earth's oxygen levels and historic deviations in global environments.

I'm this far in and already know I don't want to read on, so I skim the highlights...

Nuclear Explosions and Radiation, Electromagnetic Pulse, Firestorms and Black Carbon Smoke, Photosynthesis, Mass Starvation and Ecosystem Collapse!

"Really? That's all!" I say out loud in amazement.

The BoldWar disrupted food production, leading to widespread famine in certain regions of the globe. Starving populations consumed stored food supplies.

Forests, grasslands, and marine ecosystems suffered because of radiation and climate disorder. Dead vegetation released less oxygen.

Because of the BoldWar, the 'Oxolet', a personalised oxygen generator was developed for use by humans. Unfortunately, developers did not create such a device for non-humans.

This led to a calamitous reduction on the world's meat, grain, and fresh food supply.

TheBioSynth food systems work developed post-BoldWar to surplus the world with edible foods.

Post-BoldWar, global visionaries conceived the Central Government, leading to the conversion of countries to cantons and the merging of certain countries to become new cantons.

Post-BoldWar also brought about a monumental shift in the world's power supply. Now the world runs on solar, generating powerful Solar Grids. Some say this may be the only positive, if there is any positive whatsoever, to stem from the worst 22 days in the history of mankind and the planet Earth.

I just keep on reading. More and more information. I've got what the Mighty5 call, TO, Temporal Overload! Must. Stop. Reading!

"ENOUGH!" I tell myself out loud.

I can't flic my BTN off fast enough; all the updates evaporate. Did I truly need to read all that!? No wonder they say my dad's invention of the Oxolet literally saved the planet from complete annihilation. "Good job, OZ," I say under my breath.

I shake it off. That was too much to take in all in one sitting, and I can see why I have bypassed this conversation, and education, my entire life.

I dare look up to the sky, so dark, foreboding. An off shade of grey, with thick, swirling clouds that block out any trace of the gleaming sunlight seen just days before. Lightning flashes unceasingly, illuminating the devastation being wrought by the storm. I look down to the ground far below and can see trees uprooted, buildings being pelted by debris, and flotsam flying. And certainly no sign of eVTOL's.

As I look closer, I can see water cascading down the side of our SkyRise. Not rain. Water must be splashing from the pool above, hurtling to the streets below. The very pool where all this started, with an instant glimpse into the goreish nightmare besieging London.

The Thames appears angry and tumultuous, with dark, churning waters and waves crashing against the banks with a ferocity that is both intimidating and chaotic. No more floating gardens.

An image of Amelia, the enigmatic proprietor and Sorceress of Teas, flashes to the front of my mind. The fond memory of her strolling toward our table with a tarnished silver tray adorned with delicate mixed matched teacups filled with perfectly crafted scones, cream, and a variety of mouth-watering pastries with no crusts.

Then my mind flashes back like the lightning outside to reality with the crash of thunder. "This sucks," I say under my breath.

It's time for some help.

I RAP TENTATIVELY on the heavy steel door of my father's office; the sound echoing back at me like a complex chamber of secrets. The silence that follows is thick with anticipation. I take a deep breath, feeling the recycled air nip at my lungs—a stark reminder of the dystopian shroud enveloping us.

"You here, Dad?" I mutter, mustering the remnants of hope I've salvaged from the wreckage of our world.

With a push, the door groans open, protesting its own movement. The sight before me hits like a gut punch. There he is, OZ, the man who had orchestrated technological marvels, reduced to a shell of despair. He's hiding his head in his arms, his body trembling with silent tears.

"Hey, hey," I say softly, approaching him with cautious steps. "Dad, talk to me."

His head lifts slowly, and I glimpse into his face—lines of worry etch deeper than ever, eyes red and haunted. It's as if the weight of our crumbling society has settled squarely on his shoulders.

"Odezza," his voice cracks, barely audible over the hum of computers, floating monitors and tiny machinery. "It's even more severe, far more severe than what we believed."

"Tell me," I urge, pulling up a stool beside him. My heart lurches against my ribs, bracing for impact.

With trembling hands, he shuffles through the papers scattered across his desk. He writes all his thoughts, research notes, discoveries and inventions in freehand. I could hardly believe it.

With a heavy sigh, he hands me one of his workbooks filled with what looks like complex equations. Cloud formations, what seem to be laser vectors, hand-drafted images of canton outlines and more. My eyes fly across the text, deciphering the scientific jargon. But it doesn't take a genius to understand the bottom line: irreversible climate cataclysm.

OZ doesn't say a word. He doesn't need to.

"Damn it," I whispered, my mind racing. "They've truly accomplished it, haven't they? Played God with the weather."

"Seems so," he finally concedes, wiping his eyes with the back of his hand. "And now we're staring down the barrel of a disaster that could end us all."

"Okay, okay," I quickly interrupt, more to myself than to him. "We knew it was bad, but this is a whole new level of terrible."

"Roman Polotov," he murmured, the name falling from his lips like a curse. "If anyone has the resources to mess things up and not look back, it's him. We can't trust him, Odezza. We just can't."

"So you figure it out too," I stutter.

"What do you mean, 'too'?" he squeaks out.

"I accidentally overheard you and your old team chatting and, well, couldn't help but question what it was you were all talking about."

He looks at me blankly, blinking his eyes back to reality. "How, when?"

"The other day. Your massive lab door was open a jar, so TiM and I couldn't help but eavesdrop and we heard what you were talking about and figured out the rest."

His blank stare turns to a mixture of embarrassment with a twinge of anger mixed in for good measure. "Sorry, Dad," I add, meaning it with all my heart. If there is one person in the world I hate to disappoint, it's my father. I guess I don't know a teen alive that does. I had betrayed his confidence and secrecy, and I feel really poorly for that. But not that poorly, the more I beat myself up.

"What have you found, Dad, and I'll tell you what the Mighty5, my uni friends, and I have found?"

"I tapped the CG a few times," he adds with a cheeky bad-boy grin forming on this difficult-to-read-scientist-face.

"You did?" I reply, with an equity cheeky, you-sly-fox-face.

"I had to do something, right?"

I try to sound confident as I answer his query, my eyes shining with determination and pride. But deep down, I can't shake off the doubt and uncertainty gnawing at me. Were we making the right decision to break into and tap the CG? Would it all turn out okay? Oh, what to do?

"Of course you did, and I'm proud of you for breaking the habit of always doing the right thing." I end up spinning my sentence like a keenly trained canton politician.

"Trust and Polotov don't belong in the same sentence," I

shoot back, a bitter laugh escaping me. "But we need to do something. If the sky won't give us mercy, we'll have to wring it out ourselves."

Dad nods, a ghost of determination flickering in his strong eyes. "You always were your mother's daughter."

I stand up, rolling my stiff shoulders back. "Alright, let's get to work. No time for dry tears when the world's falling apart."

"Right behind you, Odezza." He rises too, the scientist in him clawing back to the surface. "But wait, you and your friends found some information too? How?"

"Determination, skills and smarts," I add. Oh for-gawd-sake, I really am turning into a damn politician. Shit!

"Okay, fine, have it your way," he says. "If you and your friends, the Mighty5, found something, let's compare notes and see where we're at," he continues, "just as long as we're fighting for the right to see tomorrow and we're all on the same team, sign me up."

And with that, we dive into the fray, two minds united against the darkening skies.

CHAPTER NINE

I tuck myself into the settee in the corner of our massive lounge room, staring across a dark Mudchute Park. Beyond the park, other impressively tall SkyRiser's cluster around Millwall Outer Dock in the middle of the Isle of Dogs. Impressive how they all seem to reach for the same thing, the murky skies above. Their sides continually lite with the best products the world offers. This time, the ever-changing windows feature daily flights to the StellaPort, dune skiing in Dubai and holiday stays in the Ethereal Tower in Nusantara. They all sound good right about now.

It's well past midnight, but sleep is a stranger to me now. My mind races, continually replaying Juice's revelations and the historical narratives about the BoldWar; the ghost stories of our tech-ravaged world. I can't let it go and now I know why I shouldn't have read it. I can't digest the information.

The stories about autonomous drones turning against us, a hive-minded army under the sway of a rogue AI, named APEX. The countries crumbled or didn't exist, governments falling, and the sky—once a canvas of blue—becoming a constant overcast of smoke, sorrow and radiation. They called it the war to end all wars. A brutal symphony of man versus machine, ending not with triumph, but a tenuous ceasefire brokered by the few who remained.

And yet, through all this chaos, sorrow and change, it forced us to reimagine our lives, our ways, to examine our use of robots and how we now use sunlight for all our energy. We almost went completely off grid, to create an entirely new grid. No petrol, no oil, no fuel as we know it. It also forced people to think of new, improved transport systems and continual globalisation.

"Humanity barely survived," Juice had said, his voice a mixture of awe and dread. "APEX went silent, but I'm sure it's still out there, lurking in the shadows of our own technology," he had added.

Crops withered under relentless droughts. Coastal cities drowned beneath rising seas. Millions of climate refugees fled their homelands, only to be turned away by those fearing scarce resources. Famine spread. Conflicts erupted. Dark days for humanity. We teetered on the brink.

Somehow, we pulled back, but the scars remain. The authorities act like the BoldWar is ancient history, a reminder of humanity's hubris. But its lessons lurk close beneath the surface. I sense the same forces in play today, obscured by propaganda and technological distractions. History doesn't always repeat, but it often rhymes.

I can't shake the images of that era. Desperate faces, hollow-eyed children, scorched earth—an entire generation scarred by relentless fear. An entire continent and a half, rendered unusable. The tales of bravery, of sacrifice, they cling to me, as if whispering from the grave: learn, remember, prepare.

A shiver courses through me, not from the chill of the night, but the weight of history upon our shoulders. OZ raised me with the warning, "Knowledge is a double-edged sword, Odezza. Wield it with care, or it will cut you deeper than ignorance ever could."

"Indeed," I murmur to the darkened room, to the ghosts of the past and the uncertainty of the future. "But wield it we must."

The sound of the slight patter of OZ walking breaks me out of my downward spiral of mental desperation, his presence as familiar as the almost imperceptible hum of my Oxolet. I hear TiM at his side, always diligent, always awake, and always so adorable!

"Odezza," he calls out softly, as he steps down into the sunken abyss of the massive room, two cups of steaming hot Old English Tea in his hands. His voice startles me into reality.

"Can't sleep either, huh?" he tries for a smile, but it doesn't quite reach his eyes. A tension in his shoulders tells of burdens carried and restless thoughts.

"Night's when the mind likes to play tricks," I reply, folding my arms over my chest. "What's on your mind?"

"Been tapping into the CG feeds again." OZ puts down the cups of tea on an angular side table made of transparent iron ore and rubs the back of his neck, where a network of fine lines maps out years spent in contemplation and concern. "The Central Government's up to their old tricks. They're faster than we thought."

I frown, leaning forward. "Faster how? Their tech or their lies?"

"Both, if you ask me," he exhales sharply, and I detect the faintest trace of fear. "The weather, Odezza. It's changing at a pace that's off the charts. The clouds are swirling in patterns no one has seen before, and what we are seeing on the News-Blogs is not even close to what the CG is monitoring."

OZ continues to share more of his discoveries and my TO shoots to new heights. I continue with more questions.

"Are they seeding them again? Like during the BoldWar?"

The question springs from my lips before I can stop it, and OZ shakes his head.

"Can't say for sure. But the public's being fed a different story. Bright sunny days ahead, according to the newsfeeds. It's all an illusion."

"An illusion that could suffocate us if we're not careful," I muse, the irony bitter on my tongue. OZ's gaze meets mine, and there's an unspoken agreement between us. We're in this together, a daughter and her inventor father, standing on the brink of a tempest that could engulf the world once more.

"Then we'll uncover the truth," OZ declares, a note of defiance lacing his words. "We owe it to them—to those who lived and died in the shadow of the BoldWar."

How does he know what's on my mind?

"Agreed," I push away from the wall, determination coursing through me like a solar flare. "They think they can cloud our skies and our minds. Let's prove them wrong."

"Let's," OZ nods, and in that moment, the weight of our shared purpose is palpable, binding us tighter than ever.

We stand together in the room, surrounded by the ghosts of the past and the storm of the future, ready to chase the truth wherever it leads. Adventure beckons, and we answer its call with hearts fierce and hopeful, undeterred by the gathering clouds.

As I leave the lounge and make my way down our massive hall toward my room, sleep-deprived and weary, I flic on my BTN.

My HelloHolo projects a polished newscaster, her perfectly coiffed hair and designer suit giving the illusion of a calm and prosperous society. She delivers false promises of clear skies and mild temperatures coming.

But behind closed doors, OZ has remarked that the government's contingency plans for food rationing, crowd control drones, and martial law are already underway. The impending doom is palpable, and when the truth inevitably surfaces, mass panic will ensue, making the BoldWar seem like a leisurely Sunday afternoon stroll through the islands that once floated on a now battered Thames.

"What can we do?" I call out to OZ as I reach my door.

Dad finally turns to me, his eyes blazing. "Expose the truth. Hack the feeds, override the fakes. Let people see reality, unfiltered. Maybe then they'll demand change before it's too late."

I nod, filled with nervous purpose. We have a mission now. The fight continues. Hope endures. But first, sleep!

CHAPTER TEN

The digits and code flash before my eyes as we race through the Central Government mainframe.

We have regrouped after a sleepless night, and at this moment we're huddled around, eyes glued to our holos.

"There!" I shout, stabbing at a line of code. "That sequence right there—it's initiating the cloud seeding."

"But the CG said it was an accident," breathes Banksia.

I shake my head. "This isn't accidental. See how the code loops? It's on purpose."

Shock ripples through the group. This changes everything.

"There's more," I say. My fingers fly as I dig deeper. "This line, this is a trigger. See it? It starts a chain reaction in the upper atmosphere."

We figured it out. We have the proof. And we all reach the same conclusion at the same instant. The government has lied to us all. All of us.

"Keep looking," says Soren. "We need to confirm who did this."

I nod and refocus on the screen. After a few minutes, I find it. The authorising signature.

"Roman Polotov," I whisper. Soren's face hardens. Juice curses under his breath.

"Polotov runs Anthro-Tech," Banksia says. "If he's behind this—"

She doesn't need to finish. We all understand the implications. Polotov has the resources and the motive to orchestrate humanity's downfall. And he has the government's help, whether they know it.

I lean back, mind racing. We're deeper than any of us realise. But now we know the truth. Now, we can fight back.

I nod, taking it all in. "What's his plan after the botched cloud seeding?"

Juice shakes his head. "With that maniac, who knows? But we need to find out."

"Agreed," says Soren. They look around, "Juice, can you dig up anything else on Polotov's operations? Any other projects he's got in the works?"

I crack my knuckles. "I can try."

For the next hour, our HelloHolo's are silent except for the aggressive huffs and puffs. We are all omitted. We know time is running short, but we're also uncovering information that could save 5.5 billion of our fellow citizens' lives. The pressure is immense, but it focuses on us.

Time continues to tick by.

Finally, I came across something big buried deep in the CG servers. "Got something," I say. "Looks like — a proposal for off-world colonisation. And the lead researcher is..."

"Polotov?" Benny asked grimly.

Soren affirms. "But it still makes little sense. Seed the clouds, force humanity to die, then flee Earth? Why?"

Silence as we ponder Soren's question. Soren breaks the silence, "then he can continue his work on cloning, AI, and who knows what else." That's a crazy statement, but what if their speculation is true?

I feel sick. This is worse than any of us imagined. But this might be a good time to work together with OZ and his old team of scientists and work on a plan where we might just be able to stop Polotov and Anthro-Tech from their crazy games. I look at Soren, Juice, Banksia and Benny, their faces set with determination. We're an unlikely team, but right now, we're humanity's only hope. Failure is not an option.

"Oh, damn," Banksia squirms.

"What, what is it?" all react in panicked unison.

She continues, "I just found another hidden document I don't think the CG will ever admit they have it on file, and how the hell they figured all this out defies any reality we seem to be in."

"Stop your poetic musings and tell us what the hell you just found," Soren barks at Banksia.

"I found a file that just popped up named Summo Secretum."

"For gawd's sake, Banksia, throw the damn thing up on our holos," I can't help but bark! This is all cascading out of control and I can't guarantee my heart, or mind, can take any more of this stress! "What. Did. You. Find. Out?"

"OMG," she panics, "shut up and stand by." Oh, great. Now Banksia's getting feisty.

Within a femtosecond, an official CG document with the words Summo Secretum pops up in front of us. We all sit erect and start reading along:

Dear Minister,

We bring to your attention the grim news that our mole has uncovered embedded deep inside Anthro-Tech. Anthro-Tech is the holding company of Roman

Polotov; a long-time supporter of yours and our governments.

Our source has revealed that Anthro-Tech plans to begin immediate work in the fields of human cloning and next-generation robotics.

"DID a government spy just figure all this out?" Benny reacts.

"Shut it, Benny," Juice snaps. "That's just the preamble." Soren reads the official document.

SUMMO SECRETUM // MINISTERS EYES ONLY MEMORANDUM

Subject: Project Aegis: Anthro-Tech's Covert Endeavours

Classification: Black Diamond

Distribution: Authorised Personnel Only

1. Origin and Mandate

Anthro-Tech, a shadow entity operating beyond public scrutiny, has embarked on a dual-pronged mission: the clandestine pursuit of human cloning and developing next-generation robotics. This memorandum outlines their activities, motivations, and the strategic rationale for conducting these operations aboard a classified space station.

2. Project Components

a. Human Cloning Division

Objective: Anthro-Tech's cloning program seeks to transcend mortality. By perfecting somatic cell nuclear transfer, they hope to create genetic replicas—vessels for ancient knowledge and memories. These clones harbour the wisdom of historical luminaries.

Sinister Implications: The bioreactors aboard the

space station are not mere organ farms; they are conduits for stolen souls. These "space-grown" organs hold more than tissue; they will cradle the essence of long-departed minds.

b. Robonauts: The Soulless Enforcers

Objective: Anthro-Tech's robotic division hopes to design adaptable, lethal machines. The Robonauts, trained in zero gravity, will serve as assassins, resource extractors, and collaborators. Their cold efficiency knows no bounds.

Resource Efficiency: Solar panels, regenerative life support systems, and closed-loop recycling will sustain the Robonauts. They are the harbingers of a resource-hungry future.

Human-Robot Hybridisation: Anthro-Tech experiments by merging cloned minds and robotic bodies— an unholy fusion that defies ethical boundaries.

3. Space Station Nexus

Isolation: The space station provides an impervious veil. Earth's laws will not extend to this cosmic outpost. Anthro-Tech's work can remain hidden.

4. Legacy and Warning

As Earth descends into twilight, Anthro-Tech's space station glows. Clones whisper forgotten truths, and the Robonauts dance their deadly ballet. The company's new tagline will echo across the void: "Where Science Meets Damnation."

5. Findings/Recommendations

• The cloud seeding operation was not helped bring rain to the Sub-Saharan desert, as was first revealed, but as a purpose-driven trigger to eradicate the human species. Recommend immediate closure of the Cloud Seeding Facility in Malta, the only operating facility we have found to date!

- Besides the Maltese cloud seeding facility, we recommend the immediate closure of all Anthro-Tech R&D facilities, including Tanzania, Turkey, Portugal, Tonga, and Venezuela.

END OF MEMORANDUM

Note: Unauthorised dissemination of this information will cause immediate termination.

We are all tired after tracking along with this frightful memorandum! We are speechless. All of us. And speechless is not a word we use for ourselves.

Benny jumps in first. "We have to tell the Central Government right away. They need to know Polotov's full plan."

Juice frowns. "That memo is from the CG, so are you sure about that? We don't know how deep this corruption goes. Plus, do I need to remind you that this is an official government memo? What can we tell them? They don't already know? Oh—" he continues, super cross, "...and numb nuts, how do we explain how we came to this TOP SECRET SUMMO SECRETUM report in the first place?"

Tensions are rising around here - I need to get ahead of this.

"It's a risk we have to take," I kick in. "The CG will need all the help we can get."

"Oh, so now we're government sympathisers, too?" Soren crunches.

I hesitate. Every instinct tells me we can only rely on each other.

"Alright," I say. "Let's bring this to OZ. And keep scanning for anything else useful."

Everyone nods. "We've got this," Soren says in a less aggressive manner.

"Benny, I'm sorry mann eller fyr," Juice adds in a calmer tone.

Inside, I'm scared like a small child. But the clock is ticking - the torrential rains won't stop. We need options and we need help - the help only OZ can offer.

We all flic off our BTNs. That was getting intense, but that memo would set anyone off.

The fate of the world rests on what we do next. Failure is not an option.

CHAPTER ELEVEN

After a day filled with stress, storms and systematic repetition that seamlessly merged into a shockingly restless sleep; my mind still weighs heavy after yesterday's news about Anthro-Tech.

Like an enigmatic harbinger, it lingers in my thoughts, casting a shadow over the start of my day. I've lost track of how many days it has been since we first saw that odd and crazy cloud formation. I can feel the tension in my muscles and the pit in my stomach as I slowly sit up, dreading facing the reality that awaits me outside the serenity of my bed.

The world seems to hold its breath, waiting to see how this news will unfold, if it unfolds at all, and the impact it will have on our lives if Roman gets away with this diabolical plan. My mind races with questions and fears, unsure of what lies ahead for me and those around me. It is a tense and uncertain time, and I can't help but feel overwhelmed by it all.

And, if I'm being honest with myself, I can't believe Juice tapped as far in as he did. Great work, Juice, but geez, what if the CG does a reverse-tap, leading them directly to us! Oh, no, my mind's running round looking for rabbit holes to scurry.

"one diabolical problem at a time", I say under my morning breath.

I head down the massive hallway, adorned with famous artwork from today around 600 years. Yes, it is a side hobby of Dad's after he became Oxolet-rich, as his friends at the time called it. I don't know all the artists by name but I know the collection includes Paul Gauguin ("Bathers"), Vincent van Gogh ("Young Peasant Woman"), Edvard Munch ("Madonna", Willem de Kooning ("Woman III"), SystemM ("Elevated Waterfall") and a super recent piece by a young up and coming Czech, who goes by the name of, Hollis! No named art is his kick and collectors spend millions on his work. It frames an interesting start to my morning each and every day.

I find the kettle boiling in the dimly lit kitchen and quickly make some Old English.

On heading to my dad's office/lab/lair, I hear him humming some Daft Punk. That's my dad for you. The world is crashing around his ears, but the bloke still has time to find joy in the simplest of things; old school House Music!

"OZ?" I start, entering his now not-so-guarded office, my voice barely above a whisper, "there's something you need to see. Oh, and good morning."

He looks up and greets me with a fatherly smile. My guess is he's been up for hours.

I flic on my BTN and show him a copy of what our team had found last night.

I can feel the significance of it pressing against my chest. You can see the cogs swirling inside OZ's cerebrum. His gaze locked on the spectral display as I narrate the contents, each word tasting like ash on my tongue.

"Anthro-Tech's been playing God," I say, my fingers dancing through the projection to highlight text. "Your initial thoughts were correct. They've purposely tinkered with the clouds and their experiments are sending the weather spiralling out of control."

His deep gasp punctuates the air, a soundtrack to the dread that now binds us together. The Central Government's narrative is crumbling before our eyes; and the cantons are teetering on the brink of disaster. And here we stand, at the epicentre of mayhem, with little more than our wits and unyielding resolve.

"Things are bleak," I admit, but there's no room for sugar-coating the truth. My mind races, thoughts tumbling over one another like dominoes in a ceaseless cascade. "But I've got an idea."

The room becomes silent, as if someone has vacuumed all sense of sound from the air. The tension is palpable as he awaits my next words. I take a deep breath, allowing the cool air to fill my lungs and steel my nerves.

OZ stops me, squelching my drama-boarding statement. "Hang tight. I want my team to hear what you're just about to say. I don't want to repeat it and risk missing anything, including your intensity and ardour for this newfound subject."

Time seems to slow down as his BTN comes to life. But I can't help but be drawn to the shiny alloy object, which catches my attention. It's unlike anything I've ever seen before. It looks like an Ocelot, but its design is unfamiliar and unique. As my curiosity grows, I can't help but wonder what secrets this new technology holds.

Focus, damn it, Odezza. Focus!

"Hi there," Dad says to his group. "I have invited Odezza to join us this morning as she has something to share, something her team, the Mighty5, as they call themselves, discovered last night."

My empty stomach drops. I have never seen these people for real, in person, well, over a HelloHolo. I've only eavesdropped on them. They all look so wise, seasoned, smart, and intimidating. What the hell am I doing here? This is not me. I have classes to attend, my mind to expand, and lessons to learn.

"Hi!" I blurt out, my gaze sweeping across the unfamiliar faces. "It's time to join forces with OZ's legacy team. That's you. Let's craft a plan to save our world."

"Odezza," Dad cuts in, almost laughing, "please back up a moment and tell my esteemed colleagues what your team discovered last night." Shit, I think to myself. Calm down, be yourself, stop being awestruck and piece this together like a normal human, not a RoboChimp on helium!

"Yes, sorry Dad, I mean OZ," oh, this is going so well so far. "My team has been tapping the CG for the past few days, learning the art of both cover-up and espionage at a lighting rate." Oh, this is no time for puns, ya stupid idiot!

I have to recover and do it now. "Last night, things got really interesting. Juice, on our team, went on a mission and man, did he hit the jackpot. He uncovered a top secret memo from a GC spy within Roman Polotov's Anthro-Tech organisation."

I go on, trying to keep calm and not get caught up because we discovered such an important piece of this emerging puzzle. They hang on to my every word as I recap the memo. There's a beat, a moment suspended in time where doubt could creep in—but I won't allow it. Instead, I harness every ounce of intellect handed down from my father, every lesson learned from swimming against the tide.

"Optimism is our starting block," I state firmly, concluding my diatribe about the memo. "We'll build from there." The team nods, their expressions hardening with determination. "I suggest we pool our efforts. I suspect you've also been tapping the CG, so let's put our heads and minds together to figure out a plan that has us united in the reversal of the botched cloud seeding and see if we can stop Roman from getting off planet and leaving us all here to die."

And so, we begin. With the nodding of heads, this motley crew is bound by a common goal: to unravel Anthro-Tech's tangled web of deception and weave a new tapestry of hope for mankind. Together, we're more than mere humans; we're architects of the future, and our blueprint starts now.

AFTER CALLING the Mighty5 back together and calling in OZ's legacy team, I sweep a hand across my HelloHolo display, scattering the virtual piles of data and reports that have been haunting me for hours. The room is a cacophony of clicks, whirs, and low mutters as we dig deeper into the mire, searching for redemption in rows of encrypted messages.

"Guys," I say, voice edged with urgency, "the more I see this, the worse it gets." My eyes flic to the surrounding faces. My team. No, our team now. The Mighty5 merged with OZ's old guard, a coalition of the willing and able. I'd like to think we are now the MightyLegacy.

"Can we really do this?" Benny murmurs, voicing the fear gnawing at the edges of our resolve. We're David facing a Goliath of our own making, armed with slingshots against a leviathan of tech-gone-wild.

"Remember?" I counter quickly, refusing to let the seed of doubt germinate. "This Anthro-Tech's spy memo is not just bad, it's officially apocalyptic. But we've stared down dooms-day's before. Well, we haven't, but I'm guessing the Legacy Team has, yes?"

"Right," the female on his team echoes. My father had introduced his team mates as Artemis and Ekon.

"We're not superheroes," Banksia adds, the weight of our humanity a tangible thing in the air.

"Superheroes?" I scoff, injecting a dash of levity into the tension.

"Please, they wear capes." Banksia bounces back. "We wear smarts and sheer stubbornness."

A chuckle ripples through the holo, brief but life-affirming. We need that—a reminder that the gravity of our task has not crushed our spirits.

"Okay, brainstorm time," Soren announces, preempting what I'm sure OZ was just about to announce. "First step, saving the world: admitting it's royally screwed. Second step: unscrewing it. Any bright ideas?"

"Let's get technical," I continue, trying to maintain momentum. "We analyse, strategize, and mobilise." Again, sounding more like my father than myself. "No dark corner left unlit, no stone unturned."

"Sounds like an election slogan," Ekon quips, and I grin despite the gravity of our situation.

"Vote for survival, eh?" Benny snorts. "I'd say it has a nice ring to it."

"Alright, enough with the stand-up routine," Soren chides. "Time to get serious. We have a world to save, remember?"

"Starting with..." My voice trails off, the enormity of our undertaking suddenly looming large. Where indeed do we begin? "Starting with the first step," I finally say, squaring my shoulders. "We take it one move at a time, like a game of 3D chess against fate."

"Except fate doesn't play fair," Banksia points out in the most poignant of ways.

"Neither will we," OZ shoots back, conviction hardening like steel in his veins. "We'll rewrite the rules if we have to."

"Then let's write a damn good story," comes a collective call to arms, and it's all I need to hear.

"Perfect," I say, my brain's gears whirring faster. "Our

prologue starts now." And with that, we dive headfirst into the unknown, penning the future with every breath we take.

I sweep the room, taking in the fierce resolve that has ignited across every face, Legacy and 5. We're a fierce assembly of brains and bravery, not one of us untouched by the world's frantic free fall into chaos. The air crackles with the silent promise of action—a collective unspoken oath to bend the arc of history back towards salvation.

"Okay, team, let's blueprint our ark," I declare, my voice a beacon cutting through the storm clouds of uncertainty. "We're building more than just a plan; we're crafting humanity's comeback."

Heads nod, eyes spark—there's a hunger here, a shared appetite for change. We're parched for progress, and hope is our wellspring.

"But where do we start?" murmurs Benny, hesitant yet hopeful.

"Where every grand adventure begins," I respond, feeling my pulse quicken. "With a map and a destination."

"Destination: future," Banksia adds, the word resonating, a shared vision of tomorrow.

"First step; I suggest we all look at these challenges through our own expertise; our own lens, if you will."

OZ, who has been letting me take the lead to this point, and has been awfully quiet, finally chirps up, "I agree, let's look at this like any science innovation; what would each of us do to solve the problem?" He looks around the room, seemly looking at each of us. "So first steps first, what are we trying to solve?"

Soren beats Artemis to the punch. "We need to figure out how to stop Roman from going off planet."

Juice quickly adds, "And stop all this gawddamn rain! That seems like a must."

"I'm going to suggest," I continue the conversation toward

a conclusion, "we attack each one in the order you see best, as they are both essential to the survival of the planet. Just keep focused." Although I'm pretty sure that's an overstep, it felt right in the moment.

I can feel the shift, the tangible uptick in energy. We're molecules vibrating at the thought of the impossible made possible.

"Then let's chart our course," I urge, pulling up data streams and projections, laying out a blueprint.

"Science and a dash of audacity," OZ adds, a twinkle in his eye.

"Nothing worth doing was ever done without it," Benny jokes, already immersed in algorithms and environmental models.

"Alright," I say, rolling up imaginary sleeves. "Let's turn this dystopia into utopia—one byte, one breath at a time — and meet back here in 24 hours."

And just like that, we're off—optimism, our engine, determination, our fuel. A band of mavericks riding the edge of a knife, carving out destiny from the clutches of doom. We're not just dreaming of a new world; we're engineering it, each of us a cornerstone on the foundation of a rejuvenated Earth.

As I feel I can finally relax, if only for a moment, I plonk myself down in the lounge room. TiM is by my side. I'm ready to work when my BNT pings me. As I look, it's an incoming holo from Benny. I activate my HelloHolo and am greeted by a grim face. "Dezzy, I'm terrified."

CHAPTER TWELVE

The darkness clings to London like a shroud, ever-present, relentless. It's a thick blanket that smothers the city. I'm sitting here at the window, my gaze fixed on the inky void where the sun used to reign. Dad's in his office grappling with shadows, just as we all are. And the Mighty5, those brave souls, they're scattered to the winds, each fighting their own battles against this unending night.

I can't help but brood, the weight of the perpetual gloom pressing down on me, drowning. It's like swimming across an upside down river—no light, no warmth, just an abysmal cold that seeps into your bones. I trace the outline of raindrops racing down the glass, their journey as futile as our search for daylight.

"Odezza?" says the metallic voice of my BTN, materialising from the silence of the room. "Incoming news updates."

"Hit me," I reply, welcoming any distraction from the oppressive dark.

"Severe storms reported across multiple locations globally," the BTNews informs me, its tone clinical, detached. "Turkey, New Guinea, The Netherlands, Peru, and Slovakia are experiencing catastrophic weather."

"Define catastrophic," I demand, leaning forward. Because what's one more calamity on top of another?

"Extreme wind velocities, widespread flooding, infrastructural damage, casualties—"

"Enough," I cut off the conversation with a sharp gesture. Casualties. That word hits hard, a punch to the gut. These aren't just data points; their lives unravelled, homes torn apart, futures snuffed out by this chaos we've all been thrust into.

"Any word about what's causing these storms?" My voice is steady, masking the turmoil inside.

"Speculation varies," my BTNews replies. "Some attribute it to natural climatic cycles, others to aberrant atmospheric phenomena. There are whispers it might be connected to the perpetual darkness—"

"Whispers won't help us," I snap. OZ always says speculation without evidence is as useful as a solar panel in a blackout. "Keep digging."

"Affirmative."

I push away from the window, my resolve hardening. This isn't just about overcoming darkness anymore; it's about facing down these literal and metaphorical storms. Dad will have dived headfirst into the fray already, his intellect a beacon cutting through ignorance and fear. And here I am, his daughter, ready to do the same.

"Let's get to work," I murmur, more to myself than the BTN. If this darkness is a puzzle, then I'll find the pieces. If these storms are a code, then I'll crack it. It's not just about hope; it's about action—smart, decisive, relentless.

"Odezza, additional reports—"

"Later," I interrupt, already pulling up schematics and data streams. I have storms to chase and darkness to dispel. "No, wait," I recoil. "Tell me more about these storms—"

"Here is what I am currently finding," the system announces, as calm as always. "NewsBlogs are calling this: The Great Tempest of '88. I have found this news despatch from seven minutes ago GMT. Shall I continue?"

"Yes, forgawdsake, yes," I scream as if I have an imaginary petulant younger brother to push around.

"Very well," the system continues, ignoring my tantrum. "Let me continue—"

Sven-Erik, NorLand News Despatch: "Extreme Wind Velocities"

The winds are howling like vengeful spirits, tearing through cities and forests alike. Their velocity defies reason, reaching speeds that mock our feeble attempts at shelter. E.R.M.E.S.S., the innovative risk assessment software, is warning of the impending gales. It integrates global- and canton-scale hazard maps, meticulously tracking cyclones, hurricanes and tornadoes. Buildings like the Sky Mile Tower in Next Tokyo are swaying out of control, foundations tested to the limit. Fragile structures are crumbling throughout Southwestern Europe and Northeastern Africa, while the robust ones cling to survival. The air seems to have become a weapon, uprooting trees, flinging debris, and leaving scars on the landscape.

Widespread Flooding

A massive cold depression is currently hovering over the southern tip of South America, and a deluge is descending upon that area, relentless. Rivers are swelling, swallowing towns and villages up and down the southeast coast of Brazil. Coastal cities, once bustling with life, now lie submerged beneath murky waters. The 2068 South Asian weather and climate disasters in which the world lost hundreds of islands and tens of thousands of people, pale compared to this watery onslaught. Floodwaters are breaching dams in New Zealand. Streets have become canals, and SkyRise rooftops; desperate islands. People around the world are clinging to the slightest thread of hope, while rising tides threaten to erase our coastal existence.

Infrastructural Damage

Once-mighty cities such as Singapore, Beirut and Budapest bear the scars of a weathered battle. SkyRisers, such as Akon City, the modern symbol of human achievement, now stand like hollow shells. The Vänskap bridge between Sweden and Estonia has collapsed, its steel sinews strained beyond endurance. Solar grids are faltering, plunging entire regions of East Africa into darkness. Dams are buckling, rendering travel treacherous. The very fabric of civilization is unravelling as we watch. Engineers and architects are working around the clock, attempting to shore up the crumbling edifices. But the relentless forces of wind, rain and water mock their efforts.

Casualties

The human toll is staggering. Cantons divided, families torn apart, lives extinguished. Emergency services are straining to cope with the influx of injured and displaced. The elderly, the young, the vulnerable— all swept away by the tempest's wrath. The death toll continues to climb in every corner of the world, and grief hangs heavy in the air. Those of us who are left mourn our losses, but also find solace in acts of heroism. Strangers become saviours, pulling each other from the maelstrom. During this darkest hour, we uncover the unyielding spirit that unites us all.

Sven-Erik, NorLand News Despatch: Disconnect

First, I ask about the BoldWar, which put me in a spin, now this. "I probably shouldn't have asked," I say under my breath. Things are going to get worse before they're going to get better - time to shape-up and get back to work!

AFTER A QUICK RUN to the kitchen and other places, my fingers fly back across my luminescent screen. I pull up the latest broadcasts from GON (Global Oceanic Network) on my BTN. Images flicker into view—satellite data, oceanic charts, a swirl of currents turned chaotic. The Atlantic Conveyor Belt and Indian Ocean Gyre are all over the place, like someone threw the ocean into a blender and ramped it up to max. Not good.

"Ocean currents are the earth's heartbeat," I whisper.

"Show me the Gulf Stream deviation?" I command the BTN, my voice a notch sharper than intended. Graphs and arrows spill onto the screen, painting a grim picture. The warm water flow that once tempered climates is now a wandering vagabond, leaving Europe to shiver in its absence.

"Environmental domino effect," I mutter, connecting the dots. If the currents falter, so does everything else. Fish migration patterns go haywire, weather systems unhinge. It's not just about putting on an extra jumper; it's about survival.

Change of subject. "BTN, please assess the societal impact of perpetual darkness." The request hangs in the air, almost tangible in its urgency.

"Compiling data," the BTN responds, tone neutral yet somehow reassuring.

New charts cascade before me: reports, interviews and analyses from every corner of the globe. They tell a story of adaptation and despair. In the far north, communities celebrate the extended 'nightlife,' but the novelty wears thin when vitamin D deficiencies spike. A gnawing fear—that the sun might never return.

I can't help but scoff at the irony. People used to dream of endless nights, warmth, and parties that never ceased. Now they crave a single ray of light, like it's the last drop of water in the desert.

The BTNs monotone voice betrays any emotion as it delivers more alarming statistics. "Energy consumption has increased by thirty-eight percent," it announces. My eyes dart to the holo charts projected ahead of me, showing a sharp incline in energy usage. "Solar grids are failing," the cybernetic voice continues, devoid of any hint of concern. "Global reliance on solar is maxing out." I feel a pang of anxiety as I am reminded of the strict ban on fossil fuels after the devastation of the BoldWar. The world had turned to renewable sources of energy before then, but those were banished because of a GC decree. I can't imagine a world with cars, planes, and other technological advances fuelled by oil and petrol. That was before my time. But I also remember the destruction caused by their use and understand why they were outlawed.

I snarl, my frustration bubbling to the surface. "Just what the world needs," I spit out, "a scarcity of energy collectors that rely solely on the sun for power." The weight of this realisation hits me like a ton of stone, and I feel a sense of helplessness wash over me as I think about how dependent we are on this one source of global energy. The rays of sunlight that once seemed so warm, comforting and plentiful now hold an ominous weight, reminding us of our precarious situation in this strange world.

My fingers drum against the tabletop, restless. We need action, not academic musings.

"Record note," I say, voice firm. "Research artificial light sources capable of simulating the sunlight spectrum. Investigate alternative biofuel as a stopgap for dying solar grids?"

"Note recorded," comes a prompt reply.

"Also, add a reminder. Reach out to OZ. He might have insights from his oxygen elevation projects."

"Reminder set."

I lean back, a rare moment of stillness amidst the chaos. Hope is a luxury, but it's one I cling to. There's got to be a way through this darkness, both literal and metaphorical. And if anyone's going to find it, it'll be the ones who dare to ask the bold questions—the ones who refuse to accept 'impossible' as an answer.

"Let's keep digging, BTN," I say with newfound determination. "There's a solution here. We just need to shine a light on it."

"Understood, Odezza. Continuing search."

With that, I'm back in the game, chasing answers, fighting for a future where the sun rises anew with light and heat. Trying to let my harsh surroundings fuel me, not fail me.

I want to Punch my BTN off and give my head a rest, but I must. Keep. Going.

The next prompt I blurt out, my mind recoils at the implications. "Create predictive models for the effects of darkness on people, plants, algae, and animals."

My stomach lurches at the thought, a knot of dread forming in my gut. The prospect of delving into the unknown horrors that darkness may bring sends shivers down my spine. But I steel myself and proceed, determined to uncover the potential devastation lurking in the shadows.

A microsecond later, my BTN displays its predictions:

Human Despair:
Year 2090: The sun's absence has plunged

humanity into perpetual twilight. Cities lie abandoned, their once-bustling streets now echoing with the footsteps of the desperate few who remain.

Year 2095: The last flicker of artificial light will fade. Families huddle together, their breath visible in the frigid air. The concept of daylight is now a myth, whispered by elders to wide-eyed children.

Plants' Struggle:

Year 2090: Photosynthesis ceases entirely. Trees stand as skeletal sentinels, their leaves mere memories. Moss and lichen cling to life, their colours drained to grey-scale.

Year 2095: The last blade of grass succumbs. Earth's green mantle turns to ash. The soil, once teeming with life, crumbles like ancient parchment.

Algae's Dim Glow:

Year 2090: Algae, once vibrant in oceans, now drift as spectral wisps. Bioluminescence wanes, leaving the seas eerily dark. Fish navigate by instinct, their scales lifeless.

Year 2100: Coral reefs, once kaleidoscopic wonderlands, bleach to bone-white. The last jellyfish pulses feebly, its glow fading like a dying star.

Animal Extinction:

Year 2090: Nocturnal creatures, bereft of moonlight, hunt blindly. Wolves, eyes vacant, howl at unseen moons. Birds plummet from the sky, their wings clipped by invisible sorrow.

Year 2095: The last polar bear collapses on ice that no longer reflects sunlight. Insects vanish, leaving silence in their wake. The final elephant trumpets a mournful farewell.

Desperation and Decay:

Year 2100: Cannibalism becomes the norm. Families consume their own, driven by hunger and madness. Shadows dance on cave walls, telling tales of lost warmth.

Year 2110: The prophecy of a child born with eyes that pierce the darkness persists. Pilgrims search, but hope dwindles. Madness seeps into their souls.

The Final Curtain:

Year 2118: The last heartbeat echoes across a barren landscape. Earth, a tomb of frozen memories, spins silently in the cosmic void. The universe weeps, and entropy claims all.

I'M stunned and totally speechless. Sadness is weaving through my cells. Why did I have to ask that question? Third time's a charm for asking gloom-ridden questions with catastrophic answers. I wasn't ready for that answer either and feel it knocking me back, working as a wake up call centred around my audacity!

Neither my friends and I, nor my dad and his team, think we can turn all this around. Stop the unlawful cloud seeding, help a lame government see its ways and stop an insane person who wants to destroy us all and replace us with Robot Clones! That's not just audacity that is complete and utter lunacy.

As I sit back, I close my eyes, doubting all of this, and wish I could be in my safe, warm pool, doing laps, TiM watching.

"Damn it," I mutter to myself, "run another report. Another prediction model, please?"

"READY!" Red lettering pops up on my holo - here goes nothing! "Please run a predictive model if the solar grid goes down?" Talk about going down a gawddamn rabbit hole.

Another microsecond later:

An unyielding shroud of clouds blankets the world as we currently know it, and humans will continue to face a dire predicament. Our once-celebrated Global Solar Grid (GSG), the pinnacle of human ingenuity and the heart of all energy production after the BoldWar, teeters on the brink of collapse.

The relentless cloud cover, a thick, smothering veil that the sun's rays cannot penetrate, will continue to plunge the world into a perpetual twilight.

Our current global solar network will continue to be starved of sunlight and become little more than relics of a brighter past. The power reserves, meticulously stored during our era of abundance, will continue dwindling at an alarming rate.

"This is a time of abundance?" I say under my breath, rolling my eyes.

Predictive models show that societies accustomed to the luxuries of endless power will continue to be thrown into chaos as the grid falters, causing widespread blackouts, crippling the very fabric of rebuilt civilization.

Predictions also show, as desperation mounts, cantons will scramble to find a solution, but the relentless clouds will mock their efforts, ensuring that no ray of hope—no spark of sunlight—can revitalise the dying solar cells.

The world will stand on the precipice of a new dark age, an era in which the absence of light has become the omen of an uncertain and ominous future.

"Shall I continue?" my BTN shakes me out of my focus.

Oh, forfuckssake! Was it my gawddamn problem right now? I need to get out of this negative spiral, or reality as the case maybe, and get back to thinking of a solution. I know that since the BoldWar, people have rarely used wind power because of the lack of breeze (oh, the irony). But what about other alternatives to solar? I don't know enough to be dangerous right now, but I need to know.

"Run one more search? Please provide alternatives to the crashing and burning scenario you just reported about an alternative to the GSG? Have any cantons been researching alternatives in the past few years?"

A microsecond later:

"Yes, here are three alternatives and the cantons testing these non-GSG energy sources:"

Geothermal Energy: This is energy is obtained by tapping the heat of the earth itself, both from kilometres deep into the Earth's crust or from shallow grounds. People can use geothermal energy for heating, cooling, and electricity generation. Stromboli; Italy, Fagradalsfjall; NorLand, and Nyiragongo; Congo would make effective test sites.

Biomass Energy: Biomass is an organic material that comes from plants and animals, and it is a renewable source of energy. When we burn biomass, it releases the chemical energy as heat. Very rare since the BoldWar. The Valdivia Temperate Rainforest; Chile would make an effective test site.

Fuel Cells: Through a chemical reaction, these devices convert the chemical energy from a fuel into electricity. Fuel cells, unlike batteries, need a constant supply of fuel and oxygen to sustain the chemical reaction, whereas batteries internally store energy. Hydrogen, natural gas, methanol, and other types of fuel can power fuel cells. Muscat; Oman and Sanaa; Yemen would make effective test sites.

"Is any of this helpful?" I say out loud.

AFTER RETURNING from the kitchen with a freshly brewed pot of Old English tea, trying not to let the past half an hour of information get under my skin, and trying desperately not to look outside at the perpetual gloom, I summon the strength to get back to my research.

I flic open my BTN console again, diving into the global NewsBlogs. My eyes flit from server to server, a digital spectre, hunting for truths hidden in the shadow of this new world order.

"Show me the latest from The Guardian," I command, my voice barely above a whisper, but the BTN obeys with unerring precision. Columns of text and intense images cascade down the transparent holo, a waterfall of spewing information.

"Next, Al Jazeera. Le Monde. The Australian." I command, each name summoning a fresh stream of reports and editorials. Voices from around the world unite in a chorus of concern, their stories painting a grim tapestry of life under the continual gloom.

"Perpetual Nightfall Reigns," one headline declares. "Global Solar Grid Collapse Imminent," warns another. Everywhere I look, it's the same bleak narrative: weather wreaking havoc, complete darkness, people clinging to hope like a lifeline.

"Anything else?" I murmur, not expecting much.

"Accessing alternative sources," the BTN responds.

That's when I stumble upon it—a research paper tucked away in an obscure scientific journal in Egypt. It's like finding a particular needle in a haystack made of needles, but there it is, stark against the dim light of my workstation.

"Download complete," announces the BTN.

I pivot from the BTN, my heart thundering in a rhythm that screams action. My fingers dance across a holographic keyboard, summoning schematics and data projections into the surrounding air. The room—a nest of tech and shadows—becomes an extension of my thoughts, flickering with potential solutions to the darkness that has swallowed our world.

"Artificial light sources," I mutter, the idea sparking like a live wire. "Simulated sunlight. It's possible, isn't it?" I recall Dad's musings on human adaptability and his insistence on innovation as our greatest survival tool. I seize the concept with a determination that feels like a legacy; like destiny.

"Let's start small," I decide, focusing first on urban agriculture. "Without sunlight, what little crops we have are failing, food shortages looming like spectres over the already bleak horizon. "Hydroponics, vertical farming—but they'll need light." My mind races through equations and energy requirements. "LEDs? No, too power-hungry for the dying grids."

"Think, Odezza, think!" I urge myself. A breakthrough dances at the edge of my consciousness, teasing, elusive. Then it hits me: bioluminescence. Nature's own luminary trick—could we harness it? Engineer plants to glow, to feed themselves in this sun-starved world?

"Brilliant!" I can't help but admire the audacity of the idea. But there's more to consider—the cities, the streets, the faces of children straining to see in the dimness.

"Viable alternative solutions," I muse. Yet not nearly enough. We need something radical, something... "Fusion," I breathe the word like a plea to progress. "It's always been on the brink of tomorrow, but maybe now it's time."

"Time to shine," I say, rolling my shoulders back. Time to

craft a plan, to reach out, to ignite a spark of hope. Perpetual darkness has met its match.

"Let's make some light," I declare, buoyed by adrenaline, on purpose. This is more than theoretical science now—it's a lifeline, a promise. And Odezza, daughter of OZ, a scientist in her own right, doesn't break promises. Not when the world needs her most.

Fusion, bioluminescence, artificial photosynthesis, geothermal energy, biomass energy - too many options. So which one can I take back to the team? What might make the biggest difference in the shortest amount of time?

"Artificial light might also just be the band-aid," I mumble with heightened delirium. I'm so tired, and my head hurts from all this thinking. My head wants to be on my down pillow so badly, but no, not yet! More work to do.

I pull up schematics, dive into chemical compositions, and toy with theoretical physics. It's a puzzle, alright, one that humanity has never faced. But that's what science is about— solving the unsolvable, reaching for the stars even when they're hidden behind an impenetrable veil.

"Artificial light from fusion; maybe bioluminescence; could happen, artificial photosynthesis; maybe geothermal energy; unlikely now that I have crunched more data, biomass energy and fuel cells; given the infrequency that cantons are using it, time to forget about those two. There's got to be a fusion of ideas here somewhere." I speak to the silence, but it feels like the entire world is listening, hanging on the brink of my breakthroughs.

The night outside doesn't relent. I'm as stubborn as I am. But beneath the BTN's glow, under the watchful gaze of equations and theorems, I piece together fragments of tomorrow. One idea leads to another, and another, until the blueprint of a plan crystallises.

"Okay, Odezza, let's make some light," I say, emboldened

by the thought that maybe, just maybe, I can outshine this darkness.

I'm just about to Punch off my BTN when 'incoming messages' reverberates through my head! "Yes?"

"I have discovered a RedMemo; the CG has announced the discovery of an Elops!"

End of Transmission.

CHAPTER THIRTEEN

It's another gloriously crappy morning in London. The lightning and rain are bad today. I see TiM staring out the window, trying to make sense of what he's looking at and probably wondering why we haven't taken him down to the river for his daily stroll.

After finding and grabbing a cup of Old English, I make my way to Dad's office.

I hear him humming Around the World by Daft Punk.

Every time I step into his hideaway, my eyes immediately fixate on the old Daft Punk poster adorning his wall. The man clearly has a fondness for the French electronic duo, who I know very little about, except they wore helmets or masks or something. Was that a thing back then? I ask myself.

My musical preferences lean more towards today's ECHO, with its catchy beats and pulsing bass. But there's something infectious about his love for Daft Punk that always puts me in a good mood. The walls seem to vibrate with the thumping rhythms of their tracks, creating a lively atmosphere that I can't help but bask in.

I perch myself on the edge of a stool; the place vibrating

with the silent hum of a dozen tools scattered across workbenches like metallic confetti. He's buried in the guts of his latest brainchild, fingers dancing deftly over components that promise to be our salvation—or at least, I'm guessing that's his plan. He's done it before, so I know he can do it again.

"Watch your head," he mumbles without looking up as I duck under a low-hanging oscilloscope arm. His eyes locked on to the device sprawled before him, its innards splayed open like an intricate puzzle begging to be solved.

This contraption, it's a marvel really—a symphony of wires, chips, and shimmering panels. There's a central chamber, crystal clear and pulsating with a soft blue light that reminds me of bioluminescence—nature's own way of thumbing its nose in darkness.

"See this?" Dad points to a spherical part nestled in the device's heart. "It's an atmospheric equaliser. If I've done my computations right, which I have, it'll recalibrate the ion distribution up there." He gestures skyward.

"Next to it, that's the condensation catalysts." Dad's fingers tapping a pewter coil, sleek and serpentine. "It should, in theory, kick-start a reversal in the cloud formations. No more acrid monsoons, if we're lucky. There's just one insignificant minor challenge," OZ gives a fake cough, clearing his throat, "it needs to be pointed toward a break in the clouds for it to work.

"Hope's not a strategy, Dad," I can't help but smirk, even though the gravity of what we're doing presses down on my chest like I'm diving under the sea. "And what's that part about needing a gap in the clouds?"

"Working on it, Odezza."

"Well, let me not stop you." I go to walk out.

"Since when did you become such a cynic, Odezza?" He throws me a look over his shoulder, a mix of exasperation and affection.

"Since I started understanding the stakes." I step back into the room and move closer to the device, peering at the network of tubes that weave through it like veins. "And what's this bit?"

"Ah, that's the pièce de résistance." Dad's pride is almost tangible as he holds up a tiny chip etched with microcircuitry. "The solar synapse. Without sunlight, nothing works—not Oxolets, but you already know this. This baby amplifies whatever light it can scavenge, keeps the entire show running."

"Brilliant," I breathe out, the word feeling like an understatement. This device isn't just some gadget—it's hope, distilled into a fascinating and daunting form. It's a chance to undo what Roman has done, maybe to give us back a world where the sun doesn't play a game of hide and seek behind man-made clouds gone rogue.

"Remember, love, brilliance is just persistence wearing a fancy hat," dad winks, returning his attention to the device, his hands never still.

Persistence. If there's anything dad has taught me, it's that. And as I watch him fasten, code and calibrate, I know that we might have enough of it together to make a difference. The thought sends a shiver of excitement racing down my spine, chased by the shadow of the monumental task ahead.

"Ready to test it soon?" I ask, the question laced with anticipation and a twinge of fear.

"Getting there," Dad replies, his voice steady as a drumbeat. "We just need to find a hole to try it on."

"By the way," OZ asks, "where did your research lead you last night? I've not talked to the others, but I'm curious about what you found."

My mind is a carousel of formulas and untested hypotheses, spinning faster with each step. "I've been dissecting our options like a malfunctioning bot—Fusion, bioluminescence, algae, artificial photosynthesis. But the data, it's like trying to read the wind."

"Bioluminescence?" Dad arches an eyebrow as he wipes his hands on a rag, leaving streaks of metallic residue. "That's quite the leap from standard solar energy sources."

"Exactly!" My voice pitches with enthusiasm. "Imagine harnessing living light. It's not just about illumination—it's about symbiosis, energy independence. And fusion? Well, that's the holy grail, isn't it? Infinite power, zero waste. But the calculations are stubborn. They need more crunching."

"Stubborn can be good," Dad says, nodding thoughtfully. "Means you're onto something complex. What about algae? Any breakthroughs there?"

The excitement deflates from me like air from a punctured tyre. "No. The news is worse than a black hole's appetite. Algae... they're suffocating. The thing that brings us 70% of our oxygen is dying right in front of our eyes." I let the gravity of those words sink in. "And if the algae fails, we fail.

"Damn the BoldWar," Dad's voice is a low growl, his frustration echoing mine. "We knew meddling with nature would backfire, but this—"

"An ecosystem out of sync, and us without a paddle." I slump against a table, feeling the weight of every failing tree and struggling for a breath of air. "Without the oxygen, we might as well be living on a barren rock hurtling through space."

"You mentioned something about Oxolets a moment ago. What are you worried about?" Truly not sure I can handle the answer, a little reminiscent of last night's research pilgrimage.

"Oxolets," he murmurs, more to himself than to me, "they're our lifeline, but they're not built for eternal twilight." The thought hangs heavy between us. "Without sunlight," he explains, "these bio-engineered marvels might, no, will fail. As every human receives one at birth, we're talking about everyone! It's like we're on a sinking ship, and someone just pointed out the lifeboats might be full of holes.

"Then it's a race against the dark," I say, forcing levity into my voice, trying not to freak out. No time for doom and gloom; Dad's already got enough of that for both of us.

He doesn't smile, but there's a fierce spark in his eyes as he reaches for a delicate filament, no thicker than a strand of hair. "Exactly. We can't let the shadows win."

"Have you considered—" I begin, but he cuts me off with a raised hand.

"Every possibility, Odezza. This has to work." His voice is a mix of adamant conviction and something else—a whisper of fear that he usually keeps buried deep.

"Good thing you're a genius then," I quip, trying to inject some optimism into the dense air of the lab/office. The joke lands with a thud, but I press on. "I mean, who else could make heads or tails of this — this splendid mess?"

"Splendid mess?" he repeats, a half-smile finally breaking through as he looks up from the device. "I suppose that's one way to describe saving the world."

"Hey, do you have a name for this thing yet?" I say, cutting through the silence a little more abruptly than I'd imagined. He slides a microfilament into the device's core, the ultimate piece. "I was thinking about the Atmospheric Re-calibrator—or AR. That's what I've been calling it in my mind."

"What a silly name," I spurt out.

"How about the PlanetPreserver? What do you think?" he retorts.

I look at him like TiM would, head tilted, totally judging the man! "No! Try again, OZ."

"WorldWarden," he says with a straight face. Is he serious with these names? I just keep my head cocked, sending a silent signal that he's got to be kidding. "Third time's a charm," I chide.

"How about the ClimaSphere?" he asks coyly.

"I was just about to blurt out EcoStabilizer, but I like The ClimaSphere," I add quickly. "I really do."

The ClimaSphere - it's got a cool ring to it. And that was a fun little game that no one in the world will ever care about, so I snap back to reality.

"By the way, I have the latest readouts on the storms," I announce, tucking a strand of hair behind my ear. A flurry of holographic charts and graphs blooms before us, painting a grim picture of weather gone wild. "The storm patterns are speeding up, OZ. And the oxygen levels... they're dropping faster than your mood when CG bureaucrats blather."

He doesn't look up, too engrossed in his work, but his voice is steady. "Not good! Keep on monitoring the changes."

"Will continue crunching the data," I commit.

Dad pauses, finally locking eyes with me, "We need more time, Odezza, but the luxury of time is exactly what we don't have. If this new machine doesn't work, the Oxolets won't be the only thing we'll worry about failing."

"Understood, Captain," I salute him with mock formality, then get back to my station. We've got algorithms to refine and simulations to run. The world outside is a canvas of chaos, painted by humanity's own greedy hand—to think cloud seeding might have been our salvation, instead it became our damnation.

"Pass me the micro-torque, Odezza," he says without looking up, voice a mixture of command and velvety reassurance.

"Here," I reply, sliding the tool across the table with deft fingers. "Dad, we're close, aren't we?"

"Close?" He pauses, glancing over with those eyes that have seen too much yet still gleam with promise. "We're on the cusp of something monumental."

"But before we go too much further, I need to put some

fail-safes in place, in case something happens to them, what did we call it?"

"ClimaSphere", he mumbles.

"Think it will really work?" I dare to ask after what feels like an eternity.

"Still too soon to tell."

OZ's words hang in the air, heavy with exhaustion and uncertainty. We have depleted all options, but he refused to give up ambition. I can see the weight of responsibility on his shoulders, torn between wanting to believe and not wanting to disappoint. It's a difficult balance, one that leaves us both feeling conflicted and unsure of what comes next.

We also need to get the teams back together and catch up on what's happening.

"Hey, OZ," I add, "what's an Elops?" The question escapes my lips before I can stop it—a stray thought amidst the chaos.

Dad looks up at me slowly, now his head is at the same tilt as TiM's and simply says, "a what?"

CHAPTER FOURTEEN

As my HelloHolo jumps to life, the scene unfolds with me virtually wedged between two equally exhausted teams—Legacy on my left, Mighty5 on my right. We sprawl across our cyberspaces command centre. It's like watching historians and hackers swap notes. We're piecing together a jigsaw puzzle with half the pieces missing, trying to find some alternative to the sun that's playing hide-and-seek behind relentless layers of spirited storm clouds.

"Geothermal's a bust," grumbles Soren. "Not without drilling deeper than we've got time for."

"Wind energy is also a bust, having no time to set up equipment from scratch. Plus there might be a tad too much wind to deal with now. It's like the sublime to the ridiculous," I toss in, even though it feels like suggesting a band-aid for a severed limb.

"Agreed," Ekon counters. "What about biofuel?"

"From what? Everything's flooded or flattened," Benny says, tinged with defeat.

"Then there's only one option left," I say, meeting eyes around the room. "We need to go unconventional. Be creative." But I'm distracted. "I'll be right back." OZ gives me a funny look.

I step outside dad's office to make out what the loud sound is. The weather is throwing a tantrum. I peer out at the grey fury beyond the family room windows—a window turned wide-screen display for the apocalypse. The cityscape that once stood proudly against the sky is now a jagged horizon of destruction. The SkyRise next to ours has become a twisted metal skeleton.

Rain and hailstones are lashing against our enormous windows with the ferocity of a wild beast, clawing at the barriers between us and oblivion. I can see boats on the Thames, meant for leisurely cruises, bob helplessly amidst the debris, turned into lifelines for those caught in nature's upheaval. AeroCars seem to be submerged, their promises of safety and autonomy drowned beneath murky waves.

"Look at that," I murmur, more to myself.

I scurry back, returning to the group. I am met with curious looks. "The Thames has burst its banks, reclaiming its ancient, broader bed, indifferent to the centuries of human meddling. It's an eerie sight—waves where streets used to be. Greenwich landmarks are being reduced to barely recognisable islands in a churning sea." I cannot overlook the irony that the water is sweeping away The Old Royal Naval College buildings, which once protected it.

"Odezza, focus," snaps OZ.

"Right. Power," I reply, jerking me back to reality. "We keep looking. There has to be something we missed, some stone unturned."

"Or some cloud unhung," Banksia jokes weakly.

"Time's running out," I say, ignoring the poor attempt at humour. I look at OZ, reading his mind about his disdain for short-sighted solutions and his belief in the improbable. We need one of his impossible ideas now more than ever.

"Let's regroup in an hour," OZ suggests, agitated. "Fresh eyes might find fresh solutions."

"Or fresh disasters," I mutter under my voice.

As everyone disperses from sight, minds whirring with possibilities, I can't shake the image of the ravaged city outside. My home. My London. My world! But we're not done yet. Not while there's still breathe in our lungs and fight in our hearts. There's power out there, beyond the traditional, waiting for us to seize it. And I'll be damned if we don't find it.

WE REGROUP AS PROMISED. Time to change subjects and check in on everyone's weather report.

"Broadcasts are coming in from all over," I say, flicking through the news streams on my wrist screen. "It's chaos out there."

"Define 'chaos,'" Benny murmurs, his voice tinged with a mix of sarcasm and genuine dread.

"Picture this," I start, painting them the verbal picture unravelling across the globe. "Autonomous vehicles jammed bumper to bumper in Paris, their AI brains overloaded trying to reroute around flood zones that pop up like whack-a-moles."

"Sounds like a regular Tuesday around the Arc de Triomphe," Artemis quips, but no one is laughing.

"Electric vehicles fare slightly better in Nicosia," I continue, "but only because they're sitting untouched in garages. Owners are panicking, unable to brave the new waterways we call streets and, with the solar grid completely down in Cyprus, and other places, those cars aren't going anywhere soon."

"Hyperloops?" asks Benny, his voice hopeful.

"Stalled." My single word hits the room like a lead weight. "The rapid transit saviour of ground transportation can't hack the power outages. Seems like those smart highways weren't smart enough to expect an apocalypse."

"Great, so what about getting off-world? The rich must have a Plan B, right?" Soren snarls.

"Ah, the exodus strategy," OZ muses aloud. "Rich folks flocking to Germany, Belize, Mozambique, Japan, India, New Zealand and Australia – anywhere with a spaceport. But Mother Nature's having none of it. Rain, clouds, wind; the perfect cocktail to ground all rockets."

"Guess money can't buy clear skies," Dad scoffs, his disdain for the elite's escapist fantasies as palpable as the tension in the skies above.

"Suborbital spaceflight is a no-go too," Banksia confirms.

"Let's not get ahead of ourselves," I interject, before despair paints us into a corner. "We're not out of moves yet."

"Right," Juice echoes, the word hanging uncertainty between hope and resignation.

"Keep your eyes on the skies — and the news," I add. "Something's gotta give."

"Or break," comes the dark-humoured response from Ekon.

Rueful half-grins flash around the room, the camaraderie binding us tighter than any Hyperloop track ever could. We're the MightyLegacy after all. If the world's going to hell in a high-tech handbasket, we'll be the ones giving it a run for its money.

More updates are streaming in. The world's unravelling at the seams, and even from everyone's high-tech bunker, we can feel the tension vibrating through the concrete walls. On the holo, a mosaic of distress broadcasts from every canton, a global patchwork of panic.

In South Africa, once dry metropolises are flooding

with more than just water; fear saturates every corner. Johannesburg's elevated highways, those marvels of modern transit, are strangled with autonomous vehicles stalled in gridlock, their systems overwhelmed by the deluge.

Poland's gone frigid, Warsaw enveloped in an unseasonal deep frost. The high-speed trains meant to whisk citizens away to warmer regions are frozen on the tracks, their sleek forms turned to ice sculptures.

Hong Kong's vertical cities are swaying, not with the rhythm of life, but with the tremors of earth unsettled. Their Hyperloops, those veins of progress, lie dormant, silent, waiting for a pulse that doesn't come.

Cuba's coastlines, once the envy of the Caribbean, are besieged by rising tides. Havana's streets, where electric cars used to hum and AeroCars flew, now echo with the splashes of desperate footfalls as people seek higher ground.

Bangladesh, already intimate with nature's fury, confronts a new enemy: relentless rain that's turning rivers into monsters and homes into memories.

The sheer volume of water outsmarts Dhaka's smart street systems, its algorithms useless against the ancient rage of the elements.

"Seen enough?" I ask, my voice steady despite the chaos unfolding before us.

"More than enough," Soren mutters, their gaze still locked on the screen displaying Next Tokyo's skyline.

"Speaking of which," I say, clearing my throat, "has anyone here heard of an Elops?"

Heads turn, brows furrow. Soren nods, "Yeah, I came across that word while digging through satellite feeds. Thought little of it."

"Think again," I tap the screen, bringing up an image of a vast, clear circle amidst the oppressive cloud cover. "I just heard the word, and not knowing what it was, did some CG tapping of my own."

"So," Artemis asks, "what's an Elops?"

I continue, "From what I can tell, they look like Fallstreak Holes, or Cavum clouds, except they're not." I can see some of the team already looking up those two terms. "These are larger, eerier, like the sky itself is winking at us, offering a glimpse of blue in a grey world.

"Near Tokyo," I continue, "has an abnormal hole in the clouds. That's evidently an Elops. If we're looking for a sign, this might be it."

"An invitation, maybe?" Benny quips, half-hearted humour laced with intrigue.

"Or a chance," I say, feeling a surge of something unfamiliar. Hope? Maybe. But there's no denying the pull of possibility. "Whatever it is, it's our best shot. Better than us trying to figure out alternative power sources." I know that was a lot of work for everyone, but we have to pursue what's right in front of us currently.

And just like that, the HoloRoom's atmosphere shifts from despair to determination. When the world gives us an Elops, we don't just stare—we leap.

The word "Elops" hangs in the air, a tangible promise of the impossible. I meet OZ's eyes across the room; there's a spark there that ignites something within me. His gaze is electric, mirroring the shock and joy coursing through my veins.

"OZ?" I breathe out, hardly believing the serendipity. "It's a hole in the clouds... it's exactly what we need to test the new machine."

His nod is vigorous, almost childlike in its enthusiasm. "Exactly, Odezza! The universe couldn't have aligned more perfectly for us."

Around us, the teams display a mix of confusion and curiosity, their heads snapping from OZ to me like we're tennis balls volleying back and forth over the net of this mad revelation.

"New machine?" Soren echoes, scepticism lacing their tone as they lean forward.

"Uh-huh. New tech," I clarify, a smirk playing at the corner of my mouth despite the gravity of our situation. My heart pounds with the drumbeat of adventure, an echo of the adrenaline-fuelled escapades my father loves to recount from his pre-cataclysmic days.

"OZ, care to elaborate?" asks Juice, his fingers tapping impatiently on his forearm interface—a nervous tick he never shook off.

"Right," OZ clasps his hands together, his eyes gleaming with the fervour of a man who has just been handed the keys to redemption. "I always thought the Oxolet would be Dad's legacy," speaking as if he isn't standing two metres to my right. "However," I continue, gleaming like the proud daughter I am, "he has developed a machine that could reverse the rogue cloud seeding process."

OZ just stands there - he doesn't have to say a word. He apparently has his own personal spokesperson.

"Wait, seriously?" Juice interjects, scepticism giving way to intrigue. "That's a game-changer! It is true, OZ?"

OZ simply nods. A sly grin forming at the edges of his mouth. This is a proud moment for him.

"Game-changing, world-saving," I add, the words tasting like ambition on my tongue. I continue on my dad's behalf. I can't stop beaming as I had wanted to spill this news earlier. "OZ has never stopped believing in a solution, even when everything else seemed lost. We just need a break in the clouds to test it. The Elops."

Hope is a currency we thought bankrupt, but here in this dingy room, with OZ's revelation hanging between us, its value skyrockets. Our collective breath catches, teetering on the edge of possibility. Despair has beaten us down, our spirits weathered like the battered landscapes outside our windows. But now—

Silence.

"Where do we sign up?" quips Banksia, the first to break the quiet, her voice a melodic challenge that ripples through the group.

"Consider this your enlistment," OZ finally speaks, grinning despite the weight of responsibility settling on his shoulders. "This is still in proto form, but with some more tweaks, I am optimistic. We've got work to do, people."

"MightyLegacy," OZ declares, standing tall amidst a saturated world. "Let's make history and see if we can save this planet and its madman, Roman."

And just like that, we're a team fuelled not just by necessity but by the sheer, audacious wish that maybe, just maybe, we can fix this broken world.

"Does it have a name?" Benny chirps. I'm so glad someone finally asked.

"The ClimaSphere."

CHAPTER FIFTEEN

I want to Punch off my BNT and take a break from the anguish. I have Temporal Overload and need to SlackBrain for a bit. This is when I would dearly love to hit the pool, but there is no way I'm heading upstairs. As it is, half the water is washed out and down the side of the building, plunging to a watery death.

I'm also dying for a HoloFlix and watching a PeterG movie, but can't seem to switch gears to that either.

"MightyLegacy," OZ says, urgency threading every syllable, "it's the Oxolets. They're giving out."

Evidently, there is no time to celebrate the concept of the ClimaSphere, so we're just on to the next manic subject - this all seems so brutal!

"What?" Benny splutters, "all of them?"

"Potentially," OZ replies grimly. "Dad," I say in front of everyone, "that's a brave claim. Are you positive? Do we need to assume they're all compromised?"

Our little group huddles closer around the holo screens, each face a mask of creeping dread. For twenty years, the Oxolet has been our lifelines, filtering the toxic sludge we call air into something manageable in the bloodstream. Without them, we might as well be fish on land, gasping for an ocean that's long gone.

"OZ, come on, there's got to be a backup, right?" Ekon asks, trying to keep the shake out of his voice. Smart banter, that's what we need—keeps spirits up, even when belief seems like a fool's game.

"Backup plans are luxury items now," he retorts sharply, his eyes—a mirror of mine, wide and anxious—flicker with something close to resignation. "They're not going to all give out simultaneously, but they will certainly start going out given the time without sunlight." OZ continues on, "and the CG keeps saying there's no problem with them, however—"

The team huddles together, instantly diving deep into the endless stream of news blogs to verify OZ's speculation.

As they read, everyone's expressions shift from curiosity to anxiety, mimicking the panic that is spreading across the globe. News anchors' once smooth and polished voices now falter as they report on the catastrophic failure of Oxolet's all around the world. But amidst all this chaos, OZ remains calm and collected, his prediction proven right with undeniable evidence at hand.

"The solar-powered devices were a product of necessity, born from the aftermath of the BoldWar and the ever-present rays of the sun that enveloped the world. Their sleek design and effortless installation made them a global necessity for survival, with the added convenience of easy charging," OZ says in a straight and deliberate tone. "Despite their impor-tance, it is an embarrassing oversight on my behalf to have overlooked such an obvious issue."

Our eyes lock in a tense, stunned silence. His words hang heavy in the air, creating a sense of unease and uncertainty between us. We struggle to process the meaning behind his mystifying statement, our minds racing with strife-filled emotions. How could he possibly say something like that? What does it mean for us? We are like everyone else, wearing the same tech all over the globe. We are not immune, or special; we are just people wearing a lifesaving instrument that is apparently conking out as we stand here.

I ponder for a second exactly what OZ just said, trying to think of an immediate solution. Like I can come up with something that fast!!! It is funny how one's brain works under pressure and panic. The first, and I will admit, only thing that comes to mind, is putting us all on the next TerraTube and heading to the closest stop to Mt. Everest, Numbur Station. But I do a quick calculation in my head. That damn thing is 7,846 metres high. The cloud seeding has mixed Cirrus clouds (at 12,000 m) with Noctilucent clouds (at 80km), so there isn't a mountain high enough to escape to. No wonder no one in this group ever mentioned it. They'd probably already pondered it and I'm just late to the gawddamn party.

"London to Lesotho, chaos is the new norm, as Oxolets fail," I mumble, running a hand through my hair as I try to piece together the semblance of a plan. The buzzing in my head grows louder than the alarms sounding outside.

"Is this it then? Are we really the beginning of the end?" That's Benny, always the one to voice the thoughts we're all too scared to admit we're having.

"Endings are just beginnings in disguise," I say, more to convince myself than anyone else. "We've got to work with what we've got."

"Which is what, exactly?" That's Soren, their dark eyes flashing with the same fierce determination that convinced me to join Mighty5.

"Brains, guts, and each other," I reply, forcing a grin. It feels hollow, but it's better than nothing.

"Plus whatever OZ has in his bag of tricks," adds Banksia, ever the optimist despite the odds. This, ClimaSphere.

"Let's go back to the depleting Global Solar Grid," Juice asks, trying to get away from the dreaded news of everyone's life support systems crashing in the not-so-distant future.

Leaning over the holographic blueprint that flickers before us, I can't help but feel like we're five kids and three adults trying to piece together a shattered Ming vase—knowing full well we can't even find all the pieces.

"Could we reroute the power from the auxiliary grids?" I suggest, more out of desperation than any real hope.

"Grids are failing faster than my patience," Soren mutters, flicking through data streams with a swiftness that belies our dire situation. "We're patching up a sinking ship with sticky tape."

"Sticky tape won't hold back the ocean," Juice chimes in, leaning back, eyes scanning the ceiling as if it might suddenly reveal an answer.

"Or a sandstorm," I add, thinking of the howling winds that had replaced the gentle breezes of my childhood.

"Ocean, sandstorm—does it matter? We're still drowning," says Ekon, his voice a low rumble of frustration. He's the realist among us, always ready to ground our flights of fancy.

"Or being buried alive," offers Benny, his usual bright tones dimmed by the gravity of our predicament. He's fiddling with a small gadget, hands working on autopilot while her brain races for solutions.

"Morbid much?" I quip, though the humour falls dead in the thick air of our conversation. I'm grasping at straws here, trying to keep spirits afloat when mine is already taking on water.

"Let's focus," I continue, rallying the teams. "We've got the whole world gasping for air. There has to be something we can do."

"Short of inventing a giant Oxolet for the Earth itself?" Soren asks, eyebrow raised sceptically.

"Earth-sized problems require earth-sized solutions," OZ muses, not quite joking.

"Which would need resources we don't have and time we can't spare," Artemis points out, ever the voice of reason—or doom, depending on how you look at it.

"Then what?" I ask, throwing my hands up in frustration. "We stand by and watch the countdown to our last breath?"

"Never said that," Artemis replies, her gaze meeting mine. "But we need a game-changer. Fast."

The holo room goes hollow, each of us lost in thought, the weight of humanity's plight pressing down on us. Our great ideas are mere whispers against the roar of a dying planet. And time—time is the fire in which we burn.

"Okay," I say, breaking the silence. "Let's break it down. What can we actually control?"

OZ chimes in, "only our own actions."

"Right," I nod. "We start small. We do what we can. And maybe—just maybe—we spark something bigger."

"Like a chain reaction," Banksia adds, catching on.

"Exactly," I agree, feeling a glimmer of hope pierce the gloom. "We act, and we inspire action. It's not about fixing everything. It's about igniting the first flame."

"Before the world snuffs it out," Benny interjects, but there's a new light in his eyes—a challenge.

"Then let's get to work," I declare, standing tall. "Mighty-Legacy doesn't wait for miracles. We make them."

"Starting with what?" Juice questions, his practicality reeling me back in.

"Starting with us," I affirm. "And that's no small thing."

"Wait," Banksia gasps, her tone trembling with urgency. "We're perceiving this all wrong." Instead of standing around, wasting precious time trying to figure out how us mere mortals could invent a new power grid for the betterment of the Earth, whilst our Oxolets begin failing, why aren't we rushing to Next Tokyo to test out the machine? Every moment counts and we can't afford to waste any more time!"

She seems to have said all that in one long breath.

How can we devise a plan, test it and implement it in time to save the planet?

"Gawddamnit, Banksia's right." I let out. "We are thinking way too big, thinking we can conceivably pull this off. We need to get to Japan and test The ClimaSphere. It is a logical play and one I think we need to do, and do it fast."

"What are we waiting for?" Juice bursts. "I just looked it up. We all need to get our asses on the next TerraTube and make our way to the Tsukuba Space Centre (TSC) in Tsukuba; in Ibaraki Prefecture."

With eyes glazed, Juice stares greet his command. "Grrrrrrrrrrr." Oh, now he's getting aggravated. He slows to a deliberate trickle. "Wherever you guys are, just head to Old Tokyo TT station in the next 48-hours, we will all regroup there and take the TT3 up to the TSC."

In my head, I was really hoping he would have said: 'Take the TT to the TT2 up to the TSC ASAP', but he didn't; that's just not his style. But it would be mine. I must be feeling a little more excited or a little more SlackBrain.

"I'll start putting the final touches to The ClimaSphere," OZ states proudly, "and report my progress over the next 48 hours. Great thinking, Banksia and Juice, and thanks for keeping this all in perspective and the MightyLegacy on track."

"Out!" I say to the group as the HelloHolos turn into good-bye-for-now-holos!

CHAPTER SIXTEEN

After OZ and I indulge in a satisfying synth-lunch, we eagerly reconvene, determined to maintain the strong pace we have set.

The energy and excitement from before the break carries over as we dive back into our tasks, eager to continue making progress. The smell of freshly brewed tea lingers in the air, adding a sense of alertness to our renewed efforts. We come together with renewed determination, ready to conquer whatever challenges lie ahead.

As our HelloHolos spring to life, there is an urgent discussion that allegedly Artemis and Juice had finally tapped into the CG's Elite-Subframe after days of trying. We never thought we'd make it this far, but there was no turning back now.

"Juice," Artemis murmurs, her eyes glued to the screen in front of them, "I think we're on to something big here."

"What do you mean?" I ask, peering at her seemingly endless rows of code running across our holos.

"Roman," she says simply, and my heart skips a beat. To

me, Roman is quickly becoming a riddle, wrapped in a mystery, inside an enigma.

"Look at this," Artemis says, tapping on a specific line of the cipher. "It's an encrypted message." But with her expertise, she can decipher its contents quickly.

"Juice, do you understand what this means?" Artemis questions, excitement and dread clear in her voice. "He's planning to go off planet."

"Leave Earth? But how?" I inquire, my mind racing.

"Check this out," Artemis replies before pulling up another file. "This one contains detailed schematics of a rocket, unlike any I've ever seen before. It looks like it is designed to be launched from the Japanese Tanegashima Space Centre, located just north of Next Tokyo. Right where the Elops is!"

"If he gets off Earth, there's no telling what he could do," Soren mutters. Anxiety is twisting my insides. "We have to stop him."

"Agreed. But we need more information. Why now? And what's his endgame?" Artemis questions, her fingers flying across the keyboard.

"Keep digging," OZ urges.

My heart is pounding with anticipation. The future of our world could very well depend on what we discover next. And it seems up to us to ensure that Roman's twisted plans never came to fruition.

"What's this?" I ask Artemis, pointing at a section of the report examining Roman's potential destination.

"StellaStation3," she reads aloud, her voice heavy with concern.

"Yep, it's an unoccupied space station in Earth's outer orbit."

"Wait, outer orbit? Why would he go there?" I query, trying to piece together Roman's plans.

"From what I can gather, it's the perfect hideout," Artemis says as she pulls up more information on the space station. "It seems Roman is planning to take 60 of his people with him, including some of his most trusted goons."

"Damn," I curse under my breath. "If they make it there, they'll have all the time they need to plot their return and unleash whatever horrors they have planned for Earth."

"Exactly," Artemis agrees, her eyes scanning the screen for any more useful intel. "We need to figure out how to stop them from reaching StellaStation3."

"But how?" Benny wonders aloud, his thoughts racing. "Our resources are limited, and Roman has an entire army of cronies working for him."

"Let's wrap our heads around this new information," I suggest, already feeling the weight of responsibility settling on my shoulders. "The sooner we act, the better our chances of stopping Roman and protecting Earth."

"Good idea—" Artemis pauses momentarily before continuing, determination clear in her voice. "Roman may have the resources, but we have something he doesn't — hope. And we'll use that hope to fight for our world and everyone in it."

"Hope," I echo, feeling a surge of energy. Roman's plans are terrifying, but with MightyLegacy, I can't help but believe that we have a fighting chance. Maybe.

"Alright, let's get to work," Artemis says, her fingers continually flying across the keyboard once more. "We've got a madman to stop, and Earth's future is in our hands."

My heart hammers in my chest as I skim through the Central Government's Elite-Subframe Files. They're like pages ripped from a dystopian sci-fi novel, only this isn't fiction – it's our reality.

"You guys, look at this," I declare, pointing to a section of the report. "Roman plans on taking a group of highly skilled engineers and developers with him."

"For NextGen robots?" Ekon muses, pondering the possibilities. "He's really not playing around, is he?"

"Definitely not," I reply, shuddering at the thought of what Roman could accomplish with an army of advanced machines under his control. "These are some of the best minds in their fields. Roman must be planning something huge."

"Something even bigger than just escaping Earth," Artemis adds, her eyes scanning the text. "And that's saying something."

"Wait, there's more." I scroll down the page, feeling a chill run down my spine as I read the CGs report about Roman's interest in human cloning. "Biotechnologists, genetic engineers, reproductive biologists...."

"He's going to do human cloning for sure," Dad's declaration stops us dead in mid thought.

"Cloning?" Banksia's voice trembles with disbelief. "That's... inhumane. Not to mention, illegal."

"Roman doesn't strike me as someone who cares much for ethics or legality," I retort, feeling a wave of anger wash over me. "He's playing God. And if we don't stop him, who knows what kind of world we'll be leaving behind for future generations?"

"Wait," I cry out, stunned at what I am reading. "This report also says Roman expects to take mechanical engineers, electrical engineers, computer scientists, and artificial intelligence developers. According to this, he and his team of scientists, or rather, as Benny quips, mad scientists, are working on designing, constructing, and operating NextGen robots. So it is true."

"Shit!" OZ proclaims.

"We have to bring this information to the NewsBlogs,"

Artemis insists, her hands clenched into fists. "We need their help to stand a chance against Roman and whatever twisted plan he has in store."

"Agreed," I say, my resolve growing bolder with each passing second. "We can't let him turn Earth into his own personal playground."

"Let's get to it, then," Soren says, already pulling up a secure communication channel to contact certain key News-Bloggers. "Time is running out, and every second counts."

OZ cuts in, seeming less out of it and back to his old self. "What's his endgame? Let's figure that out. Why? I get what he is doing is wrong, but why go off planet to some abandoned space station? Aren't there lots of places right here on Terra firma, like up in some hidden cave, or within some secluded mountain, in some secret lair? I just don't get why he needs to move, particularly when it is so difficult to lift a rocket off right now."

"I think I know," Soren says slowly and deliberately. "Roman wants to wipe out the entire Earth's population, yes? It seems like he wants to start fresh with his own army of cloned humans and NextGen robots."

"Earth2?" Juice mutters, shaking his head. "The arrogance of that man knows no bounds."

"I sensed something was wrong when they utilised cloud seeding for destruction rather than precipitation. But to think it was all part of a calculated scheme... it's delusional," OZ adds.

"Insanity or not, we need to stop him," Juice asserts, his face etched with resolve. "And we need to do it fast. We have little time before he launches from Tanegashima Space Centre."

"Agreed," Soren says, clenching their fists. "We can't let Roman get away with this. Too many lives are at stake."

As silence descends upon the holo space, my thoughts

race, grappling with the enormity of the task ahead of us. How do you stop a man who has the resources and power to attempt something so monstrous?

"Let's start by reaching out to the world's remaining NewsBloggers and share this information," I add.

And with that, we set to work, united in our quest to save Earth – and all those who still believe in a better future.

CHAPTER SEVENTEEN

As I flic on my BNT, the holo before me glimmers, casting a dim glow through the cavernous lounge room. Perched on the edge of the huge white settee, my heart is pounding in sync with the rapid-fire news reports streaming in from around the world.

"Breaking news," declares a solemn-faced anchor, their voice quivering slightly, "the Global Solar Grid continues to fail, plunging entire cantons into darkness. Hundreds of millions are now without power."

As I stare at the holo display in front of me, chaotic scenes fill my vision. Hospitals overrun with sick patients, AeroBulances speeding over flooded streets, and transportation systems at a standstill. Formerly bustling cities now resemble war zones, with buildings crumbling and debris scattered everywhere from the unrelenting storms. Below our lofty flat, I can hear screams of sirens and howling winds fill my ears, making it hard to focus on anything else. This dystopian world feels like a nightmare, but unfortunately, it is our new reality.

The correspondent's face shows fear as he reports,

"Infrastructure is collapsing in every direction." Communications networks are failing. Utter chaos. People are turning against each other in desperation."

More flipping around. "Tragedy upon tragedy befalls us. Reports of Oxolet malfunctions are streaming in at an alarming rate. Families are being torn apart as their loved ones suddenly lose their last source of oxygen." The gravity of the situation weighs heavily on her words as she struggles to maintain her composure.

I think to glance at my Oxolet that encircles my left wrist, the miniature green light reassuring me of its functionality is still good — for now.

Tears prick at the corners of my eyes, but I blink them back. There's no time for sorrow, not when every second brings us closer to irreversible destruction.

"Massive storm clouds continue to converge," warns a weather expert, gesturing to a swirling mass of ominous grey hues on the screen. "No one has ever seen this phenomenon before. It's as if the very atmosphere is rebelling against us."

"Is there any hope?" I whisper, my voice barely audible above the cacophony of despair filling my HelloHolo. I close my eyes, searching for solace in the depths of my soul.

"Swim," says a quiet voice within me, echoing one of my father's favourite sayings. "When the world is sinking, swim."

I open my eyes and take a deep breath, steeling myself against the tidal wave of fear and desperation that threatens to engulf us all.

For now, the world is drowning. I will swim and won't stop until I've saved us all.

I turn back to my HelloHolo, taking in even more chaotic scenes as blood and violence unfold before my eyes. People are truly fighting and stealing functioning Oxolets. As I take in the scene before me, I can sense the terror people are going through, their locations thick with the stench of fear and desperation, mingled with the metallic tang of spilt blood.

Bodies seem to move like frenzied animals, their primal instincts taking over as they claw and stab at each other in a ruthless battle for survival. Why can't I turn this damn thing off and walk away?

In every scene they show, bodies are writhing in agony or lying still in pools of crimson, their once-human faces twisted into grotesque masks of pain and terror. I can hear screams and weapons clashing, echoing through streets around the world; drowning out the dull sound of dismay.

It is a nightmare come to life, a frenzy fuelled by desperation that shows the darkest side of humanity. Amidst it all, the expired Oxolets lay forgotten and trampled underfoot, a mere object that, for twenty years, saved our lives. Now, our lives are being killed for simply for a few more hours of oxygen and a lung full of life.

CHAPTER EIGHTEEN

"Odezza," comes a familiar voice. I turn to see my dad in the doorway, grease staining his lab coat, eyes alight with that mad scientist gleam. "Join me in the lab, please. I have something to show you."

He disappears down the long art-adorned hallway before I can respond. I sigh, smoothing my rumpled clothes as I stand. The office of fantastical inventions awaits.

There, on the central table, sits the strangest contraption yet. Two contraptions, to be precise. They are slender metal bands with a tiny glass orb sitting on top like a diamond on a ring, filled with a shimmering blue liquid. Watching the liquid move is mesmerising.

"Behold, my dear! Another answer to our current troubles." OZ sweeps his arm dramatically. His eyes shine with pride as he gazes upon his newest creation.

I stare at the tiny devices, a faint flicker of optimism rising within me. Perhaps this is what I noticed the other day. But I don't know what it is, but I can tell Dad is excited about whatever it is.

"OZ," I ask with all humility, "what the heck is it? It is stunning, but I don't know what I'm looking at."

"It's Scandium."

Like I know what that is. "Okay, smartass, but what is the thing I'm looking at here?"

"I call it the Oxy-Stabiliser," he announces, practically glowing. "A breakthrough in oxygen enrichment technology. It can increase oxygen levels in the immediate vicinity by up to 20%."

He grasps the invention gently, holding it up. The blue liquid glimmers. Then he takes off his Oxolet and replaces it with the glistening one.

"But how?" I ask. This seems impossible, even for my brilliant father.

"Ah, therein lies the genius!" He taps his temple. "Applying newly discovered aeroscopic compression principles, I have created a self-contained system that draws in ambient air, enriches it, and releases the oxygen-concentrated result in a steady emanation field. And it's pretty to look at, right?"

I nod my head in wonder. If this works, it could be revolutionary. A portable, self-powered way to combat the oxygen loss afflicting our world. And replace the current, dying Oxolets we all wear.

OZ clasps my shoulder, his exuberance dimming. "I know you have always been a big fan of my inventions; my biggest fan, Odezza," he says with a tone of seriousness. "This could change everything. No more reliance on solar. Clean, oxygen, whenever we need it. Just imagine! Without the use of the sun."

His fervour and positivity reignite my buried aspirations. Maybe OZ is onto something. With this groundbreaking invention, we can control our own fate and escape the need for the sun's rays to keep us alive. We have the power to not only save ourselves but also to rescue the remaining inhabitants of this world.

"How on Earth did you do this so fast?" I ask in complete and utter amazement. "I mean—"

"Our conversations with the MightyLegacy fuelled me, excuse the pun, to do better, so I worked faster to think outside the band; pun intended."

"What do we do now?" I ask.

Dad's eyes remain a fervent shine. "Now, we test it. And we spread the word - cautiously, of course. The Oxy-Stabiliser will not remain secret for long."

"Any chance we can change the name? Like the BlueOx?" I beseech.

"That sounds like an ancient Himalayan animal," he smirks.

"Oxo2?" I continue thinking.

"That's not bad," Dad adds, "I don't hate it. Let's do that instead, it's short, and it makes sense. Well done and thank you, as always."

For the first time in forever, I feel a smile growing on my face. There might be some prospects still left in this world. And my brilliant, eccentric father has found it.

I am curious about how OZ has thought through manufacturing and distributing these things in time to replace everyone's dying Oxolets. However, I hate to ask and ruin his moment of triumph.

CHAPTER NINETEEN

As I slowly awake the next morning and take in the immediate gloom and doom outside my bedroom windows, it dawns on me the irony of the building we live in: Cloud Haven. In some ways, it is a haven, a fortress from the relentless rain, and wind and hail and hell! Yet, on our floor, we are closer to the clouds than ever. Oh, to be on a beach in Ibiza, sun on my skin, wind in my—enough!

As I wrestle my mind back to this new melancholic state of reality, it begins to replay the cryptic information from Juice. Could Roman and his crony crew really be going off planet and leaving the rest of us to perish? This thought lingers in my thoughts like a puzzle waiting to be solved.

This entire notion settles heavily on me, and I can feel the tension building within me as I try to decipher the consequences. My heart races with apprehension and dread, unsure of what this new information could mean for our already precarious situation.

I head to my wardrobe. Finding nothing that piques my interest, I throw on yesterday's clothes and run a brush through my hair.

The rest of the MightyLegacy are already gathered around their holos as mine comes to life.

Juice stands, practically vibrating with nervous energy. His eyes seem bloodshot and his hair sticks up at odd angles. Clearly, he was up all night.

"Alright Juice, what's the juice?" I ask. I finally got to say it. "What did you discover?"

He takes a deep breath. "I did something crazy last night. I tapped into the AnthroTech mainframe."

We all gasp. Breaking into AnthroTech has to be nearly impossible given their ultra-sophisticated security protocols. If Juice got in undetected, he's even more of a genius than I realised. Or just plain gutsy.

"There were encrypted files on Roman's private server," Juice continues. "Schematics, research data, correspondence. It paints a deeply disturbing picture."

He pauses, and the silence hangs heavily over us. My heart hammers against my ribs. Just what exactly did Juice uncover? And what does it mean for our mission?

Soren leans forward intently. "Go on. We need to know everything if we're going to have a chance at stopping his plans."

Juice nods, his expression grim. Apparently, what he discovered shook him to the core. I brace myself as he opens his mouth to continue. Juice takes a deep breath and begins.

"I found definitive confirmation that Roman's end goal is indeed to eradicate Earth's population and essentially start over," he says, his voice taut. "Once the cloud seeding task is complete, and the planet becomes inhospitable, he and a select team will escape off-world. They'll wait in an orbital station while the biosphere collapses and the clouds return to normal levels."

We are all stunned and rendered speechless. So the worst news has been confirmed.

I feel my stomach drop. Beside me, OZ gasps and grabs my hand. Destroying life on Earth as we know it? It's almost too horrifying to grasp.

Juice goes on, "It gets worse. Roman plans to return with his team eventually and repopulate the planet as he sees fit. And he'll use," Juice hesitates, "he'll use human cloning and his Gen14 robots to do it."

The words land like body blows. Human cloning. An army of robots. Roman would hold the fate of the new earth in his hands, with no one to oppose him. It would be his kingdom to rule as he pleased.

"So, the GC spy's report was correct?" Soren asks.

My mind reels. How can one man have such a twisted vision? So willing to sacrifice billions of lives for his own deranged purposes?

Benny's voice trembles. "What are we going to do? This is way bigger than us. We're just a handful of university students and your dad and his mates."

The odds seem insurmountable. But we can't give up hope. Too much depends on us exposing Roman's plans and finding a way to stop the atmospheric reaction he's triggered.

I squeeze my dad's hand back. "We'll keep fighting," I say firmly. "Whatever it takes."

Somehow, against all odds, we have to bring down, or at least stop Roman and save the future of humankind. The weight of it falls heavy on my shoulders. I can feel it, but lifting my eyes, I see the same steadfast courage shining in the faces of the MightyLegacy. We're in this together. And we won't stop until we've won.

"There's more," Juice says grimly. "I found plans in the AnthroTech files. Roman intends to take over the Central Government and eliminate their power over the cantons."

Shocked silence blankets our virtual space. The Central Government in Bonn has overseen world affairs for two decades. Despite recent tensions, they've tried to maintain stability between the cantons and done a pretty decent job.

If Roman seizes control—it would throw the entire world into upheaval. Some cantons would resist, while others might side with him, sparking violent conflicts. Everything could devolve into chaos. That would lead to more fighting and escalate the current bloodshed we've been witnessing.

"He wants absolute power," I say bitterly. "With no one left to oppose him and no one left on the planet to ultimately stop him."

OZ slams a fist into his palm. "We have to stop him. But how?"

"We may be small in number," Banksia says, "but we have something Roman doesn't - conscience. However we do it, we have to expose his plans and shut him down before he destroys everything we hold dear."

I meet each of their eyes, seeing the fear but also the resolve. "Roman has the resources, but we have the truth," Artemis adds. "And in the end, truth and conscience are stronger than any madman and his makeshift army of scientists. If we stand together, we can do this."

We all nod, steeling ourselves for the monumental task ahead. The odds seem ludicrous, but we're not giving up.

Somehow, we'll find a way. The fate of the world depends on it.

I take a deep breath. "OZ, show everyone what you showed me last night? Your new tech."

OZ's eyes light up. "Yes! Great. Good reminder, Odezza. I've done it - I've developed what we're calling the Oxo2."

Dad goes on to show the group as he geeks out about the tech behind the new life support band.

"No sunlight required," OZ wraps up. Everyone's mouths are ajar.

Soren lets out an impressive whistle. "A renewable energy source immune to the clouds … this could change everything!"

"It's ingenious," Banksia marvels. OZ flushes with pride.

"This is the prototype," he says. "But with Roman's solar collectors down, a larger version might be possible, one that could energise an entire city block and eventually a whole city; keeping the lights on, climate control running - it would save so many people."

We all nod in unison. "You're right. If people see we can still thrive without sunlight, it undermines Roman's whole doomsday narrative." I am in awe.

"Exactly," OZ says. "His power comes from fear and despair. This technology can take that away."

Real excitement stirs in me for the first time since we learned Roman's plans. "

"You're a genius, OZ. This might just save us all," Soren says.

He smiles. "Now we have two secret weapons. The Oxo2 and the ClimaSphere. Now let's put them to good use."

Excitement courses through me. The battle is far from over, but with OZ's two miraculous inventions, we finally have a fighting chance.

CHAPTER TWENTY

The holographic screen flickers before me, and I can barely contain my excitement as the data streams in. "Guys! Are you seeing this? Let me throw it up." I call out to my fellow MightyLegacy members. They gather around, their eyes widening as they take in the same news that has my heart racing.

"Two more Elops?" Banksia asks, her voice trembling with a mix of disbelief and hope.

"Seems like it," I confirm, my fingers deftly navigating the holographic interface to zoom in on the locations. "And they're huge."

The images on the screen show gaping holes in the omnipresent gloom suffocating the world. The size of these new Elops is astonishing - easily three times the diameter of the original one discovered near Next Tokyo. Through them, the once-mythical celestial bodies are visible - stars glittering like diamonds scattered across the black canvas of the night sky, an almost full moon casting its serene glow upon the landscape below.

"Look at that," Soren whispers, awestruck. "You can almost feel the fresh breeze just by looking at it."

"Amazing," Ekon breathes, his eyes fixed on the alluring glimpse of a world we've not seen in quite a while. "But how did these appear? What's causing them?"

"Still working on that," OZ admits. "For now, let's focus on spreading the word and helping people get there. We can worry about the 'how' later."

A flic to map mode. I zoom in. "It looks like there is one near Punta Lavapie, Chile. The other seems close to Dar es Salaam, Tanzania."

"How big do they measure?" Benny asks.

OZ chimes in, "I can't be completely accurate at this stage, but by my calculations, maybe 10km."

"Oh, that seems large," Banksia adds, surprised. I'm not sure what she is comparing it to.

We can see Artemis flic to a different screen on her Hello-Holo. Restless and tense, the streets of Punta Lavapie display remnants of modern tech decaying alongside crumbling architecture. The CCTV streaming feed reveals a cacophony of voices and the rumble of desperate people pushing and shoving to make their way toward the Elops. The sun, a sickly yellow disc in the sky, casts a haunting light over the chaotic scene unfolding before us. A similar scene plays out on the coast of Tanzania. Boats. People. Discord.

Families cram themselves into makeshift AeroCars, at least the ones that still have power, piling high with hastily packed belongings. Others are on foot, clutching children or whatever possessions they can carry, their faces etched with exhaustion and determination.

"Can you believe it?" Soren exclaims, their eyes wide with disbelief. "Thousands of desperate people, all converging on these locations like moths to a flame."

"Desperation has a way of making people do the unthinkable," I reply, my eyes scanning the mass migration.

"Look at them," Banksia says quietly, her gaze fixed on a group of elderly people struggling to keep up with the frantic pace set by those around them. "They're risking everything for a glimmer of blue sky. But to what end?"

"Hope. Hope can be a powerful motivator," I respond, my heart aching for them. "But how did word spread so quickly? And what if this journey is all for nought?"

"Word travels fast when there's something worth chasing," Ekon replies. "And as for the risks — they're taking them because their Oxolets are fading and they have nothing left to lose."

"Still, we need to find out more about these Elops," I say, my resolve growing stronger. "If we can understand their origin and purpose, maybe we can help these people."

"Agreed," OZ concurs. "We'll gather as much intel as we can, but our priority should ensure that these people reach the Elops safely."

"Two scenarios come to mind," I say, jarring myself back to reality whilst trying to piece together how these Elops came to be. "First, they could be a natural phenomenon, like some sort of atmospheric pressure shift. Or second, someone or something is creating them deliberately."

"Either way, we can use them to our advantage. We need to try out the ClimaSphere," OZ says, his determination unwavering. "We need to get there, safely and quickly, and see if this machine really will reverse these holes, like my calculations show."

"Agreed," Soren chimes in. "But how?"

"Leave that to me," Juice says, his eyes already scanning his contacts. "I may have a way."

Soren takes on a puzzled look. "But let's get going to Japan first, as that's the first one and we have to assume Roman is heading there too."

"Perfect," I reply. "Soren and I will help work on a plan for Next Tokyo."

As I Punch my BTN, I steel myself for the challenge ahead. Leading people through storm zones that could look more like war zones with so many people clambering to see the blue sky and smell fresh air seems daunting. But it's nothing compared to the oppressive cloud cover that's choking our planet. The clear sky and fresh breeze promised by these three Elops are a beacon of hope in this dystopian world, so we must seize this opportunity – for ourselves, and anyone and everyone that is left breathing.

"Here's to taking risks," I whisper, more to myself than anyone else.

CHAPTER TWENTY-ONE

What I am watching, hearing and feeling on my BTN is beyond disturbing.

The glow of the NewsBlog casts a soft light on my dimly lit room as I scroll through the latest headlines. From here, tucked away in a cosy corner of England, it's almost surreal to think about how much chaos seems to unfold across the globe. A sharp contrast to the constant patter of rain against the window.

"Central Government admits potential global crisis," reads one headline. "About time," I say to myself. It's taken them far too long to acknowledge the severity of what's transpiring. It's like they've all got their heads buried in the sand, pretending they're not liable for the mess we're in.

"CG urges cantons to maintain calm and civility amid growing unrest," I snort. Of course, they would ask for calm and civility when finally admitting that there might be a problem. It's just like them, trying to keep up appearances while everything crumbles around them.

I swipe to an image and information about das CG Gebäude, a building that always makes me think of the Pyra-

mide Inverse do Louvre. It is a colossal inverted pyramid structure, a marvel of modern architecture and engineering. Smart
glass clad the building's exterior, a material that can change its
transparency and insulation properties in response to environmental conditions, optimising energy efficiency.

Carbon nanotubes reinforced with graphene compose the
structure's framework, making it incredibly strong yet light-
weight. This allows for vast open spaces inside with no
internal support columns. The interior is a blend of natural
and synthetic materials, with aerogel for insulation and self-
healing concrete for the foundations, ensuring longevity and
durability.

The building is a government facility and a symbol of
technological advancement and sustainability. It harnesses
energy from integrated solar cells and piezoelectric materials
that convert mechanical stress from wind and rain into electricity. Within a closed-loop system, the building recycles and
purifies water, while vertical gardens line the interior walls,
contributing to air distillation and providing green spaces.

This inverted pyramid stands not just as a seat of power,
but as a testament to our era's commitment to innovation,
environmental stewardship, and the welfare of its citizens.

I see on multiple NewsBlogs that this modern marvel is
flooding, its thousands of occupants trapped inside. I can't
help but wonder if this monument will soon become a tomb-
stone for a dying system.

A part of me wants to laugh at the absurdity of it all.
These out-of-touch politicians never saw it coming – or
perhaps they did, and they just didn't care. I can't say I'm
surprised; their incompetence has been glaringly obvious for
years.

For too long, those in power have ignored the warning
signs, dismissed the cries for help, and turned a blind eye to the
suffering of their own people as the world turned to a dust

bowl of unhappiness. Now, they're the ones trapped, facing the consequences of their actions.

And as much as I'd like to step in and save the day, a part of me wonders if maybe this is what the world needs — a fresh start, a chance to rebuild without the weight of a broken system bearing down on our shoulders. Maybe, just maybe, this is the beginning of something better.

But not on Roman's watch. Never!

CHAPTER TWENTY-TWO

The storm rages like a beast outside, its roar muted by the thick, reinforced glass of my enormous bedroom windows. Lying in bed, I blink away the remnants of a restless dream, that same dream, the kind that leaves you gasping for a reality check. My eyes focus, and through the blur of sleep, I catch the rhythmic flash of lightning—an elevated ECHO dance floor, just for me. I push myself upright, noting the familiar hum of energy that seems to throb with life itself. It's Dad, in his element, oblivious to the chaos of nature's tantrum.

"Music's got me feeling so free," his voice filters through the walls, muffled, but unmistakably giddy. "We're gonna celebrate, celebrate and dance so free."

I can't help but smile sleepily as I swing my feet onto the brushed concrete floor. One More Time, Daft Punk's classic anthem to euphoria echoes from OZ's office, an odd contrast to the dystopian backdrop we've woken up to daily for the past few weeks. As if on cue, the chorus swells. You can hear him singing at the top of his lungs like a man who's just solved the world's biggest puzzle. 'One more time, we're gonna celebrate. Oh yeah, alright, don't stop the dancing'. My smile continues until the end of the song and his singing.

"Morning, Dad," I whisper to myself, shaking my head. His joy is infectious, even through a maze of thick walls.

A sudden knock halts the rhythm of my heart. Standing, I smooth down my rumpled shirt, part of the uniform I've adopted since diving headfirst into this research. The door swings open, and there's OZ—wild hair, crinkled eyes, and an almost boyish grin plastered on his face.

"Odezza!" he exclaims, his excitement palpable. "You've got to come to the lab. I think—I believe we're onto something potentially game-changing."

"Good news?" I reply, my voice laced with hope and a tinge of scepticism. "In this weather? That's a first."

"Trust me," he says, his hand gesturing towards the long hallway, urging me to follow. "Today might be the day we finally give this storm a run for its money."

"Lead the way, Captain Optimism," I chuckle, trailing behind him. The space between us feels charged, crackling with the potential of his latest breakthrough, whatever that may be. I can't shake off the thrill, the thought that maybe, just maybe, we're close to turning the tide in this endless battle against a world that seems determined to undo itself.

As we move through the dimly lit corridor with its recessed lighting magically leading the way, the weight of our mission settles over me like a second skin—reverse the rogue cloud seeding process, restore balance, and save the future. And despite the enormity of it all, I can't deny the rush, the adventure that pumps through my veins, a legacy handed down by the man leading the way.

"Ready to see what your dear old dad has cooked up?" OZ asks, pushing open the massive, thick doors to a world of possibilities.

"Always," I announce, stepping into the lab/office/lair, ready to face whatever comes next—one more time.

A whirl of gears and the hum of machinery greet me as I step into the lab, the scent of ozone heavy in the air. Dad stands amidst a chaos of screens and cables, his eyes alight with that mad scientist spark I know all too well.

"Odezza," he begins, barely containing his excitement, "I've done it—or at least, I'm on the brink of doing it. No! I believe I've done it," correcting himself, gesturing toward the ClimaSphere, its surface gleaming even under the fluorescent lights.

"Last touches?" my heart races, anticipation building like a static charge.

"Exactly." He hovers over the device, hands gracefully dancing across its interface. "The ClimaSphere's algorithm needed finessing. But if my calculations hold up—" His grin is infectious. "We're ready for a field test."

"Seriously?" I can't help but mirror his smile. This could be it—the answer we've been searching for since the skies turned on us.

"Seriously." He nods, conviction etched into every line of his face.

"Let's not pop the bubbly just yet," I caution, though I'm already mentally uncorking the bottle. "But this—this could change everything."

"Ah, my ever-pragmatic daughter." OZ chuckles, but there's pride shimmering in his eyes.

"I just need to put one last failsafe in place and I believe we have what it will take to reverse the collision of clouds and piss off Roman," he adds with a sinister chuckle.

We wait no longer, pivoting to our HelloHolo's, the sleek devices coming to life at our touch. I ping the group chat, the display casting a soft glow in front of our dimly lit faces.

"Guys, you won't believe this," completely forgetting my

manners without saying good morning. My face lights up with a beaming grin, "dad's cracked the stubborn challenges with his reversal machine. The ClimaSphere is ready to rumble."

Even through the digital space, I can feel the group's excitement, their hope. It's a tonic against the storm raging outside.

"Testing soon," I add, followed by a crossed-fingers emoji for good measure.

"Stay safe." Soren says, underscored by their characteristic coolness.

"Always do," I shoot back before going to sign off.

"Optimism suits you, kiddo," Dad says, reading over my shoulder.

"Learned from the best, didn't I?" I give him a quick hug, feeling the solidity of his presence. In this moment of shared triumph, the world outside—with its howling winds and relentless rain—feels a little less daunting.

"Wait!" I snap. "Soren, what am I talking about? We're all going," looking around the holo. "We're all going to Next Tokyo, together — we hope to leave tomorrow."

"Wait," chimes Benny, "we are ALL going to Next Tokyo tomorrow? Why?"

"Got something better to do than save the damn planet and the few billions remaining," Juice snaps, coming to my rescue, the early adopter he is.

"Good point," Soren adds, "it's not like we have uni. We haven't had it in weeks."

"But—" Benny tries to continue.

Banksia quickly follows up, "If you guys are going, I'm certainly going. Count me in."

"We're going to sit this one out." Ekon and 3 both speak together, almost in perfect unison.

"Afraid of a little rain?" Soren snarks.

Artemis adds solemnly, "I think, and I'm speaking for

both of us, we're just a tad beyond our years for taking on battles bigger than ourselves, and you kids know more about the tech OZ has built and certainly can move around the TT and Japan with more ease than both of us. Sorry, but support OZ, bring about the change we so desperately need right now and make us all proud."

I look at OZ, as he looks at them. "Godspeed, and thank you for getting us this far, my friends. We'll celebrate together soon and dance to some Daft Punk."

"Not sure everyone's on the same page with your ancient tomes of '90s House Music," I grin, "but nice try, Dad."

I can see Benny is finally getting on board with the shock and awe of this whole notion, "Okay, we need to go, Odezza. If the ClimaSphere works, we need to see it happen firsthand and OZ might like the company, right OZ?"

OZ simply nods a polite 'thank you'.

"Let's map this out. We will all obviously be taking the TerraTube," OZ draws invisible lines in the air, and the Holo mirrors him, sketching our routes across the globe. He continues, "Juice, looks like you'll be heading to Next Tokyo, via the metropolis of Hanoi City."

"Bet he'll stop for the pho," Soren jokes. Juice cracks a lame smile.

"Wouldn't put it past him," Dad grins, adding virtual pins and strings to our digital command centre. "Odezza. You and I, London to Next Tokyo with a changer over in New Taipei."

I give a prompt nod.

"Hope they've got good boba tea?" I question, picturing the bustling streets and neon-lit night markets. A world away from here seems unreal.

"Always about the food with you," Benny teases.

"Focus, we're talking travel strategy." Soren charges.

"Can't strategize on an empty stomach," I counter. "Besides, travel's part of the adventure, right?"

"Right, you are," OZ nods.

"Banksia's taking off from Doha," Dad says, tapping the air where the Arabian city pulses on the map. "Banksia, you'll be making a pit stop in Hong Kong before joining us." The virtual pin drops, a beacon for Banksia's journey.

"Shopping spree or dim sum?" I muse, knowing Banksia's penchant for both.

"Definitely both," Banksia chuckles.

"And Soren?" I ask, the image of the Paris skyline sprouting behind their image. I have been reading about the torrential rain and massive flooding Paris has been receiving. The Seine breaking its banks has resulted in people being unable to see the curvature of the river, and major landmarks like the La Tour Eiffel have been cut off.

"Ah," OZ remarks, "Soren will also grace New Taipei with her presence." Another pin marking their layover. "Soren's probably looking forward to some quiet time at the Longshan Temple, away from all this chaos, right, Soren?"

"Or you're just in it for the night market snacks, if they have survived," I quip, linking my desires to theirs. Somewhere beneath the adventuresome spirit, we all crave those minor comforts, even if we don't admit it.

"Speaking of snacks," Dad winks, "we should pack some tea from The Time-Traveller's Tea House. Might as well bring a taste of home along with us."

"We've got work to do, supplies to pack and a world to save. But first, rest," Dad continues as he goes to Punch off his BNT.

As our HelloHolo's fade to black, OZ and I find ourselves lost in our own thoughts. A rarity lately.

"Love you, Dad," I say, wrapping my arms around him in a hug that feels like clinging to hope itself. "I'm proud of you for everything. You have saved the world before, and it looks like you're going to do it again."

"Sleep well, kiddo," he replies, his embrace a fortress against the storm. "Tomorrow, we make history."

"Can't wait," I answer, pulling back with a grin. "Goodnight."

"Goodnight," echoes his voice, filled with the same thrill that sparks through me. Tomorrow can't come soon enough.

MOTTLED MORNING LIGHT filters through the storm-riddled clouds, just like the last umpteen dozen mornings; casting a grey pallor over what once would have been a bright, sunny day. I shuffle into the kitchen, TiM at my heels, his mechanical tail wagging in a rhythmic whir of servos and gears.

"Morning, TiM," I mumble, the words lost in a yawn. Our RoboDog responds with a series of happy bleeps, circling around me, his sensors fixed on my mood. It's a routine dance we've perfected over time—his attempt to inject some cheer into the monochromatic dawn.

The kitchen is so quiet. Too quiet without the usual hum of OZ's latest experiment or the scent of burnt faux toast that often accompanies his absent-minded attempts at breakfast. I notice the counter where our ancient Time-Traveller's Tea House teapot sits, an oddity among the sleek modern appliances.

Beside the teapot lies a note. A handwritten script, so difficult to read, on old parchment paper. TiM cocks his head just as I am.

"Odezza," it begins, and I can almost hear Dad's voice, "I've taken the morning TerraTube to the Elops hole in Japan to test the ClimaSphere."

My heart skips a beat, then steadies, then sinks. Classic Dad, passionate as ever, charging ahead with the fervour of a man possessed by his mission. The ClimaSphere, his brainchild, is ready for testing, and not even the fury of nature's worst tempest could keep him from seeing it through.

"Wait!" I say out loud. "Why am I excited? He's taken off without the rest of us." An inquisitive look staring up from TiM.

"Test the ClimaSphere," I read aloud, letting the reality sink in. A frown works its way across my forehead, frustration nipping at my heels. It's just like OZ to leap before looking, driven by that same spark that fuels the storm outside.

TiM tilts his head more, optical sensors blinking in silent query. I pat his metallic flank, reassured by the cool touch of his composite armour. "He's gone to try to save the world, TiM. But without the Mighty5."

For a moment, there's a hollow feeling in my chest, a space where anger and pride swirl in a dissonant dance. But it's over-shadowed by the love and admiration I have for the man who'd throw himself into the eye of chaos if it meant giving humanity a chance.

I flip the note over, but there's nothing more — just the looping scribble of his farewell. "Wish me luck," it reads, a cheer in the curve of each letter that doesn't quite reach my heart. "Love you, Dad" — a term of endearment he's never outgrown. "Oh," he added, "and look after TiM."

The words hang between me and TiM, our Robot Dog now entrusted to my care. I swallow hard, feeling the knot in my throat tighten. What's he thinking, zooming off without a word? The parchment feels like a relic, an echo of ancient times clashing with the hum of our tech-laden kitchen.

"And look after TiM," I mutter to myself, glancing at the machine creature whose head cocks to the other side, awaiting instruction. His loyalty programming is top-notch, but right now, I wish for something less mechanical — a warm, living presence to share in the sudden desolation of OZ's absence.

"Smart move, Dad," I say, the words laced with sarcasm

he's not here to appreciate. Sadness tugs at me. But beneath that, a simmering frustration boils up. How could he leave without me? Without the team.

"Seems like it's just you and me now, buddy," I scratch behind TiM's sensor-laden ears, finding comfort in the routine gesture. His tail wags in response, a programmed happiness.

"Let's get cracking then," I announce with a forced bravado. My voice echoes against the sleek surfaces of our home, a shrine to future possibilities, now feeling colder without OZ's frenetic energy.

"Next stop, Next Tokyo," I declare, though the adventure seems less thrilling without my scientist-in-crime. Still, we have a mission — correction, I have a mission — correction, the Mighty5 has a mission. To follow in his footsteps and help save the world.

"Stay charged, TiM," I add, a playful wink thrown at the RoboDog, who can't appreciate the humour. "We've got a dad to catch and a planet to fix."

"Love you, Dad," his salutation still tugging at me. Why would he go on without us?

And with that, I turn away from the note, from the lingering scent of The Time-Traveller's Tea House brew, and focus on the horizon stretching out before us. There's work to be done, storms to quell, and a father's faith to justify. It's a lot for a sixteen-year-old to shoulder, but then again, I'm not your typical sixteen-year-old. I'm Odezza, daughter of OZ, and together — or apart — we're going to change the world.

CHAPTER TWENTY-THREE

The moment I read the note from Dad, I can't help but feel my heart leap into my throat. He's taken off to Next Tokyo alone? With everything going on in the world right now, it seems senseless. I flic on my HelloHolo and call the Mighty5 immediately, my hands shaking as they flicker in and out of view.

"Guys," I gasp, "OZ is heading to Next Tokyo without us, and I don't know what his plan is. We need to find him!"

"What do you mean, he's heading to Next Tokyo without us?" Benny asks, his voice laced with alarm.

"We, TiM and I, just found a note he left in the kitchen. He apparently couldn't wait for us, so yes, he's taken off."

"Odezza, calm down," Soren tells me, their holographic face filled with concern. "Let's figure out how we can track him."

"Oh forgawdsake! Good question. Let me try his tracker," I say under my breath. I'm obviously a little emotional, having forgotten to do the obvious thing. "Let me check."

"Well?" Benny exclaims impatiently, like he's out of breath.

My hands tremble as I stare at the blank tracking screen in front of me. This is impossible. We have all the technology to track anyone, anywhere, anytime. So why am I unable to see Dad?

OZ's silence only adds fuel to my growing panic. It's a foreign emotion, one that I may have never truly felt before. But now, it consumes me and I can't help but hate it and the uncertainty it brings.

"I'm looking too," Banksia adds, "and I see nothing."

"He seems to have disabled his tracker," I point out. I, too, sound like I'm out of breath. What the hell is happening right now? It's not like him.

Juice suddenly receives a news ping, a RedAlert, and his eyes widen in shock.

Oh, I really can't stand any of this!

"Hang on. Something's coming in about a TT crash. Stand by."

"What?" my voice cracks, an octave higher than usual; fear clawing at my insides. "Which track? Is it the one OZ is on?"

"Can't tell," Juice replies, scrolling through the NewsBlog. "They're not releasing that level of information yet. There are something like 150 tracks around the world, Odezza. It might not be the same one."

"Can anyone track him somehow?" I ask desperately. "We need to know if he's okay!"

"Odezza, we're trying our best," Banksia says reassuringly. "Our trackers can't seem to pinpoint him, but we won't give up."

"Find him!" I don't mean for my voice to come out as a command, but it does. It's all I can do to keep from breaking apart. "Please—"

"Hey, don't worry, Odezza," Benny chimes in, attempting to lighten the mood. "We've got your back."

"Thanks, guys." I force a smile, but it feels more like a grimace. "Let's keep searching, okay?" As we all work together to locate OZ, I can't help but think about the rogue cloud seeding process and how much he despised it. Even though he is a brilliant inventor, he loathes the futuristic technology causing so much chaos in the world. And now, with him missing and possibly in danger, I'm more determined than ever to reverse the damage that's been done.

"Come on, Dad," I whisper to myself, my eyes scanning through endless streams of data as my heart clenches with fear. "Send us a signal that you're okay."

"Guys, we might run out of time," Juice continues, "I just saw another announcement pop-up that the first Elops at Next Tokyo is closing. And closing fast."

Could this morning get any worse? Even if Dad is okay, will he know their Elops is closing? Although I have never been on the TerraTube, I have to imagine it would have the latest tech on board, so hopefully he is seeing the news feeds too.

The crazy thing is, it won't take long for him to get there. I need to look closely at his exact arrival time. I have to stay calm and figure this out. His TT would have left an hour and a half ago, from Central Portal London. It should take about two and a half hours to New Taipei Main Station, with a half hour layover, then about an hour and a half up to New Tokyo. Damn, that train is fast! So let's call that six hours' total travel time.

What to do?

Then I realise. I have a cousin in Next Tokyo. How had I never thought of her before now? Amira. At least OZ always called her my cousin. Now that I reflect, I never took the time to inquire about our relation – Focus, Dezzy!

"Guys, I need to Punch and work on an angle for a

second. Let me get back to you shortly, okay?" And with that, I am left in my bedroom by myself and my thoughts, trying to put all the pieces of this puzzle together.

"AMIRA, this is Odezza - your cousin in London. Your itoko." I start, really not sure if Amira had even heard about me.

"Ah, yes, Odezza. Konnichiwa." Amira adds in the most polite way. "How are you and how is your father, Ozwald? It has been far too long." Well, at least she recalls OZ.

"Well, funny you should ask. He is heading your way, and I hope you might do me a huge favour?"

"Of course, anything for kazoku; for family." Amira affectionately offers.

"Well, it's a super long and rather complex story that just might include a part about saving the planet and its inhabitants, but for now, my friends and I are trying to find him. He left this morning for Next Tokyo with a new machine he invented that he, we, hope will reverse these Elops, these holes, these kubomi, and transform the clouds and bad weather back to some type of normalcy."

"There isn't a direct TT from you to me. Which layover did he choose, Odezza?"

"We believe it's New Taipei Main Station."

I can hear Amira thinking. "So he could be here in the next couple of hours?"

"We think so, yes," I add softly. "Where are you, Amira?"

"Right now I'm in The Sky Mile Tower, floor 396. I considered going up to the top floor, Floor 421, but that seems really frightening to me."

"Probably a good idea. I should have asked first, how is the weather there?"

Amira looks hesitant to go on. She seems scared. She takes

a gulp of air and says in her best English, "Imagine the sky over Tokyo Bay as a canvas of turmoil. Ominous clouds have rolled in, swallowing the light overhead, turning day into night. The air is electric here, charged with great scariness."

Suddenly, a jagged bolt of lightning splits the sky behind her, a brilliant flash illuminating the afternoon gloom. I can also hear thunder rumbling, a deep, resonating growl that seems to shake the very foundations of the building. And I can see the horizon move behind her. That building is swaying.

Amira continues, "rain is lashing down in torrents, relentless flooding that's destroying the streets far below and seems to whip the water's surface into a frenzy. Hailstones, like icy marbles from the heavens, are pelting the side of our building like a moth and a moth-swatter, clattering against windows and shattering on impact. The wind has been howling all day and all night, a fearsome gale bending trees and sending debris flying like missiles."

This can't be easy for Amira to talk about, but I also don't interrupt. It sounds horrid, but her poetic tale is mesmerising.

"The storm is a beast, untamed and wild, unleashing its fury with a power that is both awe-inspiring and terrifying. It's a reminder of nature's might. This force commands respect and holds the power to transform the familiar into chaos. This is not just a storm, Odezza; it's a cataclysmic event, a tempest that will be etched in the memory of all who witness its wrath for a long time."

Amira continues with even more grim weather news, "I saw a NihonNewsBlog this afternoon that out of the 14,125 islands in Japan, approximately 530 have disappeared under water. Luckily, most are inhabited. Even so, things are seigyo funō dust - out of control," she translates.

"I'm systems," Amira ends sadly, which I think means I'm afraid. After that description, I can see why. I would be too.

I know in Japanese culture, politeness and clarity in

communication are highly valued, even when discussing powerful emotions like fear, so I know that it took a lot for her to share and admit.

"I have never felt such swaying. And did you hear the first Elops is closing just north of us, Odezza?" Amira continues, taking a sip of water from a long, graceful glass.

"Yes, we just heard that, too. The challenge is that Dad was heading to that Elops to try out his new machine. However, we don't know where he is, as he has turned off his tracker, so we don't know if he is aware of this news about the closing hole or not."

"Wait, it just hit me. He is taking the TerraTube. Did you hear about the one that just crashed?" Amira is being overly courteous about the way she asks.

"Yes, we also just heard that, but the CG is not disclosing where the accident happened, so my uni friends and I are trying not to panic, but without all the information, it is difficult not to."

"I should have asked, sorry. How can I help?" Amira asks, again, so very politely.

"If it is not too much to ask, can you please head out to the Tokyo Main Station and keep an eye out for OZ?" That was difficult to ask for. "I will Flip you a recent photo. Do you have 'waiting boards' at your station?"

"We have a system like that, yes. As people disembark the TT, they walk through a circular scanner, which reads their information, including their name and where they have arrived from, and it appears on a massive screen in Japanese and English. Yes, is my answer - I can certainly tell when he arrives, on what platform and exit he is heading for. I will keep a close eye out for your father and let you know the moment I see him."

Progress! "Domo arigato gozaimasu," I say in thanks,

bringing a small grin to the edge of her mouth. It's the little things OZ always taught me.

As I Punch my BTN, and say under my breath, "Where are you OZ? I'm worried about you, Dad. Send me a signal that you're okay!"

CHAPTER TWENTY-FOUR

I flic on my HelloHolo. The screen flares to life with a whir of pixels. "Juice," I blurt out, "I need your help to crack into my dad's office. Think you can help me?"

"What's going on and why are we breaking into OZ's lab?"

"We need to make sure he is almost in Japan. Then we need to get after him and join him there. And I can't tell if he knows the Elops he is heading toward is closing. So yes, we need to get moving fast, but I want to look inside his office to see if he might have a second ClimaSphere. A back-up unit. I know it's a long shot, but if there is a secondary version, I want it in hand just in case anything goes wrong."

"Also," I continue, "I just got off a call with my cousin in Japan to see if she can help."

"Hold on, you have a cousin in Japan?" Juice interrupts.

"Yes, yes, I have a cousin." We never talk about our families, so she has never come up. "We've also never met, but Dad has told me about her. Her name is Amira. She told me she lives in The Sky Mile Tower in Next Tokyo. I think she is originally from Q. When she was born, it would have been called

Qatar. OZ told me she moved with her parents a few years ago - anyway, I tracked her down. I've asked Amira to keep an eye out for OZ when he gets off the TT. She'll report back in a few hours."

"Anyway..." I take a long breath and continue on, "like I was saying, I went to see if OZ has another ClimaSphere - from what I'd heard, he often made a back-up, as a back-up."

"Odezza?" Juice says with concern. His voice is quick, laced with consternation. "Breaking into your dad's lab is serious business — but what does the lock look like?"

"Only the latest tech, from what I can tell." I rush toward the door, the Holo hovering in front of me, its sensors humming softly. My fingers tap against the cool metal surface as I inch in closer, giving Juice a better view.

The locking mechanism glints back at us. A sleek panel of encrypted defiance—a Gordian security knot designed by the best. I swear I can feel the weight of its challenge pressing against my chest. Juice whistles low, impressed or daunted. I can't tell.

"State-of-the-art," I confirm, a wry smile tugging at my lips despite the tension coiling within me. "But if anyone can crack this code, it's you, right?"

"Flattery will get you everywhere," he quips, but there's an edge of seriousness to his tone. Juice's eyes are laser-focused now, flicking over the details visible on the tiny holoscreen. It can't be easy doing this via one's HelloHolo.

"Can you get in closer by chance?" he asks. "I want to cross-reference the model with known vulnerabilities."

"Okay, let me push in closer," I reply, my voice barely above a whisper. The silence around me feels too loud, the empty halls echoing with ghosts of conversations past.

I am as close as I'm going to get. I can see his fingers dance over his own set of keys, a symphony of clicks and taps that hold within them the hope of unlocking secrets. Secrets and duplicates that could change everything.

"Ready?" Juice grins through the holo, his exuberance infectious.

"Born ready," I reply, the familiar surge of adrenaline coursing through me.

"You know, he's an enigma to me," I confess, the words spilling out before I can stop them. "My dad, my hero. The man can do anything we put his mind to. That's kinda cool, right?"

"Yes, I guess so, but heroes have their secrets," Juice muses, his voice a lifeline through the digital ether. "Even more reason to get inside, right?"

"Right," the word tastes like determination. But there's a tremor in my hands that betrays the fear niggling at the edges of my mind.

"Please check the power source," he suggests, all business. "Any redundancies or backups? They might give us an angle."

"Looking." My fingers trace the sleek matt black panel, feeling for the telltale hum of concealed energy. I press here, prod there, hunting for the weak spot in my father's citadel of solitude.

"Anything?" Juice prompts, his voice a thread of urgency in the quiet.

"Nothing obvious," I admit, frustration knotting my brow. "It's clean. Too clean. It seems to be part of the wall."

"Okay, think Odezza," Juice coaches. "Your dad had a style, patterns. You know them better than anyone."

"Patterns, right?" I chew on my cuticles, casting my mind back to the quirks and idiosyncrasies of OZ's designs. What would he do? What has he done?

"Got it!" A spark of inspiration flashes brightly. "Dad hates the obvious, the blatant, but he loves puzzles. He'd call it a 'flawed concept dressed in caution's clothing'." I relay my epiphany, the corners of my mouth lifting in a half-smile.

"Classic OZ," Juice chuckles. "Alright, let's exploit that singular focus. If there's no backup, then every part is essential. Find the keystone."

"Keystone..." The notion sets my thoughts racing. I scan the doorframe, probe the interface, search for the linchpin of my father's genius.

"Pressure points," I murmur, my fingers hovering over a section of the panel that appears identical to its neighbours. Yet, intuition screams it's different. Something about the way the light doesn't touch it is quite the same.

"Talk to me, Dezzy," Juice says, anticipation lacing his tone.

"Hey, you are the puzzle wiz. Have you studied the history of gaming in your classes?"

"Yes," Juice says, "a little. Why, where are you going with this?"

"Have you ever heard of a game called Tetris? It's old."

"Is that the game where you move the coloured boxes around the screen?"

"Yep," I add, puzzled by what I'm looking at. "Take a close look this keypad. When you touch it, there aren't numbers that appear. Look. They are small coloured blocks. What if the code to get in is the same as the game? You know how OZ loves old crap; strange oddities the rest of us don't quite understand or, in my case, appreciate."

"Interesting notion," Juice adds, tilting his head like TiM does. "Let me check something real quick."

"Very interesting indeed." I acknowledge.

Juice seems to have discovered something. "And?" I quip.

"This concept seems to blend physical security with a bit of fun. Very OZ. From what I can tell, this idea is really rare, so again, very OZ. It looks like he has indeed built a custom electronic keypad and locking system. With that screen and input controls, my guess is you're correct. You can run the keypad just like a Tetris game. I believe the lock's software should be programmed to identify the game's completion or the correct sequence of blocks as the unlocking mechanism."

I think Juice is loving this little quest we're on, particularly given what he's studying at Tokë: Meta-Game Theory. This sounds like a dissertation he could write for class.

Juice continues, "OZ has built a customisable system where each Tetris block configuration represents a different number or letter in a code sequence. To unlock the door, we need to input the correct sequence of Tetris blocks. This is like a dynamic challenge." OMG, he is loving this. "I'm thinking we need to complete one or two lines to unlock. Seeing as this is yet another OZ invention, the reset is establishing a unique challenge for each entry attempt." Oh, he is so in his element right now. I've never seen him in a zone like this. The door might unlock if we score a certain number of points within a time frame. Oh, your dad is good. This is adding an element of skill and speed to the unlocking process."

"You make it sound easy," I say in admiration.

"Let's try some colour combos and start playing his game." Juice is really on a roll now.

After a few tries, all of which fail, you can feel the frustration rising in both of us. This might be a lot easier if Juice were in the room, but he isn't, and we don't have time for him to get here on the TT, so we must keep trying.

"Okay, sorry, I can't seem to get this," Juice says with a serious look on his face.

"Look, try this sequence. A thread of code just popped up with a thing called a 'T-Spin Triple'."

"Excuse you?" I quip.

"Do this," he continues, not allowing my sissiness to distract him. "Rotate the T-shaped block up and to the right. It looks inaccessible, but I think it will—"

"Hang on," I cry out with a newfound sense of exhilaration rolling over me. "Look, something's happening. Are you seeing this, Juice?" Forgawdsake, this might be working.

We both watch as the blocks move into place. That T-Spin thingy seems to work. I can hear something moving inside the massive door, like cogs being awakened from a deep slumber. "Are you hearing that?" I blurt out.

"No, but you can hear something?" Juice remarks, excitement in his voice.

"Yes. Stand by. Something is certainly happening here and the Tetris pad has now gone back to its blackened state." As I speak those words, the noises stop and I see the door click open. "Ohforfuckssake, we did it. We've actually broken into my Dad's inner sanctum.

"Brilliant," I breathe out, the finality of the unlocked door before me both thrilling and daunting. With a steady hand, I push it open, stepping into the chancel that houses my father's dreams.

"Thanks, Juice. Couldn't have done it without you." Gratitude spills from me as naturally as breathing; he's more than just an accomplice—he's my lifeline in this chaos.

"That's exceptional, if you ask me. A Tetris Lock. Anytime, Odezza. Happy hunting finding a replica ClimaSphere." Juice's voice is all business, but I catch the undercurrent of concern. He knows how much is riding on this.

"Want to stay on the holo with me and check it out?" I blurt out, not really thinking through my request.

"Happy to. Let's look around."

The office greets us with stone silence. This is a stark contrast to the cacophony of innovation that reverberates when Dad's working. My gaze sweeps over familiar equipment, each piece a fragment of OZ's continual puzzle. But I'm searching for something specific—a trace, a hint, of another ClimaSphere.

"Check the bench by that left wall. Looks like a compartment?" Juice suggests his observations serve as a map to navigate my father's organised chaos.

"Right," I stride over, ruffling through handwritten papers and futuristic hardware, my heart racing with anticipation. Every second counts and the air feels charged with the weight of potential discoveries.

"Anything?" Juice asks after a moment that stretches too long.

"Nothing yet," I reply, but then my fingers brush against cold metal, half-hidden beneath a pile of schematics.

With every cluttered compartment and bestrewn shelf, desperation claws at my patience. Juice's voice crackles through the static of my HelloHolo, a lifeline in the growing storm of frustration.

"Check behind everything, Odezza," he urges, his tone laced with an urgency that fuels my frantic search. "Every nook, every cranny."

"Trust me, I am." My words are accompanied by quick puffs of breath as I shove aside biochips and blueprints, seeking what feels like an apparition. Dad's lair is dense with the residue of his genius, yet the ClimaSphere proto remains elusive, a ghost in the machinery.

"Could it be—I don't know, camouflaged?" Juice speculates, grasping at straws as much as I am.

"Camouflaged?" I scoff, though the idea ignites a flicker of intrigue. "Like hiding a tree in a forest?"

"Exactly! Or a safe behind a—"

"Poster!" We say it in unison, our minds syncing even across the digital divide.

I pivot on my heel, my eyes locking onto the old Daft Punk poster clinging to the wall. It's an artefact from another era, one where electronic beats filled the air rather than the hum of quantum processors. A memento of Dad's love for the old, perhaps, or a clue so obvious we've overlooked it until now.

"Rip it down, Odezza. There could be a wall-safe," Juice suggests, the mischief in his tone a stark contrast to the gravity of the situation.

"Oh no, Juice, it's signed!" T. Bangalter and G.H de Homes-Christo! Daft Punk. "Forgive me," I mutter, reaching for the tattered edges of the poster. With a swift yank, it gives way, fluttering to the ground like a defeated flag, but unscathed in its retrieval from the wall.

"Anything?" Juice's voice is tense, expectant.

My hand hovers over the exposed wall, feeling along the cool, smooth surface. And then, there it is—a faint outline barely perceptible under the dim recessed light. A hidden door within these walls, a secret kept even from me.

"Juice, you're a genius." My heart drums a frenetic beat against my ribs.

"Hey, it takes one to know one," he quips. I can see a satisfied grin on his face.

We might just pull this off after all.

My fingers tremble as they trace the edges of what looks to be a safe, its presence both reassuring and terrifying. "Okay, Juice. You're up."

"Alright, give me a clear view of the lock," he instructs, his voice crackling through the HelloHolo.

The device in my hand casts a bluish glow over the keypad, the light dancing across intricate circuits that would make lesser minds swoon. Juice's face, pixelated but focused, examines the feed from the other side of our connected worlds. "It's a ZephyrLock 3000," he says, a whistle of admiration escaping him. "Top-notch security there, Odezza."

"Can you crack it?" My question is more of a plea. This isn't just about breaking into a safe; it's about unlocking the past to save our future.

"Let's find out," Juice's fingers dance on his own keypad, a symphony of clicks and taps that heralds our hopeful breakthrough.

Seconds stretch into eternity. The occasional buzz and beep from Juice's end punctuates the prolonged silence.

"You will not believe this, but it's a hand scan locking mechanism."

"But we don't have my dad's hand here, so now what? How are we meant to break in?" I say as a sense of dread falls over me like the gloom of the sky right outside our flat.

"Try it with your hand and see if it opens," Juice responds.

"There's no way my hands will work, Juice, sorry," I say with defeat.

"Odezza, try it. What do you have to lose? Maybe your dad thought about a moment like this."

"Well, if he had, wouldn't he have made breaking in the front Tetris door a lot easier?" Now I sound mad.

"Try it, Dezzy, please," he says calmly.

I roll my eyes and place my right hand upon the blackened door's cold sleekness. Nothing.

"Odezza, are you left-handed by chance?" Good question Juice, I think to myself. Clever lad.

"Yes, let me try that." As I reach out, I notice my Oxolet green dot is fading and changing to a deep orange colour. I hadn't looked in a while. Forgawdsake! Flashing red is next, and that means one step closer to expiration. "Really?" I say under my breath. Now is when I have to look at that damn thing. Concentrate!

My left hand applies itself to the door — "Nothing," I share with Juice.

"Damn," is his only response. "Wait," he adds. "Let's try something super strange, just in case OZ really thought through this day. Put both hands up there."

"That's utter nonsense," I scald, "who's ever heard of a two-handed sensor?" I scoff rhetorically.

"Just try it," Juice says firmly, snapping me out of my obstinance.

I lean over my dad's messy workbench, trying this stupid idea when... "Oh! My! Gawd! I just heard a sound."

"What sound?" Juice almost screams edgily.

"Hold please."

"Ah, baloney," I say, shocked and alarmed, "the door, it's opening. It worked. Your strange idea totally worked."

The door swings open with a sigh, revealing its secrets.

"Juice, you're beyond a genius." I can't help the laugh that bubbles up, an echo of relief amidst the tension.

"Save your praise. We've got work to do." He's right, of course. "What do you see?"

Inside the safe, I see a treasure trove of history before me. Books with worn spines, their pages filled with dad's scrawl—notes on experiments that never saw the light of day. But hidden behind them, almost shy in its placement, is the Oxo2 prototype. And another ClimaSphere.

"Look at this, Juice."

I carefully extract the items, my breath caught between awe and reverence. The Oxo2 is sleek, the metal is cool against my skin. And then there's the other ClimaSphere. It looks like the one Dad has, yet not quite the same.

"Is that — another ClimaSphere?" Juice leans closer to the holo, squinting as if he could reach through and touch it.

"Yeah. It's here. He really had a back-up, but it looks different to the one he has with him." My voice is barely above a whisper, as though speaking too loudly might shatter the moment.

"And there's the Oxo2," Juice adds, amazed at the treasure trove we just uncovered.

I can't think about the Oxo2 right now. I need to focus on the ClimaSphere, as there surely seems to be something different about it. With careful hands, I transfer the proto sphere to the workbench, the clutter of tools and gadgets now pushed aside to accommodate this new puzzle.

"Something's off about it," I muse, turning the ClimaSphere in my hands, feeling for any give, any hint of what makes this one unique. Whatever secrets it holds, I know they're vital. It's just another piece in the increasingly complex jigsaw of my father's world.

"We'll figure it out, Odezza. We always do," Juice says, confidence lacing his words. "At least we found a proto. That's worth something. And we also have the Oxo2. That's also a big deal."

"Right. We will indeed need to figure this proto out," my gaze hardens with resolve. This is no longer just about curiosity — it's about survival. And we won't let anything stand in our way.

I trace my fingers over the ClimaSphere's smooth surface, feeling the cold bite of metal against my skin. A small terminal catches my attention—a keypad with numbers and symbols that gleam under the lab's sterile light. I had only seen the original for a few moments, but this is a stark contrast to the version dad took with him, which had no such feature. My heartbeat quickens, a mix of excitement and trepidation pulsing through me.

"Juice, do you see this?" I tilt the holo so he gets a better view. "There's a keypad here."

His brow furrows on the screen. "Didn't have that before?"

"Definitely not." My mind races, thinking about what this enhancement could mean. The room feels smaller somehow, the silence heavy with the weight of unanswered questions.

"Could it be some sort of lock? Security measures?" Juice suggests, his voice crackling with static through the HelloHolo connection. "Or another Tetris game."

Juice laughs. "Too soon," I scold him, almost laughing at myself.

It has to be a lock. But there's a gnawing thought that it's something more—something crucial.

I glance around the lab, seeking anything familiar yet out of place. Then I spot it—an open notebook on Dad's chaotic side table, its pages a mess of scribbles and diagrams. A rough diagram of the proto. I snatch it up, leafing through the contents as my eyes struggle to decode the scrawl that is unmistakably Dads scribbled handwriting.

"Look at this," I say, holding the notebook up for Juice to see. As I turn the pages, there are other hand-drawn images of the ClimaSphere, surrounded by annotations and arrows. "These schematics differ from any I've seen before."

"Can you make any of it out?" Juice leans in closer, his forehead nearly pressing against his own holo-screen.

"Only bits and pieces. Dad's handwriting is always more code than script." I squint at the page, tilting it, hoping a change of angle might make the words clearer. "It's not a hologram, you idiot," I say under my breath. But it's no use; the writing remains stubbornly cryptic.

"Let's not panic yet. We're good at puzzles, remember?" Juice keeps the tone light, but I can hear the underlying strain. Time is slipping away, and every second we spend deciphering is a second closer to catastrophe.

"Right. Puzzles are our speciality," I force a half-smile, but the gravity of our situation hangs over me like a storm cloud ready to burst. Dad's work, his cryptic mind. It's all here—

somewhere between these lines of ink and the mysterious keypad on the ClimaSphere.

"Okay, Odezza, now that we have found it, pack it up and let's get back to the original rendezvous plan, finding your dad and saving what we can of the world that remains."

Yes, the plan. We need to keep on moving forward, find OZ and get back to the work at hand - reversing the Elops.

CHAPTER TWENTY-FIVE

I hold the new Oxo2 in my hands, feeling its sleek, cylindrical shape and cool, unfamiliar surface, a stark contrast to the old Oxolet that has been my lifeline for as long as I can remember. Swapping out Dad's legacy for this updated model feels like a betrayal, especially since it was hidden behind his precious band poster. But the world doesn't have room for sentimentality, not anymore.

"Okay, old friend," I murmur to the older device, "let's give you a well-earned rest." Precision guides my fingers as I disassemble the Oxolet, my tactile memory recalling each step Dad taught me. I integrate the Oxo2's core into the framework of the old device. It is cold. Foreign. It hums to life, an infusion of new vigour in a familiar shell.

"Odezza, you genius," I tell myself, my heart thrumming with success and a surge of adrenaline. The Oxo2 could be the breakthrough we need—if only we had the time to mass-produce it, to get it onto the wrists of the suffocating population outside these walls.

The colour is completely mesmerising. It is the most

incredible blue you can imagine. The fluid is profound, vibrant azure, reminiscent of a clear London spring sky just after dawn, or the rich hue of the ocean seen from a tropical beach. It's a shade that feels alive, full of depth and tranquillity. It is breathtaking. And I have the only other one. And it will never need solar energy to power it - a schizophrenic juxtaposition for sure.

Meanwhile, on my right wrist, the NewsBlogs blare incessantly from the BTN's holo-screens, tales of desperation and violence due to depleting oxygen supplies and life-sustaining Oxolets. There are reports of black-market Oxolets, rigged to squeeze out another breath of life at the cost of someone else's. It sickens me. And worse still, people are killing people for their Oxolet, if only to bring the thief half an hour of stolen life.

"Got to think bigger, faster," I mutter, pacing the cluttered expanse of dad's lab/lair/office. My mind races through possibilities—3D printing en masse, underground distribution networks, even barging into CG headquarters in Bonn, sodden as they are, and demanding action. But each thought slams into the same wall: time is slipping away, and lives with it.

I can't seem to prioritise which is more important and or which can be done quicker: developing a new global energy supply to bolster the flailing solar grid, developing these next-gen Oxolets, or moving as fast as possible with the newly discovered, but yet to be figured out, ClimaSphere and the Mighty5 to the next Elops. OR— "forgawdsake, Odezza," I say to myself, how about we find OZ and then take some of these on! I just want all this to be over, but I know deep in my heart we have come too far to turn around now.

Ah, it is helping to think through this and what I think we can accomplish - Dad first, then the next Elops, working with Dad and his own ClimaSphere. Good. If we can do that, and his machine works as he thinks to take advantage of these holes and turn things around, then we can think about improved energy sources and Oxo2's later. Yes. Feeling a little better - family first. Dad always has a plan or is working on a plan.

Amid this maelstrom of thoughts, an icy splinter of worry pierces my focus. Amira. She should have checked in by now; her silence is as loud as the storm raging outside our sanctuary.

"Amira, where are you?" The question hangs unanswered, a ghostly whisper in the chaos. I'm not a fan of radio silence. I try her on my BTN.

"Come on," I urge the universe or whatever powers might be listening. "Don't do this to us."

No answer.

I glance back at the Oxo2, now pulsing rhythmically, a beacon of hope amidst the encroaching despair.

"First things first," I tell myself. "Find Amira, save the world. No pressure, Odezza."

Still no answer. I disconnected.

The ever-present chime of my HelloHolo starts up, its static crackle filling the air and serving as a harsh reminder of my isolation. It's the team, the Mighty5, perfect timing. "Any word on OZ?" Juice asks, throat tight with the weight of unspoken fear.

"Nothing," comes my terse reply, my voice also dry and brittle with concern. "Nothing from OZ or my cousin."

"You have a cousin?" Banksia adds.

"Yes. She lives near the main TT station OZ is heading to, so I have asked her to go down to the station and collect him when he pulls in."

"His very own greeting party," Banksia laughs.

"Yep, she's letting us know as soon as she has him safe and sound."

Benny shifts the subject, "CG's being as transparent as tar

again about the TT accident." His words are laced with a bitterness that mirrors my own.

"Maybe they don't even know," Banksia muses aloud, ever the devil's advocate.

"Or maybe they just won't say," I counter, adjusting the settings on my BNT, scanning for any shred of information, anything that might tell us where the TerraTube accident happened or if Dad... No. Can't think that way.

"Guys, focus," says Soren, their tone cutting through the haze of our collective worry like a beacon. "First, we stabilise the situation here, then figure out the next move."

"Right," I affirm, pushing down the dread to let my brain do its crucial work. We need plans, not panic. "We need to get to OZ first. That's our priority. However, if we can chat with him, maybe we won't go to Next Tokyo, we will meet him at the next Elops. We just have to pick which one is the highest priority.

"Okay, weather check," I command, bringing up the translunar feed. The images flicker to life, showing the clouds swirling wildly above us, a nightmarish ballet of nature's fury unleashed.

"Looks like it's getting worse," Juice observes, and I nod. The world outside is an abstract painting gone mad, the sky an angry artist splashing grey upon darker grey, the clouds running in reverse, defying gravity and reason.

"Same here," confirms Soren. "The clouds are practically dancing a jig, a jig played by the devil."

"Anyone else think Mother Nature finally lost it?" Benny jokes halfheartedly, but there's no genuine humour there, just a veneer covering the dread.

"Let's not give her any ideas," I quip back, trying to inject some levity into our grim reality.

"Stay sharp, everyone," Soren warns. "We don't know what's coming, but we need to be ready for anything."

'Anything' feels like a vast, gaping unknown, stretching out before us, each possibility more daunting than the last. But the Mighty5 doesn't cower from challenges; we run headlong into them.

"OZ is out there, and we'll find him," I vow silently to myself, a promise that I'll keep searching until we have answers. For now, though, the immediate threat looms large and ominous. The storms are getting worse, a testament to the changes tearing through our planet.

We all continue to look at the weather wrapping the earth. "Look at them," I murmur, half to myself.

"Like a symphony written by a mad composer," comes Soren's response, their voice crackling with static.

"Or nature throwing a tantrum because we've been naughty children," Benny adds, finding humour where there seems to be none.

"Either way, it's a mess," quips Banksia.

"An artful mess," I counter, unwilling to let the dread claw its way back in. "We need to understand it, not just fear it."

"Understanding might be a stretch," says Juice, his tone grim. "Surviving is more like it."

"Survival's the baseline," I shoot back. "We aim higher."

The wind howls right outside my window, a banshee cry that joins the cacophony of our uncertain future. It pounds against the thick windows of the penthouse, demanding entry, but we are steadfast. The storms beyond are not just meteorological anomalies—they're the physical manifestation of our world's ache, the pain of progress gone awry.

"We've got to survive this upside-down river show," Juice points out, a note of concern lacing his usual bravado.

"Let's hunker down," I suggest. "Keep your comms open and stay safe. We'll ride this out together."

"Always," they chorus back, and despite everything, despite the monstrous sky and the missing pieces of our puzzle, I believe us. Together, we're the Mighty5, and we've got this.

"Hope's all we've got left," I whisper to the wins, though it's snatched away by the howling gales outside. Still, hope clings stubbornly within me, a flame refusing to be extinguished. It's the one thing this storm can't touch.

CHAPTER TWENTY-SIX

My fingers drum a staccato rhythm on the metal surface of the console, each tap echoing the tick-tock of impending disaster.

"Any word yet?" Juice asks guardedly, seeming not to really want to ask the question.

"Nothing," to the shimmering avatars of my team projected around me. "Not a blip, not a whisper."

"Odezza, we need to keep focused," Soren's image insists, their tone firm yet tinged with the same undercurrent of worry gnawing at my insides.

"Juice, any chance you can triangulate his last known coordinates?" I ask, turning towards our tech guru's image. His avatar is bent over a virtual keyboard, fingers dancing across keys that only he can see.

"Already on it," Juice replies without looking up. "But all we really have to go by is the TT he was on and his estimated arrival, which has not passed. Between those two points, it's simply like he vanished."

"How is that possible? Could the Elops be messing with signals?" Benny's question hangs between us, unanswered.

"Maybe," I concede, "we really don't know enough about

those damn things, but that doesn't explain why OZ or Amira haven't reached out. They know the drill. Comms is key."

"Speaking of drills," Banksia cuts in, her voice slicing through the tension, "we've got bigger fish to fry. That Japanese hole has almost closed, and our window to hit the Elops over Isla Santa Maria, Chile, could also be shrinking."

"So we know exactly where that is now? Not Punta Lavapie, but Isla Santa Maria?"

Banksia connects the dots. "Yes, it's just off the coast of Punta Lavapie, in Southern Chile.

"Right," I snap back into leader mode, pushing down the dread for OZ and Amira. "That's a good point about the Elops. We need to let OZ know about the change of plans. He shouldn't be meeting us in Japan. We need him to redirect to Chile."

"Agreed. Japan's off the table now," Juice finishes my thought, his Scandinavian lilt grim.

"Juice, blast a high-priority message to OZ's last comm link. Let him know we're rerouting to Isla Santa Maria in Chile. The last thing we need is him popping up at an old, dried-up Elops."

"Sending now," Juice confirms, and I imagine the digital waves piercing through the stratosphere, if they can even make it that far these days; searching for the man who once scoffed at the very tech that might save his life now.

"Alright, Mighty5," I declare, steeling myself against the silence that answers our call to OZ. "Let's prepare for Chile and keep hoping that OZ gets our message and Amira finds him wandering around the station."

"Hope is a luxury," Soren says softly, "but it's one we can afford. For now."

"Then let's not waste it," I reply.

We wrap for now, but I need a change of tactics and have

just the idea. Let's go fishing. Or at least send Juice on a fishing expedition.

"JUICE, WHAT DO YOU HAVE?" The digital labyrinth of Anthro-Tech unfolds before him like a neon-drenched spider-web, each strand pulsing with secrets meant for shadows. I can see he's in, slicing through their firewalls with the finesse of a surgeon and the ferocity of a storm. Code dances across the screen, a silent symphony to breach the unbreachable.

"Patience, O," Juice says, head down, in a pure state of concentration. "It's not like they exactly keep their dirt by the front door or send a note when they update their secret files. And what exactly should I be looking for?"

"Anything you can find on what Roman is currently up to," I blurt out. "Anything. Just— just find something juicy, Juice." Oh, I didn't just say that again, did I?

His fingers are a blur over the holographic keyboard. And then, buried beneath the clutter of corporate espionage and technological blueprints, he hit pay dirt.

"Got something — oh shit! Shit! Shit! Shit!" he mutters.

My heart quickens as I scan the notes popping to life.

He hesitates at first. "It looks like they knew OZ would be on the TerraTube to Next Tokyo. It's all here—dates, times, even his seat number."

"Impossible!" I feel like I was just hit by a TT. I can hardly breathe. "How did they tap into his schedule?"

"Better question," Juice interjects. "What else have they tapped?"

"Who knows? It could be everything or hardly anything. We have no way of knowing, do we?" I say flatly, the realisation dawning like a photovoltaic flare. "But what do they want from OZ?" I can't imagine he is on anyone's radar. It's been twenty years since he released the Oxolet and no one knows about the ClimaSphere.

"Well," Juice continues grimly, "it looks like they have OZ's comms, his personal logs. They've been shadowing him for days."

"Which means," I cut in, a steely resolve hardening my voice, "they're onto us too. We need to assume our plans are compromised."

"Then we change the game," Soren declares, already initiating the wipe sequence to cover our tracks. "We stay one step ahead."

"Good plan," Juice agrees.

"Wait a second," I cry out, watching the code flash by our eyes.

"Is that...?" Soren trails off, unable to finish the question hanging heavy in our virtual meeting space.

"OZ's Oxo2," Benny confirms, his usual playful tone now dipped in gravity. "They've got everything. Diagrams, codes, schematics, hell, even annotations in his handwriting."

"Roman's been playing us for fools," Banksia says, her avatar pulsing with contained rage.

"Focus," I snap, more harshly than intended. "We need to understand how this fits into their plans. How they intend to use the Oxo2. And is that really the reason they tapped OZ?"

"But OZ has nothing to do with cloning and next-gen robots," Juice sparks. "And we read Roman wants to go off.... wait...I think I've got it. We read he was heading to the Next Tokyo Elops, and we know he has a rocket on standby there, but with that Elops closing, he's panicking."

I see lots of nods.

Soren picks up where he left off, "and, without knowing exactly what Elops to get to next and not knowing if he and his team can even have a rocket at the ready, he is developing a contingency plan."

"He wants the Oxo2 to keep him—" Benny starts, but Banksia finishes his thought, "to keep his people alive until he can safely get off planet."

Stunned silence greets the holo space.

"Forgawdsake," I finally squeak out! "That bastard!"

"It seems Roman's got ambitions that stretch far beyond corporate greed," Soren adds.

"Then we top his plan," I say, forcing conviction into my voice. "We have to."

"Always one step ahead, right?" Juice grins wryly, but it doesn't reach his eyes. We all feel the weight of our newfound knowledge; it's a shadow looming over us, threatening to swallow us whole.

"Always," Soren echoes. They continue erasing our digital footprints from Anthro-Tech's servers. As if we were never there.

My voice trembles with determination as I urge my companions to stay alert and hidden from Roman. Our mission is clear: find my father, inform him of the situation, and share our revised plans for Chile and that secondary Elops.

But above all else, we ensure that Roman and his cronies can not intercept our messages. That is our top priority now. The thought of them developing their own Oxo2 fills me with dread and fuels my resolve to protect my father at all costs.

CHAPTER TWENTY-SEVEN

I try not to get sucked into the continual gloom of the outside world as I sit alone with my thoughts in our enormous lounge room.

My BTN casts an eerie glow on my furrowed brow as I scan through the latest NewsBlogs. "Forty-five centimetres," I mutter to myself, shaking my head in disbelief. Ica, a town that once cradled ancient mummies and whispered secrets of a bygone era, is now gasping under the weight of cascading waterfalls. Who would've thought? Penguins might have paddled there aeons ago, but today's deluge is no place for flightless birds.

"Freezing temps in Peru," I read with a shiver despite the cosiness of the flat. I am not oblivious to the irony as I huddle closer under my blanket. I spare a moment's thought for the sufferers, their lungs probably yearning for that parched air they once cursed.

I swipe left, and the BTN obliges with a sombre pirouette of pixels. Al-Kufrah now paints my screen—a tableau of snowy banks where sand dunes once stood sentry. "Fifty-two centimetres..." My voice trails off as I envision the oases, those desert lifelines, now unrecognisable amidst the flooding. Dates, peaches, apricots—I can almost taste their sweet memories, now just remnants beneath the icy grasp of change. The people, the animals—all scattered like seeds in the wind.

"Evacuated, all of them," I whisper to the silence of my desolate domicile. "Wise move." There's a tinge of respect in my tone, for the human spirit that endures, that adapts. But there's also a pang of loss—for the land that moulded their lives, for the certainty that crumbled like the desiccated earth they once trod upon.

'Adapt or perish,' Dad always says. He'd know; he's been swimming against the current longer than I've been alive. My DNA is woven with his tenacity, forming a tapestry of grit and wit. I suppose that's why I don't crumble at the prospect of our world turning aquatic. Instead, I smirk at the challenge, roll up my sleeves, and dive headfirst into the fray.

"Great, the globe's running on fumes," I scoff, adjusting the settings to conserve energy. "And here I am, plotting course corrections for humanity."

I lay back against the white plush cushions, my new Oxo2 glistening, feeling somewhat guilty about my one-of-a-kind lifesaver. My eyes glance up, tracing the light patterns on the ceiling, mapping out strategies and contingencies. "Hope's a tricky beast," I muse. "Gotta chase it without scaring it off."

My heart races as I continue to flic through the NewsBlogs, each headline forming a dreadful narrative of urgency and disaster. My mind reels at the news of the first Elops in Japan, a symbol of hope now snuffed out. Panic grips my chest as I watch footage of panicked crowds in the thousands, surging like frenzied swarms, their Oxolets blinking red with low-battery warnings or turning solid red, signalling their imminent demise. The sight sends chills down my spine.

While I scan the continuing NewsBlogs, I see that many heading for Japan are now changing course, joining the desperate throng headed towards Isla Santa Maria in Chile and Zanzibar in Tanzania. These two islands are now rapidly becoming lifelines for those escaping the chaos. I can't help but note that all three locations are islands - an interesting coincidence?

"Come on, come on," I mutter, tapping at my BTN, willing the images of people flailing to get back up and take another breath. But the stream of people is as erratic as the heartbeat of the world—flickering, failing.

Half the blogs are static, dead air where voices used to be. We're losing our narrators, the storytellers of our downfall, and camera ops, as the solar grid gasps its last breaths.

"Typical," I sneer, the paradox not lost on me. "The sun gives life, and now it takes it away."

"Focus, Odezza." My voice cuts through the silence of the penthouse, sharp and clear. There has to be a thread to follow, a pattern in the chaos. My father could see it, the order in the disorder. I need to get away from the doomsday visual and see what our lame government is saying, thinking, and doing.

Delving into the CG mainframe requires a certain finesse, a delicate touch amidst the digital anarchy. And there it is, something I had not seen when I last dived into this dark array of information and disinformation — a whisper among the screams, a rumour of salvation flickering in the outback of Northwest Australia. Could it be? A fourth Elops? Now that's a big island!

"Ha!" I bark out a laugh, a mix of triumph and disbelief. "What's one more miracle in a world gone mad?" Maybe it's a wild goose chase, or maybe it's the break we need. Either way, I'm all in. That gives us three choices now. Options are good.

"Game on," I announce to TiM, a grin splitting my face. This is it, the adventure calling my name, daring me to dive into the unknown. My heart races, ready for the challenge. Because if there's one thing I know about adventures, they don't come knocking politely. They roar up in a storm, demanding to be chased.

"Let's see what you're made of," I whisper to the phantom Elops. It's just me and the Mighty5 plotting a path through the tempest. "Let's plan to visit all three Elops; Chile, Tanzania and Australia if we need to," I tell myself. I can feel the cogs moving within my skull and can feel why they call it Temporal Overload - but it also feels good, plotting and planning.

I need to get the Mighty5 on the Holo and finish this with them. And look at that TT chart, as I know some of these Elop destinations aren't conveniently located directly above main TT hubs. We will have to take TT3s. Slower trains going around 3000 kph and probably even TT2s at their slower speed of 2,000 kph, and then from there, I can't even imagine how we will get to some of these destinations. But for now, I can tell I'm getting ahead of myself, thinking too much without the help of the team. I need to be pragmatic. Think through the plan and plan for the journey.

But then I realise, why am I looking at these newsfeeds, CG secrets and TT travel plans? I am woefully under-prepared. I need to do is find OZ, wrap my arms around him, tell him, as sappy as this may seem, that I love him and we need to all get to the task at hand! Saving the planet and the dwindling population that remains. Oh, and kick some Roman Polotov arse!

CHAPTER TWENTY-EIGHT

As the last specks of twilight fade from the skyline of a dystopian London, I swipe my hand through the air, summoning the familiar glow of our virtual meeting space. The HelloHolo's hum to life, connecting the dispersed members of the Mighty5. Soren's avatar pops up first, their smirk as audacious as ever, followed closely by Banksia's warm grin and Benny's earnest face. Juice joins last, his features drawn, tension etching lines into his brow.

"Hey," I begin, unable to mask the tremor in my voice. "Any word from OZ or Amira?" My heart hitches with hope, but their silence, palpable even through the holo screens, slices it to ribbons.

"We were going to ask you the same question," Juice kicks in.

Soren shakes their head, their expression grim. "Nothing. It's like they've vanished."

"Or thick air," Banksia quips, trying to inject some levity into the weighted air. But even her sunny disposition can't brighten the encroaching darkness of uncertainty.

I interject, eager to divert discussing the abyss of our

worries, "I've been scouring every news feed available. And let me tell you, this is Temporal Overload to the max." I force a chuckle, hoping it sounds more convincing than it feels.

"Speaking of TO," I remark, "what I wouldn't give for a cuppa Time-Traveller's Tea House brew right about now. A little sip of the past might do me some good."

The team laughs, a chorus of melancholy notes that still carry camaraderie's warmth. We're a family, bound not by blood but by purpose, and in moments like this, I feel it down to my bones.

"Though," I continue, "everything outside our little circle is falling apart. The feeds are half static, half despair. But here we are, fighting the good fight, right?"

"Always," Benny affirms, his voice steady.

"Right," Banksia echoes. But what else can we do but agree? To press forward is the only option we have.

"Alright, team," Soren chimes in, their tone all business now. "Let's buckle down and keep searching. They're out there somewhere. We just need to find them."

"Okay," I whisper, more to myself than to the others. "Let's get to work."

And with that, the Mighty5 dive back into the fray, each of us seeking answers in a world that seems increasingly devoid of them. Our avatars flicker with determination as we parse through the digital ether, hunting for any sign of our missing friends.

"Juice, you're awfully quiet," Soren observes. "What's brewing in that Scando-Baijan head of yours?"

"Something's not adding up with OZ's disappearance," he says, his avatar leaning closer as if to share a secret. "I've got this itch, right? And it's telling me to dig deeper." He flashes a grin that doesn't quite reach his eyes. "Gonna tap into Anthro-Tech again. They won't see me coming—not this time."

"Be careful," I warn. We can't afford to lose another one of us to their clutches.

"Always am," he retorts with false bravado.

"Let's hope they haven't upgraded their firewalls since last time," Soren mutters, scepticism lacing their tone.

"Trust me," Juice says. "I've updated our encryptions. There's no digital breadcrumb leading back to us, or for that matter, OZ's computer."

We all nod, but unease coils in my stomach. It's one thing to chase after phantoms; it's another to invite them into your home.

"Good," I say, swallowing the lump in my throat. "Let's get to work."

Juice's fingers dance across his holo-screen, a silent fugue of taps and swipes. Soren watches with hawk-like intensity, while Banksia takes notes, their face a mask of concentration. Benny paces within the confines of his avatar, unable to sit still even in virtual space.

The seconds stretch into minutes, which might not seem like much, but when you're looking for your dad, it feels like a lifetime of waiting.

Silence blankets us, heavy and expectant, as Juice's skills carve a path through electronic fortresses.

"Anything?" Banksia asks hesitantly, her voice a thread of sound in the void.

"Working on it," Juice mumbles. His physical intensity, palpable.

The tension ratchets tighter, anticipation and fear mingling in a toxic cocktail.

"Wait," Benny exclaims, his avatar freezing mid-pace. "There."

On the screen, a flicker of something—a clue, a ghost of a trace. But before we can grasp it, before we can shout victory, the unthinkable happens. The raw edge of tragedy slices through our ranks, and silence descends like the final curtain on a play whose ending we never wanted to see.

"Juice?" I whisper his name, more of an appeal than a question.

He doesn't answer.

"Juice!" This time it's Soren, panic edging their voice.

Still nothing.

"Anything?" I murmur, my voice barely a thread in the digital tapestry that connects us.

"Wait," Juice cuts in, his attention riveted to a cascade of images blitzing across his screen. "I'm onto something."

We huddle closer to our own displays, the silence stretching taut as a wire. The only sounds are the soft clacks of Juice's fingers dancing over the keys and the distant hum of the city outside, unaware of the drama unfolding within our midst.

"Talk to us, Juice," Soren insists, their tone tight with urgency.

"Top-secret footage," he says, breathless, as if he's run miles instead of sifting through data. "From the TT crash. There's so much here—it's like looking for a needle in a haystack made of needles."

"Juice, what exactly are you hunting for?" Banksia asks, her voice steady, but her brow furrowed in consternation.

There's a pause, heavy and expectant before Juice finally responds. "It's OZ. I've got this nagging suspicion that he was on that TT," he confesses, "the one that crashed."

It feels like the temperature just drops several degrees.

Every muscle in my body tenses, my breath catching in my throat. We exchange glances, each of us silently grappling with the indications. Juice continues to sift through the deluge of images, the tension among us rising with every second that passes.

"Find him, Juice," Benny says, his jovial facade slipping to reveal the steel beneath. "Find him."

Eyes glued to our screens, we watch as Juice combs through the chaos of the CCTV footage, a silent sentinel in search of the lost. Glimpses of lives, moments frozen in time, flit by in a relentless stream—a woman laughing, a child asleep, a couple arguing—all underpinned by the constant thrum of unknown peril. All playing out like an ancient silent movie.

"Come on, come on," I whisper, more to myself than Juice. The weight of hope and dread is tangible, pressing down on us with merciless gravity.

"Stop!" Benny exclaims suddenly, an uncharacteristic seriousness in his tone. He points to a screen where a solitary figure lounges, engrossed in a book.

"Is that—?" Soren begins, but they don't need to finish.

"OZ," I confirm, a lump forming in my throat as the image stabilises on the screen.

"Juice," Banksia says, "you found him."

There he is, just sitting there, reading his novel. OZ always found comfort in the classics, a stark contrast to the high-tech world he helped create. The way he sits amidst a sea of futuristic chaos is almost comical, lost in Jules Verne's Journey to the Centre of the Earth. In another life, he'd be chuckling at the irony.

We watch, captivated. There's something tragically serene about seeing OZ in his element, oblivious to the turmoil surrounding him. It's as if he's found a pocket of peace in a world hurtling towards doom—a peace we are desperate to preserve.

"Look at him," Banksia whispers, her voice tinged with reverence. "Even now, he's teaching us. Escape when you can, where you can—even if it's just in your mind."

"Always the dreamer," Soren adds softly, their avatar giving a sad smile that reflects her real-life counterpart.

"Guys," Juice says, his hands still but his avatar's eyes sharp and searching. "There's more here. We have to keep watching."

"OZ—" My voice cracks, betraying the turmoil within. A hero in repose, a visionary caught in a snapshot of normalcy that belies the darkness creeping ever closer.

The room falls silent. The only sounds are the faint whirring of TiM's servos and the muted shuffle of our own breaths. We stand together, united not just by our mission but by the raw, unspoken grief that threatens to overwhelm us.

"It's getting fuzzy. Play it through," I finally say, the command barely a whisper.

The footage blurs into focus, and the collective breath of the Mighty5 catches in a silent gasp. Tension coils in the virtual space where our avatars stand shoulder to shoulder, eyes riveted on the scene unfolding before us.

"Wait," Benny murmurs, his avatar pointing with a shaky hand toward the train aisle. "Who are they?"

Six figures emerge from the scrolling blur of passengers, their movements deliberate, cutting through the crowd like sharks through water. They're heading somewhere with purpose, with intent. Our eyes track their progress, narrowing as they converge upon one man—OZ, oblivious, lost in his paperback.

"Something's wrong," I say, my voice barely above a whisper. Logic wars with dread in my mind—this can't be right.

"Juice, can you enhance this?" Soren's voice is steady, but I can hear the undercurrent of urgency.

"Working on it," Juice replies, fingers washing over his controls. The image sharpens, bringing the group into clearer view, but the lack of sound turns their approach into a silent nightmare.

"Here we go," Banksia says, her words tight with tension.

The six moving figures terminate at OZ. In seconds, their

hands are on him. No warning, no conversation—just sudden, violent movement. The attack is swift, brutal, and we can only watch, powerless, as OZ tries to fend them off. But he's no fighter.

"What's going on? Why are they attacking him?" my voice cracks, the strain of witnessing my father in peril cuts deep. The rest of the team is equally shaken, the camaraderie that usually fills our conversations replaced with a palpable sense of fear.

"Can't tell..." Juice trails off, his avatar frowning in concentration. We watch, hearts hammering, as the fight escalates. OZ faces outnumbered opponents but is not outmatched.

"Come on, OZ," I stammer, as if my words could somehow reach back through time and space to lend him strength.

"Guys, look at his stance—did he know this was coming?" Soren analyses, their sharp mind dissecting the scene even as their voice wavers.

"Knew what was coming?" Banksia asks, her gaze never leaving the holo.

"Whatever it is, he's fighting like hell to stop it," I reply, feeling the helplessness settle like lead in my stomach.

"Keep watching," Juice commands, though none of us needs the reminder.

Our avatars stand frozen, a digital vigil for a man caught in a struggle we can not comprehend, trapped within a moment we can not alter. The weight of what we're witnessing presses down on us.

We are the Mighty5, a team bound by intellect, adventure, and now, collective heartbreak. As we watch in horror, the vibrant tapestry of our friendship frays, thread by thread, with each blow that falls upon OZ.

"OZ—" I whisper again, the name a plea, a lament, as we

witness the impossible. My hands clenched into fists at my sides.

The scene continues to play out, an unwelcome odyssey that we're helpless to stop. And as the final frames stutter and vaporises to black, our connection does more than falter—it shatters. We are left adrift in a sea of shock and silence, our mission, our hope, eclipsed by the raw reality of loss.

We are all glued to our collective screens. Mesmerised. Disturbed. Appalled.

At that exact moment, my BTN flashes at me. I have an incoming HoloMessage from Amira. "Right now?" I say out loud.

"What's happening, Dezzy?" Benny asks quickly.

"Juice, can you put that on pause? Amira is calling in — finally."

I can see Juice trying to no avail.

"Hi Amira," I finally answer, "kinda busy watching some footage of OZ on a TT with some thugs. "What's going on?"

Amira shares with the team that she was really sorry for not having found my dad and even more sorry for not getting back to me sooner. I try to listen to her but watch the screen that Juice can't pause, looking at the most dreadful scenario unfolding before our very eyes.

As Amira continues her story, I don't have the heart to cut her off. Meanwhile, my mind is racing as I see what seems to be a metal case under Dad's seat on the train? We all watch as OZ grabs it like it were the most valuable thing on the planet, which I'm guessing it is. Given the case size, I guess it contains the ClimaSphere.

Our eyes are glued to the screen while I still can't seem to hang up on Amira's long-winded, yet ever so polite story of how many times she had gone to the main TT terminus in Next Tokyo. This is all too much for my head to take.

As we look, we see my dad's assailants are all wearing

uniforms. Juice is seeing the same thing and although he can't pause, he can zoom in. And there it is, stark against the fabric —the Anthro-Tech emblem emblazoned on the attackers' tops. A chill runs down my spine.

"Amira, I hate to cut you off, but I must run. Thanks for everything. Chat soon." I feel rude after all her help, but forgawdsake. What's going on here?

"Anthro-Tech? But why?" Benny picks up where my brain left off. The question hangs in the air, mingling with the collective disbelief. His avatar, normally the epitome of cool, now mirrors our shared confusion.

"Whatever it is, he's fighting like hell to stop it," I reply, feeling the helplessness settle like lead in my stomach.

Our avatars stand frozen, a digital vigil for a man caught in a struggle we can't comprehend, trapped within a moment we can't alter. The weight of what we're seeing presses down on us, and we lose our usual witty banter, replaced by a shared grief that no words can bridge. We are completely helpless; a foreign place for all of us.

We are the Mighty5, a team bound by intellect, adventure, and now, a collective heartbreak. As we watch in horror, the vibrant tapestry of our friendship frays, thread by thread, with each blow that falls upon OZ.

There he is—Dad is, locked in combat, his motions desperate, protective. His focus never wavers from the metal case, the object of this violent tug-of-war. And then a chilling moment unfolds before our eyes. A man breaks free from the scuffle, grabbing his Oxo2 clean off his wrist.

"Noooooo!" I gasp, the warning useless as it escapes my lips.

But time, cruel, refuses to heed my pleas. The gunshot echoes silently through our shared imaginations, an invisible shockwave that shatters our resolve. OZ stumbles backwards, a look of surprise etched on his face that mirrors our own disbelief.

As the one person walks away with the prized Oxo2, looking like they've stolen the Crown Jewels. "Someone else is pulling a gun and aiming at — from down the—d" Benny starts, but his words are cut off by the abrupt static that fills our vision.

The screens crackle, lines of interference dance wildly; a maddening cacophony of pixels that robs us of sight. The cacophony crescendos, a visual scream, and then... darkness.

"Juice—" I breathe out, "what happened to the feed?"

Silence blankets our group, thick and suffocating. It's a silence filled with things unsaid, futures unmade, and dreams undone. We stand, or rather, our avatars do, in stunned still-ness, the distance between us now feeling insurmountable.

"Did they just—?" Banksia's voice trails off, unable to finish the thought, unwilling to give it life.

"Is he—" Soren can't complete the question either; the possibilities are too grim, the implications too dire.

"Can anyone rewind? Enhance?" Benny implores, grasping for any thread of denial that might unravel the tapestry of tragedy before us.

"Nothing left to see," Juice replies, his voice hollow, the usual mischief snuffed out.

"Anthro-Tech — why?" I murmur, my mind grappling with the scene we've just witnessed. But deep down, I know. It's always been about control, about power. And OZ, the thorn in their side, held something they wanted. Something worth killing for. And not the ClimaSphere. They must not have understood he was carrying such a lifesaver. His Oxo2.

"OZ—" Banksia whispers once more, her avatar slumping as if the weight of our collective grief has finally become too much to bear.

"OZ—" I echo, letting the name hang in the air, a tribute.

"Turn it off," I snap at Juice, "turn off that gawddamn static! What just happened? What did we just witness?

"Was all that for real?" I beg.

Our eyes remain locked on the HelloHolo's flickering light, the afterimage of the chaos we've just witnessed burning behind our retinas. No one dares to speak; the silence is a vacuum, sucking away the remnants of bravado that usually defines the Mighty5. We're scattered across the globe, but in this virtual space, distance means nothing.

I feel the weight of everyone's stare from the square on my screen. I can imagine their thoughts, believing that no sixteen-year-old should be exposed to such turmoil. The shadow of my loss, our loss, sits heavily in my eyes that are typically filled with scientific curiosity.

Benny's brows are knitted together, his usual amiable smile replaced by a tight line of concern. Juice's avatar is static, but I can sense his mind whirring, trying to make sense of the impossible. Banksia's face is a mask of stoicism, but even she can't hide the tremble in her lip. And Soren, they just seem to be numb.

We're about to disconnect, to retreat into our own corners of grief, when Soren's holo blinks with an incoming transmission. The CG emblem—ominous in its simplicity—flashes before it opens into a memo. We lean closer as if proximity could lend clarity to the confusion.

"Roman—dead?" Soren's voice cuts through the stillness. More statement than question. The CG memo claims Roman perished in that same Next Tokyo-bound TT crash, but we know better. Propaganda, that's all it is. A story spun for those who don't know to look closer.

"Can't be," Banksia chimes in. "We saw it with our own eyes. The fight. Roman wasn't even close by, but I'm guessing he is not the type to shy away from the action."

"Right," Benny's nod is almost imperceptible.

"Could be a cover-up," I suggest, my mind racing. "Throw us off the scent."

"Or to incite fear," Juice adds. "Classic CG move."

"Roman wasn't on that TerraTube," Banksia asserts, sharpening her words. "The thugs—those Anthro-Tech's henchmen. They were there for one thing: the Oxo2."

I lean forward, gripping the edge of my desk as if it could tether me to this reality. "But why cut the feed? Why then?" I press, needing answers more than oxygen.

"Because," Soren proceeds, their theory slicing through the fog of disbelief, "a bullet fired in a TT at those speeds... It's a death sentence. The whole thing would be an instant disaster —"

"Like the old jets before the BoldWar," Juice picks up, his face ghost-pale. "A complete and utter annihilation."

Benny's fist clenches visibly, and Banksia whispers something that sounds like an invocation. We're a crew adrift in an ocean of unanswered questions and dawning horror.

"OZ—" I can't finish; his name is a boulder in my throat.

"Was he protecting the Oxo2 from them?" Soren's voice is a scalpel, cutting to the heart of it all.

"Must have been, even though at first it looked like he thought they were after his metal case and the ClimaSphere," Benny growls, the fire we know so well flickering behind his eyes. "They knew. Roman knew OZ had an updated Oxolet."

"Which means they'll be coming for us next," Banksia adds, her voice steady but her eyes betraying the storm within.

"Assuming he knows, OZ often built a backup. We'll be ready," I declare, the words tasting like ash. There's no going back now, no unseeing the truths we've uncovered.

Their nods are solemn, an unspoken vow passing between us. We have suddenly become the keepers of OZ's legacy, the guardians of a secret that could either save or doom us all.

But as the conversation dwindles and the weight of our

new reality settles heavily on my shoulders, I reach out and flic off my Holo. Darkness engulfs the room, punctuated only by TiM's soft whirring beside me.

"OZ—" My whisper is a surrender to the void.

TiM nudges against my leg. His sensors dimmed to a comforting glow. I sink to the floor, the cold concrete leaching the warmth from my skin. Surrounded by complete darkness, I surrender—a sob convulsing my body, echoing through the stillness.

He's gone. The man who was my anchor in this tumultuous sea of chaos—my father, my mentor. Gone.

My tears fall uncontrollably, a torrent of emotions that I can no longer contain. My spirit is broken, and the weight of our failure weighs heavily, like a shroud of guilt. The once powerful Mighty5 is now reduced to mere shells of our former selves. And yet, we must press on. We must continue his journey and his optimism, even though it feels futile at this moment.

But how can we move forward without him? How can we face the unknown trials ahead while still mourning the loss of our leader? Time will continue to march on, indifferent to our pain and grief. However, tonight, we have no choice but to rely on each other for comfort as we navigate conflicting emotions and uncertain futures.

CHAPTER TWENTY-NINE

I can't bring myself to leave my bedroom this morning. The emptiness feels suffocating, a constant reminder of all I have lost. OZ was more than just my dad. He was my mentor and my companion in every aspect of life - from taking me on my first AeroCar ride when I was two, and sharing the fundamentals of science, to our faux breakfasts together and sipping our Old English tea. Losing him feels like losing my best friend, leaving me with a gaping void that I'm not sure how to fill. I know I need time alone to mourn, but I also can't bear the thought of being left alone with my thoughts.

Suddenly, a sharp and unexpected chime jolts me back to reality as a HoloNote pings in on my BTN. I rarely receive these messages, so its arrival catches me off guard. The sound echoes around my room. The baron walls and the ultra-high ceilings and windows reverberate in my ears, causing temporary disorientation before I refocus my attention on the device on my right wrist hand.

As I open it, I see it's from— "It's from Dad," I whisper and gasp. There is a note.

"Odezza, my precious daughter, if you are reading this, it

means that I am no longer alive. My heart aches at the thought of leaving you behind, but I have prepared for this moment. I synchronised my Oxo2 and BTN to trigger a message after 48-hours of the Oxo2s failure. I will always love you. Now our family legacy must continue with you. Stay strong, honey, and never forget the love that binds us together."

My heart aches as I read the words in front of me. Despite TiM's comforting presence by my side, I can't hold back the tears. How could this have happened? I can't decide whether to stay and read my dad's note and face the reality of his death, or run away without ever looking back. Sadly, I can't escape the pain and confusion that consumed me. So I choose the former and read on—

To My Starlit Daughter,
In the silent lab, my final words are penned;
A love in formulas, from a father and friend.

Our bond, deeper than genes, could ever say,
In each discovery, you were the light of my day.

Bright as a star, my guide through the night,
We spoke in science, a bond so right.

Now, I'm a whisper, but remember our time,
Our lives entwined in rhythm and rhyme.

I leave you my legacy, in every lab's part,
In each trial and error, you'll find my
heart.

Look to the stars, there's no need to roam,
In the cosmos above, you'll always find
home.

My essence remains: in the science we adore,
I'm the constant in your heart, forevermore.

Keep changing the world, let your dreams
soar,
My love is the beacon, now and evermore.

Farewell, Dessa, in time's grand design,
Our love, the prime constant, eternally
entwined.

With all my essence,
Your partner in tea. It's always been you
and me.
Your Pal. Your Dad.

CHAPTER THIRTY

Slouched against the plush white cushions of the main living suite, I flic on the HelloHolo. Holographic team members pop in—Soren's furrowed brow, Benny's half-grin, Juice's smirk. Even Banksia's eyes are alight with a mix of determination and anxiety.

"Alright, team—" I start, my voice slicing through the static silence, "—we're off to Santiago, Chile. We're not packing for a picnic, so only one rucksack each."

"And space-saving snacks only," Soren chimes in, "Dried fruit, nuts, those protein blocks that taste like cardboard."

"Well," Banksia slides in, "I've also made a quick list of food. Can anyone get these at their individual locations before you leave for your TT?"

With an instant frown, Juice retorts, "This'll be good—pray tell."

"Well, I did some quick research and yes, we can get food on any of the four types of TTs we'll be taking, but I thought we'd also need more."

"We need nutrient-packs that are travel-friendly, perfect

for our global escapades, oh," she interrupts herself, "and don't forget to bring your warmest, most waterproof slickers."

"Really Mum?!" Soren snarks.

"Okay, where was I?" Has she lost her mind?

"Yes." She has apparently remembered her mind-thread. "Quantum Quinoa Bars," she begins. I've never had these, but if memory serves, they synthesise these bars in quantum food labs for perfectly balanced nutrition. Each bar contains faux quinoa, chia seeds, and spirulina. They're compact and light-weight. Good start, Banksia.

"And NanoFruit Spheres," she continues. Yum, These I've had. Their tiny, gelatinous orbs that burst with flavour when you pop them in your mouth. I read scientists engineer them to provide essential vitamins and antioxidants. "They come in Nebula Berry, Solar Citrus, and Wormhole Watermelon, so order what you can, but make it fast."

And Hydro-Grown Algae Chips she tells the team. These I've had too. They're like a potato chip - which we have only heard of. These are algae crisps that are cultivated underwater in floating algae farms. Banksia has certainly done her home-work. These guilt-free snacks pack omega-3s, chlorophyll, and a touch of bioluminescence, so they look as good as they taste.

Banksia has even more thoughts, as she spills out, "and don't forget Syntho-Nuts and Vita-Gel Capsules." Okay, also good choices.

Syntho-Nuts are like crunchy 3D-printed morsels from sustainable protein matrices. I think I've had the Neutron Nut, and Electron Almond. They're interesting as they require no chewing, thanks to nano-digestion. And Vita-Gel Capsules are translucent capsules containing a week's worth of nutrients compressed into a single dose. All we have to do is swallow one Vita-Gel Capsule with a sip of antimatter-infused water, and we'll be set for a while.

"Well done, Banksia," I say with an abundant amount of pride.

"Hey, that's a helpful list. We won't starve," Benny interjects, his tone light. "And pack light, right? Just essentials?"

"Exactly," I nod, feeling the weight of our task. Only what we can carry on our backs as we venture to save a world shrouded in perpetual rain-soaked twilight.

"Routes?" Juice asks, snapping us back to the present.

Banksia proceeds, "I'm currently in Doha." Man, this chick moves around a lot. "I have to route through Abuja, Nigeria. I've never been before, so—"

"Paris to Praia, Portugal," Soren cuts her off impatiently, brushing a lock of hair from their face with a grace that seems out of place in our dystopian setting. "Then straight under to Chile."

"Rabat's my current STAC," Benny says, his compact frame somehow conveying readiness even through the hologram. "Praia for me too, then joining you all in Santiago."

"Juice?" Benny asks with the usual TiM-style cock of the head.

"I'm coming from the Maldives Floating City and I have to go through Lagos, Nigeria."

I pick up the thread. "I'm tunnelling in from London, obviously," trying desperately to ignore the flutter in my stomach at the thought of the trip. Without OZ. "This is my first time on the TT. Should be a thrill. I'll be joining everyone via Caracas, Venezuela."

"Thrill is one word for it," Juice says, a wry twist to his lips hinting at stories untold. "Just wait 'til you hit 4,000 killomeres an hour."

"Can't wait." I mutter, more to myself than anyone else, the sarcasm lost in the whirl of emotions.

Juice continues, "then there's the rest of the trip. First, we will head down from Santiago on the TT3 down to Los Angeles. That's only 3,000 km an hour, so much slower."

Slower?

"Remember," I add, trying to bolster the group's spirits, "it's about getting to Los Angeles together." There's a chorus of affirmations, each of us silently acknowledging the weight on our shoulders.

I glance at my lonely LunaRed TravelAll rucksack, packed and ready. It's just me, my bag, and the ClimaSphere safely encased in a titanium carry case. With a deep breath, "see you all tomorrow in Santiago."

"Safe travels, Mighty5," Soren says softly, their image winking out first, followed by the others, until only the quiet hum of my flat remains.

"BON VOYAGE," I whisper down to TiM. "I will be back soon, okay boy." Hoping my promise to him is a truism.

I scratch his cold metal posterior. The tiny TM, Trade-Mark symbol is still on there from the day OZ brought him home for me. I was four. Dad asked me to name the Robo-Pup. I was only just learning to read. I thought his name was TM and pronounced Tim. I still recall OZ laughing, but not understanding why. It's funny now, but not when you're four.

TiM looks up at me, acknowledging that my salutation is genuine, though not comprehending the fear in my voice.

"Here's to bringing back the sun," I murmur, grabbing the handle of the titanium case and my LunaRed TravelAll rucksack. It's time to face the storm, to brave the wilds of this fractured earth. For dad, for us, for the flickering hope of sunlight on the other side.

The front doors close with a hiss. I plummet down the side of the building. Let the saving of the world begin.

The RedEl floats beneath me, its suspension silent against the storm's tantrums. London sprawls below like a brooding beast, shrouded in rainstorms and regret. I clutch my rucksack to my chest, the other hand cradling the ClimaSphere.

Not long after boarding— "Next stop: Triple Tee," the automated voice cuts through the hum of the bus, indifferent to the gravity of my mission. The station looms ahead, a cathedral of steel and glass amidst the ruins of old-world charm. My heart hammers against my ribcage as if trying to keep pace with the thoughts racing through my mind. This is it—the leap into the unknown.

Stepping off the RedEl, the chill bites at my cheeks, a stark contrast to the artificial warmth that awaits within Kings Cross TT Terminal, the Triple tee. The station swallows me whole, a futuristic belly gleaming with holographic ads and the soft glow of bioluminescent lighting. People bustle around, their faces etched with the same determination that fuels my steps. We're all chasing something—maybe redemption, maybe escape, could be desperation.

My EstateTrackBoot's stomp on the polished concrete floor, each step a drumbeat counting down to departures.

The TT beckons, its sleek form promising speed beyond comprehension. I've studied the specs, know the science behind the marvel, but the reality is daunting. This isn't just about velocity; it's about vaulting over the chasm left by Dad's absence.

"First time on a TT?" The question comes from a fellow traveller hurrying by me. A pale skinned woman in her forties. Her eyes were kind and curious. "You won't notice the speed, as you won't be able to see outside to see how fast you're really moving," she adds.

Well, that's a tad odd. No windows.

"Is it that obvious?" I manage a half-smile, feeling the tremor in my fingers as I adjust my rucksack strap.

"Only to an old pro like me," she chuckles, then winks before merging back into the flow of the crowd. I wish her words could steady the flutter in my stomach, the gnawing anxiety that nibbles at my resolve.

"Odezza," I whisper to myself, channelling my dad's inner spirit, hoping it will summon some coating of his courage, "you were born for this."

But am I? My pep talk with myself didn't last long.

Beyond the TT's promise of comfort and speed, I steel myself, setting my jaw. There's no room for doubt when the stakes are this high—not when the Mighty5 count on me, not when every breath of wind howls for salvation.

"Time to shine, girl," I say, stepping toward the platform. My first TT awaits, and so does destiny. Dad always said, "great leaps are made by those willing to take them."

Well, OZ, I'm leaping.

Gleaming like a metallic serpent, the TerraTube stretches before me, its sleek lines promising unfathomable speed. I hoist my rucksack higher onto my back and approach with reverence the titanium case containing Dad's proto ClimaSphere clutched in my other hand.

"Boarding for Caracas," drones an automated voice, emotionless, as if it's announcing a schedule rather than a leap into the future. My ticket automatically pops up on my BTN and activates with a blip of acknowledgement from the transparent aluminium ticket reader interface.

The doors part with a hush, beckoning me inside.

As I step aboard, I am greeted into a whole new world. The interior is a sleek capsule of purpose; seats moulded to embrace passengers, seemingly not attached to the floor of the TT, but suspended, levitating, consoles aglow with soft light – all designed to cocoon us from the reality of the velocity we're about to endure.

I find my place, heart thrumming in tandem with the hum

of the TT powering up. It's a lullaby for the brave, or perhaps a prelude to a storm.

The walls are a crisp, immaculate white, like some type of hard enamel, punctuated with hidden strips of soft blue recessed lighting. The furnishings and decor are sleek and modern, unlike anything I have ever seen before. It all feels unreal, like something in a futuristic PeterG movie set.

"Secure your belongings, please," instructs the invisible robo-voice. I tether my rucksack to the seat, the titanium case snug between my feet. "Please prepare for your passage."

"Ready as I'll ever be," I mutter, the words escaping into the charged silence.

Then it begins. My gut wrenches under the pain of last seeing OZ on a train just like this. My heart is so broken. But I am English forgawdsake; suck it up, chin up, spirits up, shut up!

Acceleration seizes us, a titan's hand propelling us forward. My breath catches. We are a bullet fired from the chamber of human ingenuity, piercing through the belly of the North Atlantic Ocean.

The pressure mounts, an insistent whisper at first, then a crescendo presses me deep into my floating seat. But there's a whisper of wonder beneath the roar and the rush.

An hour and a half later – the span of a movie – now the measure of distance between continents. Time wraps around me, a bubble of anticipation. I close my eyes, feeling the superficial vibrations sing through my bones, and imagine swimming through the currents far above, free and relentless.

The sense of smoothness is unreal. I have experienced nothing quite like it before. Although the holo windows take me a minute to get used to. That woman was right. We are so far underground, under the ocean, that there is no need for windows. From what I'd read in preparation for this trip, windows would make a weak point in the train's structure, if you can call this a train.

A robo-cart stops by twice on this brief trip. I let it pass and dig into my rucksack for a Vita-Gel Capsule. That should keep me going for a while. I am thankful Banksia had done her homework and my stash arrived before I left the flat.

When the deceleration tugs gently at my senses, announcing our arrival, it's almost a disappointment. Almost.

Caracas greets me with the Libertador Simón Bolívar Railway Station, a cathedral of transit. As I depart the TT and rise from the depths of the station on perhaps the steepest escalator I've ever ridden, light pours through its immense stained glass veins, reflecting off highly polished alloy, casting prisms on the stunning marble floors. The architecture here sings of progress, of humanity reaching skyward despite the earth's turmoil. I step off the escalator, the cool air a contrast to the heated pulse of travel still resonating within me.

I pause, taking it in. This is no King's Cross; it's something else entirely – a monument to what we can achieve when the world demands it. And the world has demanded much from us over the past twenty years. I adjust my grip on the titanium case, its contents suddenly heavier with responsibility.

This is the largest TT terminal in what is now the capital of the seven South American cantons.

"Next stop, Chile," I remind myself, a mantra to propel me onward.

Switching trains becomes a dance amid the grandeur, each step a note in the harmony of movement that surrounds me. Bodies blur past, a myriad of lives intersecting momentarily with mine. We're all hurtling toward different destinies, yet for a fleeting moment, we share the same path.

"Keep moving," my inner voice chides, commanding focus. "There's work to be done."

The TT3 carriage seals with a hiss, a cocoon of sleek

design. I settle into the contour-hugging seat as it moulds to my frame, the familiar grip of my rucksack nestled between my legs. Not the same levitating seats we enjoyed on the last train from London, but still comfy.

The train surges forward, lurching me into the unknown at 3,000 kilometres per hour—I'm not sure I can tell the difference. All I know is the shorter the run, the slower the train. The word slower seems to be relative at these speeds. But again, if I wasn't told the train was going this fast, I really don't think I could tell. These really are a marvel and to think this global network of trains and tubes was all built around the same time as the BoldWar. A testament to mankind's colab under the toughest of times. Robots started the entire system, but it had to be finished the old-fashioned way, by humans. It was a promise of a world to come as the governments of the world had shut down air travel. They deemed air travel as a pollutant versus the TT system, which was faster than any plane could ever hope to be and solely ran off the solar grid. However, I noticed many of the TTs, TT3s, and TT2 lines starting at King's Cross had 'CLOSED' signs at their gates and I have just noticed the same situation in Caracas. A bad sign the grid is continuing to fail on a global level. We really couldn't have waited any longer to start this journey and reverse all that Roman had started.

Around me, the world is in motion but oddly static; passengers are locked into their own orbits. A woman taps incessantly on her holo-screen and a child giggles at something flickering in their retinal projector. Those are really new. I don't even have one yet.

The air is thick with the sterile scent of metallised recycled air, mingled with the cloying sweetness of someone's overpowering perfume. I reach for my PRLZ, pop them around my ears and flic on my BTN, settling back in my seat.

The low hum of ECHO music fills my mind, providing a

calming background to my much-needed rest. As I closed my eyes, I could feel the weight of exhaustion lifting from my body. The world outside may be chaotic, but at this moment, I welcomed the tranquillity of my safe little bubble.

"Próxima parada (next stop), Santiago, Chile," the AI conductor purrs, its voice a soothing balm for travel-jangled nerves. Seventy-five minutes to the rendezvous—the thought sends an electric shiver down my spine and I'm asleep in a quadrillionth of a second.

I WAKE WITH A START! Santiago station looms, a hive buzzing with anticipation. I step off the train and head up one level to our designated meeting spot. And there they are, my fellow engineers of salvation, the Mighty5, assembled for the first time in the flesh.

We're a patchwork quilt of humanity, stitched together by necessity and the faint pulse of hope.

Juice towers above us, his height a SkyRiser among bungalows. Oh, wow, I notice he has a mechanical left leg, a marvel of engineering I had not known about. It whirs softly as he shifts his weight. It's a symphony of carbon fibre and hydraulics, a testament to human resilience—or stubbornness, depending on who you ask.

Then there's Soren, whose mere presence seems to still the air. Ambiguous beauty radiates from Soren, drawing curious glances that linger a moment too long. In a world craving definition, Soren defies it, a comet streaking across the dusk of our norms.

Beside them, Banksia seems almost ethereal, her slight frame defying the gravity of our situation. She moves with grace, a reed in the wind, yet her eyes hold the steel of someone who has weathered storms.

Benny, compact and powerful, stands with the assurance of a man accustomed to being underestimated. Muscle bundles under his shirt like coiled springs, ready to unleash. He is short, yes, but built like he could go fifteen rounds in a ring—and probably win most of them or be in a rugby scrum.

"Odezza," Juice booms, his deep Scandinavian voice echoing off the high ceilings. It's still strange to look at someone who is clearly Azerbaijani, but with that Scando-Baijan accent. "The prodigy herself."

"Prodigy? More like work in progress," I quip, unable to suppress a smile despite the sombre task ahead.

We exchange no handshakes, no hugs—such things feel trivial when the sky itself is our enemy. But our eyes speak volumes: determination, fear, camaraderie.

We spend a few moments in awe, simply looking at each other, taking each other in. The HelloHolo had done our group an injustice. We are truly a force to be reckoned with, and it feels astonishing to finally meet. We have much to catch up on, but we can do it on the next leg of our journey.

"Alright, Mighty5," I begin, our codename feeling more real now than ever before, "let's book it to the platform, save the world." The weight of our mission feels tangible as I should my rucksack with a grunt, as though I'm carrying more than just essentials.

I am a tad sad not to get outside the station and check out Santiago as I have only ever heard amazing things. Super modern SkyRisers are surrounded by sun-kissed hills and snow-capped mountains in the distance. Well, probably not sun-kissed anymore, so I leave my sightseeing daydream alone for now and keep on moving.

"Lead the way, Odezza," Soren says. Their voice is calm in the tempest of my thoughts.

"TT3 this way," Banksia chimes in, squinting at the signs

above us. Her fingers dance over her BNT, pulling up schematics like she's hacking the very air we breathe.

"Keep pace, everyone," Juice commands, his mechanical leg whirring softly. His towering frame cuts through the crowd, parting it like some ancient sea.

"Feels like we're headed to the centre of the Earth," Benny quips, his eyes twinkling with that infectious humour I expect from him. He's right. The descent to the platform is steep, an angular wound in the city's underbelly.

The TT3 station unfurls before us—a cavernous space pulsing with the heartbeat of Santiago. Glass and a palladium arch overhead, a testament to the will to endure. Our footsteps echo, joining the cacophony of sounds: the distant hum of trains, the murmur of travellers, the subtle vibrations of a world on the move.

"Ever think we'd end up here?" Banksia asks, "together," tilting her head back to take it all in.

"Never," I admit. "But then, I never thought I'd be trying to reverse-engineer the sky."

"Speaking of which," Juice nods toward my titanium carrier, "that ClimaSphere proto had better work miracles, kid."

"It will," I say, but it's more hope than certainty. A gamble against the odds. I just need to figure out the codeword, which so far has eluded me. What was OZ thinking putting such a failsafe on this proto? It seems he never thought I or the Mighty5 would find it or need it.

"Seventy-five minutes to Los Ángeles," Soren notes, checking the time. "Can we sync our BTN-watches?"

"Synced," Benny confirms, tapping his own device.

"Then let's not waste another second," I say, stepping onto the platform where our ride awaits—the sleek, bronze bullet of a train designed to shoot us under the spine of this fascinating country. I notice the Chilean flag on the side of the bronze beast. The flag comprises two equal-height horizontal bands of white and red, with a blue square the same height as the white band in the canton, which bears a white five-pointed star in the centre. "I don't think I'm in the UK anymore, Toto," I say under my breath, an expression I picked up from OZ, or at least my version.

"Here goes everything," I mutter, feeling the familiar flutter of nerves. But as I glance at my companions, their faces set with resolve, I find a steely determination within myself. This motley crew, the Mighty5, together for the first time, ready to brave the unknown.

CHAPTER THIRTY-ONE

We zip up our bags, the collective whirring of zippers sealing fate. There's a thrum in the air, a vibration of adventure that sets my heart in a staccato beat. I sling my pack over my shoulder and grab the titanium lifesaving case. Banksia, Juice, Soren, and Benny are all geared up, their faces etched with commitment and determination.

"TT3's ready to roll," announces Soren. We nod, a silent pact forming as we step onto the new train, sleek and silver, like a sleek rocket destined for liberation.

"I'm excited to see Los Ángeles," says Benny. Not the city of angels we know from tales of old, but a beacon in Chile's BíoBío Region. We settle into our seats, the plush cushions a stark contrast to the chaos of the world outside we have been travelling below.

The TT3 heaves forward, accelerating at a blinding pace. My stomach lags for a moment before catching up with the rest of me, hurtling through landscapes transformed by nature's relentless hand. Santiago's urban sprawl quickly fades into memory.

We can 'see' the majesty of the Andes, an omnipresent

backdrop painted with the purest snow. A lot of snow. But the windows we are looking through aren't windows at all - they are ultra thin flexible and rollable transparent monitors. I only know this because I just saw an ad for this tech on one of the London SkyRisers. The 'windows' on the train show the outside world in staggering detail; thanks to hundreds of 22K cameras seamlessly attached to the outer belly of the train. And when we dive underground or under vast oceans, it replicates the area above us. Like a show. That tech I don't get, but I know OZ would have loved all this.

"Look at that," murmurs Juice, gazing at the monitors. We all take a gander. The once-thriving vineyards roll by, dormant fields promising resurrection beneath the deluge. "I bet those used to be amazing vines."

Banksia, her gaze following the trails of water that surge along the paths of rivers and streams, swelling with purpose and power, "so sad."

Forests of pine rise like emerald spires, piercing the grey veil of the sky. The train, a vessel of progress, glides alongside the untamed wilderness. Could it really look like that outside? The land is alive but on the edge, breathing in tumultuous gasps as we streak past hamlets where life clings to normalcy, lights flickering defiantly against the encroaching darkness of failing solar grids.

"It's oddly beautiful, isn't it?" I say more to myself than to the others. "Even in the rain, even now."

"Chile's got guts," Benny chimes in, a grin spreading across his face despite the ominous skies.

We ascend higher into the embrace of the Bío Bío Region. The world unfolds around us—a tapestry of swelling rivers and stunning peaks; verdant valleys giving way to the rugged bones of the earth. The mountains stand guard around us, stoic sentinels of stone and soil. Some things never change, even under the relentless craziness of the suffocating clouds.

There is a certain juxtaposition between the beauty of this area, which is torn at by the relentless rain and storms.

"This seventy-five minutes is going by fast," Soren ponders, ever the navigator, eyes fixed on the digital display charting our course.

As the TT3 carries us on steel wings, the incongruence of our mission and the world outside fuels the fire within. Adventure beckons with each kilometre, each glimpse of Chile's fierce heart beating beneath the brutality of the weather. We ride the edge of tomorrow, chasing down the second Elops, our spirits undaunted by the whirlwind of challenges we face.

And there, on the periphery of sight and sense, the tornado rages, a reminder of nature's might and the urgency of our quest. But for now, inside the TT3, we propel ourselves in motion, driven by our relentless pursuit of a future where balance is restored, and nature reigns once more.

"Ever seen a tornado up close?" Soren's voice cuts in casually, as if discussing the weather on a HoloBlog. We all take a closer look out the left side of the train and the faux panes.

As the train curves to the west, circling around an incandescent lake, our eyes scan the southern horizon where a dark behemoth twists, an angry column clawing at the sky. "Let's not add 'storm chasers' to our resumes," I mutter, half-joking, praying our path steers clear of the tempest's dance.

"Damn, that thing is massive. How far away do you think it is?" Benny ponders.

"Far enough," Soren says wisely.

Our TT3 vacuum hums around us, a technological marvel slicing through the rain-soaked air at speeds that defy nature. We are a blur as we swing back toward the south, a whisper of movement against the lush backdrop of Chile. The Andes loom like ancient guardians, their snow-crowned peaks majestic in their silence.

I open the titanium case and twist the ClimaSphere between my fingertips, the surface slick yet inscrutable as I probe for any hint of its secrets. Is it a riddle etched in its code? A series of passwords to unlock the storm-breaker? The device is as enigmatic as my father's last notes—dense with potential, yet silent in guidance. His notebook is truly of no use to me and is about as helpful as the secretive pad adorning the proto ClimaSphere. "How difficult can this truly be?" I mumble under my breath. Apparently, it's more difficult than I presumed it would be. How can we be heading toward our first glimpse of a real-life Elops, just for this gawddamn thing not to work?

"Los Ángeles coming up," Soren announces as we begin our descent and deceleration; the city unfurling before us like a vibrant soaked tapestry. Houses drenched with colour peek out from the embrace of pine-encased forests, their red-tiled roofs a stark contrast to the verdant green landscape.

Our display windows showcase the Laja River slicing through the city, a gentle giant cradling its bursting banks. In the distance, the Antuco volcano stands defiant, its silhouette a testament to nature's eternal strength.

"Let's find our way to Punta Lavapie," I say, clutching the ClimaSphere tighter. "The future awaits, hidden within its depths on the journey ahead."

As we spill out of the TT3, the whirr of its doors announces our arrival. The air is thick with the scent of pine and an impending storm, a heady concoction that fills my lungs and sharpens my senses. I glance at the team—Banksia with her hair bouncing as she checks her gear, Juice fiddling with his handheld weather tracker, Soren's brow furrowed as they tap away at their BTN, and Benny, ever the optimist, scanning the horizon with a determined squint. Probably looking for tales of the tornado.

"Shit! Look at that station sign? The TT2 to Punta

Lavapie is down, as in, not working," Soren announces, their voice cutting through the gusts that tug at our clothes. "No juice, no ride. Pun intended, Juice." Soren smiles.

"Oh, no!" Banksia mutters, hitching her pack higher onto her shoulder. "So, what's Plan B?"

"Walk?" Juice suggests, only half-joking. He receives a chorus of groans in response.

"Thirty-eight hours on foot," Soren says, not missing a beat. "If we don't sleep or encounter any—surprises. That number doesn't include crossing the BíoBío River."

More groans.

"Or surprises like that?" Benny points toward the ominous swirl of the tornado, still visible in the far distance, scarring the sky with its furious dance.

"Let's rule out 'walk' as Plan B," I interject, trying to keep the mood from plummeting. "There has to be another way." I sweep a gaze over Los Ángeles; the ghostly quiet of the city unnerves me. Has everyone headed to the coast and Elops #2? This begs the obvious question: if they have indeed fled to the west, how did they get there?

The few lit buildings stand like lighthouses in the gloom—beacons of civilization in a world succumbing to nature's wrath. Most houses and buildings have no light at all. I do like how some of the newer homes seem to be constructed using 3D printing, built to look like the ancestral homes of their forbearers. That's very cool. But the solar grid continues to fall to ruin under our feet, jarring us back to reality and instantly adding to the pressure of what we five need to accomplish and no, walking 38 hours won't cut it.

"Anyone up for commandeering a boat?" Banksia asks, eyes glinting with mischief.

"Or even better, find someone crazy enough to fly a eVTOL in this weather," Juice quips, always one to raise the stakes.

Soren points out pragmatically that both plans require finding someone who hasn't fled or isn't holed up waiting for the end times.

"Which means we need to start looking for Plans X, Y and Z," I conclude, feeling the weight of responsibility settle on my shoulders. "We can't afford delays, not with the fate of those Elops—and potentially the world—at stake."

"Alright, Mighty5. Let's split up, gather intel, and rendezvous back here in one hour," I specify, trying to sound more confident than I really feel. "Keep your BTNComms open and stay alert."

The group nods, a pact as tight as ever. We're in this together, come hell or high water—or both, by the looks of it.

"Be safe," I add, watching them disperse into the shadow-laden streets.

I turn my back to the wind, face the remnants of civilization in Los Ángeles, and wonder if its deserted confines hide the answers we seek. My mind races with possibilities, each more improbable than the last. How do you traverse a broken world when time itself is the enemy?

But there's no space for doubt—not now, never. Adventure calls, and I can't suppress the thrill that zips through my veins despite the uncertainty. Time to get creative, Odezza.

A cliff looms ahead, and I'm about to leap without knowing where I'll land.

CHAPTER THIRTY-TWO

The world has ground to a halt. The AirStreams are as barren as the roads that once crisscrossed this dystopian landscape. AeroCar's and eVTOL's have become relics of a forgotten convenience. Even many of the TT2s sit silent and still. Our window of opportunity is quickly shrinking, and the rugged mountains and the mighty Río BíoBío wait impatiently to our west.

"Estamos en un aprieto," I mutter under my breath. This certainly is a predicament.

"¿Punta Lavapie?" The question hangs in the air, laced with urgency as Juice approaches some locals looking up at him under the weight of rain-soaked awnings. Their laughter ripples back at me in Spanish, echoes of disbelief.

They find humour in our haste and you can tell what they're thinking: who are these topsy-turvy bunch of strange-looking imports that just got tossed out of the last TT2? "Rápido, rápido," he insists, his hand gestures painting desperation in the rainy air. Seventeen languages in his arsenal, and it's his body language that seems to speak volumes right now.

"¡Imposible!" They laugh, shaking their heads as if we're

children chasing a fairy tale across the pages of some worn-out adventure novel. But ambition hasn't left us yet. Not when the planet's destiny hangs by a thread so thin it's almost invisible against the backdrop of this stormy sky.

We've got to cross the BíoBío, and get to the Chilean coast pronto. The challenge is, apart from not wanting to walk, Banksia read on the way down here that the engorged floodplain has washed out the six bridges across the river.

"Un Milagro," one local finally says, not unkindly, his eyes softening with a touch of empathy. Maybe he sees the determination in our eyes or the weight of the world on our shoulders. Or maybe he's just entertained by the spectacle of it all.

"Un Milagro," I echo back, the words tasting both bitter and sweet on my tongue. We need a miracle, but miracles are as scarce as functional transport in these parts.

The laughter of the locals still clings to my ears when a pint-sized figure sidles up beside me. Juice, our linguist, leans down to hear over the howling wind. The boy's voice is like a reed in a storm—small, but unyielding.

"Si yo fuera tú, volaría a Punta Lavapie," he says earnestly, his gaze piercing through the veil of disbelief that seems to hang around us. Did the little lad just say, if he were us, he'd fly?

We all chuckle, mirth bubbling out uncontrollably. "Fly?" I ask. Might as well sprout wings. But Carlos, as he introduces himself, isn't sharing in the joke. His eyes don't waver, and there's an old soul living in that boyish frame, a determined spark that catches our attention.

"Volando no, pero en el carro de mi abuelo, sí," he continues, pointing toward an old barn that looks like it's barely clinging to the present, let alone the future. "Carro."

"A car?" I repeat. An ancient word for an ancient mode of transport.

"Un Suburban viejo," Carlos clarifies with a nod. "Dos

tanques llenos de gasolina. Mi abuelo los guardó... antes de que su Oxolet muriera."

"Juice? Did he just say what I think he said? That there are two tanks of gasoline, petrol? And something about his grandfather kept them, and I presume a car — before his Oxolet died along with the grandfather?" Just three days ago, I think soberly, the world lost another of its dwindling sparks.

Juice nods back at me. Maybe this is a Milagro.

At this stage, the locals have scattered into thin air. "Tell us more, Carlos," I prompt, and the Mighty5 huddle around, the laughter fading into the background like the last notes of a forgotten song.

"Es fácil," Carlos starts, his demeanour shifting into one of an instructor despite his tender age. "Giran la llave para encenderlo y apretan el pedal para moverse. Es como los Aero-Cars, pero sin levitar."

That was a bit too much for me. Juice turns to translate. "You turn the key to start it and press the pedal to move. It's like the AeroCars, but without levitating."

"Wait, back up - did you guys say Petrol?" Soren mutters under their breath, a touch of wonderment in their voice, blended with a good amount of fear. We've heard of the substance, of course—fuel for the relics of the past—but none of us has ever seen it, or used it.

"Y cómo lo ponemos en el carro?" asks Banksia, her brow furrowed in concentration.

"Con un embudo," Carlos explains, miming the action with his small hands. "Asegúrense de no derramarlo; es valioso." "With a funnel," Carlos slowly says in English, "make sure not to spill; it's valuable."

Ohforfuckssake, who is this 'hombrecito'? I think to myself, he's adorable.

"Valuable indeed," I muse. We stand on the cusp of a

history lesson turned reality check. "All right, Carlos, lead the way."

He grins, satisfaction spreading across his face, and beckons us to follow. We, the Mighty5, trail behind him, about to embark on an adventure that feels like we have plucked it from the pages of a dusty tome labelled 'Yesteryears'.

"An ancient Suburban," I whisper, trying the words on for size. "Who would've thought?"

"Who indeed. But what's a Suburban? Juice asked his questions with a fervent gleam in his eyes.

"Let's hope this car of yours knows the way to Punta Lava-pie," I say to Carlos, but deep down, I'm banking on more than optimism. Because if we can master this relic, we can master anything the future—or the past—throws our way.

The mud kicks up underfoot as we tread the path to the grandfather's house; the ochre coloured barn looming in the distance like a forgotten monument to a bygone era. "Just a little further," Carlos assures us, his Broken English brimming with an eagerness that contradicts his years.

"North, to Aeródromo María Dolores," he says, pointing toward the invisible line where earth meets the sky, up a winding track and over a slight hill. "No one uses it anymore."

"An airport," I echo, the concept so alien yet thrilling. We've heard stories, legends of the days when humanity soared above the clouds, not just skimmed them with our tech-laden AeroCars.

"They outlawed planes, right?" Banksia chimes in, her curiosity piqued. "After the BoldWar?"

"Si, pero mi tío..." Carlos trails off, a conspiratorial glint in his eye. "He kept his own plane hidden. A treasure from before."

"Hidden treasures, huh?" Juice says, half-smirking, half-in awe. "This day keeps getting better and better."

"Or crazier," Soren adds, but there's no fear in their gaze, only the fire of challenge.

"Carlos?" Banksia asks, "are you suggesting we take your grandfather's car, fuel it up and take it to an airport?" She seems somewhat embarrassed to ask, but I was thinking the same thing. Where is this all leading us?

Carlos seems to ignore us, continuing to lead us into the shadowy depths of the barn, where the scent of age, goats, and, I'm guessing, petrol fumes blend into a heady cocktail.

It's here he shows us the Suburban. We all look at each other, then back to the beast of an American machine that seems more myth than metal. It surely lived a rich life given its pale, wearied red exterior, blended with a fresh coat of rust.

We all stand there, probably thinking the same thing— people used to ride around in these? How prehistoric!

"An ancient chariot for modern warriors," Benny quips, running his hand over its cold, dusty surface. "Dudeeee," he says in his best American accent. Our Benny is always a character.

"Or a bunch of lunatics," Banksia retorts, but her smile doesn't quite reach her eyes.

"Let's get this creature roaring," I say, more to myself than anyone else. "Then to the airport."

"Wait," Benny kicks in. "Does anyone even know how to run this thing? I assume it's something that runs, or does something like that, right? And when we get it to run, then we take this behemoth to Aeródromo María Dolores? I'm kind of confused."

"Let me check my BTN for some instructions," Soren adds quickly, trying to provide Benny with some peace of mind. "This won't take long. How hard can it be?"

"Claro que sí," Carlos nods, seriousness settling onto his tiny shoulders. "But the plane— it may not even work."

"May not?" I repeat, turning the phrase over in my mind.

"But it's a chance we have to take, right?" I look for confirmation from the team.

"Through rain or whatever else this world throws at us," Soren affirms, meeting each of our gazes.

"We'll make it fly. We just need to see it first. Soren, let's look up how to fly an ancient, illegal plane from days of yore when we get there," Juice declares, the determination in his voice leaving no room for doubt.

Soren acknowledges the idea.

"Alright, team," I say, clapping my hands together, the sharp sound reverberating through the barn's ancient timbers. To reach Punta Lavapie, we just have to embark on a bumpy journey in a behemoth of a relic, followed by a visit to a crumbling aerodrome where an elusive plane may or may not be waiting. Let's not keep adventure waiting."

We can hear Soren speed reading the truck instructions, "1976 ... 350 V8 ... 400-cubic-inch ... carburettor ... four wheel drive ... blah, blah, blah..." It all sounds like a made-up language to me.

As we all walk around this thing, it feels like it's going to pounce on us. All I see is a massive clump of rusting U.S. Steel. Soren sees potential. Benny is almost as tall as the bonnet, and the entire thing seems as long as any eVTOL is wide. The entire body of the truck stands so tall. The word 'sleek' doesn't jump to mind, but the word Chevrolet is prominent on the front. Overall, this thing looks more like an aged brick you'd find in an old London "two-up, two-down" row house. And the tyres are enormous. Black, rough, but still filled with air—sort of.

I find and twist the fuel cap off with a hiss, and the acrid stench of petrol pricks at my nose. It's an ancient scent, heavy and foreign, nothing like the sterile electric bouquet of modern-day transports.

Carlos helps Banksia find the two red cans of fuel. Within

minutes, the amber liquid glugs rapidly into the Suburban's tank, sloshing echoes of a bygone era when engines roared and exhaust fumes clogged the skies.

"Smells like history," Soren comments dryly as they hop into the driver's seat, using a handle to lower the window. "Or just plain old pollution."

"Both, I'd wager," I reply, sealing the cap with a satisfying click.

Carlos pushes the massive barn doors as open as they will go, then clambers into the colossal passenger seat beside Soren. His eyes alight with the thrill of aiding our improbable quest. His small hand points northward. We follow suit, clamming into the back rows of dusted and worn cloth seats.

"Do you know what you're doing?" Juice asks Soren in all seriousness.

Soren provides a negligible nod, but with a sense of brewing confidence.

And with the turn of a key, the old beast shudders to life.

"Oh, that's really loud," Benny squawks as he jumps in the far back row of the monster.

As we slowly rumble out of the barn, thick, dark smoke belches from the rusty exhaust pipe of the old engine, staining the air with its greasy film.

"We are moving," I say to myself. We are seriously moving in a machine we can only have seen on our holos.

A few miles up the curvy, muddy and barely worn track and over the crest of the hill Carlos had pointed out earlier, we encounter a worn sign, 'Maria Dolores Aeroport'. A graveyard of aviation dreams looms before us, its long, flat runway cracked and overgrown with greenage. Weeds have claimed this place, wrapping their tendrils around the skeletons of long-grounded aircraft.

"Looks like it's been asleep for ages," Banksia murmurs, her voice tinged with awe.

"Time to wake it up, then," I joke, scanning the tarmac for Carlos' grandfather's treasure.

"There," Carlo calls out.

We follow his gaze and there, under a soggy and faded black tarpaulin, lies an old relic of an aeroplane.

We pile out of the truck and all rush to pull the tarp off the plane. As we unveil the sheath, Soren aims their BTN at the ancient winged beast and reports in a few seconds, "It's a 1990 Cessna 208 Grand Caravan."

I can feel the anticipation reaching my empty stomach. I miss OZ and this is one of those moments I miss him more. OZ's eyes would be wide with boyish excitement, taking in every detail of the old aircraft and this abandoned airport. I find it creepy. OZ would find it adventurous. He'd have a grin on his face, his head turning from side to side, trying to capture every angle. He would study every inch of the old Grand Caravan, imagining all the flights it has taken and the journeys it has been on. His regard for the old always cracked me up, but it made him who he was.

With the cloth pulled back, the word 'EJERCITO' stares at us, 'ARMY': a reminder of a conflict that grounded these birds forever.

"Pre-BoldWar indeed," Juice says, running a hand over the camouflage paint that's seen better days.

"Let's hope it's got some fight left in it," I mutter, peering around its mass. 1,2,3,4,5,6,7,8,9— I count more than enough seats. Perfect. It's like a flying Suburban.

"Fight or flight," Soren corrects, lips curling upward as they tap at their BTN again. Data streams across their screen —manuals, checklists, procedures, videos—all in a language they're about to translate into action.

The old bird sits like a forgotten relic, in muted greens and browns, its high wings outstretched as if waiting for the signal to take flight once more. Its metal body bears the scars of years of use and, I'm guessing, abuse, but there was still a glimmer of pride in its stance, a hope that it could still serve its purpose.

Eight grubby windows peer back to us and three large tyres seem to have seen better days, but preserve some ancient air. If it could talk, it would dispense some rich and elaborate stories.

I see Soren's hand move along the body of the ancient plane. They find a latch and, with a quick twist and a tug, reveal a wide door that pops up, reaching for the sky.

"This looks promising," I whisper under my breath.

With no sign of steps or a ladder, we jump up into the opening. The long-lost scent of mustiness fills the air mixed with avgas and engine oil. The worn cloth seats hug the windows, with a tiny aisle running up the middle. With the low ceiling, we hunch over, looking for a seat.

As we store our gear and sit in what seems like a centimetre of soot, Soren and Juice make their way to the cockpit. Dusty and untouched instruments and controls stare back at us, worn down from years of use. Some popped out, others missing.

"Who knew we'd be time-travelling today?" I muse to no one in particular. This is not a scenario they offered at the teahouse.

"First a car, now a plane," Juice chuckles, shaking his head in disbelief. "What's next, an undervannsbåt?" A submarine.

"Let's not jinx it," I counter.

I watch as Banksia and Benny wander off toward a large cylindrical metal canister, sitting on the muddy ground, propped by three rusty, old, dilapidated legs. The words AVGAS 100 and Prohibido Fumar are plastered in enormous block lettering on the end. I get it — don't light a fag. But after the war, they banned cigarettes, so there is little hope that anyone will pull out a pack right about now.

I realise this is the fuel depot for the plane, and as we can't take the plane to the fuel depository, we have to bring the fuel to the plane. With buckets in hand, they locate a decrepit fuel pump and start the laborious task of hand-pumping the precious fluid into their handheld canisters. Six in total.

"Feels like stealing fire from the God's," Banksia calls out with a grunt, hefting a brimming pail toward the plane's fuel port atop the high wings.

Soren, all business, chimes in, "It says here it takes 1,257 litres of fuel. How much are you carrying?"

"I do not know," Banksia adds, "I'm just carrying buckets. It's tough to tell." She and Benny pass them up to Juice, who is now standing on the right wing, awaiting the AVGAS 100. With three emptied canisters, they move to the left wing and complete the task of fuelling this baby. But now I'm worried about the inaccuracies and guesswork behind the six buckets versus the amount of litres Soren had just called out.

Suddenly, I see Carlos standing there, excited for us, yet I can feel a sense of forlornness. Maybe he is sad to see someone take off in his grandfather's old flying jalopy or sad he made new friends who are literally taking off before his eyes.

What an amazing young man, to help complete strangers from a distant land and get this far with two antique solutions. He is Un Milagro.

Those of us who are not on fuel duty, shower him with hugs and thank you profusely for rescuing, directing, and providing for us. This is a moment in time I won't soon forget.

"Adios," he spills out and runs off down the muddy road. And just like that, he's gone.

"Keep on bringing buckets over, okay?" Soren calls out, "I know we don't have a lot of time to burn, but we also don't want to crash because there is not enough AVGAS."

"Yes," I think to myself, "top-shelf idea, Soren."

"Alright," announces a few minutes later, the BTN

clutched like a talisman. "That's good with the fuel. Now let's see if we can make this girl sing."

My heart pounds a relentless rhythm as we all prepare to defy gravity—and perhaps sanity—in a machine that none of us were ever meant to touch, let alone see; let alone fly. But here we are, teetering on the edge of disaster and discovery, fuelled by more than just AVGAS. We have audacity and a dash of madness.

Juice slides comfortably into the co-pilot seat, the right seat, the leather cracked and worn like a map of a long-forgotten world. You can see his fingers dancing over controls that belong in a museum. "Ready to defy history?" he quips, flashing a grin that doesn't quite reach his eyes.

"Only if history's ready for us," I call out, trying to soak up the bravado oozing from Juice's every pore. The rest of the Mighty5 faces expressing a mix of determination and faintly veiled terror.

"Okay, just so we're clear," Benny says from behind me in the third row, his hands gripping the back of my seat as though it's a lifeline, "why aren't we flying straight to Muelle on Isla Santa María?"

"Because," Soren answers without looking up from the BTN, "Muelle is runway-challenged. And by that, I mean it doesn't have an operable one.

"Right," Benny nods, though his furrowed brow suggests he's picturing our landing on a dirt road or a beach—crash and burn style.

"Let's focus on getting airborne before we solve the landing conundrum," I suggest.

I can see both Soren and Juice flipping switches with more confidence than I feel is necessary for two people who have never flown a plane before, let alone seen one. Some gauges flicker to life, a choral of green and amber lights that might as well be alien code.

I can hear them chatting, "Okay, Juice, ready to see if we can learn a new skill today?" Soren says with warmth and heart. Juice nods with anticipation.

They call out instructions with one eye on their BTN, another on the gauges and another on Juice.

Soren charges ahead. "Flight prep: aircraft fuelled. Check. And all systems are functional. Check."

"That might be pushing it," I think to myself. They don't all look like they are functional, but hey, I'm not the pilot. We'll soon see.

"Review our flight plan and weather," Soren continues.

"It says to review the flight plan and weather?" Juice questions.

I almost start laughing. The weather is crap and from what we know, and we need to head west from here. That is one hell of a flight plan.

After flipping a few more switches and turning a couple more knobs, Soren turns a solitary key in a keyhole, and the engine slowly springs to life. The blades of the single prop swirl as black and grey exhaust kicks out the side of the engine. Well, that's something.

"Ready?" Soren asks Juice, now having to scream over the whine of the nose-mounted engine.

"Yes. Next."

"Now we push the throttle forward. It's that black rod on the dash between us both. I have my feet on the pedals, which act as breaks," Soren yells. How on earth did they learn this so fast? They don't even seem flustered forgawdsake!

"Okay," Soren continues, yelling louder with every passing minute. "Time to taxi, which I guess means to drive the plane over there."

I see Soren pointing to the derelict old runway. I see a huge 'ONE EIGHT' at the foot of the aged tarmac. The numbers are as old and faded as this plane.

"We need to request clearance from the tower to taxi," Soren resumes, looking squarely at Juice. "I think that means getting permission for takeoff," I hear them state, receiving a blank stare from her co-pilot. "Okay. Never mind," a smirk crossing their lips, "I'm sure if this is an abandoned airport, there's no one around that even cares, let alone to give us clearance."

Juice simply goes along. Not totally sure if Soren is serious or being sarcastic. I know I can't tell, but I'm back in the peanut gallery.

They are doing a good job and seem to manoeuvre the rowdy plane with little difficulty. At least we haven't hit anything yet. They move the steering mechanisms around in unison. I would call them wheels, but they look more like the letter 'H'.

"Head toward that number 18 over there, I think. Then we should be able to line up on the runway, or at least that's what the quick guide says to do. I also looked up instructions for Aeródromo María Dolores," I overhear Soren discuss, "and it says we should see the numbers 18 and 36 on either end of this runway and take whichever heads into the wind. As we seem to be in a perpetual storm and have never done this before, let's stick to the closest one the 18. And now that I think about it, Juice, the other plane instructions mentioned something about a pre-flight check, but we all got on so fast I didn't do that, not that I even know what to do. Think we'll be okay?"

I see Juice ponder this question for a moment, then simply give one long nod.

With this reassurance, they get back to it. "It's saying we need to verify engine parameters such as RPM, oil pressure, and temperature, but I do not know what that means right now. Watching the propeller circling around, I think we'll be okay."

Again, one long nod of confirmation.

"Do you think we're lined up?" I hear Soran ask.

"Yes," I hear him promptly confirm, "then let's apply full power - push on that black bar forward more and keep the plane straight as we pick up speed," Soren directs Juice.

The plane moves faster along the runway; although having just ridden a TT system, faster is relative.

"Somewhere in this sea of little round clock-looking faces is a thing that shows our knots, Juice. If you can see it, look for 85kts. And hang on to that steering wheel," Soren continues, barking over the noise of the old plane. And do you see anything marked FLAPS?" Soren adds.

No answer from Juice. Just pure concentration.

"Okay, I see it, there, it's showing 79kts. Wait, now it's 83... okay, now what?"

"Pull back on the steering wheel. We will pull it back together... NOW!"

The old plane heads up at an angle I'm pretty sure it's never achieved before. "Shit!" I hear Benny say under his breath. Agreed!

"Keep on climbing, Juice," I hear Soren snap. "When you see the dial read 110 kts, level off. That means push the—Got it," Juice exclaims. "And no, I see nothing that says FLAPS, sorry. Do we need them?"

Nothing from Soren. You can feel the tension, which I guess is normal. I'm just glad it's not me up there faking to fly.

I glance over at Banksia and observe that her eyes are sealed shut. I don't blame her. Mine should be too, but I can't help but look out the dusty windows as the land below pulls further away.

"Forgawdsake, we're flying," I scream out.

For a moment there, I thought I saw both Soren and Juice smile. Now, that would be the miracle of the day.

We continue to go up, closer to the bottom of the clouds,

so I see them both push the steering H forward and the plane levels off. I can't honestly tell if this is fun or frantically crazy. No time to think about it, which I'm assuming is probably for the best.

"Nothing like a bit of pressure to make you learn fast," Banksia pipes up, her eyes squeaking open a fraction, her voice steady but laced with adrenaline.

"Pressure makes diamonds," Juice murmurs, adjusting dials with shaky hands. "Or explosions."

"Opting for diamonds today," I declare, faking a casualness that fools no one. My heart is a hammer against my ribs, but there's no backing out now. Not when the fate of the planet hangs in the balance, not when every second counts.

"My stomach feels weird," Benny squeaks out.

"Everybody buckled in?" I call out, and a chorus of affirmative responses crackles through the cabin. For a moment, we are one—a team united by the impossible.

"Then here goes— everything," Juice says, and with a collective deep breath, they engage the throttle a little more.

As we bank toward the west, the old army plane groans beneath us, a beast awakening from a long slumber. It shudders, hesitates, and then surges forward, propelling us toward the coast. Outside, the world becomes a blur of grey, a dystopian canvas rushing past as we barrel toward an uncertain horizon. The clouds are so close that I feel like I am back in my pool.

"Here we go!" Juice yells, pushing on the steering wheel, making the plane go flat and level.

And just like that, we're soaring. A Grand Caravan full of crazy misfits.

I can see Banksia's face glued to her dust-caked window off her left cheek, "It still there, that massive tornado."

We all look out the left side of the plane, which isn't a

smart thing, as the plane leans in that same direction. Physics, people, physics. So I let Soren and Banksia take a peek.

"That is a huge funnel," Soren yells out. "Banksia, any way of telling how far away it is?"

"No boss," she calls back, "but my guess is it is moving east by the looks of it, so we might be fine."

Might, I think to myself. But none of us are experts here, so little good it would do questioning her. Better to trust and let her make the call.

It is so rough up here. How did people ever do this? "It's called turbulence," Soren yells back from up front, as if they can reread my mind. Well, turbulence, I'm not a big fan of yours.

As this is no TT, nor is it adorned with modern instruments, we do not know how long this trip will take. However, I can feel us all settling in for the ride, all the while taking in the sodden ground below. As I look forward under the high wing, a mixture of farming textures like an old quilt. Just then, I can feel my eyelids getting heavier and heavier until I'm out like a light.

CHAPTER THIRTY-THREE

I awake to a jolt. Spittal on my cheek. The Mighty5 sits in silence, tucked away in the old flying tube, each of us lost in our own thoughts. We all seem to gaze out over the swollen Río BíoBío far below.

From our vantage point at 3,600 metres, the river looks like an obese silver serpent, its scales glimmering in the mottled sunlight as it roils and rages below, engulfing land at every turn. The wild ripples catch the light, creating a dazzling display. But all the granjas, the farms, they seem dead. And where are all the people? We see some on roads and tracks heading west, but so few. My guess is, that the two are heading toward the open hole of hope but are having a difficult time of it, like us.

"Would you look at that?" Juice muses, his nose pressed against the smudged glass, a portal to the chaos. The river below reflects in his pupils like a captured storm.

"Looks like the river's taking a long sip but choked," Soren quips beside him, tapping away at their holo-pad, trying to make sense of flying this outmoded creature. My hope is she is figuring out where we are going and how to land.

"Too much to swallow," I reply, leaning over their shoulders to glimpse the furious waterway. "It's like the planet's crying, crying out for help."

"Or throwing a tantrum," Banksia chimes in, her voice tight. She is sitting back, scrolling through NewsBlogs with such intensity you'd think she was going to burst.

"Anything not apocalyptic?" Benny asks, half-joking, half-desperate for good news, as he looks at Banksia. His fingers dance across his own screen, pulling up feeds that flicker with scenes of disorder and disaster.

"CG's telling everyone to stay calm. That's new," Banksia says, her words dripping with sarcasm. "As if that's going to stop people from panicking. Bit late for that, wouldn't you say?" she says rhetorically.

"Because 'stay calm' works so well when you're watching your world wash away beneath you," I mutter, turning away from the BíoBío.

"Right," Benny agrees, his gaze still locked on the unfolding drama. "If you can keep your wits about you while all others are losing theirs and blaming you, the world will be yours and everything in it—" he trails off.

"Is that a poem?" Juice asks, momentarily distracted.

"Rudyard Kipling said that way back in the day and it seems to be poignant today."

"Certainly seems like a mantra for our times," Soren responds, never taking theirs off the sky ahead.

"It's getting kind of heavy around here," I laugh, trying to lighten the mood, even though my stomach twists tighter with every mile we cover and every pocket of turbulence we tumble through.

Why would the CG take so long to step-up and organise a way to save the people still living? I'm sure at some point, OZ was going to reach out and give them the Oxo2 tech, but they'll never know how close they were to saving millions of lives. I want to say, shame on them, but they are the government - what else would you expect? If history has taught us anything—

"Here's something else I just read on the CG NewsBlog," Juice adds, his blue eyes fixated on his BTN, "and it's kind of interesting given where we are. They just flashed a News-Burst that said that the Atacama Desert, that's right here in Chile, is forecasted to receive 55mm of rain tomorrow. That might not seem like much, but it says here that until last month, the Atacama received less than 5mm; that's for the entire year!"

I can see Benny is doing the maths in his brain, then just shaking his head in horror.

"Alright, team," I say, clapping my hands together for attention. "Let's focus on what we can control. We've got a job to do you two up front. Let's trust you can land this gawdfor-saken tube of ancientness."

"Saving the world, one disaster at a time," Benny adds, his usual spark reigniting.

"Better than sitting around waiting for someone else to fix it," Soren nods.

"Or worse, waiting for it to fix itself," Juice concludes.

"Is that ever going to happen?" I ask, hoping my voice doesn't betray the doubt creeping into it.

"Who knows? But we'll be there to see it, either way," Banksia responds, her voice firm, grounded.

"Count on it," I affirm, meeting each of their gazes. Whatever Roman Polotov and the rest of the world has planned, we are the Mighty5. Together, we'll face it head-on.

And the plane flies on.

"I have an idea," Benny says out of the blue, his voice low, a conspiratorial whisper drawing us closer. He's got that glint in his eye, the one that usually precedes a breakthrough or a brilliant prank. I watch as his hands dance across his portable keyboard, sequences of code cascading down his holo-screen like a waterfall of neon glyphs.

"Cracking into Anthro-Tech?" Banksia leans in, intrigued. "What's the play?"

"Truth," Benny responds simply, the word hanging in the air like a spell.

A moment later, Benny freezes, his eyes wide. "Guys... Roman Polotov is alive."

"Alive?!" Our collective gasp could've filled a vacuum. The CG had been so adamant, broadcasting Roman's demise across all media channels, a victory for order over chaos.

"We're not surprised by this, are we?" Soren spills, always the voice of reason.

"Doesn't die easy, does he?" Juice quips.

"I agree with Soren. We never believed it." I add. "There was no way he was on the same TT as OZ. Being the mastermind behind all this, he had to have orchestrated what went down."

"Does it mention where he's headed?" I ask the question, thrumming with urgency.

"Here's the kicker," Benny turns his screen to face us, "he's en route to this Elops, the same coastal stretch we're heading to."

"Great. A reunion tour nobody asked for," Soren deadpans.

"Question is, why this Elops?" I rub my temples, trying to piece together the puzzle of a madman's motives. There's no obvious strategic value, no off-planet launch pads, no weapon caches or even tech vaults, just miles of battered Chilean coastline.

"Maybe he fancies a swim?" Juice offers, but even his humour feels stretched thin.

"Or there's something we're missing," Banksia interjects, her analytical mind already sifting through possibilities.

"Something only Roman would want," I muse aloud, feeling the weight of our responsibility pressing down. We're the barrier between Roman's machinations and whatever shred of normality the world clings to.

"Guess we'll find out when we land," Benny says, flicking off his BTN. His usual smirk has waned, a sign of the gravity gripping us all.

"Let's keep our eyes open and wits sharp," I declare, meeting each gaze, fierce and unyielding. "Whatever game Roman's playing, we're not letting him win."

"Game on," Juice affirms, his determination infectious.

"Checkmate's the only move we play," Soren adds, a warrior's promise.

"Then let's prepare for one hell of a rumpus," Banksia concludes, shutting down her NewsBlogs with a decisive flic.

And with that, we fly onward, the Mighty5 bound for an uncertain confrontation, where hope wrestles with fear, and the future hangs by a thread. Whatever awaits at Elops2 high over Isla Santa María, we'll face it together. It's what we do. It's who we are.

CHAPTER THIRTY-FOUR

Lightning forks the sky, jagged scars across the heavens, as the single propeller of our rickety aircraft continues to slice through the downpour. My fingers tap-tap against the Clima-Sphere, my father's last and most enigmatic invention, nestled in my lap. The digi screen glows defiantly, insistent on a password I can't crack—a digital sphinx guarding the secrets of reversing this engineered apocalypse.

"Any luck?" Juice shouts over the roar, his eyes fixed on his own BTN.

"Still nothing," I reply, frustration tightening my voice. I brush wet strands of hair from my face, courtesy of the leaking cabin roof. It's like trying to pick a lock in a hurricane; each failed attempt feels like another betrayal of my father's legacy.

"Keep at it, Odezza," Soren calls from the cockpit, struggling with the yoke as higher gusts buffet us sideways. "You're the brains here."

"Brains that can't communicate a simple password," I mutter under my breath, glaring at the proto ClimaSphere. I envision my dad's knowing smile, a silent hint from beyond, urging me to see the pattern he always insisted was there.

"What are you looking for?" I yell up to Juice.

"We don't know how to land a plane, let alone this plane, so I'm taking a crash course on landing before we crash, of course." Was that an attempt at humour from the big Azeri? And of all times to be rye.

I need a distraction, so I try to change the subject away from crashing. "Maybe the password is 'doomed' since that's what we are if I don't get this thing open."

"Try 'curiosity'," Soren suggests, the word nearly lost in the surrounding cacophony. "It worked for Pandora's Box. No, wait, I remember what happened after they opened it."

"It released curses upon mankind." Benny points out. "Might not be the best correlation. Sorry, Soren. And did you know that the word "box" was actually translated as a large jar in Greek?"

Not now, Benny, not now!

"Right. Something about unleashing all the evils of the world," I point out. But I type in curiosity, anyway. The ClimaSphere blinks, unimpressed. Of course, it's not that simple. Forgawdsake OZ, what did you use?

"Hope's not supposed to be simple," Banksia chimes in, ever the optimist, even as her white knuckles suggest otherwise. "It's about believing despite evidence to the contrary."

"Alert!" Banksia's voice cuts through our banter and the tension of the storm's raging force, her knuckles white as she grips her seat. "My BTN's flashing red with an Isla Santa Maria Elops report!"

I look around and all of our BTNs are lighting you like the sky outside.

"Red? As in red equals closed? As in closing of the Elops?" Benny turns from his window, where the relentless storm paints the world in furious strokes of grey and water.

"Closed or closing?" Juice barks, swiping urgently at his BTN screen. "We're running out of time and potentially fuel faster than we thought, so we need to know now."

Soren looks. "This says it is closing, and closing rapidly."

We all fall silent, dumbfounded by this news.

Soren and Juice look at each other, trying to read each other's minds. The rest of us stay silent while they ponder our next move.

"We need an alternative route. And we need it now, Juice snaps, not looking up, still scanning his BTN.

"Better buckle up, we're heading back," Soren warns. "This ride's about to get bumpier."

"Wasn't it already at maximum bumpiness?" Benny shoots back, and adrenaline courses through his veins.

As Soren changes our route, banking to the left, the storm snarls outside, a grey beast gnashing at the windows of our battered craft. "Forty kilometres."

"That tornado's picking up a real appetite," Benny calls out.

"Can we even make it back?" Banksia's voice wavers over the roar of wind and engine. "The AVGAS—"

"Calculated optimism, remember?" I force a grin, though my stomach knots tighter with each drop in altitude. "Do we have enough fuel —"

"Juice, nothing!" Juice interjects, his attempt at humour replaced by a hard edge. "We're running on fumes. Someone miscalculated the buckets."

"Guilty," Banksia confesses, swallowing the lump in her throat. "I guess numbers are more stubborn than I thought, but to my defence, I never calculated for a moment a scenario where we would have to turn back."

"Don't blame yourself," Benny jumps in, but there's no hiding the tension in the plane.

"Focus on the horizon," Soren commands. "We'll ride the storm like we own it."

WHEN ALL THE CLOUDS COLLIDE

Soren continues to turn the bulky old Cessna around. The turbulence seems even worse now. We all go silent for the duration of the bank back to the east. Then, out of nowhere, the plane drops what feels like three dozen metres. "What on earth—" I yelp. "I can see why people don't fly these things anymore," I mutter under my breath.

We head back over the raging BíoBío and watch as people continue walking toward the west like Lemmings. Maybe they haven't yet received the closure warning. How will they know? Where will they go? My mind is churning like the water below. Oh, to be back in London sipping tea with OZ.

"Between that last turn and the headwind, our bearing has shifted. We are off course," I hear Juice call out to Soren. "Follow the river, south. It should lead us back toward Los Ángeles.

"But that will have us heading toward that tornado," Soren realises, fear finally crossing their face. That's not a look one sees every day.

"We only have to head south for a few nautical miles, then we keep on turning back to the east. It will be close, but I think we'll be okay." Juice adds. Did he just say, 'think'? How about 'know'! Juice? Know would be a better word to use.

"Storm or no storm," I declare, feeling the last reserves of courage surge within me, "we're landing this bird."

But my bravery is short-lived.

Looking dead ahead through the gunky cockpit windows is the terrifying sight of that tornado. Our eyes enlarge with the look of this swirling beast. I know it is not close enough yet to draw us into its deadly tentacles, but the optical illusion of sight makes it feel like we can reach out and touch it. I agree with Benny's earlier remark about OZ. He would have been losing his mind with excitement just about now.

As the plane soars through the sky, its metal wings slice through the underbelly of the clouds. The world in front of us transformed and transfixed. A tempest of fury and chaos unfurled—a tornado, a monstrous column of twisting wind, water and debris, reaching down from the heavens to touch the earth.

From my vantage point, nestled within the aircraft's belly, I watch in awe and uneasiness. The tornado is a living force, a primal dance of air and earth, a reminder of nature's raw power, and unheard of in Chile. Its dark funnel churns with malevolence, a vortex that defies reason, daring any mortal to challenge it.

Then Soren yells back to us, calm and collected, "Ladies and gentlemen, we have an unusual sight ahead. A tornado. We'll be altering our course to avoid it. Please fasten your seat-belts." Are they also attempting humour? Why do the two driest people I know think now is a good time to practise their comedy routine?

Our eyes widen with a mixture of fear and fascination, daring not to dart away from the horrifying deed straight ahead of us. Everyone clutches their armrests and seats while Benny presses his face against his window, seeking a glimpse of the elemental beast. I, too, lean forward in my seat, drawn by equal parts curiosity and trepidation.

It has to be 200 metres wide and ten times that in height. I can see why they are called twisters. The clockwise movement of the air extends from what looks like a thunderstorm right above us, reaching for the sodden ground below. And that funnel-shape is terrifying, bending and yielding to its own free will.

The plane veers and jostles as we bank to the left. The wings tilted as if paying homage to the tempest. We are now parallel to the tornado, close enough to feel its pull—an invis-ible hand tugging at our metal cocoon. The wind buffets us, and the cabin screams with tension. Outside, debris dances—a ballet of shattered homes, uprooted trees, and torn dreams.

This is the most violent thing I have ever witnessed. Its anger and brutality scare me to the bone. I have never cried, but right now, I am close. The sound is so violent from outside and inside the plane, as the fuselage vibrates under the strain of the gripping tendrils of the tornado.

Soren continues to bank, turning away from the tornado's path. As the world tilts, land passing by our left windows, my stomach tilts with the plane. The vortex slips from view, its fury now a retreating spectre. But even as we escape its clutches, I can't tear my eyes away.

Benny wasn't ready for such a steep arch and almost toppled out of his seat.

As we levelled out, we glimpse the devastation left behind —a scar on the land, a testament to its immediate wrath.

At that moment, I understand. We are fleeting visitors in its domain, insignificant against the tempest's might. And yet, as the plane carries us back to our original destination, I feel a strange kinship. We, too, are forces of nature—curious, resilient, and forever seeking the edge of possibility.

Moments later, I see Juice's brow furrowed in concentration. He doesn't seem perturbed or unnerved by all that happened around us. "Landing gear, check. Flaps, yes, I found them, check," he says with a Scandinavian smirk.

Outside, the world is a blur of sullen greys and violent gusts, an angry canvas painted by the storm's unforgiving brush. Soren grips the yoke like it's the last solid thing left on Earth, muscles taut under the strain.

"Steady, Soren," Juice says, his voice barely rising above the din. "You've got this."

The plane bucks wildly, a bronco with wings, each dip and soar wrenching my stomach into knots. I tighten my grip on the armrests, nails digging into the faux leather—a futile anchor against the tempest outside.

"Anytime now, Juice," Soren shouts, casting a desperate

glance at him. They seem to be looking for the runway. "I'd rather not test my swimming skills today."

"I see it. 15 degrees off your port side!" Juice's eyes are wide, reflecting every soul on board. "Runway instructions coming up!"

"Hope they include a chapter on miracle landings," I mutter, glancing out the window where the tornado has moved further north.

"Less chatting, more bracing," Soren grits out as we lurch sideways, a sickening reminder that gravity is merely waiting to reclaim us.

"Bracing is my middle name," Benny replies. Fear has etched itself into every syllable.

"Thought it was 'Resilience'," Banksia offers with a strained smile.

"Today, it's 'Don't-Let-Us-Die'," I correct her, attempting a bluster I don't feel.

"Approach angle set," Juice announces, voice steady despite the sweat on his brow. "We're aiming for runway 36, okay, Soren?"

"Which is fancy talk for hold on to your bums, we're comin' in to land," Benny adds, a thread of humour woven through the tension.

"Prepare for landing," Soren barks, and we brace as one, a united front against the storm's fury.

"Here goes everything," I whisper, casting a final thought to the skies. "Let's bring this bird back home."

I see the land approach the front of the plane so fast it freaks me out. I'm just hoping those two up front have done all their homework. I see Soren pull back on the back bar she had pushed forward on takeoff, and I can hear the motor slowing. As I watch her pull back on a different black flappy handle that I had not seen her use before. "Full flaps," I hear her say to Juice. I'm hoping that's a good thing.

We can certainly feel the plane losing altitude and pointing toward the big 36 on the decrepit runway. I feel lucky we're not making a nose dive for Terra firma, but it feels like we are landing as we should. Of course, none of us have a reference point, so we can't truly tell if this is right or wrong, but where I'm sitting in the back, it feels more right than wrong.

As we pass over the massive 36, I see both of our novice pilots pull back on the yoke and as the nose points back into the air, we hear the wheels under our seats firmly strike the ground. But only for a millisecond because we bounce hard, then touch back down again. We repeat the bouncing twice more.

We hear the front wheel screech as it connects with the ground and, just like that, the bouncing stops. I see both their shoes pushed firmly down on the pedals at their feet and see Soren pull all the way back on the black handle. With that, the old plane slows down and we seem to reverse how we started not that long ago, taxiing back to the old rusty American monster Suburban.

They did it. The two of them landed this almost seventy-year-old, illegal aeronautical gem. And look, we didn't die. Bonus!

Soren pushes a few buttons and flips some switches and the plane's propeller shuts off. For the first time in a few hours, it is dead quiet. Except for the perpetual sound of rain and wind right outside the fuselage.

We all grab our bags and spill out of the plane, reversing our earlier footsteps. It's only a short slog back to the rusty truck. We all seem bewildered, completely out of it. None of us speak.

With heavy hearts and narrowing aspirations, we slowly climb back into the truck, exhausted from the adrenaline of the manic ride we just encountered. The engine rumbles to life, sputtering and coughing like an old man on his last legs. Exhaust fumes cling to our clothes and fill our nostrils.

As Juice looks over Soren's right shoulder, he breaks the oppressive silence with a precarious voice. "I'm not sure if we have enough petrol to make it back to town."

"Well," I chime in, "we can always walk if we do, unlike the past few hours."

A thick layer of mud already coats the truck, a constant reminder of our journey so far. Each bump in the road rattles our bones and threatens to shake us loose from our seats. We take one last look at the desolate landscape around us before setting off, not knowing what awaits us in town and where the next steps of our journey will take us, or at least, I'm not personally sure.

"Eleven thousand four hundred sixty-one kilometres," Juice yells back to us above the front of the truck as it makes its way back down the rutted road. "That's the distance between us and Elops3."

"How far?" I yell rhetorically, clinging to a sense of disbelief amidst the chaos. He doesn't repeat the extraordinary number.

"TTs, yeah!" Juice nods, swiping through maps and schematics. "We'll have to go subterranean—under South America, then below the South Atlantic Ocean. It's quite the shot, but doable."

I see Soren reverse our earlier course through town, returning to Estación Central de Trenes de Los Ángeles.

No sign of our little amigo, Carlos. That kid was cool.

"That sounds far," the words slip from Banksia's lips in a hesitant, almost fearful tone. As she speaks, her voice seems to waver, her trepidation palpable.

"Cosier than being tornado chow," Soren grunts, rolling their eyes.

"Okay, so we're mole people now. Great. What about

Roman?" Benny chimes in, his eyes darting around the cabin, as if expecting the tycoon to materialise any moment.

"Roman." The name hangs heavy, laced with unspoken fears. "He'll know Elops2 is off the grid. He always knows," I muse aloud, trying to second-guess a mind that plays chess while we're stuck playing checkers.

"He could aim for Elops3 ahead of us," Benny speculates, voice grave. "Or maybe he's got another ace up his sleeve."

"An ace we can vanquish bullishly," I say. If only we had a crystal ball or, better yet, a tracker on Roman.

"Elop3 and Zanzibar, here we come," Juice declares with a bravado I envy. "Let's go find a train and figure out our route as we walk."

Benny chimes in, "Did you know Zanzibar is an Archipelago in the Sea of Zanj? The archipelago is also known as the Spice Islands."

Geek!

As we wander, a ping of sadness hits me. "Hey," I yell out, "what's the date today?" It seems like such a random question amid everything we are going through.

"Wait," Benny looks, "oh, wow. Today is February 29th," he concludes.

That's what I suspected. It's not only rare because it's a leap year, but today would have been Dad's birthday. A feeling of sadness stretches through my entire being. But I don't have time to show my feelings.

"Dad, I miss you and love you," is all I can squeak out under my breath, "happy birthday, OZ!"

CHAPTER THIRTY-FIVE

The hum of the Estación Central de Trenes de Los Ángeles buzzes like a hive of metal bees as we stride in. My EstateTrack-Boot's clack against the polished concrete flooring, echoes bouncing off the grand arches overhead. Soren, Juice, Banksia and Benny trail behind me, each one's face set with that 'we're-in-it-to-win-it-and-thank-gawd-we're-off-that-stinking-plane' kind of look.

"Over here," I say, spotting an empty table tucked away from the main flow of passengers. We gather round, take a seat, and in a synchronised dance of fingers, our BTNs flic to life. HelloHolo screens hover above our right wrists—each a deluge of data, a beacon of strategy and hidden next steps.

"Okay, team," I start, my voice steady, "let's chart out this next leg of the expedition." My words are crisp, cutting through the terminal's ambient chatter.

Benny leans in, the whiz kid's mind racing faster than a train. "Looking at our options, we need to take the TT2 to Asunción, Paraguay." He suggests, tapping at his BTN, bringing up a shimmering 3D map of the regional TT system. Red, Green, Orange and Purple lines show the TT, TT3, TT2 and TT1 lines respectively. "Then we hop on the TT3 to Ascension Island."

"Sounds exotic," Banksia quips, her grin almost daring the universe to throw us another curveball.

"Exotic or not," Juice adds, his gaze hard as steel, "it's our best shot getting closer to the Elops3."

"We're off around the world to Tanzania," Soren nods, the muscles in their jaws flexing. They're the rock, unmovable in their resolve.

"Well, at least half the world," Benny adds, still doing some last-minute research on his BTN. "Our globetrotting will take us under glaciers, deserts, even lakes."

"Alright, Mighty5," I declare, standing up, feeling the pulse of possibility. "Let's catch ourselves a TT2 and ride it straight into the heart of this mess."

We are a unified front ready to traverse continents in hours, fuelled by wit, grit, and the burning need to stitch this fractured world back together—one clandestine move at a time.

As we walk, I open the titanium case and flip the ClimaSphere around in my hands, a gesture born of frustration rather than showmanship. The smooth device, no bigger than half the face of a cricket bat, its exterior a matrix of intricate patterns and tiny blinking lights, remains as unresponsive as ever. I should feel a rush from this challenge, the same exhilaration that surges through me when diving into uncharted waters. Instead, a knot of anxiety tightens in my gut.

"Any luck?" Juice glances over at me.

"Still nothing," I reply, pressing down on the sphere again. It's stubborn—like my father—and just as enigmatic. "It seems to be mocking me."

"Let it mock," Soren interjects, their voice sharp, cutting through my rising doubt. "We'll figure it out. We always do."

Benny rests a guiding hand on my shoulder, grounding

me. "Your dad was onto something big, Odezza. He wouldn't leave you a puzzle without a solution, even if he had hidden said puzzle behind an ancient pop poster."

I want to believe him. I need to. With a sigh, I place the ClimaSphere back in its metal encasement. "Later," I say to the case as it seals with a hiss. Right now, we have a train to catch.

We stride toward the TT2—a sleek metal serpent ready to devour the miles ahead with an insatiable hunger. As we board, the cool interior of the carriage welcomes us, a stark contrast to the muggy air of Los Ángeles station. We settle into our plush seats, the hum of the distant engines a low thrum beneath the soles of our boots.

Banksia opens her BTN, projecting the route onto the back of the seat in front of us. "This feels like a wild goose chase. From Asunción to Ascension Island, then Dar es Salaam and over to Zanzibar— are we sure we're not just going in circles?"

"The trail of the Elops is more of a spiral, not a straight line," I muse, watching the map pulse with our paths that lie ahead. "But spirals eventually lead to the centre."

"Deep," Benny chuckles.

As the TT2 glides forward, leaving the station behind, I lean back against the headrest. "Next stop, Asunción," I whisper, as much to myself as to the others. "Let's unravel this spiral through Paraguay."

The TT2 hums beneath us, a steel serpent threading through the bowels of the earth. We're cocooned within its sleek capsule, the world outside, geological wonders that we can only imagine lay beyond the reinforced walls. This TT2 doesn't sport the same cool windows as our last ride. So I have to picture the glaciers hanging above us like frozen sentinels, ancient volcanoes simmering with secrets, and vast deserts where the wind sculpts the sand, or probably now mud, into ever-changing art.

"Feels like we're flying through a planet's memories," I say, trying to make light of the weight pressing against my chest. Not just the pressure of kilometres of rock overhead, but the heavy frustration from the ClimaSphere's stubborn silence.

"This is how speedy moles must feel—minus the glorious seating," Benny quips.

"Plush seats don't make up for the lack of views," I mutter, my fingers continually tapping a staccato rhythm on the ClimaSphere's unresponsive surface. "And what about lakes and forests? Aren't they worth a glance?"

"Next time we'll plan a scenic route," Soren assures, though the iron in their voice belies the jest.

"Scenic doesn't get us to Asunción in two and a half hours," Juice counters. Because time isn't an extravagance we can afford—not with Roman Polotov and Anthro-Tech's sinister agenda casting long shadows across cantons.

"Speaking of scenic," Banksia points out, looking at her BTN chart, "we're passing under Laguna Mar Chiquita now." The words hang in the air, evoking images of the vast salt lake somewhere far above us, hidden yet visceral.

"Bet it's beautiful on a sunny day," I muse, earning a smile from Banksia that crinkles the corners of her eyes.

"Everything is beautiful when you look hard enough," Benny says, a mantra that feels especially poignant in our subterranean race against the clock.

"Even the Paraguay River?" Juice asks, voicing the shared anticipation of emerging into daylight once again.

"Especially rivers," I affirm. "They carve paths where none existed, just like us."

When the TT2 finally eases to a halt, we disembark into the heartbeat of Asunción. The station throbs with life, a hub of comings and goings that mirror the river's own current.

"Twenty minutes, people," Soren reminds us, their watch beeps as it syncs with the pulse of the city.

"Let's make them count," I say, leading our little band up and out into the streets. Our boots meet cobblestones worn smooth by centuries of footsteps, and the air carries whispers of history mingling with the scent of progress as the SkyRisers stretch toward the clouds like the aspirations of the people who built them. All the while, the Paraguay River rolls alongside, an old soul amidst the march of time.

"Timelessness and transformation," I note, the juxtaposition not lost on my companions, who nod their agreement.

Our time in this incredible city is fleeting, and I fear we may never have the chance to return. We're dodging between rain showers and marvelling at the bubbling clouds above. The streets are slick with water, and neon lights reflect off the glistening pavement, creating a surreal atmosphere. As we make our way through winding alleyways and bustling squares, we can't help but feel like we're part of a hidden world.

Even through the bustle, there is tension with all that is happening around us, around the globe. There is no spot on earth right now immune to the depressive nature of the clouds, the people dying from their Oxolets running out of power and the chaos associated with not knowing where to turn for help. I guess if those around us knew who we were, they would turn to us.

With one last glance at the river, we turn our backs to the staggering skyline and descend into the underground tunnels. The sound of distant music, angst-riddled chatter and skirmishes fill our ears.

"Back to the labyrinth we go," I declare with a wry grin, ready to chase down the next clue in our quest. Because no matter how convoluted the journey, hope dances on the horizon like the first light of dawn—elusive but undeniable.

Asunción fades behind us, but its spirit, a blend of grit and grace, remains imprinted on our resolve.

We hustle, our breaths short but spirits undeterred. The TT3's sleek form looms ahead, its polished chassis a promise of the velocity to come. Ascension Island beckons, a blip in the vast ocean now transformed into a pivotal waypoint on our odyssey.

"Last call for the TT3 to George Town, Ascension!" The AI announcement crackles overhead, a siren song for wanderers like us.

"Never a dull moment with us a lot," I quip, exchanging grins with my crew as we board.

"Wouldn't have it any other way," Soran retorts, their eyes alight with the thrill of the chase.

The TT3's doors slide shut with a gentle hiss, sealing us within. We exchange glances, each of us silently acknowledging the weight of our journey, the miles travelled, and those yet to conquer.

"Strap in," I instruct, my voice steady despite the flutter in my chest. "This is going to be one heck of a deep dive."

It's funny. Just as the doors close, I close my eyes briefly. As we navigate the globe, echoes of OZ singing Daft Punk's 'Around The World' spring to mind. I can still hear the repetition of the lyrics, "Around the world, around the world—" Now look at us, doing the exact same damn thing. Premonition? Coincidence? Distant memory?

We're thrust back into our seats as the TT surges beneath the South Atlantic. The hum of machinery melds with the pulse of the ocean above, a reminder of the sheer power encapsulating us. We're travelling at breakneck speed—3,000 kilometres per hour—yet inside this bullet of technology, there's an odd sense of stillness.

"9,200 metres under, huh?" Juice muses, his gaze locked

on the digital depth gauge mounted on the wall ahead. "Feels like flying without the sky."

"Or swimming without getting wet," I add, earning a chuckle from the group.

"Let's just hope Roman's minions aren't as comfortable in these depths," whispers Banksia, ever the strategist thinking one step ahead.

"Do we still know what he wants at these Elops?" Benny asks with a tone of wisdom. "There was no way to get off planet in Chile, even if the Elops had stayed open. Is there a pad where we're going?" he asks openly. Without waiting for an answer, "if not, then why? What does he want? Odezza, do you think he knows you have an Oxo2?"

"He might know about the ClimaSphere, too. Have we thought of that possibility?" Juice kicks in.

Benny offers, "We're also assuming he is heading to Tanzania, like us."

"For now, it's all just speculative. Let's just enjoy being the most advanced fish in the sea," I say, leaning back as the TT3 navigates unseen landscapes below.

"Did you know," Benny starts, his trivia as much a part of him as his unwavering courage, "that the pressure down here is like having fifty jumbo jets stacked on you?"

"What's a jumbo jet?" Banksia asks in all seriousness.

Benny raises his left eyebrow questioningly, not interested in explaining an ancient relic like a Boeing 747.

"You can seriously understand why that TT OZ was on bound for Next Tokyo would have instantly exploded like it did," Soren says in a solemn yet scientific voice. "This is a lot of pressure we are currently withstanding, yet I can't feel anything different from standing on that last TT platform."

What an interesting preponderance.

"We're essentially skipping half a continent in less time than it takes to watch a movie. Better than the ancients and flying everywhere," I interject, trying desperately to get back on track,

Soren looks up at me with a look that says, 'we were just on a plane, numbnuts, and how'd that work out?!'

WE CHAT along the way and get to know each other better. It is strange that we have been uni friends for a while, yet we don't really know much about each other personally. There is nothing quite like being stuck on a series of high-speed tubes, being jettisoned around the globe, trying to save the world, and getting to know each other.

While the group chats about their favourite sports, movies and games, I continue to work on cracking the ClimaSphere code. If I can't get this to work, all will be for nothing. Then we only have one chance left, the one rumoured to be in Australia. And if it doesn't work, then I shudder to think. We'll have to return to our insignificant corners of the world, sit in our SLABS, and watch as Roman's climate terrorism finally causes our blue orb to perish, witnessing the earth taking its last grasp.

It took a while to get it out of him, but Juice confesses he is really into Sky-Surfing on SolarWinds. I have not heard of that. He tells us that athletes, like himself, don special suits with solar sails, catching the sun's energy to glide through the sky, performing acrobatic manoeuvres. Who knows? Pretty sure he hasn't been able to play that sport over the past fortnight, but I don't have the heart to crack such a low joke.

Soren shocks us too, which I always thought would be impossible, by telling us they have been studying Lunar Parkour. I've not heard of this one either - apparently TiM and I need to get out more. Soren shares that with the upcoming colonisation on the moon, parkour artists leap across the low-gravity environment, turning the lunar landscape into an otherworldly obstacle course. None of us seemed shocked by the combination of this sport and Soren. They also share that Paris has one of only two low-gravity sims; thus the reason she'd been staying in the City of Lights.

We keep the conversation going as we stitch trains deep beneath Ascension. At this point, we're starting to think that 'once you've seen one TT station, you've pretty much seen them all'.

Banksia shares she is really into Underwater Freestyle Dancing. Now, this I've heard of. She tells us that divers equipped with water-jet packs and LED suits perform synchronised dances in the ocean depths, accompanied by holographic displays. Cool.

Then there's Benny. He reveals he is into a lot of sports, some old-fashioned like wingsuit flying and extreme fly board-ing. But Benny is also into magnetic skateboarding. This is where skateboarders ride on hoverboards that use magnetic levitation, flipping and spinning through the air on holo-graphic half-pipes. That sounds pretty cool, too.

Then all eyes are on me. Think, Odezza, think.

"I'm into AR wingsuit racing." Blank stares address my statement. "Where you don AR headsets and wingsuits and race through digital landscapes that mimic extreme conditions from around the universe. Come on, none of you have done this?"

"Odezza," Benny reacts, "why do you wear an AR wing-suit and not the real deal?"

I just look at him and bat his arm, "Because that shit's crazy and I don't have a death wish."

Gaining some giggles from the group. Look at what we have learned about each other in such a short amount of time. I am super glad we had that time to connect. It seems to truly solidify the Mighty5, not that we needed solidification.

"Dar es Salaam, next stop," the automated pilot announces, its tone devoid of the adrenaline that courses through our veins, startling us all back into reality.

"Almost there," I whisper, more to myself than to the team. The Mighty5, an unbreakable unit forged in adversity, is poised to take on whatever awaits us off the shores of Tanzania.

"Ready for the next leap?" I ask a little louder, though I already know the answer.

"Always," they respond, with unity in their voices. And with that shared conviction, we barrel onward, beneath the crushing depths, towards the unknown.

The TT grinds to a whispering halt, and I feel the inertia tug at my insides like a playful reminder of physics. "Welcome to Dar es Salaam," the emotionless voice of the automated pilot intones as the doors swish open with a hiss that speaks of secrets and hidden depths.

We spill out into the station, a modern marvel of copper, cobalt and tanzanite with the slightest specs of coloured glass. The air is heavy with brine and decay, a scent that tugs at the corners of my mind, whispering of trouble. We can already feel the sound of the approaching wind outside.

"Zanzibar's just a stone's throw away," Banksia says, squinting at the digital map flickering on her BTN. "If stones could fly over water."

"Or swim through death," Soren adds, instantly suspecting something is awry.

As we walk up and out of the Tanganyika Railway Station, total chaos and streets filled with running people instantly hit us, flashing Oxolets, fallen trees and downed AeroCars.

"What have we walked into?" Benny asks, his tone filled with instant panic.

I'm not sure what to do or which way to turn. We find

ourselves momentarily frozen, dumbstruck by the pandemonium we have materialised into.

"Is it too late to go back to the station?" Benny quips, trying to sound less scared but is fooling no one.

Juice looks around for a moment, trying to get his bearings. Just then, an elderly woman in her late 70s walks by, seemingly unfazed and unscathed by all that is going on. "Ni nini kinaendelea hapa?" I hear him ask. I'm guessing amongst the 17 languages he knows, that Kiswahili or Swahili is one of them. "Kimbunga kibaya," I hear her say in a deep, raspy voice, almost yelling over the wind and rain. "She says it's a bad cyclone," Juice translates for us. "Kimbunga Majid bin Said."

"That sounds like someone's name." I stutter.

"It is," Juice responds, still trying to figure out which way is up and down.

The two of them chat for a moment. I just heard the words Zanzibar and maji, water, but the rest is gibberish to my untrained ear. We all wait while we get the scoop. Sometimes, I hear the old woman laugh. Is Juice flirting with her and cracking jokes, or is that a nervous laugh?

Juice pulls us into a tight rugby huddle and regurgitates what the old woman just told him. "She said this storm has been raging like this all day, and is the worst storm since 1872, but somehow the Elops over Zanzibar is still intact. This sounds like a pretty manic storm. She told me the storm surge had already devastated the usually sandy beaches and low-lying areas. It's caused boats in the harbour to be turned upside down and led to the shutdown of port operations. I am not sure of the location, but apparently the Kigamboni Bridge endured a severe battering of high winds. She also told me The Msimbazi River broke its banks and exacerbated flooding in Ilala's central districts."

"That's one crazy-ass storm," Benny tosses in.

Juice takes a long breath and continues. "I asked her if

WHEN ALL THE CLOUDS COLLIDE

there is a TT to the island. She said there's generally an old train, pre-BoldWar, that runs in a tunnel under the bay, but it's been flooded.

"So we're SOL?" Benny says frustratedly.

Juice continues, not acknowledging Benny's question. "Then, I asked her about taking a boat over to the island to see the hole, and she laughed at me. She questioned why we would even want to head out in a storm like this, but I told her we didn't have a choice. That's when we laughed again and she told me she hasn't seen the shimo, the hole, but everyone's talking about it."

"So," Soren kicks in, obviously bored by Juice's details, "she said she's never seen it, but—"

"Wait, there's more." Juice is on a roll and I catch Soren rolling their eyes. "She has heard stories about an old U.S. SEAL submarine supposedly docked near or under the Tanzanite Bridge. Benny, will you look that up and see if it's true?"

Benny gives the faintest head nod.

"What's with this sub?" Soren adds with a bite.

Seconds slip by as Benny does the research.

"It looks like it might be two kilometres from here - to the North," Benny picks up the conversation.

"The sub?" Soren adds, seeming to chide Benny.

"No, the circus! Yes, the sub. That's what the local chatter says. It's apparently been abandoned for years. Let's see if we can walk up there and see what we find," Benny adds, not buying into Soren's snakiness.

"Lead the way, McDuff, and let's see what we see," I add, trying to cut between them.

As we start out, rucksacks slung over our shoulders, titanium case in my hand, we see the havoc and utter gruesomeness of this storm. That woman may have undersold it, as we climb over downed trees and around smashed AeroCars and even some dead bodies.

We keep on walking. This storm has certainly done a number on the homes and shops. Looking down a long street, we can see the left side of a hospital is completely missing and the one school we pass is missing its roof altogether.

Out of the blue, I realise we haven't seen a church. Not sure why that strikes me as odd, as there were very few left after the BoldWar. But somehow, I expected to see one or two.

We continue to walk northward in horrified silence. I'm guessing none of us have ever seen anything like this in real life.

As we hit the coastline, what we thought couldn't get any worse immediately does.

As we wander over the abandoned highway, a once inviting beach now resembles a mass grave for bloated and decaying fish. Thousands of them. The putrid stench of death immediately fills our nostrils as we look out over the once sandy shore. It was a jarring contrast to what must have been a bustling tourist destination just a few weeks ago. Now, it is nothing but a haunting reminder of the destruction that has just occurred.

Benny flic's on his BTN, "There's Yellow Tuna, Wahoo's King mackerel, Dorado and Billfish down there." He remarks solemnly. "If I am referencing this correctly, there are also barracuda and snapper, fire dartfish, octopus, moray eel and even giant grouper. I've never seen anything like this in my life." Apparently, Benny forgot to mention that he is also an ichthyologist.

"Benny, you sound like you're reading Jules Verne's 20,000 Leagues Under The Sea," Banksia scoffs. Her comment seems both accurate and amusing.

The scene of destruction is never ending. We can see a concrete and metal bridge up ahead as we continue heading north. We can see dozens of toppled eVTOL's and a handful of AeroCars haphazardly strewn upon the shore. What is all this? What did we miss?

As we continue walking, we get our first glimpse of Elops #3 over Zanzibar to the northeast. What a stark contrast to our immediate surroundings. The hole is large, like the size of three or four football pitches. And it sparkles in the bluest sky I've ever seen. What a sight. But before I get too far ahead of my eagerness to conquer the Elops, a jolt of realism rivets me. What if we get over there, and I can't get this gawdforsaken ClimaSphere to work?

The thought chills me to the bone as we travel over the deserted bridge. A bridge that will either lead us to success or to complete and horrid devastation.

CHAPTER THIRTY-SIX

As we approach the northern end of the Tanzanite Bridge, a sea cave looms before us like a gaping maw of history, swathed in shadows and secrets. We find a ladder leading down to some damp rocks below. We scurry down and as we approach the sub, my heart seems to hammer in time, waves crashing in front of us.

"Guys, you've got to see this," Soren mutters, scanning the sub and urgently thumbing their BTN screen. The Mighty5 huddles around them, our heads almost touching as we squint at the tiny, glowing text. As we huddle together, I am momentarily transported back to the way we used to meet via our HelloHolo's.

"What is this thing?" Benny asks.

"Stand by, Benny," Soren continues, scanning, their voice a blend of haste and aggravation. "It looks like you and that old lady were right about there being a sub."

None of us have ever witnessed a submarine before, so we all gather anxiously, eager to discover not only the identity of this mysterious creature but also its ability to safely transport us to our destination, without the risk of flooding like an antique bathtub.

Soren finally speaks. "From what I can surmise, it's a 1988 SEAL Delivery Vehicle," they read aloud, the words feeling alien to our ears. For all we know, it could be a gawdforsaken alien warship. "Used by U.S. Navy SEALs," Soren reads on, "for— wow, everything from the Gulf War to skirmishes in Somalia." Their eyes scan the information, taking in the historical weight of the vessel before us.

"It's like finding a relic from a halcyon era and bygone wars," Banksia blurts.

"Only this relic might save our butts," Benny interjects, his gaze fixed on the SDV with an intensity that dares it to be operational.

It is ominous-looking. Completely black from bow to stern. No markings of any type, no marine or even country designation. Nothing. And tiny slits for windows. It is intimidating and ruthless looking.

"Powered by lithium-ion batteries," Soren continues, noticeably unimpressed, "with top-notch navigation systems in their day." They tap the screen, scrolling through more data. "And it had communication tech and life-support systems. Not to mention a weapons-delivery system."

"Let's hope we won't need that last part," Banksia murmurs with a wry twist of her lips.

The CG outlawed weapons of any type in all cantons after the BoldWar, so even thinking about such things seems criminal.

"Agreed," Benny adds, scratching his head, "but how do we get this beast open and start 'er up?"

We all look around, trying to find an opening of some kind. A hatch. A door. Anything. We slap it and kick it, knock it and hammer it. It's no simple task to find an opening of some kind as we all look around. The sub sits on slippery rocks, submerged in two feet of water, but at least the water is warm.

Through all the clamouring, Juice finds a recessed handle with a button in the middle. How'd ever see that as it's black on black on black? As he pushes it, we all stand back in awe, dumbstruck by his ability to think fast and not over process. With a hard push, the button moves in taking the handle with it. Then, an enormous metal door that didn't seem to be there before, cracks, hisses and opens with a tremendous creak. It's moving slowly toward the rear of the vessel.

And just like that, there is a gaping hole opening to a seating area, and two workstations. Oh, where is OZ when you want to blow his mind?

"There are only three seats," Benny points out. As we peer in, we see this is quite right, "but there are five of us."

"We can sit on each other's laps," Banksia says with a smirk. Always the pragmatic one. "It will be cosy, but the island is just over there," as she points to the northwest.

"Keep on looking around for another button/handle combo," Soren says calmly, "as there is no way this thing only seats three. Look at the length of it."

Soren has a point. So, we all keep on pushing and probing.

Within seconds, Benny finds another entrance combo like the earlier one, this time toward the sub's stern. He follows Juice's lead, pushing hard on the button, as the handle moves into place.

This time, the massive door creaks slowly to the right, stopping within kissing distance of the first door. Before Benny can remark, we are all counting seats - five more.

"What the heck is this thing?" Benny asks, with all the zeal of a schoolboy on his first day at boarding school, wide-eyed and bushy-tailed, "and what is that awful smell?"

"Well—" Soren starts, quickly realising that was a rhetorical question.

"Since we don't know how long this thing has been abandoned, who knows what lies in there beyond the smell. Who knows what we'll encounter there?" Banksia says in the most charming manner.

"Shouldn't be bugs and stuff if that's what you're worried about, B," Juice says, always the sage. These are great seals, so nothing has gotten in or out for a while.

As we crawl and climb aboard the primitive submersible, we all keep bent over as we're unable to sit upright. It is super sparse, particularly in the rear compartment. A couple of aged dials and knobs. There doesn't seem to be too much more upfront. But there is a yolk, reminiscent of the old plane.

We take our seats. The fresh salt sea breeze off the Indian Ocean quickly flushing out the stale mustiness of years of neglect. And soon Soren and Juice take seats up front, as we all find a seat in the rear to prepare for our seaward voyage.

"Right," Soren says, always the taskmaster. "First things first. Control systems." Soren squints at the diagrams and text emanating from her wrist, then glances at the sub's interior panel, trying to match what they see to the instructions. "We need to activate the steering and propulsion controls."

"Here," Juice asks, pointing to a panel with worn labels that have somehow survived the ravages of time and saltwater.

I watch as Soren's fingers dance across the console, flickering over last-minute buttons and switches with a rhythm born of necessity. "Control systems are coming online," they announce, their voice a soft purr against the thrum of the SDV's awakened heart.

But, this is like watching the plane all over again, so let's hope it ends differently.

"Good," Soren confirms, nodding.

"Next up, navigation," Soren instructs. "We've got to initialise the Doppler Inertial Navigation System and the GPS." They pause, frowning. "Assuming they still respond."

"And life support," Juice says, his voice suddenly firm. "That's crucial. Check the compressed air supply?"

"Got it," Soren responds, left hand already moving toward that set of gauges.

"Last but not least, a final systems check," Soren concludes. "Let's make sure everything is green across the board before we dive."

"Green is good," Juice replies, offering a thumbs-up that borders on comical given the gravity of our situation.

"Comms?" Soren asks, their eyes wide with awareness, almost daring the universe to throw another spitball our way.

"Static-y, but working," Juice replies, the crackle from the speaker serving as a grim reminder of how far technology has come.

"Navigation?" Soren asks, continuing down the checklist.

"They're a go," Juice replies. "Power systems," he declares, the ultimate act before the plunge. His hand hovers over the switch that will engage the silver-zinc batteries—the heart of the SDV. A deep breath, and then contact. The gentle hum of the electric motor resonates through the hull, a lullaby for warriors about to dive into the unknown.

"Juice, we're lit," Soren says, a grin tugging at their lips despite the gravity of our mission. The old SEAL DV is alive, a phoenix rising from the ashes of forgotten skirmishes and wars.

"Steering feels good." Juice's fingers hover and then dip, his touch feather-light on the manual override.

"Propulsion?" Soren asks, their eyes alight with a rare spark—that unquenchable fire that defines every member of the Mighty5. They are quick learners.

"Like kicking a dragon in the tail," Juice replies, feeling the SDV respond to his commands, a steel beast and silence bending to our will. "Do we have a bearing?"

They must be getting close to pushing off.

"Destination: Zanzibar," Soren says, leaning in to inspect the readouts. "North, Northeast." Their voice is calm, a counterpoint to the storm that continues to rage just outside the metal frame of this prehistoric beast.

"Hope you left breadcrumbs," Benny teases, his attempt at levity a thin veil over the tension that grips us all.

"Only the digital kind," I chuck back, a smirk tugging at my lips despite the gravity of our mission. We're about to thread the needle through Poseidon's domain, and there's no room for error.

"Then let's not keep the sea waiting," Juice declares, his voice a low growl reverberating through the hull.

"Or history," Banksia adds, her hand gripping the edge of her seat as if she could hold the future in her palm.

"History can wait," I muse aloud. "It's the present that needs us."

And with that, Juice hits two large flappy panels above the controls, causing both flat doors to find their resting place along the side of the submersible. The door's seal closes, and a soft blue glow immediately emanates from the ceiling of the sub, casting an ethereal ambiance. Like fireflies in a jar, we eagerly await, ready to witness the passing of the world.

With an abrupt shove, we pull out of the SDV's hiding place tucked away in this coastal cave. We slowly slip beneath the waves, leaving the Tanzanite Bridge and Dar es Salaam in our negligible wake. Adventurers charting a course through liquid daylight, our vessel a silent shadow gliding toward destiny.

THE SDV HUMS AROUND US, a steady thrum against the silence of the deep. We've been riding this ghost sub for what seems like hours, and with every passing minute, I feel the weight of responsibility pressing down harder. Although I am working at cracking this damn code, I am yet to solve its riddle—and our window is narrowing.

I look at the nav screen Soren and Juice have in front of them. It looks like we're passing by many islands. My eyes catch sight of Tele Island, Chumbe Island, and Nyange Island. I hazard a guess that the parts we can not see must have been stunning before all the clouds collided and crazy ass storms wreaked havoc around the globe. I make a mental note to return here one day - if we all survive this mess.

"Any luck?" Banksia asks, glancing over at me. My fingers continually dance across the darkened screen, a blur of motion that speaks to urgency more than confidence.

"Still working on it," I reply without looking up, my voice a mix of determination and frustration. "OZ loved his puzzles. But I'll get there — I hope." My voice is fading away with exasperation. I must have tried a thousand different combinations of numbers and words, dashes and dots, English and any other language I recall OZ speaking, but still nothing.

"Damn right you will," Benny pipes in. "You've got your dad's brains and twice his stubbornness."

"Stubbornness might just save us all," Banksia adds, her usual humour shadowed by the gravity of our submerged mission.

Juice looks back and touches my arm, nodding toward the viewpoint as the first rays of returning sunlight pierce the ocean's depths. We must be close to the Elops. "Time to trade fins for feet, people."

Moments later, we clear the surface, the SDV breaking through into the world above like it's an everyday occurrence. The bright blue sky stretches out limitlessly—a stark contrast to the confining darkness that has enveloped us for the past few weeks. Elops #3 soars over us, its massive frame holding open a gateway between what is and what could be. It is both stunning and mesmerising. You don't know what you've missed until you don't have it and the sun and blue sky are part of that missing piece. It is staggering how fast our world, the one we take for granted, can fall to pieces so quickly, all because of a lack of sunlight and a madman's plight for world domination.

"Look at that," Soren breathes, pointing upward. "It's like the eye of some noble beast staring down, daring us to blink."

"Let's not keep it waiting," Juice says, steering us toward the Old Fort Marina. These guys did an excellent job piloting another old, out-of-date transportation relic.

"Well done getting us here, team," I pipe up. "That was a really interesting way to travel." Soren and Juice offer a polite head nod. "Remember," I continue, my gaze fixed on the two sub doors, waiting for them to open, "the Elops needs to remain open long enough for the ClimaSphere to work. No pressure or anything."

"Pressure makes diamonds," Juice quips, earning a roll of my eyes, but he gets a chuckle from the rest of the crew.

Emerging from the depths, we gently nudge against the old dock. The old sliding doors swipe to their open position, and we disembark, stepping onto Terra firma. The Old Fort greets us with its ancient walls, a silent guardian that has watched over countless arrivals and departures for centuries. Today, it witnesses ours.

Zanzibar, or Unguja, as the locals call it, greets us with its famed humidity. I guess we are officially in the tropics. Beyond the old town, I see Mt. Masingini rising like a sentinel standing watch over the island.

"Wow," Banksia whispers as we make our way through an ancient archway. People swarm all around us, a sea of faces united by hope and fear. Bustling, walking, running and riding little old motorbikes, scooters and sidecars. My guess is, everyone here is here for the same reason we are—to see if the

Elops will hold, reversersing the trends of the others. Staying open and remaining that way. What these people don't know is what I have in my sturdy titanium case.

"Never seen so many people gathered in one place," Benny marvels, shading his eyes against the glare of the sun.

"Desperate times," Soren murmurs, but there's a thread of awe in their voice, too.

"Let's not disappoint them," I say. The Mighty5, a band of uni misfits and geniuses, ready to tackle the gawdforsaken code and breathe life back into a dying planet.

"Today, we rewrite history," I pronounce in a cocky manner reserved for football players and movie stars. A murmur ripples through the masses, and heads turn our way —eyes alight with something that looks a lot like hope.

"Or at least give it a hell of an edit," Benny adds with a smirk. Everyone cracks a smile, and for a moment, the weight on our shoulders seems lighter. We're here under the breath-taking blue sky, under the open Elops, our first time seeing one, and we're not alone—not anymore. Together, we step into the heart of the Old Fort, ready for whatever comes next.

The Elops above shimmers, a wavering curtain between doom and deliverance. Desperation claws at me as I remove the ClimaSphere from its case and scan its interface once more, searching for a sign, a breakthrough, anything.

"Odezza?" a voice cuts through the din, sharp and clear. It's distant yet slightly familiar, impossible and yet unmistakable.

"Did you hear that?" I ask, my head snapping up, eyes scanning the throng.

"Did someone just call your name?" Benny asks, confusion lining his face. "But how? It sounded like... like it came from across the square."

"Odezza!" the voice calls again, louder, more insistent.

"Okay, that's no hallucination," Juice says, squinting

toward the source of the sound. We exchange looks, a silent agreement passing between us.

"Let's find out who's calling," I say, determination fuelling my steps as we push through the crowd. The Mighty5 united in purpose and perplexity, driven by hope against all odds. Who here would know my name? Who anywhere would know my name?

Elbows collide and voices compete for attention as we navigate through the bustling square, where merchants peddle their wares and the aroma of spices and humanity intermingle, while the name "Odezza" reverberates through the cacophony. I'm drawn to the source, a beacon in the turmoil, the edges of the Elops pulsing above like a living thing. The Mighty5 rally around me, our collective breaths syncing with the thrum of anticipation.

"Odezza!"

Oh, forgawdsake! What the heck is happening? The call slices through the din again, this time laced with urgency yet familiarity.

Just then, a woman in her late fifties, resplendent olive skin, short, salt and pepper wavy hair with a bright red, yellow and blue scarf around a long slender neck emerges like an apparition from the restless sea of faces. Her sea-blue eyes locking onto mine. There's no mistaking the determined set of her jaw or the fierce intelligence sparking behind her gaze – she's every inch the woman in the copper frame in OZ's lab/office. I have never been so confused. Could that really be my— my thoughts are cut short.

"Odezza?" she questions as she comes closer, her voice rich with an Espana accent, steady as she reaches me, parting the crowd with authority born of desperation. "I went by the flat in London to check on OZ and you—"

"Who are you?" Soren cuts the woman off, cross-examining her, ever so defensively. The unity of the Mighty5 is tight.

The mystery woman gives Soren a curious look. She keeps her gaze squarely fixed on me. I want to question, accuse and embrace; but there's no time. Her presence here is a puzzle piece I didn't know I was missing.

"Mum?"

"I went to your lab," she continues, pressing louder over the rumble of the crowd. "He always had a failsafe code to the penthouse."

"Mum?" I repeat, but not hearing my own words.

"Yes, honey. My name is Alice."

I can't shake off the feeling that an invisible barrier has been erected around our group, isolating us from the rest of the world. Amidst all this noise and chaos comes a deafening silence that seems to amplify my inner turmoil. How can I feel so alone in such a crowded place?

"I don't get it," I say, stunned and confused. The thought of having a mum never crossed my mind - ever! It was always OZ and me. Then OZ, me and TiM. Then OZ, me, TiM and my uni mates. But never a Mum. "I don't get it," I add.

Alice continues, not skipping a beat, "like I said, I went by OZ's lab to find more clues about what you were up to and where you were going."

"I don't get it. What 'clues'?" My voice seems to echo a sense of scepticism and trepidation.

Alice presses on with determination in her eyes. "I had been keeping tabs on your dad since I left. I left when you were four months old. I'm guessing OZ never told you." I just nod. "I loved your dad very much, but after the BoldWar, our relationship turned distant." He was always in his lab, working around the clock, and would never share with me what he was working on. He had created the Oxolet for which I and every-one, I guess, were very grateful; but what else he was working on was anyone's guess. So, with great joy, you came along, but with great sorrow, I couldn't stay. I'd had too much and felt like I couldn't raise you as a fully dedicated mother.

I can hear Banksia sniffling over my right shoulder. Keep it together, woman!

Alice, or I guess, Mum, continues, "It broke my heart to leave, but I couldn't stick around. It was all too much for me to take. I was, I am a scientist in my right and didn't want to be in the shadow of the mighty OZ for my entire career.

"So, when all this meteorological madness appeared, I knew somehow OZ would be near the epicentre of creating a solution. So, with the help of a colleague, we tapped your dad's mainframe and poked around, and put some pieces together. Which, by the way, is difficult with OZ. I can tell he must still hand-write everything down in notebooks because what we found was a pittance.

Her comment releases a tentative smile at the edges of my mouth.

"I suspect he made some type of machine that he believed could do something with these holes and put the climate straight again. Is that correct?"

As I go to acknowledge and share the frustration around the proto, Alice immediately pipes back up, "Wait? What is that on your left wrist?" she interrupts herself.

"It's an upgraded Oxolet," I say with great pride. "It's an Oxo2. Dad developed it."

"Does anyone know about this upgrade?" Alice asks. "And where is OZ, by the way?"

With that, our jaws drop open. She doesn't know. How would she?

"I assumed he was off finding a cup of Zanzibar Chai," Alice muses poetically.

"OZ is dead," Soren says flatly, before I can take a breath.
Chai?

267

"Alice, these are my uni friends," I quickly add, in a somewhat monotone voice, "Soren, Juice, Banksia and Benny."

Soren repeats, "OZ is dead."

"OZ is dead?" Alice squeaks out.

Juice quickly adds, "A few days ago. Someone murdered him on the TT heading to Next Tokyo where the first Elops was discovered."

"What's in Next Tokyo that he needed to be there?" Alice asks. "And are you doing okay, Odezza?"

I just give a slow, deep nod. This is one of those rare times I could do with a hug, but I don't know this woman from Eve, so any form of emotional compensation will have to wait for now.

Juice continues, "And your hunch is right, Alice. OZ did develop a machine that he suspected could reverse these openings, these Elops, for good. But the person—"

"It's a long story—" Benny interjects, and Juice continues, "That did the cloud seeding—which brought about the bad weather— had him killed." Juice is really struggling. "And like Benny said, it's a long story that might not be appropriate at this moment."

"What is," Alice continues, "this machine?"

"OZ called it a ClimaSphere," Banksia adds.

"Of course he did." A bitter laugh escapes Alice. "OZ, the meticulous inventor, was always good at developing catchy product names. So, did he have it on him when he died?"

"I'll just give you the punchline, as I can see where your mind is heading," I kick in. But I need to watch my tone in case this woman really is my mum? "He had the ClimaSphere on him when we died. And yes, before you ask, he made a second proto. And yes, we have one with us."

I tap the metal case, thinking that I should really try to use it instead of prattling on with this potential stranger.

"There is just one slight, ever so teensy-weensy hiccup

with this machine," I continue. "We, as in I, can't seem to make it work."

Alice greets my vulnerability with a look of scepticism.

"She can't make it work!" Soren says, always blunt and to the point.

I drag a hand down my face, trying not to think about the current conversation where I look like a gawddamn idiot, the reality of Alice's presence settling over me like an ill-fitting jacket. "You're — my mother?" The words still feel foreign to my tongue, as if I'm speaking in codes and cyphers rather than English. But there's no time for the emotional calculus of a reunion that should've been decades in the making.

"Later, Odezza," Soren mutters beside me, "just go with it for now," their voice a lifeline yanking me back to the urgency of now. Soren's right—later for family trees, when the forest is ablaze.

"Right," I snap into focus, my mind a whirring engine of analysis and deduction. I reopen the metal case.

"Let's cut to the chase," Juice interjects, his Scando-Baijan twang slicing through the thickening tension. "This thing needs to work, or we're all trapped under the clouds forever."

"Show us what you've got," Alice asks, hands stretched out in awe to receive the futuristic machine.

Alice nods at it, scientifically, unfazed. She's all business, her eyes scanning the ClimaSphere with the practised gaze of a fellow technologist. "Here." She doesn't take her eyes off the proto, as she hands me a folded piece of tatted paper, her fingers brushing mine—a touch that sparks a thousand unanswered questions.

"What is this?" I ask questioningly.

"A cypher?" Banksia asks, leaning over my shoulder.

"Where did you get this, Alice?" I ask.

"This note was among the few things we found useful

during our tapping exhibition. And, Banksia, it indeed is a cypher."

"I have spent hour after hour attempting to crack the code needed to unlock this thing, with zero luck," I add, frustrated with my meagre attempts.

"Now that I see the machine with my own eyes, let me take a closer look, Odezza," Alice suggests with total fascination and inquisitiveness. "And hand me back that note, please."

I hand the page back as Alice slips on old spectacles. Wow, I have only seen those in history Holos. No one wears glasses anymore. They're unnecessary. Not since nanobots were integrated into everyone's eye lenses. Best invention ever (apart from the Oxolet). Benny and I once got into a conversation about this exact tech. Microscopic robots gently reshape the cornea while we sleep, adapting to daily changes in vision. They're powered by our body's own bioelectric energy and can communicate with smart devices to provide real-time updates on eye health. So why on earth would Alice need spectacles?

"What are those?" Benny asks, half serious, half joking.

We all look at her over her shoulder, willing her to get to an answer quicker, but she does not understand the word on the page. Then, with the snap of her head, she looks up and turns toward us all.

"Nope, I can't seem to figure it out either and definitely can't read OZ's handwriting or his guides. I can only decipher one slight code. It might mean something, or it might mean nothing at all. A na—"

Without warning, our BTNs light up, sending out a Red Alert to everyone around us! "Don't tell me, this gawddamn Elops is closing?" I yell out.

We look up and sure enough. It is mesmerising. It is sickening. It is tantalising. It is mortifying. It is closing.

CHAPTER THIRTY-SEVEN

The Elops snaps shut above us with a roar and a shudder that seems to send a shock wave through the Zanzibar air, vibrating in my bones. I glance up—just in time to see the last of the magnificent blue sky vanish behind broiling clouds, like a gurgling river, plunging us into darkness once more. "It's like an eclipse," I say under my breath. What we just witnessed will never leave me and may haunt me for the rest of my life. Adrenaline kicks at my chest like it's trying to escape.

My gaze flicks to Alice, her face lit by a mix of sunset hues bleeding through the edges of the closed Elops. Her face is a display of utter shock and dismay, like the rest of us.

"Before we were so rudely interrupted by impending doom—" she starts, her voice steady but her eyes betraying something else—a secret teetering on the edge of revelation.

"Spill it, Alice. We're all ears," Banksia chimes in, arms folded, her stance as rooted as the trees she's named after.

Alice's fingers toy with something hidden beneath her shirt collar. Her lips part, and for a heartbeat, the utter chaos around us fades away like the light above. "I was about to tell you I think I figured out OZ's chicken scratch and why my instinct told me to travel six thousand kilometres from Valencia." Her hand emerges, clutching a pendant that glints even in the muted light, and my breath hitches. "Why did I have to meet Odezza?"

"Alice, dramatic much?" Benny quips from beside me, rolling his eyes, but I can feel the tension radiating off him.

"Shhhh," Banksia hushes him. "This is the good part." Always the romantic.

"I believe Odezza's birth name," Alice continues to all of us, her voice almost a whisper now, "is the key to everything OZ left behind. And seemingly our only chance at getting ahead of whatever fresh hell is about to descend on us."

Looking more closely at the pendant Alice revealed, "Rachal?" I breathe the name, feeling its weight, its potential power. Could it really be that simple? Or are we just clinging to hope in a world where it's in shorter supply than clear skies?

"Exactly," Alice affirms, with the certainty of someone who has walked through fire and emerged, still believing in the green shoots of new life. It's the unwavering belief that inspires—or deludes. Time will tell which side she falls on.

Suddenly, the crowd becomes a living, heaving entity; a delayed reaction of sorts. It's like a tsunami of Tanzanians. We are nothing more than flopson within it, swept up in the collective panic of the sealed Elops. My heart races, but I shove the fear back into its box. Panic is a luxury we can't afford.

"Move!" Soren barks, their voice slicing through the surrounding pandemonium. We weave through the throng, bodies jostling against us from every angle. It's how I imagine a salmon swimming upstream in a pre-BoldWar river, each of us fighting the current.

But what about my damn name? Is it the missing code for the ClimaSphere? How did Alice sense this as the solution? Motherly instinct? "Don't be stupid," I say under my breath, running, addressing no one. But we are being swept away toward the harbour like a fearless torrent, and I don't have enough time to think through what was just relieved to us.

"Where's the SDV?" Banksia yells over her shoulder, her eyes darting in search of our submerged vehicle, panic in her voice.

"Twenty metres. East Wing dock of the marina," Juice replies with calm precision, and I marvel at his ability to remain unfazed. The military in him, no doubt. He's already plotting our route, his mind working like a sophisticated algorithm.

"Got it!" Benny chimes in, following Juice.

We finally break free from the crowd's clutches, the chaotic noise behind us softening as we reach the shore near the SDV. Juice pushes the two recessed buttons and handles, and they open upon his command. The leap into the SDV is like plunging into another world. Claustrophobic yet strangely liberating as we escape the tumultuous sea of people outside the marina. I strap myself in, the familiar engine hum a welcome melody against my racing heart.

Juice asks, "Är vi alla bra att gå? Sorry," he says, repeating himself in English, "are we all good to go?"

"Everyone good?" Soren echoes, their fingers already dancing over the controls, starting a series of beeps and whirls that signify our departure from the island's chaos.

"Define 'good'," Banksia retorts from her seat, her voice steady despite the sarcasm lacing her words. She's checking her gear, always prepared for the worst.

"Breathing and not currently being crushed by locals," Juice shoots from the cockpit area, not looking up from dials and knobs.

"Then I'm fan-bloody-tastic," Benny chimes in, trying to inject a little levity.

"Focus," I snap, more to myself than anyone else. "Sorry!" asking for forgiveness for my outburst from my friends. I am on edge. I need to know why Alice risked everything to come here. It gnaws at me, an itch in the back of my mind that can't be reached without the truth.

As we pull away from the marina and the Old Fort and set a course southwest back to Dar es Salaam, I ask, "Mum, why now? Why did it come all this way for me?"

Alice's gaze holds mine, a storm of emotions swirling between us. "Odezza," she starts, her voice a mixture of strength and vulnerability that only a mother could muster. "I need to explain something about your name. Your real name.

"Real name?" Benny exclaims.

"What do you mean, real name?" I echo, but before she can elaborate, Soren interrupts.

"Approaching first junction," they announce, the SDV dipping slightly as we take a sharp left turn to the south, sweeping past the network of islands that brought us here.

I watch Alice's fingers as they dance around the copper chain resting against her chest. The pendant—unremarkable in its design yet clearly significant—catches the dim light inside the SDV.

"Rachal," she whispers, almost to herself, as she flips the pendant for all of us in the rear compartment to see. Etched into the metal is the name, like a secret finally eager to be shared.

"Rachal?" Soren parrots back, their attention momentarily swerving from the piloting controls. A frown creases their brow, a silent acknowledgement that this piece of the puzzle doesn't fit anywhere in their understanding.

And again, Alice gives Soren a stare I don't completely comprehend.

"Could it be—" Juice trails off, the gears in his brain clicking audibly, "the password?"

"Exactly," Alice nods with the certainty that only comes from connecting long-separated dots. She fishes out the crumpled note from her pocket, OZ's handwriting sprawled across it—a map of thoughts from a mind gone too soon.

"Odezza," she says, locking eyes with me, "Rachel is your birth name, and I really think, given your father's chicken scratch, that the name is the code to make your machine functional."

What's a 'chicken scratch'? Never mind.

A chill races down my spine, electric and revealing. How many times had I scanned Dad's notes, desperate for a clue? The hours working that stupid proto. Yet here it was, the answer, hanging around my mother's neck. This is making my head spin.

"Rachal," I taste the name, foreign to my tongue. A piece of me I never knew, hiding in plain sight.

"Your father left clues everywhere, mija," Alice continues, folding the note back into secrecy. "Did you notice his notes were a cypher?"

"Yes," I realise, "in a few different languages too, yes?"

"Yes, including Latin."

"I saw that too and could translate some of it, but not all of it," I continue, "not without help on my BTN."

"Well, within the cypher was Christiano Nomine. It was just concealed with really poor penmanship."

"Christian name?" Juice chimes in like he was listening this entire time. "Eyes on the water, Juice," I call out with a smile.

"Yes," Alice acknowledges, "and I'm guessing that's partially why you couldn't crack the code - you didn't know you had another name."

"Forgawdsakes!" sounding annoyed with this whole word-play game. "How would I have ever figured that out, not knowing I had a birth name?"

"Birth names," Alice says, her eyes reflecting our underwater journey. "They're like anchors to our past. Some keep them, some cast them away."

"Rachal," I repeat, rolling the name around like a strange new spice on my tongue. "So that's me? That was me?"

"Was and always will be, in a way," she replies, a wistful note in her voice.

"Then why Odezza?" I press, seeking the logic in a sea of parental whimsy.

"OZ loved the sound of it," Alice muses as we weave through the colourful underwater labyrinth. "But Rachal was your beginning—the first word in the story of you. It's the name I called you when you were born."

"Great, I'm a prologue nobody bothered to read," I quip. Still, the humour feels hollow against the urgency nipping at our heels.

"Trust me," Alice assures, clenching her pendant like a talisman, "it's a name no one will forget after today."

"And you really think that's the solution to all this - the one word that will get our ClimaSphere to work?"

"Well," Alice continues, "I can't promise anything, but I believe it to be the solution. Your dad loved cyphers; I'm guessing he made this as tough as they come. I'm thinking no one was ever intended to break this code but OZ. I knew my motherly instincts were telling me something."

"I guess you're right, Alice," Banksia adds, "I guess you're right."

"We were so close to finding out back there," Benny pontificates. "Now the pressure is really on to see if your hunch is right, Alice, and to make sure we make our next destination in time before that Elops follows in the other's demise."

Minutes turn into an hour. "Dar es Salaam, coming up," Soren announces, the vehicle humming beneath us as we slice through the water, an arrow aimed at the heart of a city gasping for air, slowing to a crawl.

"Kigamboni Ferry Terminal," Juice calls out as we near our destination, his voice tinged with relief. "TT Station isn't far from there."

Soren carefully mores the sub against a terminal pier. I don't think any of us expected to be returning to Dar es Salaam so soon after our departure. But here we are, in their principal port.

The port's smells and sounds wrap around us as we disembark onto solid ground. The Kigamboni Ferry Terminal offers old-world charm and high-tech.

We weave through the throngs at the terminal, a fluid dance choreographed by necessity and urgency. Soren's gaze locks onto the signs leading us to the Abode of Peace TT Station, their determination as an anchor in the swirling sea of restless people.

"Keep close," Juice shouts over the din, a commander rallying his troops.

"Like electrons to a nucleus," Banksia quips, her humour a spark in the dimming light of day.

"Except we're hoping not to collide," Benny retorts, his eyes scanning for threats, a guardian hawk in human form.

I catch Alice's eye. Her presence here, a living puzzle piece connecting the past to the future. She gives a small nod—subtle, but it's enough. It's solidarity, a silent acknowledgement of the shared bloodline that ties us together in this discord.

Alice is also glancing at Juice's bionic leg. She must not have noticed that before. And again, the strange sideways glance at Soren seems out of place. Even though I don't know this woman from the people we pass by on the cyclone-ravaged streets around us, I can't tell why she looks at Soren that way. Judgingly.

"Almost there," I pant, the name 'Rachal' reverberating in

my skull like a secret mantra. With each step, I'm rewriting my identity, moulding it with truths long buried.

Alice tucks a strand of hair behind her ear—a gesture mirroring one of my own. "After you, Odezza... or should I say, Rachal?"

The TT awaits, a beacon of potential amidst the growing shadows.

"Juice?" Benny cries out as we get situated. "Where are we going and how are we getting there?"

"That's a superb question," I add. "We do not know where we're all going. Do you?"

Juice seems to always be one step ahead of us, offering us peace of mind. "Yes, I do. I looked on the way back to Kigamboni Ferry Terminal. Let's find out seats and I can explain on the way to Northwest Australia.

"Northwest Australia?" Alice exclaims.

"How would she know that's our next destination?" I think to myself.

Just as we slip inside the TT, and the doors hiss their closure behind us, Banksia lets out a scream. Not a sound any of you have heard before.

"Whatthegawdamn," Banksia, Benny yells, "it's like you saw a ghost or something."

"What the heck was that all about?" I ask briskly.

"I swear, no — there's no way that could ha — but it must have been. There can't be anyone el —"

Soren abruptly cuts her off, slamming their hand on the table in front of us, obviously sick of Banksia's singular, stuttering conversation.

"I swear I just saw Roman and his thugs right outside the TT as we stepped inside. I feel like they just missed this train."

We all watch Banksia, our eyes fixed on her as if she's experiencing a surge of overwhelmingness. Could that be true?

Could Roman really be that close to us? Damn, not having windows. And the TT pulls away from the station like a bullet from a pre-BoldWar rifle.

CHAPTER THIRTY-EIGHT

"That was too close," I mutter, flicking a glance at the sealed exit.

"Roman's like a shadow with fangs," Benny says, his voice tense. "He is just tailing us for sport?"

"Maybe. Or the Oxo2 or ClimaSphere," Banksia admits, tapping her foot nervously against the floor. "He had that look in his eyes—the one that reeks of desperation and dangerous intent."

"I agree— he wants the Oxo2," Juice speculates, scratching at his stubble. "He needs Oxo2 on Dezza's wrist for his people, or he is trying to stop us from getting to the next Elops, but how would he know about the ClimaSphere?"

"From tapping OZ's system?" Benny asks, his eyebrows move to a peak.

"Wait," Alice interjects, her brow furrowed, "are we talking about Roman Polotov? The man who runs Anthro-Tech?"

"Yep, that's the one," I confirm, feeling a shiver run through me despite the warm air circulating throughout the

TT. "Enigmatic tycoon, with a penchant for world domination."

Alice's expression darkens. "I've heard rumours of his plans to overthrow the Central Government. He's a master manipulator; nothing will stand in his way."

Turning to Alice, I continue, "We learned this when we tapped the Anthro-Tech mainframe. We discovered he wants to get off planet to tinker with his next-gen robots and human cloning projects." A coldness snakes through me as I consider the implications. "Spurious cloud seeding was just the beginning. He won't stop until he eradicates all humans."

"Like an apocalyptic chess player," Soren says grimly.

"Except we're the pawns," Juice finishes, looking each of us in the eye. "We have to stay one step ahead, or we'll be the ones getting knocked off the board."

"Then let's make sure our next move is a checkmate," I say, clenching my fists. "For OZ, for the world, and for whatever shred of hope we've got left."

The TT hums beneath us, carving its path through the underground veins of a bleeding planet. I had seen a sign as we entered the platform that said Colombo, Sri Lanka. I'm dying to know what route Juice has planned. But above all else, I know one thing: Roman Polotov is the last person we want hot on our trail, no matter our route.

"Juice, you were going to tell us about our route to Australia," I call out in an inquisitive tone, peering over his shoulder at the flickering screen.

"Yes. Sorry. Colombo, Sri Lanka, then to Singapore, and down to Perth," he announces, a trace of triumph in his voice. The route is a tangled thread, each one representing a perilous leapfrog under oceans and through crumbling infrastructures.

As the robo-waiters roam the opulent corridors of our TT, all white, fresh and shiny, Juice tells us some of the alternative routes he considered, just in case we care about spheric geography and the world of subterranean TT lines. It seems he had explored the possibility of connecting through the Maldives (where he had lived), Flying Fish Cove, Christmas Island (which sounds lovely), or Port Louis, Mauritius (but that's now entirely flooded), or even Darwin, in Northern Australia (another newly formed state on the island of Australia). But as we enjoy some afternoon tea and a quick bite of faux finger foods, Juice shares that all those routes have stopped working; closed down because of a bad power grid, flooded or simply destroyed.

"Sounds like a magical mystery tour," Soren quips, not eating, but their levity doesn't quite mask the tension in their voice.

"More like a gauntlet," I amend, imagining the abandoned stations and dead zones we'll encounter along the way.

"Once we hit Perth..." Juice trails off, scratching his chin thoughtfully. He pulls up another schematic, this one barren of any helpful routes northward.

"Exmouth is going to be a shot in the dark," Soren picks up where Juice had trailed off. "No TTs of any grade, no clear path. Just us and the outback."

"An Aussie adventure," I say, trying to inject some swagger into the mix. We're the Mighty5, after all. We've faced worse—haven't we?

"Exactly," Juice agrees, though his brow furrows. "We'll need supplies, a vehicle, maybe even a miracle."

"Or two," Banksia chimes in from her seat, her gaze locked on the robo-waiters, hoping to be served next. "We're good at pulling those out of our hats, right?"

"Right," I affirm, feeling that familiar fire ignite within me. For OZ, for the world — for all the marbles, really—we'll find our way to Exmouth and whatever fate awaits us there.

"Let's focus on getting to Perth," Alice says, her voice steady and sure. "One impossible feat at a time."

"Agreed," I nod. Our gaze meets, and something unspoken passes between us—the weight of what we carry, the hope that we might still tip the scales against Roman and his twisted vision for the future.

The TerraTube carriage hums with tension, a live wire of anticipation and fear that sizzles through the air. 'Rachal' - the word hangs in my mind like a question without an answer. Could it unlock what we need in Exmouth? Or is it just a string of letters, meaningless and impotent?

"Hey," Soren's voice cuts through my spiralling thoughts, "You think Rachal's gonna work?"

I shrug as I look over at Alice. "It's a shot in the dark, but it's all we've got at the moment."

"Great," Benny mutters from across the aisle, his fingers wrapped tight around his Oxolet. "I thrive in darkness." It's meant as a joke, but no one laughs, not even him.

Then, suddenly, the calm shatters. Benny's Oxolet blinks red, rapid like a heartbeat racing toward doom. "Guys? This isn't good." His voice is steady, but his face is pale, the colour leached away by the urgency of the alarm. "What do I do? This thing is staying solid red. Don't get me wrong, I enjoy oxygen as much as the next person, but I'm really not ready to live without it."

"Damn it," Juice curses under his breath, diving into Benny's personal space to inspect the device. "That's our cue; time is slipping faster than Madagascan sand through our fingers and I'm honestly not sure what to do about you as we obviously don't have a back-up Oxolet and we can't just take Odesza's."

I offer a curious look, like, "Love you like a brother, Benny, but you can't take mine."

Juice continues with a tone of optimism, "I have noticed they don't instantly die when the red light comes on."

I roll my eyes, "Really Juice? Can you pick different vocab at a time like this - die?"

"Let me see," Banksia leans over, her demeanour calm but her eyes betraying the flicker of panic. "We need to move and fast."

"The problem is, we can't get there any faster," Soren adds. "We can only go as fast as we're going on the route Juice planned."

"I'll be fine," Benny says, sounding more optimistic than he really should be. Brave soul.

The TerraTube glides into Colombo with the hum of electric progress, and we pile out like refugees from the future nobody asked for. Once a beacon of connectivity, the station is now just another waypoint on our desperate scramble across a planet that's forgotten how to be kind.

"TT2's running on reserve power," Juice mutters, his fingers dancing over the HelloHolo screen of his device. "

"Reserve power? That sounds promising," Banksia says, sarcasm dripping from every syllable as she stretches her legs.

"Better than no power," I counter, but my optimism feels brittle.

"Roman Polotov probably has his own damn power grid," Soren muses, the lines around their eyes deepening. "Private lines for private people with private armies."

"Could he be behind us?" Alice ponders aloud, worry etched into the fine lines of her face.

"Following us, you mean?" Benny pipes up, keeping an eager eye on his left wrist.

"Next stop, Singapore," Juice remarks as we move from one platform to another. "Let's hope Roman is enjoying the scenic route and not following us."

"Let's hope he is on the scenic route through hell," Benny quips.

"Welcome to the adventure of a lifetime," I declare, as the

TT2 door's seal shut with a hiss, and we're propelled forward into uncertainty. One thing's for sure — we'll face whatever comes together, as the Mighty5.

"I'm off to take a shower," Banksia chimes in. "I read this TT2 has The Crystal on board. And while I'm in there, they can clean my gross clothes. They also have the Quantum-CleanQ7. The machine will clean them in under seven minutes. I feel gross and need to have a good wash."

I think we all need to do the same thing.

THE TT2 HURTLES through the submerged tube, a bullet slicing under the ocean's heart. I glance at Alice, who's been quiet since Colombo, her gaze distant, lost in thoughts or memories. Or maybe both.

"Okay, spill it," I say, unable to curb my curiosity any longer. "You've been holding onto something since we left."

Alice doesn't startle; she just turns those perceptive eyes on me. "I knew this moment would come, Odezza. The truth about your father— and why I left."

"Did OZ work for the UK Canton?" I blurt out.

"Yes." She takes a breath. "OZ was brilliant, but he got caught up in projects — projects that blurred lines. Robotics that went beyond aiding humans. That wasn't the world I wanted for you."

"What is beyond aiding humans? Replace them?" It's almost too much, and I struggle to keep my tone even.

"Among other things," she reaches out to hold my hands, as if to offer comfort or bridge the years of silence between us. "I had to protect you from that future."

"By leaving?" Soren chimes in, their voice edged with scepticism. "Who leaves a tiny baby, then blames their husbands' work?"

I look at Soren to drop it!

"Sometimes love means making hard choices," Alice replies, her words thick like the concrete and titanium walls outside the hurtling TT2.

"Choices that leave scars," I murmur, feeling the weight of her decision, the shape of her absence in my life.

"Scars heal, Odezza." Alice's voice is soft but firm. "And they strengthen us."

"Speaking of strength," Juice interrupts, tapping his wrist where multiple screens flicker with data, "we're about to dock at Gardens by the Bay."

"Ah, Singapore," Benny says, stretching his limbs like a cat after a nap. "Land of architectural marvels and unpredictable weather."

"Unpredictable? More like predictably stormy," Juice adds.

"Great for dramatic entrances," I quip, standing up as the capsule comes to a smooth stop.

"Or hasty exits," Soren counters, leading the way out of the TT2.

Stepping out of the station is like walking onto a futuristic film set intertwined with a horror movie—towering skyscrapers puncture the dark swirling sky, their lights defiant against the oppressive atmosphere. I can't help but gape; it's spectacular and terrifying all at once. Did we just walk into an immense storm?

"Thirty minutes, team," Juice announces, checking his watch. "Don't get blown away, literally or figuratively."

"Let's make the most of it," I propose, the scientist in me eager to absorb every detail of this techno-oasis amidst the chaos of a massive wind and lightning storm.

"Right behind you, boss," Banksia says, a sparkle in her eye and clothes that tells me she's ready for anything.

"Remember, we're here to lie low, not sightsee," Alice reminds us in a matronly manner.

"Of course, but who says we can't do both?" I reply with a grin, stepping out into the maelstrom.

I can't help reliving our prior conversation. "Mum, what was so bad about Dad's work that you had to leave us?" I ask, trying to keep the tremble out of my voice.

Alice, her eyes reflecting the storm outside and something much deeper within. She takes a deep breath and meets my gaze. "OZ was working with a team developing robotics that could manipulate human emotions and control logic and actions. From what I was told, they only made one. It was called a RoboTex — It scared me. Humanoids beyond anything we had seen before. I feared for you. For us." Her words hang heavy in the air between us, an uncomfortable truth finally unveiled.

"Control humans. Humanoid robotics? But dad —" I can't wrap my head around what she's saying. This from the man who taught me to value humanity above all else.

"Yes, he eventually hated the idea," Alice adds quickly, as if reading my mind. "But by then, I couldn't unsee his path. It was a long time ago."

Sixteen years ago!

I ponder my position as the daughter. Do I push on and ask more, or take my suggestion to Soren and leave it alone? I will take the latter for now. But I need to know more.

I turn around and take in Singapore. Its skyline is truly dramatic, with towering eco-SkyRiser's designed to withstand the forces of nature.

But as we look up in awe, our BNTs pop up with a RedAlert, similar to the last Elops closure. The alert warns of an approaching typhoon, as in now. It's 2088, and some truly innovative technology fills this city. I'm curious what they will do to brace themselves for this occurrence.

The sky darkens with ominous clouds, and the wind howls through the structures, which are engineered to sway resiliently. Rain pours down in sheets, cascading off the buildings in waterfalls that feed into the city's advanced water recycling systems.

Despite the typhoon's fury, the city's infrastructure remains unyielding. Autonomous drones patrol the skies, providing real-time data to the central weather command centre. How can they even fly? The streets, empty of people, echo with the sound of the storm, while underground tunnels provide safe passage for the few who dare to travel. We all just stand there taking in the meteorological spectacle.

It appears that they have retrofitted The Marina Bay Sands with storm barriers, turning it into a fortress against the pending surging waves. From where we had excited the TT station, The Gardens by the Bay's Supertrees light up the night, their bioluminescent leaves glowing eerily in the tempest.

As we look on in awe, the city's energy shields activate, creating a protective bubble that deflects the strongest winds. It's a testament to Singapore's foresight and modernisation, a city that learned to coexist with the capricious moods of nature. But how are they getting their power for all this tech?

When the typhoon finally recedes, Singapore emerges unscathed, a beacon of resilience and sustainability in a world where the climate has been unpredictable for many years. An anomaly in a previously arid world. The city's harmony with nature sets a model for others to follow, reminding us that even the most powerful storms can be weathered with preparation and ingenuity.

That was the craziest, quickest TT transfer stop of all time and I'm chaffed that OZ was not around to see the storm and the tech that held it at bay.

"Okay, time to board the bus for Perth," Juice cuts in,

always the voice of reason. "Once there, we'll figure out our wild ride to Exmouth."

"Bus?" Banksia exclaims, wrapping her arm around mine as we approach the TT.

'It's a figure of speech, Banksia," Juice scoffs.

As the TT propels us toward our uncertain future, I can't help but wonder what awaits us in Perth, and ultimately, Exmouth. I've never even heard of this desolate place. Will Roman beat us there? What does he really want? We know there is a rocket launchpad, so maybe that will keep his hands off my Oxo2. So many questions whirl in my mind, but for now, they remain unanswered. Only time will tell, and time is not a luxury we have. This is a 2,400 km trip, so it will be quick. Ironically, Juice tells us as we board our TT that this one goes right under Exmouth. Just another reminder of the infrastructure breaking all around us. I guess we should be fortunate to get to Perth, tucked away in the lower left corner of this massive country.

Tension crackles in the air of the TT as we hurtle closer to Perth, 4,100 metres under the Indian Ocean; a knot of anticipation tightening in my stomach. Even as the TT's hum promises swift arrival, it's Juice's words that map out our immediate future.

"Exmouth is due north of Perth, about 1,300 kilometres," he says, running his hands through his long, wavy hair—a tell-tale sign of his brewing anxiety. "We've got deserts that might be underwater by now and coastlines that will predictably be littered with what used to live in the ocean."

"Sounds like a stroll on the beach," Banksia quips, but her joke does little to lighten the mood.

"Transportation options?" Soren asks, their usual calm demeanour fraying at the edges.

"Unknown. Perth's the last stop for any working TTs, and from my analysis, Southwest and Northwest Australia are two enormous states, so we could be in for anything. Benny, you'll like this. Combined, these two states were once called Western Australia. That one vast state was ten times the size of the UK Canton!" Juice glances at each of us, as if checking we're still in one piece. "And Roman's likely aiming for Exmouth too—with a rocket launchpad there plus the Elops. The big question is, can we beat him?"

"Or find another way to put an end to his madness once we're there," Alice adds, her steady gaze meeting mine in silent solidarity.

"Let's focus on getting there first," I interject before anyone can spiral into hypothetical doom. "Exmouth won't come to us."

"Right. Outsmarting Roman is what we do best," Benny chimes in, though his Oxolet solid red glow reminds us all that 'best' needs to happen fast.

As the TT decelerates, we know the Elizabeth Quay and Swan River Stations are just ahead. A stop we hope is our penultimate stop. The Electrogravitics clock reads 6 am. As we pop out of the station, a new day greets us with its dim light, seeping through the dilapidated structures that loom over the once-vibrant city. We step onto the platform, our presence unacknowledged by the few drowsy commuters drifting like ghosts through the terminal.

"Welcome to Southwest Australia," Juice announces, sounding like a Thames River tour guide.

"It seems like a ghost town," Banksia observes, peering out towards the barren landscape.

"More like a ghost state," I correct, and despite the gravity of our mission, I'm unable to suppress a smirk. "But hey, it's the adventure of a lifetime, right?"

"Or the last lifetime," Soren muses, but their eyes are alight with a challenge.

"Only one way to find out," I say, leading our troops away

from the famed station. The salt air blended with the odour of rotting fish hits us with unexpected force, reminding us that although this world may be broken, it's still ours to save. And save it we will—against Roman, against time, against all odds.

But first, how the hell do we get to Exmouth and Elops #4. It's not like we can thumb a lift on an eVOLT or SkyAus. That's their overland high-speed aerial train. I'm not sure why they don't have the TT system throughout the country, but for now we need to figure out some form of transportation and figure it out fast.

CHAPTER THIRTY-NINE

"Alright, Mighty5, we need to find a way to Exmouth," I say, trying to sound hopeful despite the dire situation. "And fast. Roman won't wait for us."

The team nods in agreement, and we approach some locals lingering nearby in the thick rain. Their worn and tired faces reflect the oppressive conditions they've been living in.

"Excuse me," I call out hesitantly. "We're attempting to reach Exmouth, in Northwest Australia." Do you have any idea how we can get there?"

Nobody responds at first; they just look at us with wary suspicion, as if we're outsiders who don't belong here. I guess we are, in a way. But then, a young Aboriginal girl, no older than thirteen, steps forward.

"G'day! Did you say Exmouth?" she asks, her voice strong, saturated with a thick Australian accent.

"Yes," I reply, my heart racing with hope. "We desperately need to get there. Can you help us?"

The girl studies our faces for a moment, weighing up whether she should trust us. Finally, she nods and points east along the river to a distant bridge.

"Over there," she says with a lilt. "There's an old abandoned seaplane on the river. It might work, it might not. Could be dodgy! Risky! It's old, and I've never witnessed it in flight.

"Risky is better than nothing," Soren chimes in, their voice tinged with determination. "Thank you."

Another damn plane? "Really?" I question with dread under my breath.

"Be careful," the girl warns as we gather our rucksacks and follow her directions. "And good luck," she calls out to us. "It's just up there toward that island," still pointing. "But I can walk you there if you'd like."

We don't turn down her offer.

As we walk, I can't help but wonder if Roman and his team are already on their way to Exmouth, preparing to launch into space from that rocket base. This is our toughest journey yet, but we have no choice – we have to beat them there, for the sake of humanity.

"Hey," Banksia says, nudging me gently as we trudge along the foreshore. "We'll make it. We always do."

I smile at her, grateful for the reassurance. But deep down, I know that this time, it's going to take more than just luck and determination. We're going to need a miracle because we have not heard of another open Elops.

The once sun-bleached Esplanade of Perth stretches out before us, with Kings Park and Elizabeth Quay to our backs, the palm tree lined Swan River to our right and the futuristic city punctuated with impressive mile-high SkyRisers to our left.

And Banksia's correct. Where are all the people? For a massive city, there seem to be very few locals.

"Hey. Did you all know that back in 1962, this city was called the City of Lights?" Benny asks, his eyes scanning the horizon as we walk along the waterfront. "People in Perth turned on all their house lights when astronaut John Glenn flew overhead in his Friendship 7 spacecraft."

"Isn't it ironic?" Juice muses, his gaze distant. "We're surrounded by SkyRiser's with very little lights aglow, whilst heading to a rocket launch site ourselves."

"Let's hope we find that seaplane first," I say, my heart pounding at the thought of facing another flight after our harrowing experience in Chile.

"Almost there," the young girl says, her voice steady and confident despite her age. She leads us down a winding path toward an island, where the abandoned seaplane is supposed to be waiting. "That's Heirisson Island," she points out with some verve in her tiny voice.

"Do you ever see kangaroos on that island?" Soren asks the girl.

What a random question. Has Soren been here before?

"Sure do," she replies with a grin. "I thought they only lived in the bush. Good tucker. But they also live right here."

"Tucker?" I repeat under my breath.

Juice puts his hand up to his mouth like he is miming the word eat. What? Gross, poor kangaroos.

"Maybe we'll get lucky and spot one this morning," Alice says, her eyes filled with optimism, oblivious to Juice's gesture about eating kangaroos.

As we approach the riverbank, the old, faded yellow and blue seaplane comes into view, its paint peeling and its airframe rusting from years of neglect and salt water. The sight of it sends a quiver down my backbone. Are we really going to fly in that thing?

"Here it is," the girl announces, her gaze fixed on the decrepit aircraft.

"Thanks for your help," I tell her, trying to sound braver than I feel. "We won't forget you or your kindness."

"Good luck," she says again before turning, disappearing back up the path, and vanishing over a bridge.

"Alright, team," I say, my voice filled with determination. "Let's see if this thing can still fly."

We each hoist our rucksacks over our shoulders and approach the seaplane, our footsteps crunching on the river sand and gravel beneath our feet. I can feel the fear radiating off my companions – none of us are eager to take to the skies again so soon after Chile. But we have no choice. We have to get to Exmouth, and fast. And we certainly can't do it on foot or by car, although we passed a couple of old relics on the way to the plane. The placard had said, HOLDEN. I see a couple of eVTOL's on a grassy field across the south side of the river, but my guess is they have lost power and are grounded.

"Okay," Soren says, stepping forward to examine the plane. "Let's give this old bird a once-over, then we'll figure out how to get it off the ground. Or off the water," they say with a bent smile.

"Sounds like a plan," I agree, trying to ignore the knot of fear tightening in my chest.

As we begin our inspection, I can't help but think about John Glenn and his historic flight all those years ago. He had the courage to venture into the unknown, to face the vast expanse of space and all its mysteries. If he could do that with prehistoric tech, surely we can overcome our fears and save the world from its current disaster.

"Alright," Juice says, breaking my reverie. He holds up the BTN, scanning the seaplane.

Moments later, "It's a de Havilland Canada DHC-2 Beaver. From 1964. It's a STOL." Blank stares. "That's a Short Take Off and Landing. It's a true Canadian icon," Juice adds with bravado.

"Great," Banksia replies. "Now we just need to figure out how to fly it."

Soren steps forward, their face determined. "I'll scan my BTN again, like I did in Chile. We'll get this bird in the air."

"Okay team," Juice says, his eyes shining with resolve. "Let's get this pre-flight inspection underway."

We fan out around the seaplane, examining every inch of its ageing exterior. As Soren checks the wings for AVGAS levels, I can't help but worry about our chances of making it to Exmouth in one piece.

"Guys," Soren calls out, "there's definitely fuel in the wings, but we can't tell how much and how old. We'll just have to hope it's enough. And there is some gunk in the mixture, so let's hope that doesn't cause trouble along the way up the coast."

'Gunk' doesn't sound good to me, but it doesn't seem to phase Soren.

"Hope?" Benny chuckles nervously. "That's all we've been running on lately. That and a little sleep."

"Hope makes us human, Benny," Alice says softly. "And it's what's going to see us through this."

"Alright," Banksia announces, clapping her hands together. "Time to climb aboard and get this show on the road. Or in the air."

Dust fills the air as we each take our seats inside the cramped cabin of the seaplane, the weight of our mission bearing down on us. It doesn't seem like anyone has sat in these dirty old seats for quite some decades. It doesn't have to look like a lifesaver to be a lifesaver, I think to myself.

In the cockpit, Soren and Juice work together in their pre-flight sequence, preparing the seaplane for takeoff. I notice this plane has a laminated sheet of green paper they are methodically running through, setting the controls, instruments, and switches to their proper positions. Though I'm no aviation expert, their confidence and focus reassure me we're in expert hands.

"Let's prime the engine," Soren says from the pilot's seat on the left. They give about five shots of prime, then look over at Juice. "Ready to actuate the fuel wobble pump?"

Wobble pump? Now they're just making stuff up!

"Ready," Juice confirms, and together, they work to ensure the fuel pressure is increasing.

"Fuel pressure is good," Soren announces. I can sense the tension in the air, though none of us dare voice our fears. We've come so far, faced countless obstacles, but this – this final push to reach Elops #4 – feels like the most daunting challenge yet.

"Engage the starter," I hear Soren say, counting as five blades whirl into action. Next, I see them flip a switch that says MAGNETO to the ON position, waiting for the engine to fire up. The sound is deafening, but it's music to my ears – the heartbeat of our defiance against tyranny.

Minutes click by. Then comes a knocking sound as the old Beaver warms up. "Benny, pop out the door and unhook us from the dock, please?" Juice calls back from the co-pilot position.

We float away from the dock, heading back the way we have just walked. The propeller roars to life, and disgusting exhaust fumes fill the air. This time I'm sitting in the left seat as I watch the worn plane pull out into the wide part of the river. I look through the porthole of the Beaver and low and behold; I see two kangaroos sitting there, just watching us do our thing. They do not know we are trying to save the world, but I do and the pressure weighs heavily on my chest. The little aboriginal girl was right, kangaroos. Gawdamn! And I swear I see a bevvy of black swans. How could that be? I've seen white swans on the Thames, but black? I haven't seen wildlife in so long that I thought they had all died off. "How is this even possible?" I catch myself whispering under my breath.

I let the rhythmic hum of the engines drown out my worries about this flight.

The plane seems to hold up well enough as we pick up speed and skip above the calm ripples of the Swan River, but with some gauges not working, including what I believe is the airspeed indicator and compass, we'll be flying blind in more ways than one.

I grip the edge of my seat, bracing myself for the unknown. In this moment, as we ready ourselves to hurtle towards our destiny, all that matters is the mission – and the hope that will see us through.

Subdued sunlight glints off the water, casting a deceptive glow over the desolate city landscape off our right side. I can't help but marvel at the irony of Benny's words as we fly low over this once-sunny city. "Perth, the City of Lights. A fitting place to start our journey toward the stars," I muse aloud.

"Indeed," Banksia chimes in, her eyes reflecting the same determination that drives us all. "Let's just hope we find some answers up there."

"Right," Soren says over their right shoulder, then turns their attention back to the seaplane's cockpit.

"Alright, everyone," Benny says, rallying us together. "We're doing this for our world, for OZ, for our future." Alice grins. "Together, we can face anything." I still can't help but notice this growing redness of his dying Oxolet.

"Agreed," Soren nods, their resourcefulness and adaptability clear in every move. "Let's get this show on the road."

"Or in the sky," Benny quips, his humour a welcome reprieve from the gravity of our situation.

"Exactly," I say, my heart pounding in anticipation. "To the skies – and beyond."

As we gain altitude, we soar towards the unknown and a long string of white beaches. The knowledge buoys our spirits that no matter what lies ahead, we'll face it side by side as the Mighty5.

"Next stop, Exmouth," I declare, my eyes locked on the horizon as we soar toward the distant northern horizon.

"Let's just hope we get there before Roman," Benny adds, his humour a lifeline amidst the storm.

"Trust me," I say with conviction, my heart swelling with hope. "We will."

———

AS WE HEAD up the coast, sand dunes to our right, the Indian Ocean to our left, the plane flies low, lower than it feels like we should be. Soren abruptly turns to Benny, sitting to my right, and hands over their Oxolet.

"Here, take this," they say, their voice steady and emotionless.

"Wait, what's going on?" Benny asks, clearly taken aback.

"I just realised I don't need it. But you do. Sorry, I didn't think of this before now."

Benny gives Soren a look of utter surprise, as we all are. What's going on here? The Mighty5 strikes me as thankless, but not to the point where one would give up their lifeline to the world. We're a generous group of misfits but not selfless.

"What's going on, Soren? You need to keep that on. You know what will happen," I say, panicking at what is unfolding before our very eyes. "We will be in Exmouth by the end of the day, and with some luck, and my birth name, we will retreat the clouds, we'll see the sun and our Oxolets will start re-charging.

There is a blank stare on Soren's face. Then they continue, "OZ created me," Soren reveals. "I am the RoboTex prototype."

Complete and utter silence and dismay strike us all squarely in the chest. "What did you just say?" I blurt out.

"Seriously?" Juice exclaims, his eyes wide with disbelief, almost letting go of the yoke of the old plane.

"I had my suspicions," Alice quickly admits, her gaze fixed on Soren as if trying to decipher their robotic soul. "But I never wanted to believe it."

"What?" Benny pings with great abruptness. You're — a — robot? No way! No flipping way. I always thought of you as non-binary, which I never worried about. To each their own, but you're seriously saying you're a robot and a Robo-Tex? The RoboTex?"

"Systematic Operational Robotic Exploration Navigator," I murmur, piecing together the acronym. "SOREN... It makes sense now."

"Does that mean I can really have your Oxolet?" Benny questions, still gripping the device tightly. I'm not sure if this is all really happening.

"Correct. It will remain green for some time," Soren confirms. "My systems function differently. But again, I am sorry it did not cross my mind until right now. I have been preoccupied."

We all let out a slight laugh. Yes, you have been preoccupied saving our skin; I think to myself.

"Wow," Benny breathes out, staring at the Oxolet with newfound reverence. "So you've been with us this whole time, and we never knew."

"Indeed," Soren replies, their expression unreadable.

"Kind of wish you'd told us sooner," I say out loud, struggling to wrap my head around this revelation.

"Regardless," Alice interjects, her voice firm but gentle. "We have a mission to complete, and I'm grateful for your help, Soren."

"Thank you, Alice," Soren says, nodding in appreciation.

"I can explain all about this later," Soren says matter-of-factly. "But for now, we need to keep on pushing forward."

"Wait?" Juice repeats, "I don't get it." I don't think I've seen Juice this flustered or emotive before. "You're seriously saying you're a robot? But none of us could ever tell. Well, apart from Alice." Juice's voice is a mixture of shock and dismay blended with disappointment boarding on judgemental. Oh, Juice, shit happens!

As the plane gains altitude, our group remains in shock over the truth about Soren. But amidst the chaos and uncertainty, one thing remains clear: we are a team, bound by purpose and determination. And together, we'll face whatever challenges lie ahead.

"Let's get to that rocket launch site," I say, my voice resolute as we soar over the barren landscape below. "Reverse ourselves a gawddamn Elops and stop a crazy lunatic from getting off planet and taking over the world with his damn robots. Sorry Soren. Present robots excluded."

"Why didn't you tell us you were the RoboTex, Soren? That's a pretty big deal," Juice just won't let it go.

Soren's expression remains neutral as they respond, their voice steady. "My primary objective was to assist the team in achieving our goals. I did not want my identity to become a distraction."

"Man, I can't even imagine what it would be like to have your abilities," I muse aloud, genuinely impressed by Soren's capabilities.

"Could've come in handy sooner, though," Benny adds, half-joking but with a hint of bitterness.

"Regardless," Alice chimes in, her eyes focused on the horizon. "Soren has been here every step of your journey, helping. That's what truly matters. We need every advantage we can get. That's a real friend."

"Right," I agree, nodding solemnly. "Let's focus on the

task at hand. Exmouth is still a long way off, and we've got Roman and his team to worry about."

"Agreed," Soren says, their eyes locked on the controls. "We must not waste any more time."

As our group continues to chat and voice questions about Soren's true nature, I can't help but feel a sense of growing unity among us. We've faced countless challenges, both individually and as a team, and despite all odds, we're still pressing forward. It's hard not to feel a deep connection with these people – my friends.

"Let's make a promise," I suggest, glancing around at everyone's faces. "No more secrets. From here on out, we trust each other implicitly. And together, we'll save this world."

"Deal," Benny grins, extending his hand.

"Deal," Juice echoes, with Banksia and Alice nodding in agreement.

"Deal," Soren affirms, their deep blue eyes glowing with determination.

THE LONG FLIGHT up the coast continues on, shrouded in rain, sleet and occasionally hail. I had always heard of the deadly spiders, snakes, sharks, eels, and crocodiles in this part of the world, so I'm glad we are in the air, even if it is an old junker of a plane. It's still flying, so it has that going for it.

As we look out to the west, we can see a string of dilapidated wind turbines pushing out of the Indian Ocean like sentinels of a forgotten era. Their enormous blades rusting and cracking from the salty air. They date back before the BoldWar. On the right side of the plane, we pass over four consecutive nuclear plants. Also, pre-war. I can't help but wonder about the logic of the CG to only power the globe on solar. It's sad, but I can't help chuckle that if we had stayed more diversified, we wouldn't be in half the mess we're currently in. Yes, the Oxolets would still have a problem, as they don't run on anything but sunlight, but everything else? The power grids of the past would still be working. The BoldWar really did a number on the government. It freaked them out, and today we pay for their short-mindedness, literally and figuratively. Of course, it doesn't help that Roman went and royally screwed things up, but that is a distinct set of circumstances. That is pure evil, greed and world domination kind of crap! That is off the charts, and now we all are paying for his insanity. Let's hope all that ends today because, speaking for myself, I can't take too much more of this shit!

As we cross over the Tropic of Capricorn, the demarcation between Southwest and Northwest Australia, I see Juice tapping the fuel gauge. "It hasn't been working," I call up to him over the roar of the plane. My heart races, anxiety clawing at my insides. Soren must have noticed it too, because they are now tapping the same dead gauge.

"Guys," Soren calls out urgently, their voice barely cutting through the engine's din, "hear that spluttering? We're running out of fuel and fast. Brace yourselves for an emergency landing!"

Panic immediately sets in, but we trust Soren and Juice implicitly, so we follow their instructions and prepare for impact. As the plane descends quicker than I'd like, my stomach no longer sits where it should be. I grip the edge of my seat as I did on take off. The ground rushes towards us. For not having any fuel, it seems we're still going so fast. Can we really do this? Land and not end up like the other dead marine life we've spotted along this coastline on the way up here.

The seaplane skims across the water's rough surface, our left float momentarily surfing the waves, sending up spray over our dirty windows. We finally grind to a halt on the beach near what the chart says is Coral Bay. At least that gauge works.

And that was a strange sensation as I forgot we had floats, not wheels. I see why people in the modern era don't fly planes or drive cars. These things will maim you or, in our recent history, try to kill you. But here we are, on the beach in the middle of nowhere, Australia, no comms, and we still don't even know if the ClimaSphere will work or if my damn birth name will unlock the gawdforsaken screen.

Oh, I need to pull myself together. I'm losing it over here, but I can't do that. We're the Mighty5, we don't lose our shit.

"Is everyone okay?" Juice calls back, his voice shaky and adrenaline coursing through their veins.

"Shaken, but alive," Benny replies, rubbing his neck. Alice and Banksia nod, their faces pale but determined.

We stumble out of the abused plane, surveying our surroundings. By the looks of things, we wouldn't get off the beach even if we could find fuel and top this beast up. The prop's blades are deformed, and we six cannot repair the bent right float.

The beach stretches before us, an endless expanse where sand meets sea. We may be safe for now, but I'm guessing we still have a long journey ahead to Exmouth. I take a deep breath and look at my friends, their expressions a mix of exhaustion, fear, and unwavering resolve.

"Grab your stuff and let's keep going," I say, my voice steady despite my racing heart. "We've come too far to give up now."

As we gather our supplies from the plane and embark on the next leg of our journey, I can't help but feel that we will not make it. We have no guarantee that this Elops won't act as all the others have and abruptly close on us. And as we have not heard of any others opening up, this really is our last chance. We don't even know where Exmouth is and how to get there. But our determination as a team hasn't failed us yet, so I put my faith in those around me and get over my fear of the unknown as quickly as I can. There's no time for pity parties here.

"Let's find some locals who might know how we can get to Exmouth," I suggest, eager to keep my chin up.

It doesn't take long for us to encounter a couple of local blokes enjoying a cold beer outside a makeshift pub. With urgency in our voices, we explain our situation and the dire consequences if we cannot reach Exmouth.

"Camels," one of them suggests, his face serious.

"Are you kidding me?" Alice scoffs, her eyebrows raised in disbelief.

"Camels are famous around these parts," the old man insists, nodding towards the dunes. "Been 'round for over a century. Some say they're the best camels in the world. Funny looking buggers, but when all else fails, they won't. Ridin' a camel on the beach is a pretty iconic experience here in Sand-groper country."

What kind of country?

"Seems like we have little choice," Juice murmurs, scratching his head.

"Fine, let's give it a shot," I agree, my heart pounding with anxiety. "Where can we find these camels?"

He leads us on a short, muddy walk, eventually revealing a caravan of camels resting near the foreshore. Their long legs and soft, white fur seem almost otherworldly against the back-drop of the harsh, barren landscape and the enormous expanse of ocean.

"Alright, folks," Alice says with determination, "let's get these camels saddled up and moving."

With the help of the local man, we quickly become acquainted with our new transportation. Like these locals, the camels seem unfazed by the world's current state. The old man, weathered with age but still bright-eyed, collects six saddles and after watching him put the first one on, we help complete saddling the remaining five. If you had told me two weeks ago, I'd be saddling a camel...

I see Juice head over to pay the man. That's when I notice he isn't wearing a BTN. Strange. I always assumed everyone had a BTN, just as we all have an Oxolet.

After a few minutes of conversation between Juice and the local, I see Juice walking away, shaking his head and sporting an uncustomary smile. "He won't take payment." Probably can't take the payment, I think to myself. "He gave me some ideas on how to get where we are going and said he will find the camels next time he and his mates are in Exmouth." So strange.

"Can you believe it?" I say as we mount our camels like ancient bedouins, offer our salutations and head north along the coast, the sound of waves gruffly lapping against the shore filling my ears.

"Life's full of surprises, isn't it?" Benny replies, his voice tinged with sadness. "Like me needing this Oxolet. Who would've thought?" Giving a glance toward Soren, mouthing, "thank you."

As we continue our course, the devastation of the dead marine life becomes all too real. We could see this from the plane, but now, to be this close is shocking. So much has washed up on the shore.

I watch as Benny flic's his BTN on. "Look at all this death and destruction," he says, his voice wavering. "Look, there's so much black algae, a few different species of shark, two humpback whales over there, some marine turtles, dugongs, seabirds, and look — dolphins." All victims of the critically low oxygen levels in the Indian Ocean. The smell is unbearable, but we have no choice but to press north.

At long last, after five gruelling hours of swaying back and forth on our trusty camels, we move inland, away from the coast. The low sun to our back casts long shadows ahead of us as we round an imposing mountain range. Those five long hours had us traversing rivers, streams and inlets, and pushing through kilometre after kilometre of low ruddy scrub brush.

In the distance, we can make out the edge of the Elops hovering over the town of Exmouth. We find ourselves at the end of a massive spit of land jutting out into the sparkling blue waters. Our bodies ache from our arduous trek, but the sight of our destination spurs us on.

"Guys, I know we're all tired and hungry," I say, the weight of exhaustion pressing down on me like a physical force. "But we have to keep going. We need to get to that Elops before it reverses or our Oxolet's stop working. It won't be long before all ours turn red and we don't have back-ups." I give a grin to Soren. "And we definitely need to beat Roman so he can't get off planet, leaving us here to rot.

"Right," Alice agrees, her face a mask of determination. "Let's do this. Let's push for these last few dozen miles."

As we spur our camels onward and over the last range of hills standing before us, rich with deep red sand and enormous canyons, I realise the enormous pressure of reversing this calamity. I can't help but feel a flicker of hope deep within me, wedged next to a feeling of dread and despair. With the Clima-Sphere and our combined efforts, maybe – just maybe – we can set things right again. For now, we press on, united in our quest to save the world from its seemingly inevitable collapse.

CHAPTER FORTY

The crimson sun slowly dips below the horizon, far behind us, as we and our dromedaries finally crest the last peak of the mountain range. The red sand around us shifts and glows in the dying light of the day, framing a vast expanse of canyons that seems to stretch on for miles. Ahead, our destination beckons: Exmouth and the Elops #4.

"Never thought I'd say this," Juice chuckles, "but I'm going to miss those mountains."

"Let's not get too sentimental just yet," Alice says, her eyes fixed on the path ahead. "We've still got a long way to go before we reach the Elops." Her determination is palpable, and it's clear that she's deeply invested in the success of our mission, despite her late arrival to our expedition.

"Speaking of which," Soren chimes in, their voice tinged with uncertainty, "are we sure Rachal is the key to unleashing the ClimaSphere? What if it's not?"

"Rachal has to be the answer," Benny replies, injecting confidence into his voice. "OZ wouldn't have left us a clue if he wasn't certain it would help us save the world."

"I think we're just lucky," Soren says dryly. "More luck,

then OZ leaving us a clue. We would never have put all this together if it wasn't for Alice finding us. People scoff at luck, but it has brought us this far, and it's kind of cool that you got to meet your mum. We will find out shortly if the necklace is really the code breaker. I say three cheers for Alice, luck and serendipity."

Soren makes a good point, and now I'm questioning myself. The name Rachal may be the answer, but I'm not sure Dad really expected anyone to find the proto and know how to crack this damn cypher let alone his gawdawful penmanship.

"Right! For many reasons, we are extraordinarily fortunate right about now," Banksia sympathises. I can't help but smile at her enthusiasm. This ragtag group of adventurers has become my family, and together, we'll face whatever challenges lie over the ridge ahead.

No matter what, with every step forward, I feel the deed get nearer.

"Hey," Banksia says softly, nudging me with her elbow. "Don't let the doubts get to you. We're in this together."

"Thanks, Banks," I reply, giving her a grateful smile. "I just can't help but worry."

"Nobody can predict the future, Odezza," Alice chimes in, her voice gentle and motherly. "All we can do is give it everything we've got and hope for the best."

"Your mother's right," Juice grins, his optimism infectious. "We'll cross that bridge or desert or lake when we come to it. For now, let's focus on getting to Exmouth."

"Agreed," Soren says, their perfect form shimmering in the fading light. "There's no sense in worrying about what we can't control."

"Alright," I concede, my resolve strengthened by their unwavering support. "Let's keep moving, and we'll face whatever comes our way."

With renewed determination, we press on, the promise of Exmouth and the Elops #4 guiding us ever forward. And though uncertainty lingers, one thing remains certain: we won't give up without a fight.

THE VERY LAST specks of sunlight cast a fiery glow on the thousands of people we now find ourselves surrounded by as we come to the city limits. It's like a river of humanity, a torrent of desperation and hope flowing steadily towards Exmouth and the Elops.

"Look at them all," Banksia murmurs, her voice tinged with awe. "I've never seen anything like it before."

"Neither have I," Alice admits, her eyes scanning the crowd for any potential threats. "We must remain vigilant."

"Right," Juice agrees, his usual grin subdued by the gravity of the situation. "Let's stick together, no matter what."

As we weave our camels through the throngs of people, an oppressive weight threatens to suffocate us. They're clutching their loved one's close, whispering prayers to God's long forgotten. Their eyes are wide, their faces etched with fear. And who can blame them? The world they knew is crumbling around them, and the promise of salvation lies just beyond their reach.

"Excuse me," Soren says in a monotone voice. "Please make way."

"Is it just me," Benny asks, his voice barely audible above the cacophony of voices, "or does the air feel— different?"

"Fresh," I respond, inhaling deeply. "It's coming from the Elops."

"Really?" Banksia's eyes widen, her curiosity piqued. "You think so?"

"Definitely," Alice confirms, nodding in agreement. "We must be getting close."

"Good," Juice mutters, his gaze darting around the faces in the crowd. "The sooner we get there, the better."

"Keep pushing forward," Soren instructs, their determination unwavering. "We'll make it through this."

"Right," I agree, my heart pounding in my chest. The moment of truth is upon us, and I can't help but wonder: will Rachal be enough to save us all?

I've also never seen so many people in my entire life. This is utter mayhem. So many are falling by the wayside, their Oxolets turning from flashing red to perpetual red. A constant reminder that we need to keep on moving through the throng, no matter what.

"Stay focused, Odezza," Alice whispers, her hand on my shoulder. "We're almost there."

"Thanks, Mum," I reply, swallowing the lump in my throat. With every step closer to the Elops, our fate becomes more uncertain - but so too does our resolve grow stronger. We've come too far to falter now.

"Look, there's the edge," Benny says, his voice resolute. "It reminds me of Zanzibar. It's mesmerising. Let's get this done."

As we make it to the outer edge of the Elops, the sight of the rocket launch pad stops me in my tracks, my camel snorting impatiently beneath me. I blink several times to make sure I'm not hallucinating. It's a towering structure, stretching toward the open sky above, sitting on a massive man-made island just off the east coast of Exmouth. It seems to sparkle under a barrage of endless lights. It's nothing like I had imagined. I assumed it was on land, but they had to have constructed it off-site and transported it here via the sea that surrounds it.

"Guys," I breathe out, slowly pointing toward the launch pad. "Look."

Soren gazes at the structure, awestruck. "Incredible engineering," they murmur. "Yet also intimidating and, dare I say, scary how close it is to us. It is more accessible than I'd hoped."

Sitting on the platform is an enormous rocket. How did we miss that? It is perfectly black, not a marking on its outer skin. It's just sitting there, on an island in the middle of the bay. Soren's right, that is an incredible piece of engineering, but we also know who it belongs to and what it is capable of, or at least the horror it could transport.

"Uh, guys?" Benny interrupts, his voice tense. "We've got company."

My eyes follow his gaze, and my heart leaps into my throat as I spot a large six wheeled truck moving through the crowd, heading for the dock on the bay. It is old, obviously pre-Bold-War. Matte black. Difficult to miss. It can only belong to one person: Roman. It matches the rocket forgawdsake!

"Roman's here," I whisper, my pulse quickening with every beat. "We have to stop him." There is no damn way we have come this far for him to get his crew off planet and let us all stay here to die. No way is that happening on our watch.

We all look at each other for a moment. Tired, bewildered, but not overly surprised. Roman might be an evil man, trying to destroy the inhabitants of our planet, but he also turns out to be a stubborn bastard!

"Hey!" Juice shouts, his voice carrying across the crowd. "Help us stop that truck! Please!" Good thinking, Juice. He repeats the plea in several languages, imploring those around us to join our cause. If we can't halt Roman's progress, then everything we've worked for will be for nought.

"Come on, everyone!" Alice adds, her voice filled with urgency. "We can't let that truck reach the pier!"

"Stop that truck!" someone shouts in Mandarin, followed by another voice echoing the same message in Portuguese. The chain reaction of chatter ripples through the crowd, each person passing on the plea to those next to them. My heart races with hope and angst as I watch the throng of people move in unison, attempting to halt Roman's progress.

I've never felt such a potent mix of fear and resolve in my life. But it's time to do my part.

I dismount from the camel's saddle; such remarkable camels have brought us along stark beaches, raging rivers and red sandy mountains.

As I unlock the titanium case and lift the lid, I can't help but think of OZ. His brilliance, his love, his hopes for me – they're all woven into this moment.

"Ready?" Juice turns and asks, his eyes scanning the crowd for any sign that his idea is faltering. We can hear the cacophony of voices moving away from us like an echoing Doppler effect. Let's just hope it reaches Roman's menacing truck before he makes the docks.

Concentrate!

I hear myself singing one of Dad's favourite Daft Punk tracks, "One More Time!"

Odezza, forgawdsake, concentrate!

"Ready," I confirm, gripping the ClimaSphere tightly. As I input the code, I glance over at Alice, who nods encouragingly.

"Go for it, Odezza," she says, her confidence bolstering my own. "You've got this."

The crowd of onlookers stares down at me, completely oblivious to what may or may not be about to happen.

Alice watches me intently before ceremonially removing her necklace. For a moment, she clutches it tightly in her hand, as if drawing strength from its engraved letters. With a deep breath, she hands it to me.

"Rachal," she says softly. "It's up to you now."

"Thank you, Alice," I reply, my voice trembling with emotion. Taking the necklace, I enter each letter into the machine, my fingers hovering over the keys with a mixture of hope and dread.

R — A —

"Guys, we need to do something more about Roman," Soren peppers, their eyes locked on the truck, slowly pushing against the crowd, inching ever closer to the pier. "I think it's time I got involved."

Involved?

C —

"Are you sure you're ready?" Juice asks, concern lacing his words.

"Ready or not, it's now or never," Soren replies, their determination clear. "I'll push through the crowd and try to physically stop that truck."

H —

"Go for it, Soren," Banksia cheers, her eyes blazing with excitement. "We've got your back."

"Be careful," Benny warns, his voice uncharacteristically serious. "We don't know what Roman is capable of."

A —

"Understood." Soren nods, then turns to me. "Odezza, you focus on the ClimaSphere. We can't let our guard down, even for a moment."

And just like that, we watch as they push off into the sea of people, making a beeline for the matter six-wheeler.

L —

Seconds pass.

"Look!" Juice exclaims suddenly, pointing toward the ClimaSphere.

As if on cue, the device hums, and a faint light emanates from within. My heart leaps into my throat, but I don't dare celebrate yet. We still do not know if this will actually work, but this is further than this gawdforsaken machine has gone previously.

"Please, let it work," I whisper under my breath. My eyes were glued to the ClimaSphere. In this charged moment, it feels like time stands still. My thoughts race, imagining the best and worst potential outcomes. The machine hums even louder and the intensity of the internal light show is spellbinding. Oh, if only OZ were here right now. All his quick thinking and innovation and he never had the chance to try it out. And he will never know if it was successful.

The humming is growing louder, vibrating through my bones and filling the air with a pulsing energy. Suddenly, there's an extraordinary explosion of colour before our eyes, like a million tiny galaxies colliding together in a cosmic dance. It is both spellbinding and sinister in its intensity; I'm unable to tear my gaze away from the dazzling display. I glance up at those who have gathered around this spectacle. We are all tantalisingly pulled toward the mysterious source of this extraordinary light show.

The ClimaSphere's hum grows exponentially louder, like it's trying to talk to us, screaming.

And then, suddenly, everything changes. A massive white light shoots up and out of the body of the ClimaSphere. Is it meant to do that? Who knows? It's like doing backstroke on the 300th floor outdoor pool in London and staring directly up into the sun. And just then—

CHAPTER FORTY-ONE

The air crackles with raw energy, as if the atoms are realigning themselves. I squint against the brilliant white glare that shoots skyward, a luminescent spear piercing through the churning mass above us. It wraps around the sinuous curves of the Elops like a lasso around a bull's neck. I have seen nothing like it. I'm pretty sure no one has.

A collective gasp ripples through the crowd, and my heart hammers with a mix of triumph and disbelief. The ClimaSphere—it worked. Dad's legacy, his genius unfurling before our very eyes. A life-saving scientific discovery that came to him almost overnight.

"Odezza, can you believe it?" Banksia's voice cuts through the electric charge of the moment, her voice a vibrant melody over the buzz of excitement. I turn to her, and even in this surreal light, her face is alight with wonder.

"Believe it?" I manage a laugh, allowing the relief to wash over me. "I was counting on it."

Benny looks at me and rolls his eyes, not believing my words. "I should rephrase, I was counting on OZ!"

The effect the white energy beam has on the ring of the

Elops is astonishing. The ray only striking the rim, attaches itself and seemingly pushes the circle back on itself. It is not a rapid resolution of the ring, but it is certainly an obvious retreat.

We stand shoulder to shoulder, a motley crew of uni bohemians, gazing skyward as the clouds continue their slow retreat. It's like watching a theatrical curtain being drawn back, revealing the heavens and hope itself. Hope for sunlight, for blue skies, for life to return to normal.

"Look at it go," Juice says, his voice a deep rumble blending with the whispers of awe surrounding us. As he observes the phenomenon, his towering figure is still, almost reverent.

"Like watching a flower bloom in fast-forward," Benny adds, his tone light, but I catch the undercurrent of solemnity. "We've feared, we've waited, we've fought, we've hoped against hope. And now, the Elop yields, retreats, conceding that good always wins over evil."

I think of OZ, and how his befuddled scepticism of future tech didn't stop him from dreaming up this marvel. How he'd pour over the preliminary designs, his mind always ticking, always one step ahead. He'd have loved to see this, his creation slicing through the fabric of despair that had shrouded the world. "Love you, Dad," I say to myself.

"Your father would be proud, Odezza," Alice murmurs beside me, reading my thoughts as only a mother can. She reaches for my hand and squeezes it, her own strength and resilience a beacon in these uncertain times. "I am curious how he figured all that out in such a short amount of time?"

"Yeah, he would've," I reply, my voice barely above a whisper, cracking, disregarding her science question. I had wondered the same thing as the light snaked for the sky, but the science behind it will rest in peace along with Dad. A pang of loss tugs at my chest. But there's no time for sorrow—not when there's so much to do, so many to help, and a world to rebuild.

Around us, the throng of thousands erupts into pandemonium. Cheers, hip hip hurrahs, and a lot of applause—humanity's symphony of relief and joy. We've been living under a shadow, not just the literal darkness of the manic clouds, but the weighty despair that came with them. Now, it feels like an immense weight lifted from our collective shoulders.

The retreat of the clouds feels personal, a parting gift from dad, as he watches on, nudging the clouds aside, telling us all to keep looking up, and to keep reaching for the stars. And beneath the expanding canvas of twilight, with stars peeking out like shy children, I feel it—the fresh breeze, the promise of a new dawn, and the adventure that awaits.

"Time to roll up our sleeves, team," I say, turning to face my friends, their faces illuminated by the nascent glow of freedom. "There's work to be done."

"Look," Benny gasps, his voice a reverent whisper that cuts through the din of amazement around us. He points skyward, his finger tracing the familiar crux of stars. "It's the Southern Cross, the symbol of Australia. The stars on their flag."

I follow his gaze, and there it is—the constellation hanging in the sky like a promise. Acrux gleams as the brightest point, flanked by the Jewel Box cluster, with the inky smear of the Coalsack nebula a stark contrast against the celestial light show. His eyes are wide, reflecting a universe of possibilities. He is part nerd, part geek and part adorable scientist.

"Can you believe it?" I shout over the roar of excitement, my words snatched away by the wind of change whipping through us all.

Tonight, under the watchful gaze of constellations old as time, we revel in the fresh breeze and the freedom it brings. Tomorrow, the actual work begins. But for now, we bask in the starlight, hearts alight with dreams of dawn.

My thoughts race, a chaotic whirlwind, yet at their core, there's an unshakeable certainty. We trekked across continents, gambled everything on a sliver of hope and a little box OZ invented. Now we're here—in Australia's most northwesterly point. A dot on the map that's become the epicentre for mankind's second chance. Dad, your gamble paid off.

A smile tugs at my lips as I imagine the sun's first rays peeking over the bay in a few hours. Warmth will flood the streets and seep into the world's cold, fear-stricken hearts. And with it, seep back into our Oxolet's—dad's little miracle workers. They'll breathe life back into our bodies, into our lives. Like a phoenix from the ashes, or so the old tales go.

"Here's to fresh starts," I say, lifting an invisible glass to the stars. My voice takes on a solemn edge—the kind that comes when you're standing on the precipice of history. "And to you, OZ. The world owes you one heck of a sunrise."

We plop down on the tufts of grass, a patchwork quilt beneath a sea of stars. The Southern Cross winks at us from above, stitched into the night's canvas alongside the Milky Way's celestial swirl. I can't help but marvel at the sight. We just lay there, taking it all in, exhilarated and exhausted.

"Sleep well, heroes," I whisper to my companions, though they're too captivated by the spectacle above to hear me. My eyelids grow heavy, the day's adrenaline finally succumbing to the rhythmic pulse of the tide echoing in the distance.

As slumber beckons, I let myself drift with the promise of dawn's light. A new day waits on the horizon, charged with possibility. For tonight, though, we rest under the watchful gaze of the stars, cradled by the land that's welcomed us—the Mighty5 and Alice, weary travellers who've found hope in a town forgotten by the world until now.

We'll sleep well tonight.

CHAPTER FORTY-TWO

The first light of dawn spills over the eastern horizon of the bay, painting the sky with strokes of amber and gold. I blink the remnants of sleep from my eyes, propping myself up on one elbow to watch the day break across Exmouth's rugged landscape. The air is crisp, heavy with the scent of sea salt. And clear sky as far as the eye can see.

"Another day," I murmur, half to myself, "another step closer to— what's next?" We did it.

As I gaze out at the sunrise, fragments of our journey replay in my mind: the harrowing escapes, a cyclone, tornados, panicking people, dead people, thousands of miles on various TTs, two crappy old planes, learning to pour petrol into an old yank tank, encrypted messages with poor handwriting, a damn SEAL sub, people laughing at us, characters helping us, camels, hidden safes behind posters; discovering I have a mother, realising I no longer have a father, learning I have a real name, tapping others, others tapping us, one of us is a robot, and being pursued by a relentless madman. We've come so far, catapulted through a series of misadventures that would seem ludicrous if they weren't our reality.

I stretch, feeling the ache in my muscles from yesterday's escapades — what I wouldn't give for a good cup of tea. Proper tea. The kind dad used to brew before things went sideways. Heck, I'd even take our gawdforsaken faux breakfasts right now. But the small luxuries are the first casualties in our dystopian world, aren't they?

"Thinking about tea again?" Alice's voice startles me from my reverie. "Just like your dad."

"Can you blame me?" I reply, turning to face her. She's sitting cross-legged near me, her eyes still bright from yesterday's drama.

"So, what's next?" I ask her.

"Actually, I've been working on something," Alice starts, her tone shifting to a mix of excitement and gravity. "In Canton España, my team and I believe we're close to increasing the planet's overall oxygen levels. Imagine, Odezza, no more reliance on our Oxolets. Plants thriving again, animals no longer on the brink."

She looks at me with an intensity that borders on pleading. "We need help. Not from the Central Government—they have their agendas and are corrupt—but from people who truly care. The Mighty5 has shown resilience, ingenuity — would you want to join us to turn things around for good?"

The thought echoed through my mind, tempting and terrifying at the same time. Could we really go back to a world without wrist implants, with increased oxygen and no more molecularly engineered food? A part of me yearns for it, but another part fears what that world would look like. Could we even survive without our technological advancements? The idea both entices and panics me.

"Make it a happier, a healthier place." Alice nods, her hand reaching out as if to physically offer me this future.

I have so many immediate questions. We'd all have to move to España. What is the tech they're working on, how far along are they in their R&D? Who's on her team? Could they really be working on such radical innovations, and why have the rest of us never heard of these efforts?

Pondering, I say, "Count us in," and though I'm speaking only for myself at this moment, I know the others will be by my side. We're the Mighty5—a force forged through adversity, bound by a friendship that's become our greatest strength.

"Good," she smiles, relief washing over her features. "Then let's get to work."

And as I sit beside her, watching the sun climb higher into the sky, hope flutters in my chest like a bird taking flight for the first time after a lengthy storm. Maybe, just maybe, we can win this fight. Not just for ourselves, but for the entire planet. For a future where we can wake up to sunrise without fear, breathe deeply without aid, and yes, even enjoy a proper cup of tea amidst a world reborn. No need for robots or human cloning.

"Let's make Dad proud," I whisper, not sure if I'm saying it to Alice, or to the father who left me with such a tangled legacy.

"Let's make everyone proud," she adjusts gently, and together, we rise to meet the day.

"Hey," Benny's awake, his voice cuts through the calm, "do we actually have to go back to uni after all this?" His eyes gleam with the mischief that's become his trademark.

Laughter bubbles up from our group, who are all awake now; unbidden and genuine laughter. It echoes across the abandoned stretches of grass. We apparently fell asleep in a farmer's paddock.

"Uni?" I scoff, shaking my head. "Feels like another lifetime."

"Can you imagine?" quips Juice, watching the sunrise fill the blue sky with warmth and intention. "Sitting on our

HelloHolo's, lecturers blabbing about quantum mechanics when we've lived it?"

"Written exams on survival strategies," chimes in Banksia, her smile brighter than the sun climbing higher in the sky. "And we'd ace them without trying."

"Friendship and bravery, those should be the proper courses," says Benny.

The Mighty5—we've seen things no textbook could cover, fought battles, no exam could test. We've danced with dystopia, tangled with tech, and still come out breathing. Mostly because of Alice's instinct, though none of us would say that aloud.

"Remember when we thought the biggest challenge was going to be the midterms?" I muse, the absurdity is not lost on us.

"Or making it to 8 AM classes after an all-nighter," adds Benny with a snort.

"Instead, we got all-nighters sitting on TTs," I say, and a shiver runs down my spine despite the warmth of the day.

"Evading capture, decoding cryptic messages," Juice lists, his fingers tracing patterns in the sodden grass.

"Creating bonds stronger than the toughest alloys," Benny whispers. His words hang in the air, profound and true.

Juice nods solemnly, his usual bravado softened by the gravity of our shared experiences. "We've become our own kind of alloy, haven't we? Unbreakable."

"Exactly," I say, feeling the truth of it deep in my bones. "We're forged from challenges, sculpted by hope. The world threw its worst at us, and here we are, ready to throw something back. Something good."

"Like an oxygenated planet?" Benny teases. He had overheard our earlier conversation.

"Exactly," brushing the grass from my clothes. "Let's

breathe life back into this place. For the plants, the animals, for all of us."

"What's that?" Juice asks, having not heard the earlier chat with Alice. Banksia also cocks her head in questioning form.

"Alice is asking us if we want to join her team in España. They believe they are close to increasing the planet's overall oxygen levels. Benny, no reliance on our Oxolets." I try to repeat Alice's earlier words. "That means plants thriving again, and bringing animals back from the edge of extinction. Cows, dogs, sheep, doing their thing again.

Everyone nods. It seems like we agree.

I nod too, "We're the Mighty5. And there's nothing we can't face together anywhere, anytime."

"Nothing at all," they chorus. The sound is sweeter than any symphony.

In this moment, beneath the ever-brightening sky, I know that whatever comes next, we'll meet it head-on. Together.

AS WE SIT AROUND, chatting and sharing our favourite parts of our journey, the ground starts to pulsate under us, a deep thrum that climbs into my bones and sets my teeth on edge. I freeze, the elation I was enjoying immediately dying in my throat as a shadow of unease passes over us.

"Feel that?" Juice says, his eyes narrowing.

"The earth doesn't just decide to dance," Banksia adds, suspicion colouring her voice.

As we turn toward the bay, we scramble to our feet, our makeshift circle breaking. The sea, calm in the morning light, reflects a different spectacle. There it is, across the water on the isolated island: the rocket's silhouette stark against the burgeoning dawn, black metal gleaming like a premonition.

"Is it—?" Benny starts, but he doesn't need to finish.

"Yeah," I nod, my heart kicking up a notch. "It's warming up."

We've seen launches before. We're used to them—distant specks climbing the skies, heading off on journeys unknown—but this one feels too close, too personal. The rumbling grows, crescendoing into a roar that blankets all other sounds. It vibrates through the air, through the earth, through the very marrow of us.

"Guys?" Benny's voice cuts sharply through the crescendoing rumble, urgent and laced with deep concern. He's always been the jokester, the one to point out the missing puzzle piece when the rest of us get caught up in the picture. "Where's Soren? And where is Roman?"

ABOUT THE AUTHOR

Originally from Perth, Western Australian, Ken Grant has led a remarkable life. Some accomplishments include being a concert violist for the Melbourne Philharmonic, fashion model, concert pianist, composer, recording artist, teacher, TV reporter, and radio personality. He has been a successful ad exec, copywriter, and content developer, business book author, professional speaker, podcast host, auctioneer, drone operator, and TEDx presenter.

Ken is an avid sailor, adventurist, gravel cyclist, photographer, student pilot, EDM fanatic, movie enthusiast, wine-guy and speed-freak. He resides outside of Seattle, Washington state with his family.

Made in United States
Troutdale, OR
08/05/2024